MISS SUSIE SLAGLE'S

PUBLISHER'S NOTE

Works published as part of the Maryland Paperback
Bookshelf are, we like to think, books that have stood
the test of time. They are classics of a kind, so we reprint
them today as they appeared when first published many
years ago. While some social attitudes have changed and
knowledge of our surroundings has increased, we believe that the value of these books as literature, as history, and as timeless perspectives on our region remains
undiminished.

Also available in the series:

The Amiable Baltimoreans, by Francis F. Beirne
Mencken, Carl Bode
The Lord's Oysters, by Gilbert Byron
The Potomac, by Frederick Gutheim
The Bay, by Gilbert C. Klingel
Tobacco Coast, by Arthur Pierce Middleton
Watermen, by Randall S. Peffer
Young Frederick Douglass, by Dickson J. Preston

MISS SUSIE SLAGLE'S

Augusta Tucker

THE JOHNS HOPKINS UNIVERSITY PRESS

Baltimore and London

To

My Mother and Father

Originally published, 1939
Johns Hopkins Paperbacks edition, 1987

The Johns Hopkins University Press
701 West 40th Street
Baltimore, Maryland 21211
The Johns Hopkins Press Ltd., London

Library of Congress Cataloging-in-Publication Data

Tucker, Augusta, 1904–
Miss Susie Slagle's.
I. Title. II. Series.
(Maryland paperback bookshelf)
PS3570.U237M5 1987 813'.52 86–27833
ISBN 0–8018–3419–8 (pbk.)

Title page illustration drawn by Lissa Miller

All of the incidents and characters in this novel are fictitious with the exception of the four great men of American medicine, Kelly, Halsted, Welch and Osler. For them and for the institution which they founded the author has the deepest respect and admiration.

Foreword

The movie version of *Miss Susie Slagle's* was made in
1944 and released the following year. It was shot at the Paramount
Studio in Hollywood and it was the second film I had ever produced.
It was well received, but it never quite fulfilled the studio's hopes for
a blockbusting American *Mr. Chips*. Perhaps the long relationship
between Miss Slagle and the doctors and medical students at Johns
Hopkins did not altogether make up for the absence of Robert Donat
and Greer Garson and their affecting romance. Or I myself may have
been partly to blame: having recently emerged from two years of
wartime service with the Voice of America, my approach to Miss
Tucker's novel may have been rather more documentary than the
situation called for.

Our literate, humane screenplay was written by Adrian Scott, and
the picture marked the return to films after many years of the celebrated Lillian Gish. Most of the rest of the cast was determined by
the studio, which—with many of its male stars away at the war—was
desperately trying to find new faces to take their place. One such
"new face" was assigned to me as my young leading man, a very
blond, awkward, good-natured, alcoholic young giant with the unlikely name of Sonny Tufts. By way of compensation I was given
Veronica Lake (without her curl and in a part that was neither fey
nor sexy); she was flanked by a very young, honey-haired ingénue
from New York named Joan Caulfield. Other medical students were
played by a newcomer named Lloyd Bridges, Billy de Woolf (a night-
club comic), and a six-foot-seven tennis player who never acted before
or since. To these I added a few seasoned performers of my own
choosing: Morris Carnovsky, Roman Bohnen, and Ray Collins were
formidable medical figures; finally, Miss Slagle's faithful black houseman was played by J. Louis Johnson (who had been the Porter in our
Voodoo *Macbeth*).

Our director was a young man by the name of John Berry, a former
actor with the Mercury Theatre. He proved to be particularly under-

standing and sensitive in his work with Miss Gish, and he gave the whole picture a nice feeling of energy and youth.

After more than forty years I have two particularly vivid memories of our production, one trivial, the other grotesque and rather frightening. The first is of a domestic scene at Miss Slagle's in which her boarders are gathered around her piano, singing. I recall looking down and noticing a pair of huge men's shoes raised above the others by a thick telephone directory. Following their owner's legs I discovered that they belonged to Sonny Tufts (whose main quality as an actor was his height—six-foot-five), making quite sure that he would tower over the tennis player!

The other incident involved a gentleman by the name of Y. Frank Freeman, a banker from Atlanta and a controlling stockholder of Crown Cola, whose main preoccupation as head of the studio seemed to be to make sure that no black person, male or female, ever appear on the screen beside a white in any of the company's films. On this day, in the main clinic of the hospital, we were shooting a big scene in which we used a hundred or more extras. Anticipating trouble, I had taken careful note of Johns Hopkins' last will and testament, which specifically stated that the distribution of beds and other medical facilities at Johns Hopkins must coincide as closely as possible with the ratio of blacks to whites residing in the city of Baltimore.

This was the ratio we followed in our casting; I had instructed the assistant director to make sure that in all scenes taking place in public rooms we should adhere to this formula, which, at the time of our story, if I remember rightly, was about 40-60. The assistant asked me if the blacks should be segregated. I said absolutely not. Everyone should move about naturally, but, with an eye to our southern audiences, we should avoid having small blond females surrounded by large black males. I went down to the set to see how it all looked: it seemed credible and nicely composed as I watched John Berry line up his first master-shot. Then I started back to my office.

It was a three-minute walk and, when I got there, my secretary told me rather breathlessly that the stage had just called and wanted me back immediately. I returned to find the place in disorder. The hundred extras were milling around, the crew was drinking coffee. Berry was nowhere to be seen. The assistant had just begun to explain that shooting had been interrupted by a peremptory order from the Front

Office when the red telephone-light started flashing. It was a call for me from Y. Frank Freeman himself. In a voice shrill and shredded with rage he demanded my immediate presence in his office.

For more than ten minutes Freeman yelled at me, accusing me successively of imbecility, sabotage, and subversion. He charged me with criminal indifference to the feelings of southern audiences; he assured me that he, not I, had the true welfare of the "nigra" at heart; he said I was trying to ruin the company. Finally, he suggested that I was a Communist and that what had just occurred on the set was part of a vast "Commeeeoooonist" conspiracy aimed at the corruption and destruction of the film industry—not to mention the United States of America.

When I was finally allowed to open my mouth I foolishly tried to tell him about Johns Hopkins' will; this led him to suspect that Johns Hopkins himself might have been a "Commeeeoooonist," and set him off on another harangue. At last, since the delay was costing the company a lot of money, he gave me permission to resume shooting on condition that 25 percent of the blacks be removed from the set immediately and the rest be rigorously segregated.

The reviews of *Susie Slagle* were favorable, on the whole. Bosley Crowther, who was just beginning his long tenure on the *New York Times*, had kind words for director and cast. He found Sonny Tufts "disarmingly amiable," Joan Caulfield "winsome but sturdy," Veronica Lake "respectably modest," and Collins, Carnovsky, and Johnson "picturesque." Of Miss Gish he wrote that "she manages to give an impression of respectability and pride personified," and, of the film, that, although "one would refrain from recommending it as a final drama of medical school, it's a cheerful, nostalgic and personally engaging little picture of fabricated life." In the opinion of Howard Barnes, of the *New York Herald Tribune*, " 'Miss Susie Slagle's' is leisurely entertainment but it has a great deal of authenticity, considerable feeling and not a little engaging comedy."

I am delighted to learn that Augusta Tucker's novel is being reissued, all the more since, on a recent visit to Baltimore, I had the pleasure of meeting several of Miss Slagle's former boarders and discovering that the memory of her home is still very much alive in the institution she served with such devotion.

John Houseman

Miss Susie's Revisited

Miss Susie Slagle's was first published in 1939, in what was still the dawn of the era that revolutionized medical science and clinical practice. The period that Augusta Tucker's novel chronicles, 1912–1916, was in turn close to the end of another great moment in the history of the profession, an era that the Flexners, in their life of Welch, styled "the Heroic Age of American Medicine." This earlier period, presided over by the "Four Doctors" of Sargent's famous group portrait, was inextricably bound to the establishment of the Johns Hopkins Hospital (1889) and Medical School (1893). Baltimore had suddenly become an international medical center, and the center of gravity for subsequent research had shifted decisively toward the western shores of the Atlantic. It was also during the decades surrounding the turn of the century that the new image of the physician as professional and scientist emerged.

The professionalization of American clinical research and its applications had guaranteed a striking rise in the status of the physician. But it had also led to another sort of distancing, a potential separation of the "men in white" and their laboratories from the patients whom they had traditionally served. The physician as counsellor and comforter was in danger of being replaced in the popular imagination by the intrepid investigator behind the microscope. It is one of the achievements of Miss Tucker's book that it captures at a vital point some of the excitement of the "new medicine" emerging from one of the world's great centers for clinical research, while at the same time chronicling the human struggles and concerns of a group of young men who, with quite varied motives, have just embarked on careers in that profession.

Miss Susie Slagle's is a novel constructed around two centers—one the institution that shapes the lives of those who study and work there; the other the eponymous heroine who, with her staff of one, has herself become an institution. Just as the Medical School and Hospital are the focus for medical science, Miss Susie serves as the focus for the claims of sentiment that are also part of a physician's education. On the perimeter of the institutional center are the now heroic figures from a legendary past, who are still active in the Baltimore/medical world (Welch, Halsted, Mall, and Kelly). Engaged with the fictional students are the second generation of the staff, the *fictional* successors to this past (Wingate, Howe, McMillan, Andrews, Scott, Cameron, Carlyle, et al.). Correspondingly, the world of the human center, Miss Susie Slagle's, radiates out to the life of old Baltimore. The book is bathed in nostalgia—in the evocation of scenes and neighborhoods, of customs and characters from the early years of the century—while it is at the same time a lovingly researched account of a scientific institution and its impact on the medical profession. (In later years Augusta Tucker created a popular guide to this latter world, which she had celebrated in the novel. *It Happened at Hopkins: A Teaching Hospital*, first published in 1960, has since been revised and expanded to keep up with the rapid pace of medical innovation; some of its narrative and much of its detail would be familiar to any reader of *Miss Susie Slagle's*.)

In the sense that it includes much of the history of an institution and detailed period vignettes of the life of a city, the novel can be called encyclopedic. The reader will find careful accounts of the stark beauty of an autopsy, the anxieties of a first delivery, a sudden incursion of tuberculosis, and the phantasmagoria of the pathology museum; but the narrative also includes evocations of a very different sort: a pungent inventory of the Lexington Market, a visit to a German "Christmas garden," the investment of a young belle, children's street games, Alex's walks through the seasons of the city, and much table talk. These encyclopedic compilations, organized around an episodic narrative presenting a gallery of characters and types, suggest that in addition to its elements of novel and romance *Miss Susie Slagle's* has a considerable generic affinity with the Menippean satire, or what Northrop Frye in his own anatomy of fictional forms has called the Anatomy. Like this fictional ancestor, the book includes a considerable mixture of styles and attitudes, extending from the ballad of Little Elize and medical student humor in the Pithotomy Club vein (which while changing topically has hardly improved) to the language of professional idealism and heroically deferred love. Mr.

John Houseman, in his lively memoir of the making of the 1944 movie based on the book, may have been intuitively responding to this aspect of the text when he felt he was succumbing to his own documentary instinct, refined during his war-time service. This book, like the traditional Menippean satire, has concentrated elements of the documentary about it, but it is an anatomy conceived and executed with an obvious love for the subject matter. (In fact, Miss Tucker— or Mrs. Townsend, as she is better known to her Baltimore neighbors —could not include in this first novel all of the historical material related to the establishment of Hopkins and the character of its donor. In 1942 she published *The Man Miss Susie Loved*, which, as the title suggests, traces the earlier, romantic years of her heroine. It is equally engaged with the medical profession in an earlier day and the character of the misunderstood philanthropist whose gift—the largest up to that time in the history of the Republic—made possible the university and hospital that bear his name. The Epilogue of that later novel is, in fact, the Prologue of this one.)

The overture of *Miss Susie Slagle's* and its initial compositional devices suggest a Balzac novel: a young man from the Provinces on the way to the City and the education that it holds in store; the narrative camera progressively focusing in on the dining room of a boarding house as a microcosm of that urban world. But the expectant reader soon learns that Clay Abernathy is of altogether different stuff from Eugène Rastignac. Rather than affective center for the narrative, Clay proves the unattractive marginal case, the hard lesson that not all vocations can put down roots even in the best of gardens. *The Man Miss Susie Loved* begins with a wry epigram that could serve equally as a commentary on the issue of vocations: "A novel, like a bustle, is a fictitious tale covering up a stern reality." The stern reality in the case of her first novel is figured by the arid career of Clay Abernathy: not every promising student nor "successful" physician has a genuine vocation for this most demanding of professions. (And the educational system has so far failed to devise a perfect moral filter.)

It is also soon made clear that Miss Susie Slagle's is a microcosm very different from Balzac's sordid Pension Vauquer in the Rue Neuve-Sainte-Geneviève. Unlike the stale, rancid world over which the shapeless Madame Vauquer reigns, the Baltimore boarding house is presided over by two intensely caring people, and its table is one of good food, good company, and ideals not yet tarnished. While Miss Tucker's narrative genius hardly competes with the fecundity of Balzac's invention, in one category, at least, she offers a much richer gallery than the author of the *Comédie Humaine*. In *Le Père Goriot* the reader encounters but one medical student, Horace Bianchon. In the novels that follow, he is to become the most overworked figure in all of Balzac, a one-man HMO, reappearing in over thirty fictions. Thus he becomes the template physician, occasionally assisted by his old teacher, Desplein, the central-casting surgeon. (At the end of his frantic life, when his attending physicians had despaired of a cure, Balzac weakly advised them, "Appelez Bianchon.") Augusta Tucker, on the other hand, obviously delights in the variety of physicians, tracing the temperaments and typologies of the various services with a shrewd eye—observing in their larval stages the surgeon, the country doctor, the pathologist and diagnostician, the OB-GYN, the neuroscientist, et al. While her characters are perforce types, they are also case histories, that is, exemplary narratives that mediate between the particular and the general.

Two stumbling blocks to the contemporary reader of *Miss Susie Slagle's* are, no doubt, the extensive passages in phonetic dialect (German, Yiddish, Afro-American, and country-Southern) and the incidence of several racial epithets that have, happily, passed from polite use. As to the former, we are reminded that the United States shortly after the turn of the century was still very much a nation of immigrants and highly flavored regional speech. Mark Twain had elected dialect for some of his major fiction, and all comic writing of the period seemed to demand a turn at phonetic transcription. Gertrude Stein's stylistic innovations in *Three Lives* (1909), a pioneer work that could be said to spring from her clinical observations while a medical student at Hopkins, are cast in the hesitant form and linguistic contours of three poor, inarticulate women moving inevitably toward their obscure deaths. Her transcription is, however, more syntactic than phonetic. Gradually the custom of dialect writing has waned in a country that has emphasized sameness rather than difference, so that J. D. Salinger's *Catcher in the Rye* may be one of the last significant American novels using a form of dialect (and that a prep-school/urban patois that had been refined for years in the pages of the *New Yorker*).

The ethnic epithets pose more of a problem. The social historian would remark that they were the standard currency of American speech in 1912. The careful reader would observe that they are used abusively only by the most insensitive characters in the novel. The sentimental reader would remind us that those toward whom they are directed include two of its most admirable characters: the Jewish student, Isidore Aaron, who perhaps comes closest to the Maimonidean ideal of the medical scholar, and Miss Susie's black houseman and lieutenant, the cunning and wise Hizer, who is entrusted with the eloquent last words of the novel. The author, however, might suggest that the important issue here is not one of epithets but of the ideal that animated the institution she celebrates. At a crucial point in the novel, Pug Prentiss—who is not normally given to making speeches—feels compelled to cite the letter of March 10, 1873, from Johns Hopkins to the trustees of his hospital that had not yet come into being: The hospital is to care for "the indigent sick of this city and environs, without regard to sex, age, or color," and "the poor of the city and State, of all races, who are stricken down by any casualty, shall be received into the hospital without charge." Their care is to be by "surgeons and physicians of the highest character and the greatest skill." Pug concludes his version of the historic charge with a few words to his peers about what part of his education every physician owes to his patients, and how hard it is to gain the genuine respect of one's patients: "It is the negroes who helped to make Hopkins as much as the great men." (That Johns Hopkins was ahead of his time in 1873 is sadly underlined by the footnote that on September 26, 1937, the great Bessie Smith died following an auto accident because no "white hospital" in another Southern city would receive her.)

The contemporary reader may also notice a lacuna in the gallery of students in the novel. Although it is remarked that, thanks to the unswerving efforts of Mary Garrett, the Medical School from its inception admitted women on an equal basis with men, the students at Miss Susie's view their female classmates as distant and formidable anomalies. (Students from the School of Nursing, of course, play a much more visible role in the plot.) This is a pity, because the female graduates of the Medical School were a remarkable if small group.

The modern reader is twice removed in time from the events of *Miss Susie Slagle's*—from the world that is chronicled and from the world in which the novel was written. As a mythography of a profession and an anatomy of an education, however, it retains much of its original power to capture the romance of medicine as practiced at an institution that shaped the subsequent history of the profession. Augusta Tucker, writing in the year of the Hopkins Medical School's fiftieth anniversary, captured a lovingly detailed group portrait of student life in an earlier age. (By way of personal testimony, I can add that I first read the novel some years after its original publication, when—at the age of ten—I was devouring everything I could find about doctors; after that immersion, there was only one place that embodied for me the aura of the profession in its purest form, Hopkins.) Most importantly, Miss Tucker managed to fuse the personal narratives of her gallery of boarders and their surrogate mother with a compelling sense of the medical mystique that animated a great institution. Perhaps deans and mentors were never so wise, servants so devoted, young lovers so finely tuned, nor students so willing to wait, but the anatomy she offers us mediates persuasively between the historic ethos of clinical research and the more intimate, transitory romances of those whom that ethos educated and entrusted with the legend.

Richard Macksey

CONTENTS

"Live Unto the Dignity of thy Nature, and leave it not disputable at last, whether thou has been a Man . . ."

Sir Thomas Browne

Prologue

Beside the double tracks of the B & O Railroad at Mills Gap, in the West Virginia mountains, a 1912 Buick automobile came to a halt.

Upon the wide, black leather seat was a man of fifty with large plump hands, and beside him sat a boy of twenty-one.

Dr. Clayton Overton Abernathy had been silent for some time and now he said slowly, "Son, I've looked forward to this ever since I first heard you bawl. To go back to the Hopkins together!"

The boy coughed and reached for his handkerchief. His father decided to wait until they were in Baltimore and having a glass of beer at Otto's, if Otto's was still there, before he said anything more. For the next five hours, the first five, by God, since the boy was born in which they had ever been really alone, he wanted his son to think of him and remember him always as another man. Not a doctor. Not a father. Just a man—maybe a fine man.

He slid his hand along the automobile door, opened it and stepped onto the platform. Long years had taught him that action is a splendid antidote for emotion.

"Cummon, son!"

Dr. Abernathy pulled up his stooped shoulders and breathed deeply. The clear mountain air and midday warmth braced his weary muscles. Three weeks' work in forty-eight hours. Oh, Lord! But there were no babies due for ten days; and he only intended being gone two. Safe? Safe enough. Ahead lay a vacation. Take it! Beside him stood his son!

Clayton Overton Abernathy, Junior, readjusted his cravat. His father laughed uncertainly. The old station master opened the door of the one-room ticket office and walked toward them; the boy's eyes darkened with embarrassment, his pink skin and hands turning brick-red.

"Howdy, Andy," his father said.

"Hi, Doc. Hearn you and him is goin' back to med'kal school. Hit's a fine day, Doc; a fine day!"

1

The station master's faded eyes sought the mountains and the doctor replied, "Best I've ever seen, Andy. Want you to keep your eye on the car two days. How's the Limited?"

Old Andy's face lit up, he shifted his tobacco and winked: "She's on time, Doc! Ev'body on the run knows you're goin'. She's ahead o' time, I guess! Seventy-six just passed the junction t'other side Blue Falls, and Limited was spittin' at her tail then."

Through the mountains a long wide echo began to spread.

"Git ready, son!" The old man turned to the boy. "That's Seventy-six now, and Limited is right behindst her. Git yo' pa's grip, too. He's too ex-cited to do nuthin'!"

A quarter of a mile up the mountain the long fast freight began applying her brakes.

Old Andy hobbled toward the track and snarled, "What the hell they stoppin' fur? Dern Sam Hosters! He tuk on water at the junction!"

The big engine slowed, but it did not stop. The engineer leaned from his cab and when he saw Dr. Abernathy relief showed in his hard features. Then he hurled at the doctor's feet a piece of paper wound around a lump of coal, and the train roared on.

The boy handed his father the missile. The man's deft hands slipped the note from the coal. In the fast-moving freight the engineer had written:

"Mattie's started, Doc. Dr. Willis is to a wreck in Simmons Gap. I'm awful sorry."

Dr. Abernathy's shoulders sagged. His voice was quiet and slow as he said: "Twins. Due next month. Here's your ticket, son. First, you go to Miss Susie Slagle's on Biddle Street. She's expecting you. Don't try to walk. Take a cab. Then you go to the Dean's office tomorrow. Tell him you are my boy. 'Bye . . . and . . ."

The Limited hissed and slowed. Neither of them had noticed her arrival.

A porter, a conductor, two brakemen, an engineer and a fireman leaned out and watched.

They saw an awkward youth pull himself aboard.

On the platform behind, two men lifted him with their hearts.

Chapter One

SUPPER AT MISS SUSIE SLAGLE'S

"That's the house, mister, and here's your grip!" The old cab driver pulled in toward the curb, and Clayton Overton Abernathy, Junior, poked in his pockets for his wallet.

He felt detached and dizzy. The longest train ride of his life and the slow cab ride through the largest city he had ever seen, left him totally unprepared for what his eyes were now absorbing.

The door toward which the driver pointed, and which could be partially discerned in the flickering dimness of the gas-lighted street, was precisely like ten other doors in a continuous brick wall which extended for an entire block. Beside each door were two windows and above them two more and still two more and still two more, and in front of the doors were identical white stone steps. Nothing whatsoever distinguished one opening from another except the numbers in curlicue gilt on each transom.

The boy's wallet seemed as indistinguishable as the block. Feeling for it was like grabbing for something familiar in that staring expanse of brick.

Mountains, picket fences and rambling frame dwellings, had left young Abernathy unschooled in the red brick rows which stretch for endless miles in Baltimore. Years of past familiarity had made Dr. Abernathy forget to mention them to his son.

The student finally found his billfold, paid his fare, gave his tip, stepped down on the sidewalk and grasped his suitcase.

Then he moved unsteadily up the white stone steps and knocked heavily at the vestibule doors of the house indicated. He did not want to take time to fumble for the doorbell. He was afraid of the awful sameness of this street, afraid and depressed.

His knock resounded, and Miss Susie, in the process of lacing her corset, cracked open her bedroom door and called:

"Hizer! Oooh, Hizer! For mercy's sake please go to that door!"

Halfway down the kitchen stairway a muffled voice answered,
"Hizer's beating eggs, Miss Susie; I'll go."

A gasped "Thank you" descended to Benjamin Mead. The robust
young man with extended cheeks swallowed twice; the ladyfinger
in his left, then right cheek, slid down his throat. With two bounds
of his muscular legs he was up to the first floor pantry, running on
through the front hall, and examining the figure in the vestibule,
whose peddler-knock had disturbed Miss Susie.

"Much obliged, but we don't want any vanilla extract, nor needles,
nor——"

His eyes widened when he saw Clay Abernathy's new suit and
shoes. Mead's voice was apologetic as he asked,

"Are you looking for some place?"

"Yes," Clay replied uncertainly, "I am. For Miss Susie Slagle's."
Ben's big hand shot forward:

"This is Miss Susie's. Give me your bag and come on in."

Clay obeyed. Ben lifted the new suitcase and backed into the narrow hallway.

"My name's Mead," Ben said as he put the suitcase upon the worn
Axminster runner.

"Mine's Abernathy."

"Glad to know you," Ben remarked as he closed the door.

"So am I," said Clay and they shook hands.

To the left of this narrow hall, a pair of double doors opened into
the parlor, a long, narrow room with two windows in the front wall.
Opposite the double doors was a fireplace which, in the memory of no
medical student, had ever been used. In it were laid the materials for
a perfectly good fire, but legend explained that the rafters of the
second floor extended through the upper chimney, and nobody had
ever been so rude as to find out if this were true. Over the fireplace
was a gingerbread mantel with an oval mirror and many "bird
houses." It was painted white and each balcony contained some knick-
knack which Miss Susie treasured. In one was the carved red bird she
had always hung upon her Christmas tree; in another a piece of stone
from the Petrified Forest, sent her by one of her boys while he was on
his honeymoon. Other honeymoon gifts were a small Dresden vase, a
pair of Chinese slippers, and spread behind the black horsehair sofa,

two large Japanese paper fans with figures whose anatomical lines had puzzled many a trained eye. The furniture of the room was heterogeneous and prim: a red plush love seat, two badly worn morris chairs, and two carved rosewood chairs with fragile legs, which sat each in front of a lace-curtained window and were never used.

The carpet had been bought by Miss Susie's Papa for her Mamma upon the first anniversary of their wedding sixty-three years before. The feet of many medical students had suffocated most of the petals from the red roses. Two patent rockers, one upholstered in brown plush and one in black horsehair, three or four nondescript straight chairs, and a marble-topped center table completed the furnishings.

Only by the pictures could one judge the length of time the room had been in use. Two reprints of Detaille battle scenes flanked a Gibson Girl in color hung exactly below an extensive view of the Pantheon. A picture of Queen Victoria stared directly across the room at an engraving of Napoleon and never flinched. A chromo of a mother rocking a baby to sleep acted as a sacred causeway by means of which the eye approached the "God is Love" sampler which Miss Susie had worked in red silk upon black taffeta when she was nine. It was now preserved in a gilt frame with a white plush background. Between the two windows was a large engraving of "Washington Irving and his Friends"; for many years a heated debate had raged among Miss Susie's students as to whether or not Hawthorne had a pituitary tumor!

In a far corner stood a single bookcase with glass doors; it held the last expensive present Papa had given Mamma—a complete Chamber's *Encyclopedia* for 1880.

While Clay's eyes were trying to transmit the contents of this remarkable museum to his brain, the portieres in the single doorway, at the far corner of the parlor, parted.

The student who stood there was tall, black-haired and perfectly co-ordinated. The grace which seemed to flow, silently, from the crown of his high forehead, down the straight flanges of his high-bridged nose, through his controlled lips and steady jaw, radiated on into his hands as he eased his cigarette papers from a vest pocket.

"Hey, Jack," Ben Mead said, "come meet the new patient!"

When Abernathy became aware of this man he felt as baffled as he had when he saw a feud-famous Hatfield, who had, also, seemed to see what was behind, as well as in front of him, without appearing to observe either.

"Be glad to meet him," the man in the doorway drawled. His wide-set gray eyes, which had been out of reach, became circled and centered with black as he smiled and threaded his way adroitly through the parlor miscellany. Then he extended his long hand and said, "Don't mind Mead's insults, Mister . . .?"

"Abernathy," Ben supplied. "And this, Mister Abernathy, is Alex Ashby, of the Texas Ashbys, whose great-grandfather died in the Alamo, and whose grandfather ——"

"Whoa, Ben. Whoa ——!"

Mead ignored Ashby's retort, took a stance and continued, "Whose grandfather led a company of V.M.I. cadets at the Battle of New Market, and whose worthless descendant ——"

"By some miracle," Ashby interrupted, "is still in medical school and about to enter his second year. Won't you have a seat, Mister Abernathy? Mead, give us some cheroots, those two-for-five things of yours."

Clay Abernathy forgot to associate Ashby with the Hatfields when he heard his voice, again; for Alex Ashby had that rare gift of a deep register voice which can talk through all emotions and never jar. It put Clay at his ease.

As Alex took his own advice and sat down on the horsehair sofa, Abernathy did so, too. Ben Mead, who knew that Alex could get as much information by silence as other men did with words, still, couldn't resist words. He said, "Where are you from, Abernathy? And what college did you go to? If you don't tell me, Ashby will find it out without you ever knowing about it."

They waited for Abernathy to light his cheroot, on the match which Ashby was holding, and Alex confirmed what he had seen from the doorway. The brogues which covered the splay feet of the newcomer were expensive; his vest wrinkled over his stomach, which by the time he was forty would protrude into his conversation; even now his fat, soft hands circled above and below it. His light blue eyes, the Texan noted, had lids with a cow-rim of pink-white, and his gold-threaded hair was slicked, with a right side part, to his well-shaped head.

"Like butter," Ashby reflected. Then Abernathy's loose-lipped mouth parted on a row of square white teeth as he turned toward Mead and Ashby thought, "Like butter on corn—field corn."

Abernathy said, "I'm from West Virginia, Mead. Mills Gap. Got my A. B. University of West Virginia last year. My dad——"

The ringing of the doorbell interrupted, and Ben said, as he went to answer it, "Bet the little stranger has blue eyes, yellow curls, nice manners. Two bits to a nickel he'll make a swell bedside artist!"

"I'll take you up," Alex yawned. "Open the door!"

The two students on the sofa waited silently. Then as the door swung inward, Alex Ashby burst into a rippling laugh, and Ben tried to hide the new fellow behind his own bulk.

"Yes," he said loudly, "this is Miss Susie Slagle's. What can I do for you, Mister——?"

The solid, unobtrusive young man replied:

"I'm Silas Holmes and I am to board here."

"Then by all means, come in," Mead answered gravely.

"Thank you," Silas said and put down his bags beside Abernathy's new suitcase.

Alex Ashby noted that his gladstone was badly worn and the carryall had frayed corners. He also realized that the fellow was either stupid, embarrassed, or completely solid. Then he saw the microscope bundled under the old overcoat. Half a minute later when he had lifted the overcoat from the heavy shoulders and was hanging it on the rack, Alex understood why it did not fit the boy who had worn it. In the collar band was a name tag upon which was written: "Silas Holmes, M.D."

Ben had eased back into the parlor.

"That's a fine 'scope. Mind if I look at her?" Alex asked.

"Sure, go ahead."

Alex adjusted the lens to his eye: "She's a beauty!"

"Is she really?"

"Yes. Why?"

"I just wanted to know. She was my father's and I thought maybe she was worn out."

Clay said to Ben while Holmes and Ashby were talking in the hall, "Why did you call Ashby 'Jack' and then, later, say that his name was Alex?"

"If you look at him, now, you'll understand," Ben replied.

Alex Ashby was leaning over the 'scope, and the long mirror in the hatrack reflected, unmercifully, the enormous distance to which his ears stuck out.

"See?" Mead said. "I measured 'em once when he was drunk. Two inches and a half!"

"You're foolin'!"

"Try it yourself, sometime."

"Where did you go to college?" Clay asked.

"I went to The University," Ben replied.

An unenlightened look remained on Clay's face and Ben conceded the point and said, "Er—Virginia."

"Never been there."

"It's a grand place. You ought to go!"

Ashby and Silas Holmes entered the parlor.

"Mister Holmes, I'd like you to know Mister Abernathy and the man who let you in is Mister Mead; my name is Ashby."

Mead and Abernathy rose to acknowledge the introductions.

Ashby put out his hand, "Say, Mead, don't you owe me a quarter?"

"Yes, you old double-eared—" then Mead swallowed, remembered he was among strangers and turning his back upon Ashby offered Silas Holmes a seat beside Abernathy on the sofa. Abernathy said, as Silas seated himself, "Is this your first year here?"

"Hope so," Silas replied.

Ben Mead was busy passing cheroots, getting ash trays, lighting matches, and Ashby lounged against the door jamb and watched his classmate. Mead's merry blue eyes counteracted his ordinary nose and confirmed his amused sensual mouth. His perennially red neck and infectious grin were contrasted by his unruly straw-colored hair. Ben's cowlicks were as numerous as his conversations. "The affairs of humanity and the high wind of medicine blow a steady gale in Ben's vicinity," Ashby meditated, affectionately.

"Hey, Ben, that quarter is drawing interest," he said, and as Mead moved over beside him, Abernathy remarked to Holmes:

"This is my first year here, too. Sure is different from West Virginia."

"It's colder than North Carolina," Holmes said.

Ben Mead heard the words North Carolina, swung around and asked, "North Carolina, huh? Are you a Tar Heel?"

"No, I went to Wake Forest."

"Where's your home?" Mead's questions were never offensive.

"Jefferson City," Holmes replied, then closed his lips and looked slowly around the room. Ashby engaged Ben's attention again and pocketed the quarter.

Abernathy said to the man beside him, "You second generation, here, too?"

"Hopkins or Miss Slagle's?" Holmes asked.

"Either ——?"

"Both," Silas replied conclusively.

"Then, we're two of a kind," Abernathy grinned.

"Guess we are," Silas said absently, and puffed on his cheroot.

"Yes. My dad's name is the same as mine, Clayton Abernathy. Ever hear your dad speak of him?"

"No. My father didn't talk about his classmates. Never talked about anything but sick people and politics."

"What was his party?"

"Democratic, of course."

Clay shifted his hand and began flicking ashes, surreptitiously, behind the horsehair sofa. He fell silent, too. This mutt wasn't worth the effort, anyhow.

Ben, who had seated himself in one half of the love seat with his extended legs placed horizontally over the other half, asked, "Well, fellows, who threw the noose over your necks?"

"What noose?" Silas's question was solemn.

Ben shot him a startled gaze; Ashby relaxed his long body into one of the worn morris chairs, shifted his cigarette and hid a smile.

"Holmes, you're all right!" Ben Mead said. "Ten to one your grandpa's a homeopath!"

Abernathy laughed.

Silas Holmes replied, "He was the son of a country doctor and so am I."

"That's something to be proud of," remarked Alex.

Ben twisted his legs off the love seat and asked politely, "Where does your father practice?"

"He died in April."

'What was the diagnosis?" Ashby inquired slowly.

"Coronary thrombosis, whatever that is," Silas replied.

Ben Mead said, "What is it, Jack?"

Ashby answered, "I'm not positive yet, but I think it's the doctor's friend, in the same way that pneumonia is the old man's friend. Comes from long excitement and tension. Don't know the symptoms. Do you, fellows?"

Clay Abernathy shook his head and Silas sat silent.

Ben changed the subject.

"Any more fellows due tonight, Jack?"

"Don't know. Did you ask Hizer?"

"Naw."

Abernathy turned to Mead and said, "Why did you study medicine?"

" 'Cause," Ben's eyes lighted and he lifted his legs back onto the love seat, "I couldn't study anything else. Hell, I just had to be a doctor! When my little brother cut his head when he was three and I was five, I wanted to sew it up before the doctor came, and when he came and I held the wound closed while he was taking the stitches, it was all I could do to keep from snatching the needle out of his hands and doing it myself!

"Shucks! I sound like I think I'm something great. But I don't. What I want is a wife, babies and a dog—to go fishing on Wednesday afternoons, live in a town of thirty thousand people and *matter*. Medicine won't ever be a bit better for my being in it. I haven't any false notions about myself."

"The fish-and-matter-type," Ashby said teasingly.

Ben ignored him and continued to the newcomers who sat upon the edge of the sofa, "Now Ashby is goin' to be one of those three-in-a-generation fellows."

"Whoa, Ben, lasso your own ego."

Ben went on, "I'm not complimenting you, you old prairie dog, I'm just explainin' you. You see, fellows, his eye is always glued to somebody's 'scope. He's about slides like a souse about drinks. As full of whys as a bedbug is of blood.

"Now me—well, I'd rather have a nigger with a knife in his belly than all the damned slides in the Pathological Building. Just drives me crazy snooping at those things. Rather look for fleas on a hound dog! Damned if I wouldn't."

Silas and Clay couldn't speak. They were inhaling their first fumes of medical enthusiasm.

"Ben," Alex said, "I'm glad you had those hysterics. I used to think you were going to be a psychiatrist. Now——"

"Lissen, Jack!" Ben sputtered as he jumped up. "I'll stand a lot of kiddin', but there are limits."

Ashby shoved him into the other morris chair.

"Bennie, I used to lie awake worrying about you, son! But now—hell, kid, don't you know what you are?"

"Naw, I—" Ben began, his face matching his neck.

"Boy, you're a born surgeon. And I'm not joking!"

"Ah, bologny, Jack!" But Ben was pleased and his voice showed it. Silas asked Ashby, "What's the hardest subject in the first year?"

"Depends. Anatomy is a pretty steady grind. Gummy, too. The histology and neurology, I think, are more interesting."

"What do you think?" Silas turned to Mead.

"Kid," Ben said, "it's—histology, I mean—just a little more map work. Only there you work on such lousy little pieces you have to put them under a microscope to find 'em. In anatomy you just dig around and look at guts. In histology you dig in guts and look for nerves. In neurology you dig in nerves and look for—ever take a watch to pieces? Same kind of thing!"

"What," asked Clay Abernathy, "is a psychiatrist?"

Ben flung his legs asunder and emitted a loud howl.

"Well, for the love of Pete! Say, Ashby, wouldn't that hurt 'em? Son of a general practitioner and he don't know what a psychiatrist is!"

"What is it, really?" Clay blustered.

"Well, it's a specialist in mental disorders, emotional conflicts, and sexology," Ashby answered.

"Lis-sen, Jack! Tell 'em the truth. Boys, it's a specialist in everything that isn't surgical, microscopic or straightforward."

"Is it 'required'?" Silas portrayed emotion at last.

"Yeah," Ben said, "you got to pass through a course in it, so if you become a G. U. man you'd recognize a sex-repressed old maid when you saw one."

"What's a G. U.?" said Silas.

"A male gynecologist," Ben replied.

"What's a gynecologist?"

"Say boy, quit razzing me!"

"I'm not razzing you. I'm inquiring."

Silas's heavy-lidded eyes looked straight into Ben's blue ones.

Ben explained. "Gynecology (G-Y-N from now on) is a study of the female organs of reproduction and their functions. See? Genito-Urinary (G. U.) is the study of the same organs—naw—not the same organs—but male organs of reproduction and their functions. Obstet-rics (O-B) is ——"

"I know," Silas said. "Thank you."

"Ever seen a delivery?" Ben put the question eagerly.

"Oh, yes. Lots of 'em."

"Ever seen a breech?" Ben asked.

"Five," Silas answered and closed his lips completely.

"Gosh!" Ben's tone was that one uses when admiring a football player.

Clay stirred restlessly; he felt that Silas was absorbing the stage, which annoyed him. He did not know what a breech was and he did not care to show his ignorance.

"How many cadavers do you do in a year?" He shot the question into the room during the first conversational lapse.

"Depends," said Ashby. "You are required to do half of one. Some fellows do one, complete. Some, two."

" 'Fore Christmas," put in Ben. "Although you have some 'natomy in the second quarter, too."

Silas groaned dismally.

"Is the prof good?"

Clay didn't give a damn what the prof was, but he wanted to keep in the conversation.

"Not to look at!" Ben answered. "Somebody told me he'd willed his body to the medical school for a cadaver. I think they ought to take it. Wouldn't need to do any embalming, for one thing. He's all right, though. Knows his anatomy and he don't get mad. Only trouble is he spits on the back of your neck when he leans over to show you something. His teeth are false and don't fit."

"My dad says that his teacher was a peach," Clay continued.

"Who taught him?"

"A guy named Mall."

"Heh! Your dad's right," Ben said. "He shut a fellow up in a room with a cadaver, a scalpel and a whetstone and let him sweat his hair off. That's why so many of the older Hopkins men chew tobacco."

"Do they?" Clay was astounded.

"Sure, got spittoons in all the operating rooms."

"Aw, shut up, Ben! Boys, he's stringing you."

Ben looked reproachfully at Alex and continued:

"Those old cadavers, you know, were tough as dog biscuits, and the students had to sharpen their scalpels—well, you've seen men with a whetstone around a country store, haven't you? But he had the right idea. Bet your dad remembers his guts, even yet."

Abernathy smiled uncertainly. He thought, "Whose guts? Mall's?"

"Mall never believed in telling you anything," Ben went on. "Made you teach yourself and if you ask me it was a better method. You stayed taught then."

"I'm not so sure it was better," Ashby said slowly.

"Yeah. Depends," Ben mimicked solemnly.

"Why wasn't it?" Silas asked.

"Dead men's knowledge ought to be a stairway to the progress of live men."

Silas had crossed his large flat feet and sat contemplating the unesthetic length of them. His face was totally devoid of expression. He agreed with Ashby, so he said nothing.

Their silence made Clay uneasy. "How's the grub here?" he asked.

"Doctor," Ben said caustically, "never disgrace a dish, nor a gravy, nor even a biscuit from Miss Susie Slagle's table with that word! Didn't your papa tell you? The most famous thing about this dump, outside of the Big Four, is Miss Susie Slagle's table. The Dean won't allow any student with heart trouble, a tendency toward gout, asthmatic symptoms or fallen arches to board at Miss Susie's. Mean sure death if he did. Gastric suicide in six months."

Silas asked Ashby, "How many students to a class?"

"About seventy-five."

"How many make it?"

"Around sixty."

While that profoundly disturbing fact was penetrating Silas's mind, Ben's voice filled the room, answering a question which Clay had asked him in an aside:

"Your dad's right, Abernathy. The beer's the best thing about this dump. Naw, we can drink. If you'd gone to the University you'd understand: at Virginia, no fellow ever comes to a lecture loaded, and out of lectures his time's his own. It's like that here. The men who teach you haven't the time to be running up alleys looking for bad students. They are like Ashby! Got their eyes glued to 'scopes and the future of medicine."

"Sounds grand."

"Don't kid yourself. It's not. It's the toughest grind in the world, Abernathy! Medicine is!"

"Yeah, Mead, but we're lucky to get in at Hopkins and have a chance to study under famous men."

"Aw, rats!"

Then Clay put the question which had been burning within him for a good twelve hours. "Say, fellows, what kind of a town is Baltimore?"

Ashby and Holmes knew that the question had been addressed to Mead. Ben said, "How do you mean?"

"Oh, you know what I mean."

"Yeah," Ben said. "I used to know, but since I came to Baltimore I've forgot. Son, Baltimore is the slowest town God ever allowed to put on lampposts! A man's got to be downright terrible to go to the dogs in Baltimore. Boy, to raise hell in Baltimore, you've got to raise it from the ground on up, haven't you, Alex?"

"There are nearly half a million people in Baltimore," Ashby answered. "A man can see life here, I guess."

"Shucks, Alex! You talk like you've got tertiary syphilis!"

Loud guffaws filled the narrow parlor. The Christmas-tree bird swung upon its perch, and Queen Victoria's picture took a crazy slant as Silas slapped his knee. Then he looked admiringly at Ben. Whatever else you felt about Mead, he certainly was entertaining.

When the din died down Ben finished, "It's no laughing matter, fellows. It's too damned true. A man's got to be just natural-born wicked to go wrong in this cemetery. That's all it is—just an endless brick cemetery—two and three stories high. Like living in vaults."

"It's a good place to work," Alex Ashby suggested.

"How soon do you know if you fail?" Silas asked, turning to him.

"End of the first year, usually. Depends, Holmes. Some fellows get out before then of their own accord. Can't stand the grind. Did your father do much research?"

"Not much. He was too busy. But he did his own lab work, and if he wasn't sure then he sent them to the state lab for checking. Usually he was right."

"Many of the greatest advances have been made by general practitioners, especially in heart work. I wonder why?"

"Search me," Silas replied. "What part of Texas are you from?"

Ashby grinned, "How did you know I was from Texas?"

"Because you're so big, drawl and roll cigarettes."

"Fair enough, Holmes, but aren't North Carolinians big?"

"Not in the same way, but I can't explain what I mean. I can't explain much of anything. Anyhow, what's the good of explaining things, when you already know them? Explaining is to clear up what you don't know, isn't it?"

Alex's eyes studied this new fellow closely and as he opened his lips to answer, Ben's voice interrupted:

"Now, Miss Susie, you look 'em over, and if either of 'em don't suit, why I'll do just as you say."

They rose and eyed the lady who stood in the hallway.

Miss Susie Slagle was plump, white-haired, and had an hourglass figure. Her extremities were delicate and dainty; small hands, small feet. Her nerves or her shyness, Alex Ashby had long ago decided, could be read by the state of agitation of her bosom. But read alone one could never diagnose from which emotion she was suffering. Read in conjunction with her eyes, one knew immediately. When she was shy, they looked past you. When she was nervous they looked

over you. Now she was neither shy nor nervous. Something which
had become a regular event in her life was taking place and it made
her very happy. And very nearly pretty. The total lack of personal
experience left her face, under its halo of white hair, startlingly childish. And the perfect roundness of her figure, for the last forty years,
made that youthful face not incongruous, but natural; made her
upturned nose and her small-lipped mouth, with the regular pearly
teeth, understandable.

She had all the arrested physical charm of a voluptuous virgin,
coupled with the emotional unsteadiness of a woman who has never
had a beau. Up to her thirty-fifth year she had had Mamma and
Papa; and from their deaths, twenty-seven years ago, she had had
medical students. Her maternal instincts had gone into culinary
channels and though no man ever proposed marriage to Miss Susie,
she had known the American medical student for years with a pro-
fundity which would have amazed his mother and annoyed his
sweetheart.

"Miss Susie," Ben continued, "these boys claim they belong to you.
Ever see 'em before?"

Clay Abernathy shuffled his feet, but Silas Holmes's composed stillness centered her attention. She turned her larkspur eyes upon him
and said in little gasps:

"Yes, of course. Just like unwrapping Christmas packages ahead
of time! That was a nice letter your mother wrote me, my dear. She
must hate to lose you, Silas."

Silas stammered, "Thank you, ma'am."

Ashby asked, "How did you know him, Miss Susie?"

"By his quietness, I think."

Then she glanced at Clay Abernathy and said softly,

"You're a surprise. Now let me see: there are three boys, new boys,
besides Silas, and you couldn't be Elbert Riggs, because his uncle
wrote me how he looked. You are Clayton Abernathy's child, aren't
you?"

"Yes, ma'am. He sent his regards, Miss Susie," Clay replied
suavely, and Silas knew envy for the first time.

"But I thought he was coming——?"

"Somebody got sick at the last minute. So he sent his regards."

"Oh, I'm sorry. No! No, of course, I mean I thank you."

"Now, gentlemen," Ben cleared his throat, "prepare! Prepare! 'Two generations medical' means that when you come and when you graduate you rate a kiss from Miss Susie Slagle."

Miss Susie's composure disappeared. She collapsed into a chair and protested,

"Why, Benjamin Mead! No such thing! You know perfectly well ——"

"That I'm the only man alive with the courage to *demand* it!"

He leaned forward and kissed her full upon the lips. Silas sat down firmly in a chair across the room. Clay Abernathy squared his shoulders and cleared his throat.

Alex said teasingly, "This little boy wants his supper, Miss Susie."

Her maternal instincts rose above her embarrassment.

"And I want mine, too!" she said as she stood up. "Alex, you take Clay and Silas upstairs for a few minutes, while I go and make certain Hizer is ready."

As she swept down the hall, Ben called contritely, "What must I do, Miss Susie?"

"Carry the bags, dear."

Clay Abernathy laughed. They mounted the high, steep stairs, and Alex Ashby led the way. In his extended hands the microscope was tenderly balanced.

"Say," Ben said to Clay Abernathy, "d'y'ever hear 'bout what the Chinese woman said to the doctor ——?"

As in many Baltimore row houses, the dining room opened off the ell hallway; in this back hallway was the telephone, a portiere-draped parlor door, and a door into the dining room.

In the far end of the dining room were two windows reaching almost from the high ceiling to the floor and opening upon the scant backyard. In summer they commanded a faintly pretty view of a lombardy poplar. In winter, the back windows of the opposite row of houses, like the snagged teeth of rouged hags, were gaunt and hideous.

But when Clay, red with laughter at Ben's story, stepped into the room, he saw none of these things. It was night and at night this dining room presented an entirely different aspect.

Somehow, it had a way of closing in around you and calming your loneliness and fatigue, so that when you sat down at the table you always had an appetite. Perhaps the pictures and the sumptuous richness of the mahogany sideboard festooned with bunches of carved grapes created this sensation.

The pictures were uniform, very inspiring and somehow thoroughly human: they were the class pictures of every graduating class since Miss Susie had opened her boarding house. Compared with the fine oil portraits in the Medical Library, they were like nursery snapshots.

When a medical student went to the library and looked at the portraits he felt hopeless, disconnected. As Miss Susie had not entered the dining room, the boys stood in groups, chatting. Clay caught a blurred glimpse of the faces of the class of 1909, and his reaction was, "Hell, they are no better than I am. If they could do it, I can!"

As permanent as the "We beseech Thee to hear us, Good Lord," in the Litany, was the same group of men in the front row of every picture. 'Buck' Edwards, Dean Wingate, McMillan, Howe, Kelly, Welch, Halsted and with the classes prior to 1905, Osler.

The collecting of these pictures had been natural and to Miss Susie pleasurable; but she could have found no better way so quickly and so permanently to identify a medical student with his profession. It was as though eight hundred men immediately welcomed him, and welcomed him not as august and pompous superiors, but as perfectly human creatures with whose emotions and desires he was familiar. And that permanent front row, which contained four of the greatest names the profession had known, in bodies with legs crossed like the legs of other men, was of immeasurable importance.

One felt immediately: "They did it, under those men. And I'm going to do it, under them."

The wallpaper against which these pictures were placed had long ago lost its tone and color. Now it had permanent liver spots which had been occasioned by Hizer's rearrangement, according to fame and tipping peculiarities, while Miss Susie had been at a U.D.C. convention and done a round of cousin-visiting one summer. Upon her return, of course, they were rearranged according to years as was right and proper. But for six weeks the summer sun massaged them according to Hizer and the wallpaper had never recovered. At night the liver spots were not obnoxious and the rose-colored lamp shade with the glass fringe, style 1895, which centered over the table, gave the paper a pinkish tinge.

That egg-shaped table was one of the wonders of the medical world. It could seat anywhere from six to twenty-six people and had no extra leaves. The spacing of the places decided the number of occupants, and the length was never a disadvantage because the narrowness made reaching always easy. Even when the group dwindled at vacations and O-B quarters, nobody ever felt lonesome. Then you spread out and became dignified, or grouped at Miss Susie's end and were intimate; either emotion came naturally to every student she ever boarded.

Of course, upon such a table white cloths would have been impracticable, and Miss Susie had long ago worn out Mamma's supply, anyhow. After every meal Hizer scrubbed the walnut top with soap and water and then rearranged the doilies.

The construction of these doilies was the occupation of Miss Susie during her free moments, and every student of hers when he married received a full set of twelve dinner size, twelve breakfast size, twelve bread-and-butter size and a centerpiece. They literally circled the globe, and even the most elegant medical wives were never permitted to throw them away. In between times, Miss Susie's dainty fingers crocheted baby caps; she always kept a supply of these on hand. Generally within two years' time, one was dispatched to take its place beside the doilies in some medical linen closet.

The doilies in which she dropped stitches or which for some other professional reason were considered impossible for brides, were under the students' plates. To any person without Hizer's genius for organization their dispensing and the allotment of the napkin rings would have been a herculean task. But Hizer had long ago worked out a system. He collected from Miss Susie's left and dispensed from her right. If you went home in the meantime, or came back unexpectedly, you took what you got and thanked him!

With a negro's fine sense of estimate he made his character delineations with the napkin rings; of which there were three solid silver, two German silver, two bone, two wooden and one carved ivory. Miss Susie, of course, used the one with her name engraved upon it which Papa had given her. But one of the first summaries ever made of any medical student by his predecessors, was Hizer's napkin ring.

Alex Ashby had one of the silver ones; Ben Mead, this year, had graduated to German silver; Clay Abernathy and Silas Holmes, Hizer had scrutinized through a hole in the parlor portiere; for Clay he laid out a wooden ring, and for Silas Holmes a bone ring, temporarily.

While Silas was looking at his father's picture and feeling much closer to him than he had ever felt in life, the doorbell rang again. Ashby answered it. He returned as Ben Mead eased Miss Susie into her chair at the head of the table, and with him were two boys.

One was sharp featured, his nose pointed, his lips compressed. He was of medium height, well built, with reddish-brown hair and blue eyes.

"Miss Susie," Alex said, "this is Elbert Riggs."

Miss Susie's pleasant face broke into a welcoming smile. "I had a letter from your uncle. How do you do, Elbert?"

As Elbert bowed his shyness encircled him, and Hizer, peering through a crack in the pantry door, decided to give him the second German silver ring.

The other boy was tall and repulsively ugly. His face jutted from both ends. The lower lip protruded, the forehead overhung the bridge of his nose, the nose lay insignificantly between two long flat cheeks. He stood deferentially behind Alex and waited; when Hizer saw him he opened a drawer and took out the carved ivory napkin ring. He rated it. He was the ugliest man Hizer's eyes had ever beheld.

"And this," Alex Ashby announced, stepping aside, "is St. George Prentiss, Miss Susie."

The ugly youth smiled and Ben Mead said under his breath, "Huh?"

When St. George Prentiss smiled two things became apparent: he had perfect teeth, and his eyes, so green they looked blue, were filled with irresistible devilment.

Ben Mead backed into the pantry which ran parallel with the dining room and knocked Hizer against the china closet. Hizer groaned and as the swinging door slipped back toward the dining room he said, shaking his head monotonously,

"Mista Ben, dat boy's so hidjus he's lovely! If he don't be a lady-docta he's a fool."

Ben laughed, then eased into the dining room as Miss Susie said to the standing students, "Alex, will you please sit at the other end of the table. Silas, I want you on my right. Ben, please sit between Silas and St. George Prentiss. Clayton, will you sit down there by Alex. Yes, across from St. George. And Elbert, come here by me and tell me about your uncle. There's no use waiting for Minnegerode. He's in the fourth year and will probably come in tomorrow after-noon."

After they were seated, Miss Susie said grace. It was the same grace which Papa had said when she was a little girl:

"Lord, bless this food to our use and ourselves to Thy service. For Christ's sake."

A dignified "Amen" ran around the table. Then she tinkled the bell and Hizer appeared in a white coat and nondescript trousers.

He was a tall black negro with a nose almost as wide as his mouth. His teeth were as perfect as those of St. George Prentiss. His shoulders were flat and his carriage was military. His head was bullet-shaped, and his airs were a combination of the best styles in medical bedside manners of the past twenty years. He could lay aside his dignity as a white man lays aside an overcoat. But even in moments of house cleaning no vestige of it had ever been dislodged before Miss Susie. In her presence he was perfection itself: black perfection. And a perfect mirror of her religious beliefs and her moral attitude. Even the students he coached in songs, who had seen under that dignity the enormous collection of dirty jokes which had been inoculated by their predecessors, in Miss Susie's presence, never, for an instant, in-fringed on it.

At table Hizer was the servant par excellence. The white coat overlay his dignity with a grace which, later, was unconsciously copied in many halls and corridors.

"You rang, Miss Susie?"

"Yes. The napkins, please, Hizer."

He returned with the rings and placed them around the table.

"Thank you," St. George Prentiss said as he took the napkin from the ivory circle. Hizer bowed.

He had heard Alex Ashby ask, "Where are you from, Prentiss?" and he wanted to get his good ear into range.

"Nowhere," Prentiss replied. Hizer lowered his head and listened with his eyes.

Miss Susie ordered sharply, "Please bring in the supper, Hizer."

"Yassum," Hizer said and went out of the pantry door.

Prentiss continued, "I didn't mean to be rude. That's literal truth. My parents are dead, and I've bummed about since I was a kid. Been lots of places. Stayed nowhere."

"So you came here?" Alex put the question, privately.

"A Hopkins man I met in B. A. nursed me through a three weeks' fever and said I ought to study medicine. Hidden passion I had. Didn't know it myself. I've come to find out."

Hizer returned with the supper, and the conversation shifted. In front of Miss Susie he set a tureen of chicken hash. Beside it was a large dish of grits, a long boat of gravy. Halfway up the table he deposited an enormous platter of hash-browned potatoes; across, he placed a dish of green peas and a corn pudding. Then he brought in the biscuits, the two kinds of preserves, the coffee and the big dish of lettuce and tomato salad. When he returned again he had a plate of batter cakes and a large jug of molasses.

Prentiss studied the design on his teaspoon and smiled. Alex Ashby noted the smile. "Been there?"

"Three times. It's the best city I know outside 'Frisco, New Orleans is. What is a souvenir spoon doing here?"

"Medical conventions have been held in New Orleans," Ashby said. "Give yourself a few days; you'll understand."

Hizer did not remain in the dining room during meals; therefore there was no question of first and second helpings. Every boy ate as much of everything as he desired, and when Hizer came to bring in hot biscuits he took the empty dishes and refilled them.

At the conclusion of the main course, he cleared the table and placed in front of Miss Susie the large round bowl of iced custard dotted with whipped cream and the chocolate cake which was always baked in the pan in which Mamma's wedding cake had been made and therefore seemed the largest chocolate cake any of the new boys had ever seen.

The conversation had become pleasantly general. The food and the fine glow of the pictures had erased from harassed minds the unpleasantness of travel and St. George Prentiss realized that he was experiencing a sensation much more "heady" than any he had ever achieved through drink.

Miss Susie rose and motioned the students to remain seated, but Ben Mead and Alex Ashby stood up and the other boys followed.

"Please," she began nervously, "please, I want to just speak a minute to you. To all of you. About—er—about the way— My dears, it is a very great pleasure to me to have you, to feel that for at least one year you belong to me. And I hope you will understand that at any time you are welcome in any part of this house you care to enter. You are perfectly welcome to eat between meals, to have beer and cheese in the pantry; that is, of course, if you can afford the beer. I shall be delighted to furnish the cheese.

"And—there isn't anything—yes, two things only, which I am obliged to ask that you do me the courtesy to refrain from doing.

"The first is, please, *at no time* smoke in bed. I am not afraid of mice. I am not afraid of skeletons—" the group stood attentively listening and her confession seemed like that of a pleading little girl— "I have no locks upon the doors. You are free to enter and leave at any hour—but I am afraid, terribly afraid, of fire. And when you are in bed, tired and worn with study, you are very liable to fall asleep. If you are smoking, the cigarette ——

"No! I can't even picture it! It makes me shiver to try to! And therefore I want you to promise me not to do it!"

The nod was silent, universal and solemn.

"Please," Miss Susie ducked her head, "it's quite all right now, you know. Smoking anywhere, anytime, except in bed is quite all right. And now the other rule ——"

She blushed and picked under the cuff of her white shirtwaist for her handkerchief.

"The other rule is ——"

She coughed and Ben Mead said, "It is a stag house at all times, even when Miss Susie goes to the church convention!"

"Why Ben, of course nobody ever thought of breaking his promise behind my back!"

"Miss Susie," Ben soothed, "you misunderstood me. I beg your pardon. I didn't mean it that way. They understand, don't you, fellows?"

Again the nod was universal and Clay Abernathy asked boldly, "Don't we have keys, Miss Susie?"

"Not unless you want them. The front door is never locked unless both Hizer and I are out, and that hasn't happened in ten years.

"My dear, it may seem a little peculiar to you, but you see, so far as I am concerned, you are perfectly free to order your comings and your goings according to your own judgment. It has always been my belief that a gentleman needs no restrictions. You are no longer college students but men upon the threshold of your professional life. And one thing I know about the medical profession is that to be a good doctor and manage other people, a man must be first able to manage himself.

"Perhaps I'm an old maid with ridiculously lofty principles, but if I am, then it has been very dear of your fathers and your uncles and your predecessors to preserve my illusions. They have prepared me to trust you implicitly. And I do!"

Something fine and yet intangible ran from her smiling eyes into those of every boy present. Something that most of them remembered all their lives.

Mead and Ashby had heard this speech before: after a year in her house, they understood what it meant.

At the doorway she turned and said, "One more thing I'd like to ask of you is that you *do not* fail. *None* of my boys has ever failed. I—I—simply couldn't stand it! Hizer will be here in a minute with a decanter of sherry. On occasions, like this, we have it. Please, I trust you will excuse me. There is an Altar Guild meeting. But in my heart I toast, my dear boys, your futures!"

Half an hour later, Hizer, with the group in tow, was displaying his museum. The banister from the second to the third floor was a network of initials, and the new boys were calling, "Who's S.R.A.?"

Hizer's eyes rolled solemnly.

"Samuel Randolph Anderson."

"The surgeon in Richmond?" Clay Abernathy asked.

"O'course," Hizer replied deprecatingly. "An' dat lone S was done by Docta Shelter. Docta Chris Shelter whut wint to Cuba wid Docta Walta Reed an' didn't cum back. Docta Reed's initials is above hisn. Dat Chris Shelter was de funnies' boy. Seems like yestiddy he sung dem awful songs at Easta."

They mounted to the third floor. Prentiss dropped back and asked Ashby, "What does he mean, 'at Easter'?"

"Oh, wait and see."

"It's a long time to wait."

"You'll get an inkling next Sunday, perhaps."

The rooms on the third and fourth floors were small and contained ordinary cheap machine-made bureaus, tables and chairs. The beds were the ornamental features. When Mamma and Papa died and Miss Susie bought them they had been black iron. But after twenty-seven years of anatomical sketching the black paint only etched the contours of arms, legs, muscles, tibias and the instruments which had come into use in the last quarter century.

It was because she never objected to this form of self-expression that Miss Susie was held in such respect and that the only rules she ever laid down, rules upon which she could not check, were never broken. These beds and their symbols were among Hizer's most guarded possessions. He knew the history of every scratch and the present reputation of the man who made it.

Turning to Abernathy, Hizer said, "See dis bed wid all dem kinds ob forceps. Docta Ab—yo' Pa—done 'em de same fall he brung me back my rabbit foot an' dat Wes' Virginny corn."

Reaching in his pocket, he drew out the end of his brass watch chain and showed the boys the rabbit foot from which the years had rubbed most of the hair.

"Too bad you didn't keep the corn, too," Clay spoke knowingly. "Stuff they make in the mountains now isn't fit for a hog to swallow."

"How was yours, Hizer?" Ben asked.

"Whew! Strong ez a mule! If I hadn't ob hitched dis rabbit foot onto me 'fore I drunk it, I nevva would ob kno'ed where it was."

The boys snickered and Riggs asked,

"That foot bring you any luck?"

"Yassuh! It sholy did. 'Bout dat time I was tryin' to marry myself to a gal whut aftawards knifed her man, an' 'cept fur dat foot——"

The boys roared. Hizer overlooked the laughter as he opened the door of the masterpiece of those upper regions to which Miss Susie never penetrated: the bathroom on the third floor. It resembled any other large-sized clothes closet which had been turned into a bathroom along about 1890. The tub was too short to lie down in, the basin was marble and the faucets leaked. The toilet had a long chain pulley and an overhead arrangement for flushing. But the walls were unique among the bathroom walls of Baltimore. They represented the medical impression of feminine beauty, naked and unadorned, since 1890. They made the buxom blonde chromos in saloons look innocent and childish.

Some of the sketches were done with crayon and pencil upon what had once been the white plaster wall; and that of Pinkney Dourmee, who now had skyscraper offices in New York where he directed the welfare of millions of life insurance policyholders, represented an utterly ravishing female with 1903 curves. She was done in black crayon with red anatomical trimmings and all the veins, nerves and blood vessels were richly and carefully laid in. She was securely fastened to the ceiling.

Prentiss found her charming and as intricate as an etching. When he inquired into her history Hizer said, "Dat boy had de ruffes' mind. An' now he's got on spats an' ridin' in a privet car. Sum scrumpshus he is!"

The students laughed and Mead said to Abernathy, "Say, that reminds me, did you ever hear the one about the King of Siam and the urologist?"

They retired to the stairway and sat down.

Then Hizer began assigning rooms to the newcomers. It was an unwritten law that all newcomers lived upon the fourth floor. The second, third and fourth year men lived upon the second and third floors. The house champion had the bedroom over the parlor, on the second floor, while Miss Susie's room was over the dining room; and the boys doing their O-B quarter usually had the rooms at the head of the stairway upon the third floor.

"What is the house champion?" Clay Abernathy asked.

"Wait till Sunday an' you'll see," Hizer announced, peering over his spectacles in a way which stopped discussion.

"Who is it?"

"Ashby's it," Ben said. "Wouldn't ever dream he was to look at him, Abernathy! I'll never forget his song last Easter. No suh!"

"Let dead dogs rest, Ben. 'Fraid there's competition around."

"The man who can compete with or corrupt you, Jack Ashby, hasn't been born, let alone reached adolescence."

"For a confirmed joke-toter you're very modest."

"A toter's one thing, Doctor. But a composer is something else again!"

The newcomers laughed and Hizer said slowly, "You gonna make dese gentmens think us is dis-repute-able, Mista Ben, if you ain't ca'ful."

The boys roared. Ben asked, "Well, aren't we, Hizer?"

"No suh! Dis is de house ob famus doctas; o'course bein' doctas, you gotta kno' eberything 'bout eberything. Dat's all!"

"Yeah, dat's all!" Ben mimicked. "But it's a big swallow if you ask me. Let's go to Otto's and wash it down with some beer, fellows."

Chapter Two

FAMOUS MEN WERE ONCE STUDENTS

On the morning of the first of October, 1912, Dr. Howe was seated at the table in the dining room of his home upon Cathedral Street. The silver ring into which his smooth, shapely fingers were inserting a napkin had engraved upon it, "Elijah, Christmas 1872." As he put the ring upon the table and looked up, his keen blue eyes met the fine brown ones of his wife in an affectionate glance.

Then, by mutual consent, they turned to look at their only son who was expatiating to his younger sisters upon his agility as a tennis player.

Sally, now that she was nineteen, had her golden hair piled in a psyche knot and her father regretted that there was no longer a ribbon in it to match her blue eyes. She had her mother's plump figure and skin with the texture of a peach. One wanted to feel it and then to tuck her safely away.

It would have been as easy to tuck away Margaretta, who was seventeen, as to calm a tornado. Her upturned nose, flashing brown eyes and humorous mouth were as new and as intense as fresh dew. Bright red ribbons still tied the ends of her long plaits which were twined about her head. And her father remembered how, when she was younger, on occasion, she would sling those brown plaits over her shoulders with a gesture as expressive as profanity.

" 'Lije," she said to her brother across the table, "you are not as good as you think you are. Your backhand is stinking!"

"Margaretta!"

"Ma'am?" The look she gave her mother would have melted granite.

Her mother said, "Don't use words like that at this table, or elsewhere."

"Like what, Mamma?"

28

'Lije began, "Words like—" Mrs. Howe interrupted, "Don't you say it, either."

Margaretta grinned maliciously, "And if you *think* it, while you are a medical student, 'Lije, you'll have to come home and beg Mamma's pardon."

"Keep your mouth out of my future," 'Lije retorted. "Baby girls who still wear ribbons are too young to have opinions."

"Not about their brothers."

Mrs. Howe cleared her throat and her husband ordered hastily, "Gret, eat your breakfast. You're too skinny."

"Yes, sir," Margaretta answered demurely.

Then Dr. Howe looked down the table at his namesake and asked, "Ready, son?"

Mrs. Howe took a deep breath, inclined her head and her eyes, which were like 'Lije's, softened as she remarked, "To think we've really lived to see this day, son."

Margaretta giggled and Sally lost her newly acquired dignity and joined in. The round, squat face of their brother turned flannel red. Mrs. Howe fingered her pompadour reprovingly and pursed her lips. Her silence plainly said that it was up to Dr. Howe to issue a reprimand.

Dr. Howe pretended not to notice for the morning sun had begun sifting through the curtains and previous experience had convinced him that if he remained at the breakfast table until the decanter of his wife's great-grandfather, in the china cabinet, began to shimmer he was in for a marital recital of his professional schedule.

He said gruffly, "Your being in medical school won't stop our three meals a day, 'Lije! You'll get another chance at kidney stew on Sunday. I'm going over to the hospital, anyhow. We might as well go together."

Then rising and turning to Mrs. Howe he continued, "Maria, please tell Miss Barr if they want me over in Washington Saturday for that consultation about the Secretary of State to tell 'em I'll come on the nine-thirty train."

His wife kept her eyes cemented upon his face and replied, "Very well, Elijah."

"Thank you, Maria."

"Papa, let me drive you over in the automobile," 'Lije suggested. "It would only take five hours."

"My job," the doctor's nose and broad expressive mouth were stern, though his eyes twinkled, "and yours beginning today, is to save life, not to endanger it. When I'm asked to meet all the leading men in the country for a consultation, I intend to arrive with my—er—stomach settled."

"Elijah Howe!"

"Beg your pardon, Maria! Your legs collapsed on you, 'Lije? You coming with me?"

'Lije thrust back his chair and stood erect. He lacked two inches of his father's height and all of his obvious intelligence, but there was about him a kind of dynamic force. To be the elder brother of two such opposite sisters required quickness and a cast-iron vanity. 'Lije had both. He barged forward and Dr. Howe moved in front of the cabinet filled with cut glass until his son had rounded the table.

'Lije kissed his mother and said, "It was nice of you to have kidney stew, Mamma."

Mrs. Howe's lips relaxed into a natural smile. Then she drew herself up and replied, "This is an occasion, Elijah. A great occasion!"

Dr. Howe looked solemnly at Margaretta and she remained as quiet as a nun.

'Lije said, "Thank you, Mamma," and Dr. Howe's voice yanked him forward as he announced,

"It will be a greater occasion when you graduate; but you have to register first—just as a matter of form, son! In the meantime there isn't any reason why you shouldn't continue cranking the automobile, is there?"

A few hours earlier upon that same morning of October first, 1912, Isidore Aaron gazed about a five by eight room. His head rested possessively against the closed door, his eyes were liquid with pleasure, his nose, high-bridged and with an unmistakable crook, overshadowed his sensitive lips, and his entire attention was centered upon the single white iron bed with the chipped pocks.

In a delirium of unbelief his eyes turned toward the other objects which had been brought in yesterday; the golden oak desk and the armchair which matched it.

Below in the tailor shop, he could hear his father whining, "Dot seelk drezz ezz mate tarrible. I feex hit, ivvin tree dollars."

Through the single open window, he could hear his mother saying to a customer in her junk yard, "Whan Isidore stoot fust at Maryland Uniwoisity, I hesk how motch to go to Hopkinks. Hopkinks, he vant to go. De boyess ve muff hout. Befurr, Isidore navver hev a rum. You should zee de bett. No! Isidore could hev de houze. He ezz worth four hundreet feefty dollars furr tree-fovr yeaz. Yat, he veell be a grend ducturr!"

Across the top of Isidore's desk were the textbooks of a first year medical student. He had begun buying them in the spring as soon as the secondhand bookstores received them from the students. Until yesterday they had been in the safe in the tailor shop.

Their bindings were like a sheaf of autumn leaves in the dingy room. The bare floor, the chipped bed, the scratched and rickety desk, the oily odor from the fertilizer plants across the harbor, were all purified by their presence. Flanking their ends and hung above them were the three things he had purchased with the six dollars award for his essay upon Genius Through the Ages.

One was a copy of Sir Thomas Browne's *Religio Medici*.

One was a copy of Sir William Osler's *Aequanimitas and Other Essays*.

One was a postcard photograph of the painting by Sargent, "The Four Doctors."

At nine, Isidore walked north up Broadway, the boys from Miss Susie Slagle's strolled south down Broadway and Dr. Howe and Elijah, perilously perched in an automobile, approached from the west with an audible roar.

Their courses converged at the narrow concrete sidewalk crammed in between three high brick buildings.

The boys from Miss Susie's were under the guardianship of Ben Mead. Second year students were not required to attend the opening, but Ben's love of humanity had lured him along.

In the sharp features of Elbert Riggs there was a sudden flicker of disappointment. Were these boxy old buildings the famous Johns

Hopkins Medical School? These old red brick piles! They couldn't touch the University of Pennsylvania. Clay Abernathy had a similar reaction. The State University in West Virginia still smelled of new paint, had a view, looked the part.

Silas Holmes's face showed no expression. This was the medical school and after four years of college he had reached it. The whole thing was a fact.

"Second floor of the anat. building which you are passing on the left, fellows, is where we dissect."

The group glanced up and saw nothing but an ordinary row of windows in an ordinary red brick wall. Ben sensed their disappointment and continued reprovingly, "Say, wait till you see the hospital and the profs!"

They followed him up a flight of worn slate steps into the main lobby of the Medical School. The wide hall had golden oak trimmings and a floor of worn planks which had been varnished so many times that the dust crevices beneath the varnish were like white veins. It might have been the gym entrance at Wake Forest, the lobby of the Baptist Sunday School building in Wheeling, or the entrance to the City Hall in Erie, Pennsylvania.

New varnish covered with thousands of foot-prints, a winding wide stairway, radiators which had just been resilvered; it might have been a negro high school in New Orleans. Except that lining the wall of the stairway were the photographs of many of the most famous living medical men, and the most famous dead medical men of the last fifty years. These were the signed pictures of the "profs."

At the foot of this stairway was a small photograph of Sargent's famous portrait, "The Four Doctors." And then came their students: man after man after man whose name is a by-word to doctors in the four corners of the globe.

St. George Prentiss eased his tall frame into a corner and watched the hall fill with men. Fathers, sons, new students, profs. His eyes glanced up for a gas jet, to make sure that this wasn't a dream. They found one, and he saw that this stairway wound up three floors and evidently profs present and future would take their appointed stations there, presently. When they reached the top floor, what then?

Blow the roof off the world! Phoof! Medicine would have mastered man!

For the first time in his life Prentiss was tingling from head to toe; if Ben Mead had not recalled him, he suspected that shortly he might have been too dizzy to move.

"Say, fellows," Ben was announcing, "Dean's office is there to the right. Over there to the left is the lab where you go now. I'll show you around upstairs later. Ssh! That's Kelly over there. Yeah, talking to Baetjer. X-ray did it. Baetjer's had operations galore. Lost some of his fingers. And one eye. Didn't know about protection when he started. No! He hasn't quit. Still goes on. There's 'Popsy' Welch coming in the door now. Isn't he funny looking—but more pathologists worship him than any man alive. Grand fellow! Grand!"

They felt like cockney children listening to the patter of a newshawker as the royal family passed. When the crowd began to move into the auditorium, Prentiss was again amazed. It was a large semicircular room with a rostrum near the door. Chairs in tier after rising tier were placed so that the men occupying the back row half obliterated the light from the long windows and could see into the adjacent anatomy building.

In the first few rows were the professors with an occasional son inserted and above, the seventy-five men who composed the entering class seated themselves noisily; between were the men from thirty to forty-five years old, assistants, instructors, associates.

Presently the talk died, a man mounted the rostrum; then a hush descended. The big auditorium was filled with October sunshine and the silence of waiting men. The Dean motioned to a doctor in a front row, who tiptoed to the door and shut out the pictured men upon the stairway. Still, to St. George Prentiss that did not matter. Enough of the faces could be verified in the flesh for him to realize that he had seen, not imagined, this assembly.

The new varnish on the floor and the sun upon the radiator silvering made a terrible stench which the Dean prepared to ignore with words. As this was before the era when the ability to "get along with people" was the prime requisite of all public characters, the Dean of the Medical School had the privilege of being an individual. And he was.

Dean Wingate was as incongruous as the physical plant of the school to the majority of the new class. A stiffening from attention to polite inattention ran through them. Silas had no reaction; he waited, but Prentiss felt sudden disappointment.

Then Wingate spoke, and the attention grew relaxed and natural. His humped shoulders and tobacco stained clothes were, mentally, no more of an actuality than were these rickety buildings. Morally he had only one axiom, "Whatever is normal is right"; and considered carefully, it left nothing to be said. Theodore Wingate rated his job; for when he spoke, a perfect delivery, backed by a mental clarity, sharpened by a fine wit was instantly evident. In his youth, oratory had still been the accomplishment of a gentleman, and its medical pattern then was Dr. Osler. Of all the men who ever studied with him, Wingate had drawn the greatest gift. He could inspire. His ability did not stop with young men; he could inspire men as old as himself; tired men; disillusioned men. The room began to throb with his sentences.

"Young gentlemen," he said, "it gives me great pleasure and no small degree of honor to be permitted to welcome you to the Johns Hopkins Medical School. To be allowed to offer you the rare privilege of studying under the pupils of men whose names ring hourly around the medical world.

"There is only one caution I give you: have you thought thoroughly, weighed carefully, understood exactly, not only the greatness of the medical profession, but the labor? Are you aware that to be adequately prepared for the place in the profession which your records indicate may be yours, you must spend at least the next eight years in study? In constant grinding toil, with practically no monetary reward? In learning, watching, dissecting, experimenting? In hours, days, weeks of fatiguing dispensary service? Are you completely cognizant that even if your merits in the end entitle you to a coveted residency, your remuneration will not be over fifty dollars a month?

"I presume that you are. There is something beyond the labor which you will find out for yourselves in time. It makes the labor, in the end, a joy. That I cannot describe. Few men can. But it is worth the price. Well worth it, boys!

"Regarding your present, however, I desire you to remember that this school is here for your convenience. It has been built by many brilliant men, through many years, into as fine a tool as the medical world has to offer, anywhere. Behind each seat in which you sit are the shadows of fifteen other men, young today, whom you excelled. Fifteen disappointed men.

"Your chance is therefore valuable. See that you use it. Neither the men who have gone before, nor the men you excelled, nor the men here to teach you, can make a doctor out of you. You, yourself, are your greatest teacher. Observation is the cornerstone of intelligent medicine.

"Preceding that is the map of all of the past knowledge of the human body: Gray's *Anatomy*. It is the key to many of the best brains since Galen. Therefore do not be surprised if at first it seems hard to digest. But hard or easy, respect its content, and assimilate it. It is like the multiplication tables to medicine, and in fact, all of the required work of the first two years is part of that set of tables. A man cannot add or subtract without them. That is what the first two years of medicine mean. To some it is dull, grinding, frighteningly hard. But without an absolutely thorough understanding of it, observation is blind fumbling.

"You were chosen because in the judgment of men matured in the service, it was decided that you would not fumble.

"Whatever branch you, in the end, follow, the course of study is broad, pliable, flexible, so arranged that if your decision comes before you have finished medical school, your instruction may be planned to meet the decision.

"Gentlemen, I never admit a class of first year students to this medical school that I do not tingle with hope. All famous men were once students: many of them were students sitting in the same seats which you now occupy.

"I thank you."

Two of the persons present never forgot those few minutes. To Isidore Aaron they were the first glimpse through "The Gates of Learning." For the remainder of the meeting he was emotionally knocked out. A man in clothes no better than his father's, in words whose meaning and derivations he knew, had stood before Osler and was now standing before him, inviting him—Isidore Aaron—

to continue the medical tradition. It was like a quick joining, with his own, of all of the hands from Galen to John Hunter. Wingate knew the same things which he, Isidore, felt: he had explained that they were emotions which, with work, could change into fact.

St. George Prentiss had, at last, heard a man do with words what heretofore he had thought could be accomplished only by a display of physical courage. That the man who had done it and the building in which he had done it were unspeakably drab made it all the more confusing and exciting. Presently, Prentiss felt, perhaps, it would grow understandable.

In the meantime, other men were making speeches; but St. George, like Isidore, couldn't register their words. It was then that Clay Abernathy began to take notice.

"Who's that on the platform now?" he nudged Ben Mead.

"Halsted."

"Whew! Is he as precise as he looks?"

"Twice. Keeps his residents and internes years; if you are good. If you are not he'll let you out in six weeks. Best hands in the world, I guess. Look at 'em."

Clay looked. Standing, motioning, speaking, the man wasted nothing; never gesticulated a half inch too far, never carried an action past its necessary length and usefulness. Abernathy's response was one of fright. Utter co-ordination coupled with such precision he had never seen before.

To Elbert Riggs, Halsted's hands were also bewildering; he felt so hopelessly inferior in their presence.

But to Ben Mead they were sacred. He worshiped every nail and hair. They were as strong drink and narcotics. He heard nothing Halsted said. His mind as well as his eyes were centered on the man's hands.

Four rows forward, in the last row of professors, Elijah Howe had been compressed between his father and a colleague. Elijah might have been a hole in the floor, and he felt that he was. When the speeches started, his elders listened politely, but they seemed to him to fumigate through their tremendous weight of years every word anybody else said. And 'Lije was not inclined to accept any other man's testimony, whether verbal, violent, or vital, upon any subject under the sun. He was consumed with a mounting sulkiness and an insane desire to scrape his feet.

When Halsted finished, Dr. Howe said, "Long speech, for him." The whole freshman class stirred restlessly as the Dean, professors and associates rose and the meeting broke up. None of the new boys had a very clear idea of anything except that they were "in for it," and that ahead lay a four-year grind, if they were permitted to remain to grind. They felt depressed; the sunshine and the crowd did not raise their spirits. Ben Mead tried to cover their confusion with cheerfulness:

"Now that you're convicts, you might as well take a look around. Got your appointments with the Dean, yet? Better go by the office and get them first, I reckon."

"Appointments?"

"Yep, Clay. Within the first week, he sees all of the new class and gives you a once over. That is, if you are from out of town; the local boys had theirs 'fore they were admitted. The schedule is posted in his outer office. You see, this is something like college, in a way. Only worse. Cummon!"

Clayton Abernathy was first upon the Dean's list and scheduled for an immediate interview. They left him in a vacant chair in the outer office, his upper lip sweating profusely. For the first time in the last twenty-four hours he actually regretted that his dad hadn't come along. This wasn't in the catalogue and hell, he hadn't prepared any comebacks.

The other four edged and wedged their way up the golden oak stairway. This stairway was wide enough to hold four men abreast, but only the profs and practicing men had the audacity to do it abreast; occasionally they knotted into chatting groups and the students had to pass them singly.

With the exception of the profs, only one other person claimed parking privileges. Isidore Aaron, photograph by photograph, was minutely scrutinizing the teachers, and his concentration was so genuine that no one considered intruding. On the way up, St. George Prentiss took the banister side and looked over the intervening heads at the pictures and decided to follow the little Jew's lead later.

"Straight ahead, top of the steps," Ben called. "Yep, first door."

They pushed their way in and Ben explained: "Little rooms to the sides are for dog experiments. Give 'em a hypo of something, make them have a fever and then trace its course. Malaria, or things like that. You can learn what they do and what counteracts them, this way. No. Dog surgery doesn't come yet. Second and third years."

Inside they all felt a little uncertain; outwardly they were nonchalant.

"What goes on here, Ben?" Elbert asked as they entered a large laboratory directly above the assembly room. It resembled any old worn out lab in any small university. The gas tubing was relaxed with age, the benches were pitted with initials and burned holes, the sink spigots dripped, and each defect in the golden oak sturdiness was emphasized by a recent coat of glaring varnish. Three sides of the long room contained windows and those to the north gave glimpses of the city.

"Crummy!" said Clay Abernathy who had finished his interview and found the group.

"Listen, man!" Ben replied. "It may look crummy but I'm telling you this is one place where you've got to have brains just to pick up the crumbs! This layout isn't handsome, God knows. But—it's not meant to be. Every time somebody gives a little money they clap it into more beds for the hospital or research on something big. Place was built on the German idea, hospital first, and then the medical school. Bedside teaching. Time they got through with the hospital what they had left put up this. And ever since, too much important has been done here to ever remember the plant."

"Where is the hospital?" Elbert asked a trifle irritably. If they didn't "keep up their property," he wanted, with a Pennsylvanian's sense of economy, to see the justification for the neglect.

" 'Cross the street. Curb your curiosity, kid. You'll see that hospital plenty, 'fore you die. But since you've got to spend two years in the medical school 'fore you do any real work in the hospital, you might just as well get your bearings. And lissen. Don't get any false ideas about cheapness."

After a quick glance over the equipment St. George Prentiss had moved to the window and the others were attracted by his concentration. Ben said, "Well, Pug—I'm sorry, but I've called you that from the first."

Prentiss replied without turning, "Everybody always has, I'm used to it."

"What do you think of it?" Ben's tone was almost apologetic.

"The most hideous, relentless and monotonous city I have ever seen. Miles and miles of squat brick sameness."

"Row-house-hebben!" Ben supplied. "And by the time you get through the grind in this building you'll love every brick of it. Naw, I'm not kiddin'. Anything you look at while you're working hard, you get attached to."

Pug Prentiss swung around. "Say, Mead, you're a philosopher."

"Aw, hell! It's just the way it was with me. I don't see the ugliness any more. After awhile I'll be like those men downstairs this morning about the place. Cummon. Let's go to the anat. building. We'll finish this up later. Nothing much left but classrooms—and you know what a classroom looks like. By the way, those washtub things hung up there are fume-chambers, and those handles beside them are for the sprinklers. Case you catch on fire."

"Do they work?" Elbert Riggs asked.

"Why don't you try and see?" Ben suggested as he passed on into the hall again. On the stairway they met other first year men on exploration tours; their expressions of blankness came from the realization of the weight of self-inflicted drudgery they would have to endure and overcome.

Only Isidore Aaron, who was now halfway up the stairway in his analyses of the profs, seemed at home. Every room of every department of the medical school was familiar to him; during the summer when the students were gone he had made four private tours, for which he paid a negro janitor one dollar. He had missed only these photographs upon the stairway; he had not dared to loiter in the public passageway before his official connection began.

The boys from Miss Susie's passed down the concrete sidewalk and entered the building over the transom of which was written "Women's Memorial Fund Building," and Ben explained, "After the hospital was completed there wasn't enough money for this, so a rich old maid said she'd give the money if they'd let women in as medical students. And they agreed."

Silas accepted the information, but the others felt slightly uncomfortable as they entered the doorway. The hall was narrow, ell-shaped and newly varnished. Inside the door Ben stopped and pointed to the picture: "Mall."

They gathered around and scrutinized one of the most discussed anatomists since John Hunter.

"Believed in self-teaching, you remember."

And then Silas Holmes spoke. "When he came, my father once told me, they still swiped cadavers. Had to."

While that speech was sinking in, they instinctively turned back to Mall and gave him another look. Some man!

"How do they get them now?" Elbert Riggs asked practically.

"Unclaimed from city morgues all over the state," Ben replied. "Or they pay fifty dollars where the family is willing to sell."

"You mean after autopsy?"

"No, Pug. After autopsy a corpse is no good as a cadaver. Everything is gone, you see. Say, fellows, want to see the cadavers?"

"I do," Silas announced solemnly; and nobody else denied his curiosity.

"Cummon then, down this stairway."

They followed and presently came into a cold semi-dark hallway which opened onto the street level.

"Hi, Tom!" Ben said cheerfully.

A small round man, with round black eyes and a round bald head, rose from a squeaky chair.

"Hello, Mead," he replied jovially. "What can I do for you?"

"New students, Tom. Gentlemen, this is Tom. He knows them by name. They want to see the ice chest."

"Glad to oblige you, gentlemen," Tom said with dignity. He took a bunch of keys from his pocket and waddled up the hallway. They fell in behind. " 'Tain't far. Keep 'em right by the elevator, so when Doc Snell telephones can take 'em right up." Then he inserted the key in a heavy door, which Elbert Riggs thought was just like the fire-door on Snider's store.

Tom cautioned, "Awful cold, boys. Have to keep 'em that way. Better just stand in the doorway."

The door swung out, Tom reached for an electric switch and the "ice chest" was flooded with light. The students leaned forward and looked.

And again what they saw was a distinct disappointment. Two egg-shaped iron rings, braced with inside spokes attached to a revolving center, were suspended in the room. Hooks were attached to each ring and fitted over it as a coat hanger fits over a closet rod. Halfway down, these hooks divided; above the division was a small screw lever. Each division curved at the end like a human finger and clamped to the head of a gauze wrapped human body just above the ear.

Tom explained. "Can keep up with 'em this way. The gauze keeps 'em soft and pliable. First we embalm 'em, then keep them covered with vaseline, wrap 'em in the gauze and there you are. Used to put them in formaldehyde vats, but that made 'em stiff as leather. This way you can move 'em—" He lifted the arm of a gauze wrapped thing; thirty mummies swayed slightly.

"How do you tell the males from the females?" Elbert asked.

Tom turned scornfully. "They have curves, son."

A wild guffaw swayed all sixty of the figures. "And," Tom continued, "they have identification tags. See?" He reached forward, unpinned a safety pin and slipped from its length the metal number and date.

"Any old ones?" Prentiss asked.

"Not old enough to be familiar," Tom replied. "Use 'em up too fast for that. Wait till you get started. You'll see. That tag business looks swell, but it don't mean nothin'. After you get goin' you'll telephone down and ask for Buster Brown, Tige and Stonewall Jackson—they was three last year, huh, Mead?—and I'll put 'em on the elevator and—we give service, this department moves fast!"

"Many niggers?" Silas asked.

"Sometimes. But I ain't enforcing no Jim Crow law.

"You'll see 'em again, boys. But if you don't get out of this freezing air, you'll see 'em too soon," Tom ordered; and then he turned to Elbert Riggs and asked, "Ain't you kin to Doctor Himmis?"

"He's my uncle."

"I thought so, minnit I seed you. He still in China?"

"At Peking Union Medical College."

"In his day, cadavers wasn't so plentiful, I'll tell you. But out to China I hear he has all he wants."

The boys were back at the street entrance, and Tom continued, "But when he was in medical school he kept me hopping for cadavers all the time. Watched the death notices in the paper and done a chart. Tell him when you write I asked after him."

"Thanks, I will," Elbert replied stoically. The others had drifted out onto the sidewalk and he joined them and turned to Ben, "Where do you work on them?"

"Everywhere," Ben replied.

Elbert said with painstaking politeness, "I—know—that! But *where* —on the floor?"

Ben's easy smile relaxed his lips. "Oh, you mean whereabouts? On the second floor of this building, where I showed you, on tables. But listen, you Pennsylvania Yankee, you've got to talk in a lingo I can understand if you want me to tell you anything."

Riggs's face was drained of its ruddy tint. Pug Prentiss lazily rolled his eyes toward the boy and said, " 'Spose you tell me, Mead, the way to get to Otto's. Maybe he'll be there today and a little beer wouldn't do us any harm. What do you say, fellows? We'll have a round with Mead as guest."

The sidewalks were cluttered with men. Their aimless ambling harassed Riggs; but it made Pug Prentiss more at home than he had ever been. Two years at the University of California, two at the University of Mexico and then three more drifting had taught him the charm of slow motion.

Silas accepted it as a fact; while Clay watched with an embarrassed grin. Ben Mead seemed to know everybody he passed. His "Hi, kid," "Good morning, Doctor," was like marking time and lasted until they entered Otto's. Then as they leaned against the bar, Ben said casually and with hopeful reverence, "Hello, Otto."

The last word ended upon a note of pleading cheerfulness. The barkeeper's head was lowered; he raised it slowly. His eyes were black and piercing, and his chins seemed to begin directly beneath his shoe-button nose and extend in curve after circling curve. There were some fine brown patches of hair upon his head. One tuft, arched high on his middle forehead, gave to his profile an unspeakably funny quirk. It made his shoe-button nose look as if it were always ready to sneeze. His hands and arms moved with the grace of a dancing or concert master, and that, a famous psychiatrist once said, was because Otto held food and drink in the same reverence that other men did violins.

The fifth of the beer steins he was filling from the tap rose and fell upon his lower belly; then he held it carefully aloft, blew the foam and completed the filling. Afterward he shifted his attention with the precision with which a stage curtain is raised, and peered over his glasses at Ben Mead.

"Vhen did you gome back?" Otto's voice was friendly.

Ben grinned. "Aw, couple o' days ago. Brought the new fellows from Miss Susie's. Came by last night but you were out. They wanted to see your place. Heard about it from their fathers."

"So?" Otto's voice carried interest. A waiter came and passed the filled steins down the bar. Otto settled his eye man by man on the line of newcomers; at Silas he squinted and made nice noises in his throat, and said, "No. Ton't dell me. Avfta vile, I dell you."

Then he turned and watched the waiter pass the beer and a silence ran down the entire length of the bar and rebounded to the tables. Men began to stand up and shuffle forward. Otto's concentration magnetized, overawed them. At a table in a corner three doctors, in their prime, turned and waited. They had seen this ceremony before. Many times. They waited.

Otto's inflation increased. Then he began to speak and his words were handed with precision into their ears. "A medikal man shouldt oondershtand how to relax. To savvor ash vell ash safe life. He shouldt leaf for der moment. A little music, a vell-figger'd lady, vine or bier, a peevsteak." His hands embraced their minds as he continued, "Relax. Hinjoy. Savvor. A medikal man, vhen he kno's dat, ish in pozishun to progress, pro-fessionally. Derfore ash shtudents it ish goot dat you learndt dat soondt. Derfore de foorst roundt avfta you gome to Hopkindts—at Otto's—ish alvays oon de houze! I dank you."

As he had been speaking, the waiters had filled stein after stein and ranged them down the bar.

Pug Prentiss leaned heavily against the rail and inserted his upper teeth inside his lower ones; this evidently was an annual ceremony carried, with German thoroughness, through its solemn course. As the steins were passed, he noticed that Ben Mead dropped out and pushed a new boy into his place. The entire length of the rail, reflected in the long mirror behind the bar, were the faces of students he had seen at the assembly, his future classmen. They stood baffled, surprised, ill at ease. Prentiss's extreme height gave him a vantage, so that he saw the waiting interest in the three older doctors and the pleased anxiousness in Mead's open face.

Otto cut his eye down the bar, made certain that every newcomer had a stein, and then raised his own and said,

"Vour men dey call de Vour Hossmen"—his little tuft of hair rose straight up—"hafe crooshed dissease. But mooch of dat pro-gress dey hinspired hass peen made away from de hossback of medicine: it vas pegun at Otto's, py two minds at res', revealin' demselves to each oder. De Inglish hafe a vord vitch govers it—stimulation. Drue und undpelievable, like mooch of medicine. Stimulation ish de result of relaxation. Of savvoring. It hafe made medicine de vorl'-vide hope. De language onder de skin. Indernational. Indersbensible."

All of his curves lay taut and motionless. His fat and funny body was transported into pride and great dignity. He held his stein aloft and finished, "Savvor! Relax! Hinjoy! Prosit!"

The thirty steins at the bar tilted upward. The steins of the men beyond the bar tilted upward. The steins of the three doctors in the corner tilted upward. When they were set down, Pug Prentiss suggested in measured tones, "A round on the class!"

It was drunk.

Then, a quiet doctor came forward from the corner table and caught Otto's eye. The little bartender switched his back around as a spaniel might, and the doctor laughed deeply as he said, "The first was necessary."

Otto turned off the tap, gathered his head upon one side and replied, "De secund vas, too, Docturr."

"But the second makes two, Otto."

Otto turned back to the tap and made noises in his throat. But they were acquiescent noises. The doctor chuckled and eased back to his table. Ben Mead leaned forward and whispered, "McMillan."

"Who's McMillan?" Silas inquired flatly.

"Best internist in America, I guess," Ben replied offhandedly.

"We get him?" Elbert Riggs asked practically.

"Not until you work in the hospital: last two years. He's a regular guy."

Riggs turned and stared squarely at McMillan. And again he was disappointed. The man had a long plain face whose most potent characteristic was kindness, a long egg-shaped head with a thick suit of gray hair, and an insignificant, small-boned body. Prentiss leaned down and said in Riggs's ear, "Why don't you like him?"

Elbert revolved his stein slowly. "I didn't say that I didn't like him."

"You didn't have to."

Elbert's shyness burned his neck. He replied shortly, "He's too unpretentious."

"Unassuming is the word," Pug announced calmly. Then he quoted, " 'The greatest truths are the simplest: and so are the greatest men.' Since I struck this place I think that there may be something to that trite old phrase."

"I don't think there is," said a boy who had inserted himself next to Elbert and into the conversation. Pug looked down at him. It was the doctor's son he had seen, four rows ahead, in the meeting.

Otto was studying with fascination Pug Prentiss's features in the long mirror.

"Why?" Pug drawled and slipped the word like a sharp knife toward Elijah Howe, Junior.

"Because I don't," 'Lije announced loudly.

"When you are unable to back up your impressions with logical reasoning, I see no necessity to raise your voice, do you?" Pug's words were studied.

Elijah bristled, "How do you mean, I can't back 'em up?"

"Then, why don't you do it?"

There had been no spreading to spar; rather a closing in of bodies. Pug crouched so that his shoulder was level with Elijah's; Elijah leaned so that his weight was upon Pug's arm. As Pug asked his question he turned and smiled into the pushing features of the doctor's son. That terribly beautiful smile acted as a slap upon the cheek: it stung Elijah's head backward.

Otto, who had watched the entire action in the mirror, began laughing with his nostrils and laughed through chin after chin until his apron strings flung helplessly. His snorty, snickery laughter had a quality of such enormous merriment that it was infectious. Men watched him laugh and laughed at him without knowing the source of his amusement. The freshman class, within seconds, was swaying to and fro at the bar; the seconds wore into minutes, the whole restaurant rang with laughter. But nobody knew what had set Otto off and he, with German thoroughness, had no intention of revealing the cause until he had finished his laugh.

Dr. McMillan's brows knit as he made motions of rising. The colleague upon his left grumbled, "Not before these boys, Mac! Don't make a neurotic out of Otto! He is the only living creature who has spent over fifteen years around this hospital and still thinks he may die a natural death. I know about his heart as well as you do—I've watched him breathe. And I tell you to sit down and forget it. Have him sick as you are, if you aren't careful!"

Dr. McMillan resumed a dignified pose and scrutinized a wood mosaic of a street in Nuremberg which was inset in the paneled wall.

When his chins were only slightly rippling, Otto lowered his head, peered over his glasses and said, "Dat's de foorst dime I hafe efer zeen dat!"

"What?" Elijah became pugnacious. He felt in some occult way that this bartender was making fun of him, and he wished that his father hadn't gone straight back to the office.

"A shmile baralyze a man," Otto replied squarely. St. George Prentiss blushed from the tips of his fingers up and down his long body.

"I don't get you," 'Lije replied sulkily.

"But I get you," Otto announced gravely as he pushed his spectacles upward, took a deep breath and prepared to address Prentiss. Ben Mead stepped forward.

"Say, Otto," he said, "you decide. They were arguing about great men. You've known lots of great men. What're they like?"

Otto lifted his chest and settled his head. Then he spoke, distinctly, authoritatively and in sentences which ended on a rising note.

"I hafe known all de great men of dis hospital: Osler, Kelly, Welch, Halsted—und der younger great—Docturr McMillan, Docturr Wingate, Docturr Howe. Dey hafe peen alike in one ding. Dey are qui-et und sim-pell. Dey gome, und if de bar ish full, dey shtep to de end und vait der durn. Dey alvays say, 'Otto'—low like dat—no matta vot ish de drouble. Vhen Docturr Osler's foorst childt died, he gome over und said, 'Otto, you vas so in-drested, I vant you to kno' emejetly: my son did not live.'"

Silence swept over the restaurant. The old bartender's voice quivered as he continued, "'Oh, Docturr!' I said, 'Docturr!' Denn he leandt on dat rail—right der—und shmiled. 'Otto,' he gontinued, 'do poys in Germany blay marples?' Und denn ve talked of ag-gets, und how de German poys make deir ring, und how de Inglish make deirs. For half und hour ve talk und vhen he vent I had forgot—for dat half hour, I mean--dat madgic man's turrible sorrow."

Elijah Howe coughed lightly. Otto forgave him the interruption and went on, "Avfta dat, each spring ve pought marples und had a shootin' match off de colordt childrent dunn de street. De oder docturrs dey dink it vas a poy-brank. Dey didn't kno'. Only he und Otto"—his stubby thumb touched his apron—"only he und Otto knew. He vas dat sim-pell."

"Well," Dr. McMillan's colleague suggested, five minutes later as they walked toward the hospital, "suppose you had 'controlled your patient'?"

McMillan clucked his tongue slowly. "I'd have died without knowing the best of the legends."

"But it wasn't legend," the colleague protested. "The other half of it stood before you!"

"Man, haven't you ever known that he is legend, too?"

Chapter Three

A FINE ACQUAINTANCE

While the students from Miss Susie's were sauntering home for lunch, Isidore Aaron narrowed his eyes and read for the second time, "The original, loaned by the University, is hanging at present in the Medical Library." His inspection of the profs was completed; he was back again, at the foot of the stairway giving the originators a second examination when his eye lit upon that typewritten sentence under the small photograph of Sargent's "The Four Doctors."

That he, Isidore Aaron, could within a few minutes be standing in front of that painting had never occurred to him. All of the great pictures, he had understood, were abroad in the Tate and Louvre galleries. Since Sargent had done the portrait in London, he had always presumed that "The Four Doctors" hung somewhere abroad, too. He began mechanically unrolling his felt hat; it was a new hat and presently, when he arrived home, he would be distressed. But this was a new experience and must be registered upon something.

Ten minutes later, in the Medical Library, Alex Ashby decided that he had enough information upon coronary thrombosis for theoretical use and looked around for some man with whom he might see a case. Since it was the first day of medical school, the library was almost empty, only an occasional desk light was burning, only an occasional white-coated interne was visible. An air of intangible fatigue filled the long, oblong room and it was as though these books, one of the best collections of medical data in the world, weary of being pawed by people, stayed on from duty, not desire. As though they felt a relentless permanency in illness and human frailty. Here and there a birdlike little woman moved among them, sorting, cataloguing, disturbing their calm.

Alex's gray eyes wandered slowly over the dim room. No man he knew in a position to show him a case of coronary thrombosis was in sight. His disappointed attention was centered by the amazing realization that something in the left lower corner of the portrait of "The Four Doctors" had moved. Without focusing, his eyes had been resting on it for several minutes; and now something in that picture had changed location.

For the first time in his life he had a sense of fear. From where he sat he could see that the object which had moved was a head he had never before realized was there, but one which seemed to belong.

He tried to rise and walk up the aisle to see, but his legs refused to stiffen and that visual clearness which accompanies extreme fear began, feature by feature, tabulating the new and movable head. An odd thought jumped through Alex's mind, "It's like Whistler's butterfly in the corner!" Why had he never seen it before? Its fine shape added to the group an enormously impressive quality. A quality——

A student near the portrait switched off his light and thereby shifted the glare on the picture; then Alex Ashby rose and walked steadily up the aisle. But even in spite of the change in lighting, he was not certain that his eyes were seeing correctly, for Isidore Aaron's complete concentration had relaxed every muscle in his entire body. His pitiful frame with its sparrow proportions was hidden in darkness below the picture frame, only his head was visible. And in that head was centered, suddenly centered, the visionary beauty of an untried idealist. He was thinking, "No genius came from geniuses. The great musicians sprang in one generation—and so did the great doctors."

And his thoughts, through complete relaxation, illuminated his features. Upon his thin shoulders, straining their every muscle forward and making of his neck a scrawny tube, balanced that huge head.

All of this Alex had seen while still trying to convince himself that the head belonged to a peering man and not inside the frame. From where Ashby stood, the impression was of a three-quarters face with glowing eyes, shining out of the lower left hand corner of the portrait and looking toward the globe of the world which was behind Osler.

Ashby leaned against a bookcase and visited upon that new and beautiful sight precisely the same kind of concentration which Isidore Aaron visited upon the portrait. Then Isidore turned slightly and Ashby's observation began to function again.

He realized for the first time that the head belonged to a Jew. That the nostrils were flaring with excitement and emotion; that the cheeks were sallow and hollow while the mouth was thin-lipped, sensitive, cut into a pointed jaw, and the hair jet black. A Jew whose religion was obviously medicine. Whose eyes belonged to Osler.

Alex stepped forward and said softly, "Good, isn't it?"

The Jew did not change his position. He did not look at Ashby; he gave his new hat several turns and nodded. Eventually he said, "I thought it was in London."

They were silent again.

Presently Ashby explained, "Done in London. Hangs over at the University usually. They call them 'The Four Horsemen,' you know."

Isidore nodded. Then he asked, "Are Kelly's hands just like that?"

"His and Halsted's, too. Exactly."

"I know Halsted's are. I saw them this morning." For the first time Isidore's eyes left the portrait. "Do you know them? In the life, I mean?"

Ashby swallowed involuntarily. "Yes—to speak to—all but Osler. They are human. You can talk to them."

"*I* can?"

"Certainly. That is, if you are a medical student——*"

"I entered today. Do they *teach* you anything?"

"Yes. Which are you most interested in?"

Isidore turned back to the portrait. "I am not certain, yet. I don't know enough medicine to tell. Osler makes it seem so possible: medicine, I'm referring to."

"That's genius, don't you think?"

"I'm not sure," Isidore stated calmly. "I haven't ever known a genius, myself, I mean. But from reading it seems to me that genius is the ability to know precisely the right thing to do without the prop of experience." He paused. "Through medicine from the beginning it's been that. The inquiring mind. All of the great ones have had it. Leonardo, who came so near discovering the circulation of the blood. William Harvey, who actually did discover it. And John Hunter, who always told his classes, 'Young gentlemen, I advise you not to take notes upon my opinions, for by this time next year they may have altered.' Genius is that, isn't it? The man who through observation can deduce a conclusion and try it without the weight of experience to back him up."

"How do you differentiate between observation and experience?" Ashby demanded.

Isidore had become almost impatient. It was his voice which revealed his nerves.

"Easily, I think. Experience is charted observation. But observation can occur independent of experience. When Madame Curie discovered radium she knew that there must be another element with power to affect a photographic plate many times greater than uranium. That was observation—and genius. There was no experience to back her up. When Lister revolutionized the medical world with antisepsis, when Crawford Long discovered ether, when Beaumont charted so precisely the gastric functions from the stomach of Alexis St. Martin, they all knew precisely the right thing to do—without the prop of experience."

Ashby gave a half-smile and replied, "By that yardstick these men here wouldn't rate very well, do you think? They, in their formula, inserted 'luck.' All but Kelly, that is."

Isidore's brows met and he scowled. "I don't believe in luck. Work is luck!"

"But suppose Welch had worked upon public health without Walter Reed? Suppose Kelly had tried to revolutionize gynecology before, instead of after, Crawford Long? Or that Halsted had decided he was correct in his theories as to the proper operation for cancer in 1820, instead of 1888? They were great. They were and are the greatest single group which has ever been gathered together in the medical world anywhere, at any time; but for their gifts they were profoundly lucky in their age and generation."

"Including Osler?"

"More so than any of the others," Alex defended. "Osler's great forte is stimulating other men to cultivate their talents plus a natural ability for understanding people which makes all psychiatrists look infantile. But suppose he had been miscast——?"

"Can you ever miscast a genius?"

They had collapsed onto a long, worn, black leather sofa and the room and people were blurred and fading.

"Why not?"

"Because," Isidore said, "if he's a real genius he won't stand miscasting. Even temporarily you cannot fit him into a wrong mold."

"I disagree entirely. Although I grant you one thing: when part of the genius is an innate knowledge of people, so long as that man is cast in some specialty wherein he encounters people, I think he may succeed. But I do not think he will excel as Osler excels. When Osler came into power, medicine was just entering its enormous period of scientific discovery. Metabolism tests, electro-cardiographs, glandular functions and secretions, the cause and control of malaria, yellow fever, typhus, the wonderful research upon the tsetse fly and sleeping sickness, lay unaccomplished and untouched. He awoke men to research. He and Welch; especially Welch."

"Do you think," Isidore asked timidly, "there's much left for us?"

"I wish I knew. Three things certainly we can work upon: diabetes, cancer and tuberculosis. But sometimes I also think there are many, a great many other things ——"

"Yes," Isidore interrupted, "they felt complete, too, I suppose. But how could they, or how can we? I know of only three specifics in all of pharmacopeia: digitalis, quinine and arsphenamine, and the last of those three, '606' has been discovered in our own century. Instead of feeling complete, we should be ashamed! Yet, just last week I read something which encouraged me, inside. It was an old Sydenham report upon the origin of syphilis. It threw the blame here and there, and left it more or less undecided; but one argument it put forward was that the origin would be almost impossible to trace, as prior to the manifestation of a certain type of syphilis, after the return of Columbus's crews, all diseases with similar symptoms went under the general heading of 'Lues'! We may be permitting ourselves to stagger along under a similar scientific blunder in relation to tuberculosis and thereby lose centuries of research."

Alex Ashby turned his wide shoulders sideways and looked this slender, gnarled Jew squarely in the eyes. "What year are you in?"

"I've just entered," Isidore apologized.

Alex whistled softly. "Then how do you know so much?"

"I don't know much. Really much. What I know I read because I want to be ——"

The glow faded, and he extended his hands helplessly. Ashby scratched his cheek carefully. Isidore took his silence for criticism and hastened to explain.

"I like it. All of it. Medicine, I mean. I read everything I could because I like it. I like the knowing of discoveries of long ago, like Hippocrates's queer observations and of almost yesterday like this new oil treatment for leprosy. I like the fact that there is an international language in which all learned men may converse: medicine. I like the feeling that when I am a graduated doctor I shall be able to travel into almost any kind of conflict without the fear of violent death. But perhaps that is because I am a Jew. Jews fear violent death, as you probably know."

Alex smiled and said, "With ample reason."

"A very flattering way of expressing it. Some Gentiles call it the yellow streak."

"I call it common sense," Ashby said and cut his eye back at the boy again. His eyes were still alive and vivid. They found, presently, that both of them were laughing.

"To go back to genius," Alex said appreciatively. "Can one grow it?"

"Can one grow a different sized brain?"

"No."

"Can one grow blue eyes from black?"

Alex shook his head and smiled. "So you think it is, or it isn't?"

"The inherent quality, yes. The development, of course, is up to the individual."

"Well, look at that portrait again, and I'll tell you something which may amuse you. That man on the extreme right, Kelly. Do you know why he is the most discussed one of the group? Because he had the genius for excelling at many things. He is one of the best amateur botanists in America; one of the best authorities upon reptiles and reptile poisons in the world; one of the first really great men to take an inquisitive interest in cancer. And besides all of that, the person who has completely created modern gynecology. The man whose extensive genius has sunk him in the envious estimation of lesser people. He just grew too much!"

"All of them grew too much," Isidore said softly, "except, perhaps

Halsted. Osler is not only a great diagnostician: he is also a great essayist, an expert bibliophile and a fine critic of painting. And Welch, outside of his pathology, is one of the bulwarks of the Army Medical Museum and the Surgeon General's Library in Washington. Did you know that he is an eminent Miltonic scholar and has a great fund of information about eighteenth-century prints?"

"You've read all that you could about them, too, haven't you?"

Isidore ignored the note of admiration in Ashby's voice and asked, "Who'll be the most famous of them in two generations?"

"Kelly will."

"Why?"

"Because he'll have to die to get his just recognition."

"But suppose," Isidore said, "the chemistry of medicine, as you were suggesting, comes into its own. Then the diagnostician will be the switch operator of the medical world."

"But snakes and wild flowers will still remain upon the face of the earth and there will be persons left who desire to study them. Then too, if radium should really be the cure for cancer or run surgery out of the delicate tissues, or if we find some way through it to dry up the areas of tuberculous lungs, Kelly will live in three fields—and all of them fields of international scope and interest."

"Pathology and public health have international scope; so has internal medicine, and surgery knows no tongue," Isidore answered witheringly.

"Another thing," Ashby drawled. "Kelly believes the Bible verbatim."

Isidore made a motion of extreme irritation and Ashby laughed softly.

"I'm not advocating following his footsteps. I'm only pointing out that the Bible is older than medical lore, and Kelly is aboard that band wagon, too. He's got transportation into the future upon four different vehicles!"

"Osler has literary transportation," Isidore reminded him.

"So has Oliver Wendell Holmes," Alex replied. "And I think his is better transportation, too. For many of Holmes's writings are not upon his own profession. By the way, did you know that after that first operation under general anesthesia at Mass. General the men concerned asked Holmes for a name and he suggested anesthesia, anesthetic, and anesthetist?"

Isidore nodded his acceptance of the knowledge.

"Don't forget," he remarked, "that Halsted gave medicine the rubber gloves by which it is administered. He had a pair made for his wife to use when she was a nurse right here in this hospital."

"That's technique," Ashby said squelchingly. "Think it over. With the exception of Kelly they are great, I contend, because the man and the opportunity met. Welch and public health. Osler and scientific medicine. Halsted and modern surgery, and in the same sense Kelly and modern G-Y-N. But beyond that, botany, reptiles and the Bible are ancient history!"

"Why do they criticize him so, beside that, I mean?"

"Because he's a zealot. A medical evangelist. Also he has the energy of a fanatic, and a colleague with a cancer belongs willy-nilly to him for experimentation!"

"Overloaded."

"Yes," Ashby replied. "And it's as dangerous in a man as in a vessel, I guess."

"I wonder," Isidore mused. "I wonder."

"As upsetting, then?"

Isidore smiled quickly. "Oh, yes, that's true. Quite."

They sat silent for a few moments; then Isidore asked quietly, "Is a first year student permitted to take out books from here?"

"Certainly."

"For overnight?" He sat forward and awaited the blow.

"As long as the rest of us. Two weeks."

The young Jew's eyes began circling the tier upon tier of volumes. His rapture moved Ashby.

"Want to see a few?" he asked casually. They rose and went into the stacks.

"I notice," Isidore said calmly, "that the first edition of my *Anatomy* was published by Gray in 1858 when he was thirty-three, three years before he died. If there is an early edition of that——?"

"I'll see. In the meantime you are welcome to browse around."

Five minutes later Isidore Aaron was excitedly turning the pages of the third edition of Gray's *Anatomy* and Alex Ashby was looking over his shoulder.

"Mine's different, here! We've progressed. Microscopic anatomy and embryology!"

"But many of his original sketches are still in use. He had his gross anatomy down pretty well."

Isidore nodded and turned a page with infinite tenderness, and Alex received a new reverence for knowledge. As he looked at tissue under a 'scope, this fellow scrutinized words upon the printed page. Alex said: "You like books a great deal."

Isidore looked up suddenly and his eyes were shining with enthusiasm. "If a man can accomplish, in life, something worth recording in a book, he has achieved his stature, for me."

"Then action: a very competent surgeon who saves hundreds of lives is of no importance to you?"

"He has an artisan's stature. After he is dead it will sink to an artisan estimate."

"But it takes courage to be that kind of an artisan!" Alex suggested hotly.

"Of course, but you must not expect a Jew to admire only courage. A Jew admires tradition, and permanent records of advancement, not technique. And that is because we have an inferiority complex. You might tell me until you were aged that the first barber surgeon was a Jew—" Isidore threw out his hand deprecatingly, "it would never matter to me as much as your going to that shelf and picking out an insignificant volume upon the symptoms of the common cold, recorded in the eighth century by a Jew in the Orient."

"Are you implying," Alex asked, "that a Jew is not interested in doing his job well, just his job in his lifetime?"

"A man who looks at his lifetime as an important period must have a country, a background. The Jewish background is race. We must excel in ways which require recording to count."

Alex smiled and Isidore interpreted the smile into words. "You are right. That is why I chose medicine! If I do excel, I want a permanent record."

Suddenly his confidence dropped from him and he asked wistfully, "How soon can a man know if he is going to be great?"

They had dropped into a couple of chairs and were looking at the portrait again as Isidore continued, "In reading biographies, it always seems a steady stream of future happenings ran through even the earliest years. With Napoleon, with, oh, well, with people now living, too. With Wilson. All of that studying which he did at the Hopkins which is now serving him so well, did he sense then that it would matter, later? Did he?"

He swung around and pinned the question into Ashby with an intensity which left Alex hollow. He replied slowly, "Gee! I'd never looked at it that way. Where did you read that?"

"I didn't read it."

"You mean," Ashby's eyes were big and staring, "you mean you thought it up?"

"It isn't a thought, it's a question," Isidore defended.

"It's both! And—I—don't—know—" Alex answered. "Do you?"

"Osler says," Isidore suggested, "that all great men have one quality in common. They work. And do it day by each separate day, unconscious of their greatness, until presently, through the work, it reveals itself."

Alex looked at him and waited.

"I've thought about that a lot," Isidore said emphatically. "It has advantages every way 'round, because, even if you are not great it gets the best out of you in the end, doesn't it? And if you are great, the best is not lost that way, either."

Alex asked, "How long have you been having thoughts like that?"

"I guess they are kind of crazy," Isidore said.

"Crazy, my hat! They're grand. Gosh, you've said things to me and—why, I've felt that way ever since I came to this place and it's been all bottled up inside me; I didn't even know what it was. You mind if I thank you?"

Isidore turned his attention back to the book in front of him and when his eyes were centered upon the page he remarked, "I've done nothing. You've—could I take a book with me today?"

"Sure."

They descended into the room again and realized that the head librarian had gone to lunch. Alex found it was two o'clock.

"Say, I'll tell you. Take what you want on my card, and I'll help you carry 'em. Which way are you going? We'll get you a card tomorrow."

"I live on lower Broadway," Isidore said and all of this great world dropped from him like a garment. Before Alex's eyes he became a frightened little Jew, out of his element, and uneasy.

Half an hour later they began the first of their many hundreds of walks, and Ashby entered, via that walk, a new and frightening world. A world of struggle, conflict and outrageous courage.

Alex never forgot that first impression, and their conversation had not prepared him for it. Their conversation, like the splendid October air, had been mature and sparkling. Had brought to Isidore in word and presence the companion for whom, in all his lonely wanderings, he had yearned. Had cured, within an hour, his lifelong nostalgia.

A tremendous elation swept through his whole being. His nostrils quivered and his eyes shone. The queer prosaic diamond-shaped flower beds which bordered the wide concrete sidewalk, down the boulevard path in the center of Broadway, were forever after fixed in his mind as things of inexplicable beauty. He noted unconsciously, in the stress of great excitement, their every brick and blossom.

"So much of it," Alex was saying, "has come through men without advantages but with perspective only to guide them."

Isidore nodded and shifted the precious old edition of the *Anatomy* he balanced closely in the crook of his elbow.

"Percussion."

"Did it?"

"Yes. Some fellow, I'll look it up and let you know who, discovered that a barrel made different sounds when filled to different levels. If a barrel with different content did, why wouldn't a man?"

"That's interesting. I suppose I'd heard it, but I do not remember. Say, by the way, what's your name?"

Isidore took off his hat, stopped, and lifted his immense head backward so that his eyes met Ashby's.

"Where minds dovetail, names are not necessary. But anyhow, it's Isidore Aaron, and I hope yours is as indicative of your aristocratic heritage as mine is of my race."

Alex blushed and for the first time in years stammered. "What makes you think I'm an aristocrat?"

"I didn't think. I saw. I knew, and I'll never be able to tell you how; but you are. Does the name uphold the 'diagnosis,' doctor?"

"It is Alexander Ashby."

"That confirms it," Isidore replied simply, then he looked up quickly and stated, "It's the best natural advantage a man can ever have."

"Why?"

"Because you can never defeat an aristocrat. You may beat him, but you cannot defeat him."

"Why?"

"Simply because one has to experience defeat to recognize it. You may strip an aristocrat of all his possessions, but he will retire, then, into his mind, and live along until he acquires strength to recapture them. A material crushing does not annihilate him as it does a Jew."

"Again—why?"

"Inheritance. Innate characteristics, I suppose. Courage."

"There have been courageous Jews."

The fine head upon the scrawny shoulders shook slightly. "But they did not make the headlines."

"Indeed they did make the headlines. Jesus—Paul—Akiba!"

Isidore smiled quickly. "That's what I mean by aristocracy!"

"What?"

"Your saying things like that. Perhaps, in the future, when the world is healthier and Jews have some national footing, money will not be to them so vital. Money has bought them freedom from death, bondage and from battle."

"Then why be ashamed of a desire for it?"

"Because," Isidore had grown fierce, "no man rots under its pressure as quickly as a Jew!"

"Listen, Isidore," Alex pronounced the name with dignity. "Get over your—your— What I mean is that you are entering a group of men whose estimation of you will be based upon your mental capacity.

Upon your ability to deliver. Upon your knowledge of people; upon the understanding that a Jew has as a natural advantage through centuries of suffering. Medicine deals almost entirely with suffering. If you were to try to think of your heritage as an advantage, you might be pretty correct; or much more nearly so than you are now."

"Are you saying that my being a Jew could help me in medicine?"

"Sure, if you'd let it."

"I'd never looked at it that way. To me it seemed that I should always be on trial. On mental quicksand."

"If you are, it's your own fault! With that brain and that energy, the only thing which can ever stop you is yourself."

Aaron trembled unexpectedly. This was like being told that the sand which glittered in one's backyard was gold.

"What do you want to be?" Alex asked suddenly.

"It's too soon to tell. You?"

"Perhaps a diagnostician," Alex replied, "or a pathologist."

"You have the gift to be either," Isidore stated calmly. "But you will be happier, if you are a diagnostician."

"Why do you say that?"

"Because you have insight. Where did you go to college?"

Alex grinned. "Place you never heard of. Sewanee. Sits on top of a mountain in Tennessee and was founded by defeated classicists after the Civil War."

"That explains why you understand Jews."

"How does it?"

"Because a college founded by defeated classicists views life much the same way as does an educated Jew. Ignorant Gentiles think that Jews love money. They never comprehend that what a Jew really loves is erudition—he learns early that the only things which may never be taken from you are those you carry in your head."

Alex whistled softly, and then said, "That's true. But you should have been a philosopher! Why did you decide to study medicine?"

"It was not a decision. It was the only thing—since I could remember."

But Ashby afterward could never recall the rest of Isidore's remarks, for they had gone beyond the center path and were standing in front of a plate glass window upon which there flourished in gold letters:

AARON'S TAILOR SHOP,

—Prices Reasonable—

Isidore smiled caustically. "Here are my ancestral acres."

"As necessary as doctors," Alex answered.

Isidore shrugged, and Alex sensed his acute suffering.

"Come in?" The phrase was wistful and a trifle stiff. He hoped, inside, that this new god would not enter.

"Sure. If I may," Alex replied. "I'd like to see——"

They stepped inside the tailor shop, and the worn coverings of many bodies hung about them. Overcoats, men's suits—not new— there to be patched or pressed. The dowdy green dress of what was evidently a slatternly woman hung hemless on a slim, stiff-framed form. The shop was empty and the studied carelessness with which a half-made vest—its buckram and white tacking threads still visible —had been laid across a bolt of suiting was eloquent.

"Yes." Isidore's voice was bitter. "There's plenty to see."

Alex winced slightly as he answered, "I meant phylacteries and Sedar plates and——"

"Oh, so you know about them, too. I'll show you later. Will you go upstairs and wait at the top of the landing, please? Now!"

Alex sensed authority in the pleading request and approached the indicated door without turning, but he understood, nevertheless. Two voices had entered the front door of the shop and the feminine one was saying,

"Now lissen, you dirty little Jew, ten dollars is too much for that suit. The guy what gave me the goods said he could get it made for six."

Alex pulled the door outward and passed into the dark passageway, but the words still followed,

"Seex times hover mine hants feel sotch cloth today. Smuggled, I tenk."

And the other voice fitted in perfectly with the scaling wall beside the stairway which Alex was slowly mounting. "I'll pay ten, Abie. If you don't tell de cops——"

Within seconds the front door of the shop opened and closed again, and Isidore's pleading tones scorched the heavy air.

"Papa, that is my new friend. From the medical school. Please be quiet!"

"Henswer me diss," the father's voice rose with every word, "if I hev no beezness, if I hev no wukk how shutt I sent mine boy to school?"

Alex leaned against the wall, for he felt nauseated and weak. The tie of race and pride would bind those two men below forever, and the fetters of ambition and of temperament would make that binding burn and torture both of them, forever. He understood completely and suddenly what a person with aristocratic ancestors inherited. He saw, minutely, the horror of ceaseless emotional pain as related to immigrant parents and ambitious children.

"My new friend. I shall show him my books. Yes, I'll let you see him. I promise. Later." Isidore's penetrating words pacified Abie.

Alex accustomed his eyes to the dimness at the top of the stairway. The low ceilings and flimsy walls made him able to hear every syllable uttered below. As he stood on that small landing he looked into three rooms. In one, he saw four double iron beds separated by dirty sheets hung from the ceiling. The room had one window, no floor covering. The old planks were splintery and curved. Two of the sheets were slightly cleaner and gave the impression of being recently hung.

As revealing as name tabs were the shoes under each bed. Beneath the one in the far corner were a pair of slovenly red felt bedroom slippers, crumpled at the heel, and pigeon-toed, beyond, sat a pair of men's patent leather buttoned shoes: evidently, the synagogue shoes of Isidore's father!

The next bed shielded sneakers seven inches long and brand new, and five inches long and frayed at the toes. The shoes of Isidore's sisters, and one of them had just started to school! Under the third bed stood two pairs of high laced shoes with brass plates over the toes. Alex smiled and remembered; then Isidore had two brothers who had just re-entered school. From the length of the shoes they must be about eleven and fifteen.

Ranged under the fourth bed were an old woman's comforts, whose vici-kid had been scraped gray, and two pairs of high-heeled slippers worn by different persons; their heels were walked off different ways.

"Three in a bed! One an old hag; the others girls under twenty! And the breeding, rearing, all takes place in this one room!" Alex thought, and pity which carried the same sensation as agony ran through his mind. He was relieved that Isidore's father had detained him in the shop.

Alex stepped forward and entered the room to the left. He walked to the window and looked out. The junk yard, with its naked toilets and rusty springs, obstructed his view. Among them, as a queen might stand among her choice flowers, stood a black-haired woman of indeterminate age whose body had settled to constant child bearing. She was picking at her scrawny neck and haranguing a reluctant negro about some purchase.

Alex turned disgustedly away and considered the room which might have been furnished from a mail order catalogue. Golden oak chairs with gold-covered cushions tied against their straight backs. A horrible rug figured with poppies and bluebells. Two lamp shades which matched the rug.

Terror began to enter his heart. Narrow, confined and hopeless; unused, and a sanctuary of their hopes and aspirations. It was vastly more depressing than the bedroom had been. Turning from that junk yard to this room was like turning from a dung heap to a tuberose. That simile reminded him of another one. What was it the Bible said? "Like a lily in the mire——"

Isidore's footsteps coming up the stairs made Alex slip back onto the landing. Isidore rounded the curve and explained,

"Two people in a hurry came in. I had to help. Sorry. Now, I'll show you——"

His words faded. He led his guest through the third doorway. Ashby entered the bedroom with the pock-marked bed and rickety desk and said, "Gee! If I'd known first year books could look like that I'd have been scared stiff. But I never had a real desk, so mine weren't assembled!"

"Sit down!"

Alex sat in the desk chair and concentrated upon the books, but he saw that behind the books, against the wall, were scratches left by a bed, and then he understood Isidore's pride and the difference in the cleanliness of the sheets hung in the other bedroom. Isidore perched on the edge of the bed and begged, "Are they all right? With the list I had from the Dean's office, they check!"

"Check! Sure they do! And they are all the latest editions. Say, fellow, you're fixed! No, not quite. You need a medical dictionary, too. But that's lucky, because I own two."

"How much?" The words were out and ended in a frightened pause.

Alex picked up the copy of Sir Thomas Browne's *Religio Medici*. "Nothing. It's an exchange. You lend me this and I'll lend you the dictionary. Never read it and I've always wanted to."

"But I'll have to keep the dictionary longer."

"Well, why not? I own another one. Why did you get this?" He held up the *Religio Medici*.

"Because Osler likes it," Isidore replied simply.

"You think a lot of him, don't you?"

"Yes," Isidore replied slowly.

Alex offered him a cigarette and lit one himself. "Gee, this is lucky," he said. "I've got the dictionary with me," and he pulled it from his pocket.

Isidore, as soon as his fingers touched the small, five by three, red leather book, began thumbing the pages. His guest rose abruptly and said, "I've got to run! But it's been grand of you to let me into your life, and I'll see you tomorrow, and get you a library card."

When Isidore glanced up his eyes were blank and Alex laughed. "Go on reading. I can get out all right."

He closed the door softly and ran down the steps and through the tailor shop. He did not stop to speak to Abie Aaron.

Outside in the fine fall afternoon, Ashby took deep breaths and walked slowly savoring this incredible truth. For the first time in his twenty-two years he had spent four hours face to face with contrast, smelled poverty and felt genius.

Chapter Four

A BALTIMORE CHRISTMAS EVE

After two solid months of anatomy every morning from nine to twelve, the first year students at Miss Susie's welcomed the second quarter with glee. Beginning December first only three mornings weekly were devoted to anatomy, the other three they spent in physiological chemistry. When the Christmas vacation came, everybody decided to rest. Pug and Alex went to New York. The other boys, with the exception of Riggs, returned home. Elbert, however, refused to go back to Pennsylvania and be wept over by his aunts. Instead, he wanted, for once, to forget that he was an orphan, see a city Christmas and have a carefree holiday.

November and early December had passed without a single snow flurry. Christmas Eve the paper prophesied a white Christmas. As the day wore on, that quietness which precedes snow entered the air and Riggs grew eager to see how a great city might look when the storm began. With a mountaineer's instinct he knew that he must climb to see and at four in the afternoon began ascending the two hundred and twenty steps of the spiral stairway inside the column of the Washington Monument on Mount Vernon Place. The guide book in his pocket reported that this monument was about a hundred and eighty-four feet high, the first erected in this country to George Washington, and had been financed by a lottery.

Elbert, familiar with the East Baltimore views of the statue which stood on top of the column, considered the facts of its construction as he climbed. With a woodsman's instinct, the student moved quietly and he was within twenty steps of the top when the chanting, sing-song words began flowing into his ears.

"Little Choptank, Sassafras, Nanticoke, Great Wicomico, Pianka-tank ——"

He hesitated. The strange, musical words were pronounced in a clear, ringing soprano, yet they had a poignant quality as definite as

65

violin notes. His curiosity overcame his shyness and alone in the small room in the column dome, beneath the statue, he found the young woman who was singing them.

She was looking south, through the glass in the doorway, her hat held, with a gesture of peace and abandon, in her hands. Drawn back into a knot at the nape of her neck, her silky black hair nestled against the velvet collar of the long navy blue coat which she wore. Like the reflections on black marble, the sheen of her hair seemed deeply familiar to the young man. A sudden peace swept over him and although his inclination was not to intrude, he began to want, very much, to see her eyes. The views from the Monument dropped from his mind as the petite, pretty girl, unaware that she was being watched, continued solemnly, lovingly, "Tangier, Pungoteague, Occohannock—" Then the sad note left her voice, she leaned forward and exclaimed joyously, "Goody! It's snowing! It's snowing!"

"Really?" Riggs asked, for unconsciously her joy had wrung the word from him.

She swung around, the color mounting in her cheeks, and Elbert, while ashamed, was also delighted. Her eyes were as dark as her coat and he recognized her! When Ben Mead had shown him the main corridor at the hospital, she had been among the student nurses they passed and the sheen of her hair had sunk into his mind, then.

If the recognition was mutual, she gave no sign, and her eyes and her voice were icy.

"How long have you been here?"

"Long enough," he answered, ignoring her pique and blocking the stairway toward which she was moving, "to hear your beautiful words. What do they mean?"

To ask a personal question was intensely painful to this man and the girl, through her anger, realized that it was. Her indignation vanished, the crinkles about her eyes appeared.

"They are names," she said dimpling, "of rivers and places in Virginia and on the Eastern Shore of Maryland, where—where——"

With a typical woodsman's nod, Riggs sliced the information into his head and remarked, completing her sentence, "—where you grew up. If the country is like the words, it must be—grand."

"It is! You ought to see it," she answered, looking at the harbor, again. "Boats from here go up all those rivers. Down there the land and the water melt into each other and the air is kin to the sea!"

"Why haven't you gone home for Christmas?" he asked, moving over beside her at the door.

"Because I'm a student nurse at Hopkins. All the vacation I get is this P.M.—until midnight. And I didn't know I was going to have that, until this morning."

Again he cut the information into his head and decided that the recognition was not mutual.

"Where do you catch those boats you spoke of?"

She led the way to the outside balcony, pointed toward the southeast, still visible through the occasional snowflakes.

"They go from piers on Light Street. You know, the street with cobble stones where the Old Bay Line and the Chesapeake Line pull out every night for Norfolk."

"Do you mean *The City of Norfolk* and *The State of Virginia?*"

"Yes. How did you know?"

"From *The Sun.*"

"If you were a Baltimorean, you'd say the Sunpaper," she remarked. "I *know*, because my mother grew up in Baltimore and she can sit for hours talking about it. She says your front door steps and the way you pronounce the city, rate you. If your steps are wooden, you are probably poor, and the condition of their paint states the extent of your poverty. If you have dark steps, unless your house is brownstone, you are hopelessly middle class. And if you have white stone steps, your status depends on their cleanliness, and the section of the city in which they are located."

"I see. What about the pronunciation of the city?"

She chuckled. "According to mother, if you say Balt'ma, you are well-born; if you say Balt'mer-City you belong in the dark-step class, and if you say Bal-ti-moor you are either colored or Southern."

"That's interesting," he said and looked down at the miles of flat roofs, the pall of coal smoke and the fluttering flakes.

"Why did you come up here? To see the steps?" she asked.

"I came because I wanted to see how a city looked on Christmas Eve. I thought, somehow, it would be different from a small town."

"Is it?"

"Yes: more varied, larger."

"Where are you from?"

"A little town in Pennsylvania. You never heard of it."

"What are you doing in Baltimore?"

"Studying medicine," he replied.

"Where?"

"Hopkins, too."

Panic filled her features and edging downward she said, "I'll be kicked out of training if I'm seen with a medical student. It is against the rules. Good-bye!"

"Don't be silly," Elbert suggested calmly. "Use your brains. No persons with enough authority to fire us can climb this high. Their arteries are too hard. Anyhow, it's Christmas Eve," his voice grew wistful, "and I'm lonely. Please come back. Tell me what I'm seeing."

He looked out over the city again.

"I oughtn't to stay. Really——"

"My name is Elbert Riggs," he announced when she was standing by him again. "What's yours?"

"Nan Rogers. I *must* go. Somebody might see us up here."

"Nearly two hundred feet up in the air, and when it is snowing? Bosh! Now you put your hat on your head before you catch cold, and tell me if you'll go to the theater with me tonight, Miss Rogers, to see Mary Pickford in *A Good Little Devil*."

"Heavens, no! I wouldn't dare!"

Elbert saw that her dimples belied her speech. He said, "It's at Ford's Theatre. If we sit in the peanut gallery——"

"Nobody with authority can climb that high," Nan giggled.

"That's right. And they say it's a grand play. Do you like the theater?"

"I—I don't know. I've never been since I was ten. Nothing ever comes to my home town. And since I've been in training——"

"You are going tonight!"

"But——"

"When a Pennsylvania Dutchman makes up his mind, an Eastern Shore lady is stupid to argue with him. So that's settled! Now, tell me what is that tall column there to the southeast?"

"The Shot Tower. They used to drop shot down it during the

Revolutionary War to cool 'em. And just below you, here, is the Peabody Institute of Music and the Library. On the far end of the lower square is Walters' Art Gallery and over to the east, on that hill, is a place called the Johns Hopkins Hospital. Ever hear of it, Mister Riggs?"

Through the swirling snow, which was fast increasing, they could still see the dome of the hospital, with the crooked streets, thousands of flat roofs, and chimneypots in the foreground.

"The snow is coming so swiftly now, you'd better tell me the other landmarks in Baltimore, while I can still see, Miss Rogers, and forget about the hospital."

"Don't tease me," she begged. Turning toward the west, she said, "Ever so many interesting things are over there, but you can't see 'em. Poe's grave and those little, pretty parks called Union Square and Franklin Square and Harlem Park. Also, there are two iron, life-sized Chesapeake Bay dogs, on the stoop in front of a house on Carey Street. And, oh, there is Alexandroffsky, the magnificent estate which Mr. Winans built and enclosed in a mysterious brick wall seven feet tall after he made all that money out of the Czar."

"How?"

"Constructing Russian railroads. It has a ballroom with mirrors all around it, Mother says. And to the southwest, on Lexington Street, of course, is Lexington Market."

"What's Lexington Market?"

"Goodness gracious! Do you mean to stand there and say that you don't know Lexington Market?"

Her eyes were wide with amazement. Behind her, Elbert saw the hills of the city, as if stroked by a giant paint brush, lose their angles and grime, grow soft and clean under the touch of the snow. Street by street the vision was blotted out by the flakes which began to fill the air with constant, steady motion.

The knowledge that there would be a real snowstorm delighted him, and, with a teasing carelessness he said, "I never heard of Lexington Market. I don't believe it exists."

"Yes, it does! And you can't stay up here in the twilight looking at snow when you've never seen Lexington Market at Christmas! Why, why it's the most magnificent market on earth. Come on!"

When Elbert caught up with her, she had already reached the stairs. "Give me your hand," he said. "I'd rather have you go to the market, than to the hospital."

"When you grow up near boats, you don't fall downstairs," she answered, but, without further comment, he led the way and held her hand. Down on the sidewalk, with her arm locked snugly in his, they saw that the squares of Mount Vernon Place were already blanketed in white. The red bricks of the houses, the holly wreaths in the windows looked warm and glowing against it.

"People in Baltimore love Christmas," Nan's voice was gay. "There is such a large German population and Germans are home loving and like ceremonies. I know that they are because Uncle Emil is German, and he certainly loves his Christmas tree and Christmas garden."

"Who is Uncle Emil?"

"He's my aunt's husband. He used to work in Papa's drug store in Cambridge, when Papa was alive, and married my Aunt Alice. If they knew I was off duty, they'd have come for me right away."

"Why didn't you tell them?"

" 'Cause I wanted to climb up and see the water and I was sure they'd have made me trim the tree, instead."

Through the white mist figures, bundle laden, passed by, but protected by the storm and their own discovery of each other, Nan and Elbert scarcely saw them.

"What happened to your father?"

"Tuberculosis," Nan said. "And it was horrible, for months. I can't talk about it. I hate tuberculosis! Uncle Emil was—was wonderful then. Let's go see his Christmas garden. Let's go to see him!"

"Instead of the market?"

"Oh, no! We'll see the market, too," Nan's voice was firm. "You've got to see the market!"

To Elbert all of this seemed distinctly untrue. This merry girl whose arm he held with his, the miles of brick houses and the lamp lighter going from post to post climbing his little ladder, lighting the gas lamps which made the street names stand out on their red-glass plates. The glow of the lamps, the flying snow, the wreaths on the doors, the candles and wreaths in the windows, the passing wagons piled high with Christmas trees and the cessation of loneliness within himself were too fine a set of experiences to be actually happening.

"What time is it?" Nan asked.

"Five-thirty, according to that clock we just passed."

"Then we'll take a streetcar to save time, 'cause Uncle Emil makes you look at *every*thing. Nobody from Hopkins will be on the streetcar going to Uncle Emil's. Then we'll come back to Lexington Market and ——"

"Go to Ford's."

"Oh—do you think it is safe?"

He squeezed her arm reassuringly, "If we sit in the peanut gallery, I do."

Afterwards, when he relished the memory of this night, Elbert found that one of its pleasantest features was recalling their visit to Uncle Emil's. On the streetcar, Nan prepared him by saying, "Days and days before Christmas he begins work on his garden. Everybody in the family has to string popcorn, help select the tree and then saw the limbs off and nail 'em back on."

"Why?"

"To balance it, if they are too thick at the bottom and scrawny at the top. No tree ever suits him as purchased; he always wants his limbs at just a certain angle from his manger. It sounds crazy, I know, but wait until you see it. Baltimore is called the City of Homes and Germans vie with each other over their Christmas gardens. Mamma thinks that Aunt Alice should never have married Uncle Emil, and that Christmas gardens are common—but people come from blocks around to see his."

A few minutes later in the parlor of Uncle Emil's narrow row house on North Poppleton Street, Elbert saw that the furniture had been removed and a path made between the garden exhibits which extended from the hall door to the Christmas tree standing between the front windows.

The tree, nearly as tall as the room, was trimmed with tinsel ropes, popcorn chains, tiny clear-candy red and yellow animals and objects —horses, dogs, steamboats, hands, people—which had been carefully selected in Lexington Market. Atop the tree perched a cornucopia, gold-robed, sweet-faced cardboard angel, who had outstretched pink and white wings. It and the tree stand were relics from Uncle Emil's childhood. The base of the stand was walnut, the four sides were stepped back to the height of fifteen inches and put together with fine joiner work. The tree fitted in the center hole and was steadied with wooden slivers. Many colored candles were clamped on its branches; their pinch holders, with red tin poinsettia handles, Uncle proudly admitted to having made.

Beneath his tree were his Infant Jesus, Mary and Joseph, his manger, with a backdrop of Bethlehem and the small figures of the approaching Wise Men, star overhead. Made from bits of a broken pennant off a crystal chandelier, glued onto a wooden back, this star hung from a re-angled limb, twinkling like a diamond. With the true German instinct that "what is mine is good," Uncle Emil drew attention, also, to the new thatched roof on his manger, and recent additions of carved angels to his already large multitudes of heavenly hosts, suspended beyond the star. The animals about the manger had all received a fresh coat of paint and they, Elbert saw, were as finely carved as were the angels.

The exhibits which intervened between the tree and the doorway were also monuments of German ingenuity, pictorially speaking. A village of tiny, brightly painted, real houses nestled in the valley of a mountain scene and in the background was a waterfall over which real water flowed to carry out the illusion of reality. Next came two little dolls, a boy and a girl dressed to represent Uncle Emil's own children, on the seesaw in the backyard of a Baltimore row house; when the proper gadgets were worked the seesaw went up and down. Beyond them was a sight which made Elbert feel homesick: a big red barn and a windmill which "went." Then came the little figure of a woman kneeling on the white stone steps of a row house. When one wound the proper springs, she would lift her tiny scrub brush, wield it over the surface of the steps and dip it into the miniature bucket beside her.

The most popular of all the displays, though, was that of a little wooden, painted streetcar which had written on it, as destinations, "Lexington Market, Loudon Park, Paradise"; the second being the graveyard, the third a ~uburb. Such a streetcar really operated in West Baltimore and on Uncle Emil's the different men in the neighborhood had sat at the different windows for years. When one "passed on" to the real Loudon Park, it became a matter of serious conjecture for blocks around as to whom Uncle Emil would assign his seat. On Christmases following such a change, visitors to his garden were always more numerous, and the car made a short run on its specially constructed track to welcome the newcomer.

Something in every one of his exhibits "went," with the single exception of that depicting the Baltimore custom, during the week before Christmas, of taking the children down at night to view the toy windows of the department stores. Annually, along with thousands of other Baltimore families, Uncle Emil, his wife and children, made the pilgrimage. And afterwards he did a colored sketch of whichever window had received the family vote as "best." Duplicating the window scene in the few days which remained between their decision and the opening of his garden was one of his major occupations during idle moments at the store. This year Hochschild Kohn had won. He had painted a wonderful set of the miniature electric railroad, its tunnels, mountains, coaling towers, and stations, with himself and family observing. "Reproduction from a single sight" was one of his boasts and checking his accuracy was one of the rigorously observed pastimes of his neighbors.

As pleased as a child the fat, jovial druggist showed his creations to Elbert Riggs, listened to his compliments, and then insisted that they go into the dining room and drink a toast to each other in mulled wine while the women put the supper on the table.

In the dining room Elbert saw that the table had already been set to include them, and two more apples now hung in the line of roasting apples which were attached with strings from the mantelpiece, over the Latrobe stove. The red coals glowing through the transparent isinglass front of the stove, the odor of cooking sauerkraut, the smell of roast goose, and the pungent fragrance of the pine and cedar garlands draped over the windows and pictures, mingled with the aroma of the hot wine. Through this haze of pleasantness, Elbert saw Nan move to and fro, filling the water glasses, turning the apples. She was pretty, well-made, winsome.

Aunt Alice, who had long ago given up Eastern Shore viands for the savory, solid cooking of the Germans, brought dish after steaming dish, for the scrutiny of her happy husband, and placed it on the table.

Their small son, his cheeks rosy red, came in shouting, "The snow is up to my knees, now. And they've blocked off Lexington Street from Carey to Fremont Avenue for sledding. Six whole blocks! Hurry supper, Mamma. Please hurry!"

His father calmed his excitement long enough to introduce him to Nan's "young man." Little Emil pulled off his red mittens and grinned at the medical student.

His younger sister, silent and starry eyed, sat in her father's lap and watched while the small boy wound up the Swiss music box which sat against the wall on a high stand. Little Emil stood on tiptoe and peered through the glass top while the brass disk began to revolve. The lovely, lilting strains of the Blue Danube waltz floated through the odors and increased the sense of jolliness.

"They say it's going to snow all night! Snow all night!" the chubby boy told his sister, told his mother and tried to tell his father, who ignored him and continued talking to Riggs about the fine farming land and good food of Lancaster County, Pennsylvania.

When they were all seated at the table and all helped, Elbert complimented Aunt Alice's potato dumplings and pronounced her sauerkraut und speck the best he'd ever eaten. Uncle Emil beamed; then he spoke of the fine neighborhoods of West Baltimore, the spacious houses around Franklin and Union Squares and hoped that some day he would be doing well enough to set up his Christmas tree in one of them and get Aunt Alice "a girl," to make the dumplings for her.

Aunt Alice, who looked like Nan grown-up, showed him her dimples and said he deserved a better cook than she was. Uncle Emil shook his head violently.

Little Emil got up and cranked the music box again. It began to play "O Tannenbaum, O Tannenbaum." They all laid down their forks and sang:

O Tannenbaum, O Tannenbaum, wie schoen sind deine Blaetter
Du gruenst nicht nur zur Sommerzeit, nein, auch im Winter wenn es
schneit.

The famous old Christmas song seemed to pack Little Emil's meal within him, for immediately afterwards, he took second helpings of everything. His father and Elbert did likewise, and later when Aunt Alice brought on her apfelstrudel and molasses shoo-fly cake, both Elbert and Little Emil took a piece of each. Little Emil, between bites, said he hoped they never had "a girl" to cook for them and both of the men agreed with him.

When Uncle Emil learned that Elbert had never seen Lexington Market he offered instantly to help Aunt Alice wash the dishes and release Nan, so that the young people could get off right after supper.

They did so, and Elbert's last memory of the family was the sight of Little Emil, lying on his stomach, red muffler flying in the wind, shooting past on his bobsled down the hill, toward Lexington Street.

"Merry Christmas, Little Emil," he and Nan called, but the wind was cutting past the child's ears so swiftly that he failed to hear.

"Look," Nan screamed, clutching the student's arm, "the double-deckers are out! It's a really deep snow!"

They had reached Lexington Street as she spoke and down the hill toward which Little Emil had just flashed came three bobsleds fastened together with a single plank. By using a hot poker, holes had been made in this plank. The sleds were wired to it in tandem, and on the plank, their owners and their owners' friends sat erect.

"When the double-deckers are out," Nan gasped, "that means the snow is hard-packed and that sledding will be grand. Oh, I'm so glad! Aren't you?"

Her eyes danced, her dimples shone. Elbert halted their progress. "Rather go sledding?"

"No," she shook her head. "Nurses can't take chances with broken arms. Be safer at the theater, don't you think?"

"Certainly do," he said and patted the arm he held in his.

As they walked down Lexington Street, the screech of the step-scraping hoes with which the people were shovelling the snow off their "fronts" came through the still air. They saw the army of small colored boys, carrying scrapers and busted down brooms, going from door to door, ringing bells and asking ladies if they might "clean them off!"

They trudged on toward the market and Nan explained, "General John Eager Howard, whose statue is at Madison and Charles on Mount Vernon Place, gave the land for Lexington Market in 1783. One of the interesting things about it is that the stalls were auctioned off at the beginning from two to eight thousand dollars and belong to private individuals. The city only gets twenty dollars rent annually from each stall. Now, the Baltimoreans who own those stall-grants are as rich as those who own ground rents."

"What are ground rents?" To a Pennsylvania Dutchman a woman who comprehended figures, as well as beauty, was increasingly alluring, and Nan liked the admiration in his voice as Elbert put the question.

"I know all these things, you see," she said, "because Mamma and Uncle Emil have talked about them ever since I could listen. In the older sections of Baltimore, few people own the land on which their houses stand and they have to pay an annual interest rate of six per cent on the land-value to the people who do own it. 'Having a ground rent' is being required to pay that six per cent; 'owning a ground rent' is collecting it. At stated periods, if you have saved the money, you may be able to purchase your ground rent from its owner, but some of them can never be purchased and they call those irredeemable ground rents. All ground rents come before any mortgage and older Baltimoreans think they are the best investment anybody can have."

"Certainly sound like it," Elbert remarked.

"Baltimore girls, when they marry, think it's grand if a relative gives 'em a couple of ground rents. People down home think they are awful. Nobody on the Eastern Shore would think of owning a house and not owning the ground."

"That is our outlook, too," Elbert said, as they passed the bow windows, so typical of Baltimore, in a little corner shop. Peppermint walking sticks, from two to twenty inches in length, hung on a string strung crosswise beyond the glass.

Two blocks down the street, at Pine, the out-of-door market stalls began to appear and Nan announced, "The real market doesn't commence until we get to Pearl Street. Then it extends, under cover, for three blocks and Uncle Emil says if all the stalls were put in a straight line, it would be nearly three miles long. The big market days are Tuesdays, Fridays and Saturdays, but it is open every day, except Sunday. On market days, the department stores have their sales. The ladies can go straight down the hill from market and be at their doors, in five minutes."

"What was the market named for, Miss Rogers?"

"The Battle of Lexington," Nan replied, as they came abreast of the out-of-doors stalls, with their peaked canvas roofs and small charcoal braziers around which the marketmen stood warming their hands and chatting. They had shoveled the snow from the sidewalk into the street behind their stalls and strings of overhead electric lights glared down on their produce.

These were the men who owned no market stalls, in the professional under-cover sense and who brought their products, on market days, to be sold off the street.

Three and four deep against the buildings, Christmas trees stood awaiting purchasers, and near the charcoal braziers the fragrance of pine, spruce, and balsam became more noticeable. Green crow's feet garlands, sold by the yard, holly wreaths and bunches of mistletoe awaited stair banisters, vacant windows and double parlor doorways from which to hang. The men who had gathered and arranged the decorations stood by scanning the crowds for possible purchasers. As the warm glow from the charcoal braziers slanted upward and emphasized their faces, Elbert saw that many of them were tall, gaunt, bitter men—unlike the farmers of Lancaster County.

But the fragrance of the Christmas greens and the faces of their vendors were forgotten as Nan stepped forward and they entered Lexington Market. He saw that not only was Lexington Market on a much larger scale than those of Pennsylvania towns, but also that it was differently constructed. Instead of the high domed buildings, this market was one story, low peaked roofed, and the stalls, which extended in three double aisles, were brilliantly lighted by overhead rows of electric lights. Stall after stall, in tightly packed lines, the panorama stretched for three blocks, presided over by people whose ancestors had "stood in market" before them, whose descendants would stand in market after them, and whose customers remained loyal for generations.

The section they entered was given over entirely to fish and over many of the stalls Elbert saw a sign which read, "Oysters R in season."

When he inquired whether that was local spelling, Nan replied with a touch of pride, "That indicates that this is a month with an R in it. City people believe that oysters should only be eaten in the months containing an R. But on the Eastern Shore we think that our oysters are good enough to eat 'most any time. Oh, there are some Chincoteagues. Don't you want to taste one?"

The vendor, realizing by her inflection that she came from the land of oysters, said, "Pick out any you like, miss, and I'll shuck it for you."

Nan critically studied the barrel of oysters, picked one and the dealer, with his shucking knife and a deft movement of the wrist slit the shell, then reached for his bottle of horse radish.

"Please," the girl begged hastily, "don't spoil the flavor of a good oyster. I just love the salty taste of a Chincoteague."

The man grinned at Riggs, who was watching Nan, and offered to repeat the process in the student's behalf. Elbert shook his head.

"How much do I owe you?"

"Ain't anything I can charge for one oyster, mister," the dealer drawled. "Which do you like the best, lady, Tangiers or Chincoteagues?"

"Tangiers are too delicate; I like the salty taste of Chincoteagues," Nan replied, professionally. "Have you had a good day?"

"Certainly have. The Maryland Club took all my terrapin, and I sold two barrels of Linnhavens for presents for doctors."

"What are Linnhavens?"

"They are the largest oysters going, mister," the vendor replied. "Come from Linnhaven Bay, little arm off the Chesapeake, near Norfolk. And Tangiers come from Tangier Sound, and Chincoteagues from Chincoteague Bay."

"Have a good time tomorrow and thank you," Nan said and they moved on. In a tub, at the next stall, Elbert saw long, live eels swimming, while on the counters for half a block every conceivable kind of fish glistened.

"Anything you want but crabs," one hawker called. "Anything. Name it!"

"Have you a shad roe?" Nan asked softly.

The other vendors roared, and the hawker answered glibly, "Never have 'em until the horses run, lady. March and April."

"What does he mean by that?" Elbert asked.

"The Maryland tracks open for the spring racing meets along about then," Nan explained. "And the roes of the shad in the Susquehanna River and the upper Chesapeake Bay are ready for market. My, they are good! It is only during early spring that the shad run."

"I've never eaten shad roe."

"Then, we'll—you'll have to try one," she said lamely and blushed.

"We'll have to have one," he corrected. The clean, clear sea smell swept into his head as he saw the pink of salmon steak, the flaky white of the halibut and the slimy gray-black of the eels slip by. Frog legs, diamond back terrapin sold by shell length, not weight, and marsh rabbits, or Eastern Shore muskrats, known as the poor man's terrapin, were displayed, too. Shrimp from the Gulf Coast, salted codfish from New England, pompano, and North Carolina soft shelled clams made Elbert feel as if he had seined the oceans with a giant net.

Presently the shimmering scales of the fish gave way to the richer reds of the beef. He heard the phrases, "First and second rib, please," "Standing rib roast," "Nice hamburger," "Two pounds of scrapel," "Country sausage with sage," "Have you bought your kidneys for breakfast, tomorrow? Every prominent Baltimore family eats kidney stew on Christmas morning!" "How would you like a pork roast, nice fresh loin?" "Fine rump roast for your sour beef?" "Tender chops. Nice, thick tender mutton chops!" The pale pink of veal, pyramids of pigs' feet, and an occasional pig's head with ears full of parsley caught Riggs' eye, too.

Names like Schafer, Roeder, Schaar, Immler were written over the butcher stalls and faces as red as cranberries shone behind the glass cases.

In the roar and the crowd, the young couple held hands and used their eyes instead of their tongues. Overhead the festooned green garlands and the red tissue paper Christmas bells swung gently to and fro; over each stall was some special decoration.

"The market looks mighty nice this year," and "Merry Christmas to all your family from all of ours," were sentences which rang in everybody's ears.

Off the side aisles of the two solid blocks of butchers were the poultry, produce and some of the specialty people. Eggs, pullet and cooking, butter, sweet and salted, and then guineas, capons, chickens, and turkeys, all dressed and hanging by their feet came into view. People buying cream, talking eggnog recipes, lifting turkey wings, pinching chicken breasts, stood about these counters, and above them the purple brown of the guineas was a striking contrast to the dead white of the chickens and yellow white of the fat turkeys.

Nearby were the stalls where chicken heads, chicken feet, chicken giblets were for sale. Toward them wearily moved the negroes who had hoped for a stewing chicken, but been unable to meet the prices.

Because food will spoil if subjected to heat, as Riggs was aware, he saw that the only method these dealers had for keeping warm were the same type of small charcoal brazier which the men outside the market had used. In the fish section, of course, even they were forbidden, but here the market families took turn about waiting on the customers and warming their hands. All of the men clerks wore sweaters, coats and derby hats; the women clerks had thick knitted shawls about their shoulders. They too wore hats and were nodding, smiling, caring for their customers. All were red-cheeked, red-nosed, jolly. And the customers who stood on the sawdust sprinkled concrete aisle ranged all the way from Judy O'Grady to the colonel's lady; from a fireman in uniform to a lawyer with spats and a cane; from an upset housewife whose unexpected company had necessitated the purchase of a second turkey to a worn out hag who had the price of a chop. The few children, who didn't expect an early Santa Claus, took experimental slides on the sawdust and inspected side-aisle candy counters while their parents bargained with the butcher.

The side-aisle specialty people past whose counters Nan led Elbert fascinated him. At one stall was a man handling nuts only—pecans, walnuts, peanuts, chestnuts, almonds—every kind from everywhere, shelled and unshelled, roasted and unroasted. Next, was a pickle man whose buckets were piled high with sweet and sour, mustard and green, cauliflower and small gherkin, dill and cucumber pickles, and every kind of relish imaginable. Also stuffed and plain olives, all sizes.

Across from him stood a woman dealing in potato chips, noodles and salads. Potato salad, German sweet and German sour, waffle potato chips, chicken salad, sweet and sour coleslaw, vegetable salad, mayonnaises and salad dressings.

Nearby, a man was doing a brisk business in fresh prepared horse radish—"Ground before your eyes, madam, and bottled while you wait." His other product was "Freshly shredded coconut. Freshly shredded. Freshly—" Behind the shredding and grinding machines the long roots of the horse radish and the unshelled coconuts lay side by side.

Beyond his stall was a bread counter. French rolls, soft rolls, Maryland beaten biscuit, long rolls, hot cross buns, sweet buns, German coffee cake and pumpernickel, French bread, bread with and without caraway seeds, nut bread and every conceivable kind of cracker.

Appropriately, directly across from the bread lady was a man dealing solely in cheeses. To his counter came the epicures of Baltimore and to his counter from the cheese producing countries of the world, came their finest products. Elbert saw the Dutch cheeses, apple-shaped red Edams and pineapple, molded cheeses, beside the greens of Roquefort and Italian Gorgonzola. Pale yellow cheddars and huge pale yellow Herkimer County "rat-trap" lay near the Bel Paese from Italy and the white cream from Philadelphia. Small boxes of European cheeses with bright labels on their tin foil coverings blended with the red of the Edams to lend a Christmas note to the sight. Also boxed, but carefully wrapped and not displayed, were his Limburger and Camembert; when they were uncovered to make a sale the women put their handkerchiefs to their noses and the men, nearby, whiffed the air affectionately.

Here and there, sandwiched among these food stalls, would be that of a produce dealer, whose pyramids of celery hearts, ten cents a bunch, shimmered like white silk beneath the electric lights. Elbert had never seen celery sold that way. Pennsylvanians thought *all* of the sweet celery grown in the Cumberland Valley was edible. Mounds of green lettuce which had been sprinkled, caught the reflection of the glaring lights in diamond-studded leaves; the hard-hearted iceberg variety, it had been shipped from Florida. The cool palm fingers of endive shown beside "Christmas strawberries," also shipped from Florida and selling for forty cents a box. Potatoes, sweet and "white," and cauliflower, green peas, fresh string beans, added color to the sight, as did the piles of small red cranberries. The greengrocer sold herbs, too; sassafras root, thyme, and bunches of mace, sage and of soup herbs found ready purchasers. Overhead, toward the back of his ascending displays, were his array of fresh gold pumpkins, his strings of colored dried peppers and onions. He was also doing a brisk business in "kraut," as were many of the butchers, and salad people. The spicy odor of uncooked mince meat and the penetrating, tangy smell of uncooked sauerkraut vied with the clean forest fragrance of the Christmas greens.

Elbert noticed that a potato chip woman was also dealing in dried fish—herrings, pickled eels, and dried codfish cakes, ready to cook. Dried lima and navy beans were also selling, as were the pints and quarts of uncooked "big" or lye hominy which Baltimoreans like to eat, in the place of potatoes, on Christmas.

Nan, delighted by his obvious interest, kept silent, hung on his arm and watched him. At a candy counter, though, she requested that he stop so that she might show him the large assortment of clear, red and yellow, Christmas tree candies, such as Uncle Emil used. They studied the animals and objects and saw the hills of sugar covered almonds, mountains of peanut brittle and peaks of white and colored taffy which formed a background for the clear candies. White and red rock candy, chocolate drops with anise seed, plain bonbons, hard bucket candy, licorice pipes, candy Santa Clauses, blocks and blocks of fudge, with and without nuts, caramels, lemon sticks, peppermint sticks, gumdrops, and lollypops lay side by side.

He watched her wiggle her nose like a little girl as she scrutinized the display and asked, "Ever seen anything to touch it?"

"Never. What will you have?"

"I just love white taffy, but if you ——"

"So do I."

They bought a dime's worth of taffy, then the adjacent sausage stall caught Riggs's eye. With a cheek full of taffy, each of them saw the pickled pigs' feet, flaked halibut, uncooked oyster patties, servelat, blutwurst, braunschweiger, caviar, bologna, with and without pimento, and with garlic.

Their consideration, there, was purely artistic, however, and their only other purchase was made when they came abreast of the cake counter. Elbert spied some pfeffernuesse—those marble-shaped, hard, spicy tasting little cookies. He bought half a pound and they sampled them in their vacant jaws, while studying the forty different kinds of cakes, cookies and pies laid out before them. Lebkuchen, layer cakes, cup cakes, slab cakes, chocolate, Lady Baltimore (ten-cents-a-slice, lady), pound cake, angel food, sponge, fruit cake and jelly roll. "What will you have, madam? What does your husband like?"

As the clerk leaned forward and asked those questions, both the medical student and the nurse blushed red as the Christmas bell behind them. But Elbert refused to release Nan's arm, and, turning their backs on the cake man, they listened carefully to the last of the butchers in the main aisle chanting,

"Turkeys, twenty-five cents a pound. Fresh killed. Nice and tender. Chickens, geese, rabbits, ducks—just brought up from the Eastern Shore this afternoon, eighteen to twenty cents a pound. The rabbits is thirty-five each. Have a nice rabbit."

"Those are poor prices for the producers," the boy said practically, but Nan did not hear him for she had found the flowers.

Outside the Eutaw Street market entrance the snow had been cleared and stall after stall was a mass of blooms. Because snow still fell, the vendors had lowered their canvas awnings about their shelves and one entered, as at a circus, into the tentlike stall. Under the glaring electric lights, in the tall tin green containers, roses, of every shade—red, American beauty, pink, white, and even delicate yellow—lifted their heads and waited for some one to want them for a Christmas dinner table. Cup-sized chrysanthemums, burnt orange, yellows and white, vied with the potted azaleas and potted poinsettias. Plumy ferns, delicate maidenhair ferns, potted ivy, and brilliant red rose trees overshadowed cut snapdragons and cut sweet peas.

"Want some?" Elbert asked gently.

"What could I do with them?" she whispered. "But aren't they lovely. We never had flowers like these at home at Christmas. Did you?"

"No. I never saw anything like any of this. Let's buy a poinsettia to send to your aunt and Uncle Emil. You pick it out, write the card, and I'll pay for it. Then it will come from both of us."

Nan considered several before she found one which satisfied her. Then she wrote the card, Elbert gave the man the two dollars and the man gave her a choice of his roses.

She took a red one, and as they left the stall, Elbert asked curiously, "What are those?"

Nan understood that he was referring to the wreaths of red artificial flowers, some in glass-topped cases, which lay upon a nearby counter.

"Those are immortelles," she explained. "Some of 'em are made of straw flowers and wax calla lilies. See? They are for the cemeteries. Everybody in Baltimore goes to the cemeteries at Christmas and puts red wreaths on the graves of their relatives. If you don't meet your friends at market, you are sure to see 'em at Loudon Park or Greenmount."

Nibbling their cakes, munching their candy, they sauntered on down Eutaw Street toward Fayette, a distance of one block.

Elbert said simply, "Thank you for taking me." When he desired to reveal himself, he could pack more appreciation into single sentences than most men could into paragraphs.

"Don't be silly," she answered gently. "I wouldn't have missed it for anything."

As they rounded the corner and reached Ford's he asked, "If you'd like to sit downstairs ——?"

"No. I wouldn't dare!"

"Then go to that last door and wait just inside, while I go in the lobby and get the tickets, will you?"

Nan obeyed and shortly they shook the snow from themselves and began climbing, climbing ell after ell after ell up the concrete stairway. At the peanut door, the student gave the tickets to an usher who led them to center seats in the front row of the top balcony.

Nan was white as she seated herself. Elbert said calmly as he offered her a ticket stub, "If you don't talk to me while the lights are on, nobody can prove we are together. Between acts, if you want to go out by yourself and *show* we aren't together, use this stub."

Looking straight ahead she said, "No, thank you. I wouldn't leave my seat until it's over for—for anything. Afterward, I'm going to believe it really happened."

"The way to do that is to let it happen, again."

"No! I couldn't ever." Her eyes were still straight ahead.

"Please don't say that. For once I've been happy. I'll remember tonight as long as I live. When may I see you again?"

"Not for a month, anyhow."

"You have a P.M. every week, don't you?"

"Yes."

"Then let's make it next Tuesday."

"No!"

"Two weeks from today?"

"No! I'm afraid to."

"On the third Tuesday, three weeks from today, at four in the afternoon, I'll be up in the Monument waiting," he said calmly.

"Not twice, I wouldn't dare."

"Safest place in town—for us. Remember what I said about arteries."

"I won't promise. I'm——"

Elbert changed the subject, "This is a famous old theater, you know. Joe Jefferson, Julia Marlowe, and Edwin Booth have walked these boards. After his brother shot Lincoln, Booth would never play Washington so when the government officials wanted to see his Hamlet, they had to come to Baltimore."

When she made no response, he asked, "Why are you so solemn?"

"Just thinking that—that we shouldn't have chanced Lexington Market, together. Until this minute——"

"All the time," he said confidently, "I watched. Nobody we saw knew us."

"Sure?" She turned and looked at him.

"Positive," he answered and repeated it twice. Then the frown left her forehead, her troubled blue eyes grew clear again.

"That old stage curtain is famous, too. Tell me what you think of it," he said diverting her attention.

Looking at the painting to which he referred, Nan saw a woodland glen, with tall trees and fern beds as a background. The sun filtered down through the leaves onto an ox cart around which danced, to the music from the flute of a satyr, a troupe of graceful, frolicsome maidens. Clothed in diaphanous draperies, which caught the sunlight as they floated through the air, these maidens were the essence of youth—gay and carefree.

"I love it! Don't you?"

Elbert said, "It's called the Primeval Players or the Bacchanalian Scene. The woods are pretty natural, I think."

While he was speaking Nan glanced surreptitiously at him and liked again his chiseled profile, high forehead and the wave in his auburn brown hair. Then she looked out at the high-ceilinged theater with its tiers of boxes, two balconies, and long prism chandelier.

The orchestra began to play, the hum of many conversations rose toward them, and Elbert realized that the theater was as exciting to Nan as Uncle Emil's and the market had been to him.

"David Belasco," he stated, "is presenting this play. He is the best producer in New York. They say Ernest Truex, the Good Little Devil, is a fine juvenile actor. And Juliet, Mary Pickford——"

The lights in the huge chandelier and those edging the boxes grew dim, went out, the orchestra ceased playing, the curtain rose.

The play opened in a Scottish cottage where a dreadful old witch of an aunt scolded and starved her little nephew, Charles. The boy, Ernest Truex, nevertheless had friends; into his attic room, which opened out on the stars, fairies came and brought him wonderful dreams. In his troubled sleep, a tiny fairy, Thoughts-From-Afar, who had seen his mother in heaven leaned over Charles and gave him the three kisses which she had sent. "One for memory. One for love. One for courage."

The only person who knew of the gifts which the fairies brought to Charles was his blind sweetheart Juliet, who lived in a beautiful garden where chipmunks, deers, and the dog, Rab, cared for and loved her.

Charles's visits to Juliet became the only bright spot in his reality and when his aunt sent him away to a horrid school where mercenary masters maltreated him, he escaped and returned to her garden. While at the school, he was befriended by a wise, wandering poet, and the poet's epilogues, at the beginning of each act, formed an important part of the play.

Other hard experiences befell Charles, but as in all fairy plays everything, in the end, turned out for the best; Charles married Juliet, whose sight was restored by the fairies. The scenes in her garden and those where the radiantly beautiful fairies float down from the skies, heralded by chirping birds and silver bells, delighted the entire audience.

Elbert gave his silk pocket handkerchief to Nan and tightly held her hand while she wept. She forgot her supervisors. He forgot his aunts. Along with thousands of other Baltimoreans they cheered, laughed, cried and cheered some more, as the Rostand fantasy tore at their hearts.

When the woodland curtain rang down on the last act and the Primeval Players resumed their revelry, Nan whispered, "Thank you! I couldn't possibly have had a better Christmas gift!"

The actors began taking their bows, the sixteen little child-fairies came out with Miss Pickford and Mr. Truex, and the orchestra began playing.

"If you have to be in by midnight," Elbert said regretfully, "we'd better get down immediately and take a cab. It's eleven-fifteen."

As they descended the stairs, Nan reluctantly came back to earth. The snow was still falling in Fayette Street and no taxis were available. So they ran for an eastbound Number Four streetcar on which Nan insisted upon paying her own fare and sitting by herself. When the crowd thinned, Elbert moved up and sat behind her.

Looking out of the window, he said to the pane, "How old are you?"

To the pane she replied, "Nineteen."

"What year of training?"

"First."

"Good!"

She rubbed the glass, as if to see beyond it, and whispered, "I've had a glorious time."

"If you mean it, say you'll be at the Monument three weeks from this afternoon."

Turning away from the pane Nan Rogers sat erect, but presently Elbert saw her finger moving against the hot moist glass. The letters it outlined were Y-E-S.

The car began climbing the hill toward Broadway, the nurse rang the bell, and walked swiftly toward the door. As soon as it opened, she descended and began running toward the hospital.

The medical student got off and watched her run.

"Merry Christmas, Nan!" he called.

Just before turning in the iron gates, the girl stood still for a second. Through the falling snow, her gay words came back to him, "Merry Christmas to you, too, Bert!"

Chapter Five

FIRST YEAR MEDICINE

Early in January at half past ten upon a Monday night, Pug Prentiss sat naked in a foot and a half of water and mechanically lathered a washrag. A lyric for deliverance the next Sunday morning had made him forget his dirty neck. He muttered slowly, "Dame, flame, same—no!—floor, more. More! That's better. More."

But the word disintegrated into lather; Pug realizing that the light had gone out, involuntarily lifted his green eyes and peered upward.

"Gosh!" he said and then again, "Great Caesar's ——"

In the blackness Dr. Dourmee's ceiling lady still shone faintly in all of her anatomical glory. Somebody, sometime, had given her an outline of phosphorus. The washrag flapped unnoticed in the water; Pug lifted his long legs over the end of the tub and made room for his torso to recline. He laid his head against the sloping inside of the tub's back and considered her perfections.

"Lady," he said softly, "I like your geometry and as for your calculus ——!"

The door opened swiftly and Prentiss continued in an offended tone, "I'm in here!"

"Well," Ben Mead replied, "so am I. Whyn't you turn on the light? Too modest?"

"Bulb burnt out. Say, did you know about the phosphorus trimmings?"

"Sure," Ben began running the water in the basin.

"Whyn't you tell me?"

" 'Cause I have physical peculiarities which require my occasional use of this lab!"

"Bosh! Who fixed her, Ben?"

"I dunno. But Ashby always bathes with the light off. Ask him."

89

Clay Abernathy and Silas Holmes, tired of studying, and hearing voices, drifted down to the bathroom. As their shadows fell through the door Ben said, "You are too attractive, Pug. Nickel or a quarter now charged for mutual use of this bathroom while the tub is occupied, depending upon ———"

"Ben," Clay interrupted, "did Snell use to give you such rotten long assignments?"

"Rotten and long, kid. Snell's been cutting up bodies so many years that he's got no respect for anything in 'em. Not even brains."

"Cheroot, fellows?" Clay interrupted and passed a pack. Everybody but Pug took one. Pug lay back and kept his eyes fixed upon the ceiling. He did not care to obstruct his view with a cheroot.

"But didn't he get easier in the second quarter, Ben?"

Ben laughed scornfully. "Swallow it, Clay, swallow it! Snell's an easy guy compared to what you've got coming. Take this bird I had last quarter in pharmacology: Denrich. Any time he'd cocked his nasty little head on his thin shoulders and spend fifty minutes depressing us flat!"

"Snell don't depress you. He just tells you," Silas announced.

Pug wiggled his toes in the cool air and remarked, "When a man's hair line begins to recede, he's usually past learning. Snell's in that stage."

"What about the bald heads?" Ben intervened.

"They run wild. Hard to tell. One who looks like a flying buttress is apt to be a wall; and one who looks like a wall is liable to be thick. Seems to me that there are three kinds of teachers. I found them in California, in Mexico, and I'm finding them here. The first takes a cold chisel and hammers it in: perspire!"

"Like Howe," Ben said.

"The second sneers and depresses it into you by turns: expire!"

"Denrich," Ben put in.

"And the third," Pug snapped his left big toe and glared at the glowing cheroots, "makes you think this is so darn easy I've just got to get it. He always teaches the most terrible grinds, but he puts it across, all right: inspire!"

"McMillan fills that bill," Ben again announced. "Only McMillan has a mean streak, too. They say he'll ask you what you think is the matter with a patient and after you spend half an hour spieling off all the ooze in your head, he'll smile and say, 'Very interesting. You know I haven't decided what the trouble is.'"

A voice from further down the hall chimed in, "That's because his wife is an invalid." Ashby was standing with one foot even with his other knee and flat against a doorjamb, and he drawled the words.

"Your throne's unoccupied, come on in," Ben suggested.

He came, and Silas inquired, "His wife wasn't the patient, was she?"

"No," Ashby said slowly, "but she was the cause. McMillan was white-headed 'fore he was forty. She has to be cystoscoped every few weeks!"

"Gee!" said Ben. "How y' know?"

"Otto told me."

"What's that?" Silas asked.

"Take an endoscope and go into the bladder without any anesthesia. Worse pain in the world. Feels like fire. Do men as well as women," Alex answered.

"Why?" Silas asked again.

"Brings relief in certain types of nephritis."

"And nephritis is inflammation of the kidneys?" Silas inquired.

"That's right," Ashby answered.

"Maybe something like that is what's wrong with Snell," Clay remarked glumly.

Pug Prentiss retorted, "Matter with Snell is he's afraid of live people."

"Cadavers and medical students aren't elevating," Alex said casually.

"I'll say this for Snell," Ben remarked. "He's not averse to expressing an opinion. Not like Siddell!"

"How's Siddell?" Clay Abernathy said hastily. He felt that the others were giving Pug all of their attention.

Ben answered, "Always coming along and looking at a patient and just saying, 'Xstrawdn'y! Exstrawdn'y!' Teaches dermatology. In a Pithotomy show once where the students took off the professors, the fellow who played Siddell was never referred to by name. He just mimicked Siddell's motions and the audience thought that he was Siddell, but couldn't be sure. Then one of the named doctors, just before the curtain fell, asked him what he thought of a patient's condition and he said, 'Xstrawdn'y!' and brought down the house. You won't get him for some time yet."

Silas, Clay and Elbert had ranged themselves upon the edge of the tub. Ashby occupied the toilet, Prentiss still reclined in the tub, and unabashed by Ben's superiority he inquired, "How's the bird we get in physiological chemistry this quarter?"

"Oh, Patterson's all right," Ashby replied casually. "Knows his stuff."

"What else do you expect of him?" Silas's question was flat.

"I dunno," Pug said, "little more masculinity and some honesty of features, perhaps."

"He's got both, in a way," Ben intervened. "Wife has a baby every spring. Never happy less she's pregnant. From March to June —isn't it, Alex?—those unuttered sarcasms his face spends the rest of the year piling up come down on you like a ton of bricks!"

"Way you talk looks like every man-jack 'round here is 'bout to bust 'cause of some skirt."

"Aw, it isn't as bad as that, Pug!" Ashby condoled. "It is pure sciolism to presume that all doctors are either uxorious men or onagers requiring marrams."

"Hey, quit that!" Ben pleaded. "The fellow with whom you swapped queer words graduated last June."

"Keep it up," Pug suggested. "I'm fond of sesquipedalians. And I've never heard marram used in that sense, before."

"I know that uxorious means excessively fond of one's wife, and onagers are wild asses, but what is a marram?" Silas asked calmly.

"Short grass that binds sand," Prentiss replied.

Ben cut in, "Well, old Snell's no onager—and neither is Doctor Howe, the ophthalmologist. And Jack Cameron's all right. So is Halsted, even if he does have his tablecloths ironed on the table!"

"Leave the Big Four out of this," Alex ordered.

"Who is Cameron?" Clay asked.

"Teaches diseases of the nervous system," Ashby explained. "Just gives plain, straight, clear lectures. Makes it all sound so reasonable. He's married and has some children."

"And his wife has some money," Ben intervened.

"What's that got to do with it?" Alex said hotly.

"A lot," Pug announced calmly. "It's got a hell of a lot to do with everything. I've bummed. You can take my word for it. Money matters."

"Do you expect to make money in medicine?" Alex's words were cutting.

"No. But I couldn't make money out of medicine, either. My motor isn't geared that way."

"How 'bout these gynecologists?" Clay asked chattily.

"Some of 'em make money, some of 'em don't. Kelly has, but he's also given it away, too. Not just money, but health. Kelly's religious, so I guess it isn't fair to take him as a criterion!" Ashby answered.

"Thought you were going to leave them out of this," Ben said.

Another boy had joined the group. He was the fourth year student who had arrived the night after the first supper at Miss Susie's. His name was Minnegerode Otts, and he looked it. His head belonged to the Minnegerode ancestry and his body to the Otts.

"Say, Minnie," Alex Ashby asked a trifle deferentially, "you're just in time. Tell us, why did you go into medicine? 'Cause you want to make money?"

The six students waited for his reply. It came in a deep and tired rasp.

"Because my grandfather was a minister and spent his life begging parishes. My father was a lawyer and spent his begging a jury. I had to do something professional, but I preferred to have people begging me. That's why!"

Minnie Otts's answer and the phosphorus lady's hips became indelibly mixed in Pug Prentiss's mind. So mixed that afterward he usually bathed with the light on!

"Give us some more dope, Minnie." Ben's words filled the silence.

"About what?"

"That man who teaches orthopedics or some of the other fourth year profs. We don't care."

"Haven't got the time," Minnie said and turned on his heel.

"Twenty years from now some guys will be chewing the rag and saying his wife did it to him!" Ben raised his voice. Everybody laughed and Minnie slammed his door in protest.

"Pug, get out of that tub! You'll shrivel to a mummy!"

Ashby's sentence was affectionate and before Pug could comply Ben was saying,

"That orthopedist Franklin, from McGill, is some man, I'll tell you. Invented operations galore. Works eighteen hours a day. Gruff and rude and ——"

"Roving-eyed."

"Call it the inquiring mind, Ben," Pug suggested as he reached for a towel. The cheroots of the other boys glowed in the darkness.

"Excess energy," Silas's diagnosis was a plain statement of fact.

Clay Abernathy laughed hollowly.

"Another way of saying the same thing," Alex intervened.

"That women are always messin' up everything including medicine." Pug switched his towel knowingly.

"I'm going to be a gynecologist to protect myself!" Ben announced in an alarmed tone.

"I don't think!"

"Why, Alex?"

" 'Cause, Bennie, you like to talk too much to ever be a female specialist."

"Signs of a clean and open mind," Ben defended.

"Gore!" Pug Prentiss flicked his towel toward the ceiling in excitement.

"Gore what?" Elbert asked practically.

"Just something I was trying to rhyme."

"Doctor Alexander Ashby has worked out a chart of fifty words which rhyme with that. It's on file in the Medical Library, Doctor."

"But the derivations are unfortunately accessible only in the cranium of Benjamin Mead and the Orthopedic Staff," Alex Ashby retorted.

"When you get corroded, flap-ears, you're going to have a face as full of unuttered ideas as Patterson, and you better get married early, else ——"

"Else?"

"Later you'll have no excuse for your nasty expression!"

"Then I'll be more interesting. Like 'Buck' Edwards, maybe."

"How's 'Buck' Edwards?"

"Oh, he's got a face like an angel, Clay, and a memory like Ben Mead for lascivious language."

Mead had risen and turned his back. If you didn't leave Alex Ashby's presence when you first scored, you always left it a loser.

Silas turned to Ashby and asked, "Can you ever find out after the second quarter?"

"What?"

"If you fail."

"Depends."

"Like my condition, on what you've digested," Pug said jovially. "I'm hungry, fellows. Have a glass of beer and a sandwich on me at Otto's? Need to wash that faculty down with something!"

In the last few weeks Pug Prentiss had discovered that anatomy was no longer a grind. The next morning, as he walked from Miss Susie's toward the medical school, he found himself looking forward to today because today was Tuesday and the morning would be spent dissecting.

An hour later in company with Elbert Riggs, Silas, Clay Abernathy, Elijah Howe, Isidore Aaron and eighteen other boys, one group of the first year men, he picked up his scalpel again and pushed and probed. The group was divided into fours and each four was working upon a cadaver. He and Silas Holmes had "lowers," while upon the same body Elijah Howe and Isidore Aaron were doing "uppers."

The six cadavers were laid out upon wooden tables with wooden pillars under their heads. At the foot of each table were nailed two unpainted pine uprights and the heels of the cadavers were set above a row of nails about a foot from the top of the planks; then the feet had been tied in place. Ranged here and there about the room resting upon easels which resembled the type of stand a musician uses, were Gray's *Anatomies* open at whatever section the student was dissecting.

The colored plates in the textbooks were the most vivid thing in the room. The contrast of white men working upon black bodies flowing with red blood with which old prints used to abound was entirely lacking. Only a portion, usually not longer than ten inches, had been carefully unwrapped, and the student centered his attention upon that small section. Here and there a conversation flickered, but was smothered by silent exploration.

Clay Abernathy looked up from the arm of the cadaver he was dissecting next to Pug's and began to whistle. Snell had gone to Otto's for his usual morning coffee and Clay was the first person to note his absence. Here and there a student raised his eyes at the sound of the whistling, then put aside his scalpel and rested.

"Silas," Clay said, "you still in the perineum?"

Upon a stool, between the elevated legs of Pug's cadaver, Silas Holmes sat probing. His face was pleated in frowns. His big square hands were solidly busy. He did not look up. Two minutes before he had consulted his anatomy and if he looked up now he would forget the paragraph it took three minutes to read and, he reflected bitterly, probably would require the next three weeks to digest. He grunted carefully.

Clay laughed. "Bet you spend Easter there!"

"Where?" Elbert Riggs asked, glancing up.

"In the perineum!"

Most of the boys joined in the laughter.

"What are you going to do with yours, Abernathy?" Pug inquired sarcastically.

"Eat oysters."

"Gee! That reminds me," said Elijah Howe, and reaching in his hip pocket he brought out a paper wrapped turkey sandwich.

Prentiss narrowed his eyelids and asked casually, "Where were you raised, Mister?"

"Why?" Elijah mumbled between bites.

"You must have a stomach like a billy goat."

"Why?" Elijah was becoming defiant. "Think I'm afraid of Jezzie?" Jezzie was the cadaver.

Pug drawled, "How should I know what you are afraid of?"

Elijah Howe colored quickly.

Clay Abernathy said, " 'Lijah was raised in a doctor's family, too. Dead people are nothing new to him."

"Did either you ever see a man die?" Pug persisted.

"Naw!" the answer was mutual and irritable.

"Too bad you haven't; there is a proper place for everything—afterwards."

Elijah and Clay felt rebuffed and yet Pug had said nothing they could hang their animosity on. So they turned their backs and began an exceedingly intimate conversation about nothing.

"How do you like it?"

"What?"

"This grind."

"I don't."

"Why, Howe?"

" 'Cause it's so uninteresting. Who gives a damn where the biceps comes in. I ask you, who gives a damn?"

"Damned if I know!" Clay answered quickly. They had each put one foot on the windowsill as though stamping down the fact that nobody with sense did. They felt very superior and restless. If something better would come along for half a dollar they'd give up this medicine business and—but without experience how was a man to know what was better? How was he?

"I'm thinking about gettin' drunk Sat'd'y night," Elijah announced casually.

"So'm I." Clay's reply was pitched in the same tone.

"Well, how about doin' it together?"

"Right," Clay said.

A voice behind interrupted them. Isidore Aaron had looked up from his brain dissection and remarked, "The patient might."

"Might what?" Elijah asked belligerently.

"Might care. Where the biceps came in, I mean."

Elijah swung around and faced Isidore. He was fed up with expanding his brain to absorb human bone structure; with cutting up stiffs by tidbits; well, with everything. So he decided that the irritation came from having to work on a cadaver alongside of this kike. He stepped forward, then scornfully eyed Isidore's insignificant frame and smiled condescendingly.

"Aw, dry up, Aaron!"

Elijah's full lips tried to show contempt; he swung back toward the window and Clay Abernathy. The stentorian tones in which he had delivered his ultimatum and declared his social superiority left Isidore parched and chagrined. The sentence had penetrated to the furthest corner of the room. Pug Prentiss, who had drifted there, looked up just in time to catch Isidore's quick concentration upon the cadaver.

Prior to his entry into medical school, Prentiss had always lived in a world where a man ruled by his fists; here he was catching glimpses of another type of power which, innately, he admired extravagantly; and Isidore Aaron, in his estimation, was potentially such a ruler. Elijah Howe still measured by fists.

"See you later," Pug said to the fellows with whom he was talking and moved off up the room toward Clay and Elijah. When he was within arm's reach, he spun them around like tops.

Clay, who was more or less used to Pug's physical superiority, squirmed and growled, "Pug, have a heart!"

"What the hell?" Elijah blustered, then his voice cracked as Pug smiled carefully down at him; he cleared his throat and continued, "Who do you think I am?"

"I know"—Pug lowered his own voice so that it was like an iron bar connecting their minds—"the famous doctor's son. The precious puppy—the Crown Prince, himself." His voice rose word by word; interest in the other sections of the room was centering toward them. Pug lowered his voice again. "Going to apologize?"

"To—whom?" Elijah spit the words.

"To Aaron," Pug said levelly. Then, he smiled again.

"What for?" Elijah asked bluntly.

"Snobbery." The word was audible only to Elijah, and he colored quickly.

Clay Abernathy, talking loudly, was vainly endeavoring to center the attention elsewhere. He did not succeed. Again Pug spoke to Elijah quietly.

"Being the son of a famous man is going to be just as much of a disadvantage to your success as being a Jew is to his. You're quits there. Mentally he can lead you around by the nose and always will. You don't have to apologize in words, you know. Come on!"

They swung around and the groups down the room knotted again in disappointed conversation. Isidore, really oblivious, hung over his cadaver's head and peered. After Elijah's estimate, two courses were open to him. Fight and get thrown out. Or go back to work and forget it. He had chosen the latter.

"Howe," Pug said casually as he and Elijah joined Isidore, "did you ever see Rigman operate?"

"Sure," Elijah replied flatly.

Isidore's scalpel quivered out of the opening and his eyes glittered. "You've seen——"

"Yeah. Take you sometime if you like. Next time my dad observes we'll go, too."

Pug sauntered away and Elijah's loud voice followed him.

"But you'd better not sneeze. He's touchy as a cat. Absolute silence. Stops in the middle of an operation to give a nurse plain hell for handing him the wrong thing."

Isidore's nostrils began to expand as he replied, "It's new, you see. And terribly dangerous, brain surgery is. Before Cushing nobody ever did—much."

"Doing it don't mean they know a hell of a lot about it, now." Elijah cocked his head knowingly. "Dad says it carries a fierce mortality."

Isidore narrowed his eyes and he picked up his scalpel, began gently severing and said, "I'm listening."

Elijah jogged his elbows against the edge of the table on which Jezzie lay.

"If I had a brain tumor, I'd keep it. Even the ones which get up are never right again. Dreadful depressions. Melancholia." He reeled it off with parrot-like precision, but Isidore absorbed it as sand does water. Elijah was flattered.

Clay Abernathy glanced from a window and called: "Snell's crossing the street."

The chatting groups separated and went back to their dissecting. Elijah lifted up his scalpel and leaned over the kinky-haired Jezzie.

"Let you know," he said flatly.

"Thank you," Isidore replied solemnly.

The concentration in the room moved to the long gauze wrapped bodies. Elbert Riggs leaned over the muscle he was dissecting and decided that he might as well face it and be done with it. Cadavers left him cold. From a practical point of view they had to be understood and mastered, but outside of that they were not only nasty but utterly uninteresting and took too much time to cut apart.

Across the torso from him, Clay Abernathy's fingers pushed and felt. "Hell," he thought. "Hell, it's all right to talk about that Big Four and hard work. But Osler won't get me anywhere. The younger men now teaching decide my fate—guys like Howe's dad."

Silas sat upon his stool and probed. He was not thinking. He was co-ordinating parts with pictures. His flat feet weighed heavily upon the old worn floor.

Beside him Prentiss leaned over the vitals of Jezzie and thought, "Ashby's right. That Jew is a genius."

Old Snell's weary footsteps penetrated Pug's brain. He stood over him and sputtered through his false teeth, "Getting along, Prentiss?"

"I hope so, sir."

"And you, Abernathy?"

"All right so far."

"How about you, Riggs?"

"Thanks."

The old man walked along to the other tables and watched. Then he came quickly up the aisle and leaned over the head of Jezzie. His fading eyes checked Isidore's progress, and his own head nodded involuntarily.

"Nice."

One word, "Nice," but it made more good surgeons than any other method for a generation. Then he peered again and said in the same casual tone, "Very nice—ve—ry nice!"

Prentiss smiled; he leaned forward as though confiding to Jezzie, "Snell thinks so, too."

Chapter Six

SON OF A FAMOUS MAN

At eleven-thirty the following Saturday night in his private office, Elijah Howe, M.D., sat in the worn leather chair which during daylight hours was always occupied by some patient. The oriental rugs upon the polished floor, the rows of medical treatises lining the walls, were in shadow and wreathed in smoke. Only the green-shaded desk light was burning, and Dr. Howe had eased it to the edge of his desk so that it centered upon the glazed photograph proof which he balanced in his finely tapering fingers. It was an advanced proof of a photograph of himself to be used in the Journal of the American Medical Association; under it were a short biography and a statement that he had been made vice-president of the American Medical Association.

Dr. Howe's eyes for the tenth time scanned the biography and found the words, "Ophthalmologist-in-Chief of The Johns Hopkins Hospital, and one of the most renowned medical men in the United States."

"That's not so," he muttered to himself. "They always have a Hopkins man in office and everybody else has served." Still, by means of a good cigar his brain inhaled and buried the words in that part of his interior where an honest surgeon keeps his private pride. His broad lips worked the Corona Corona slowly into the corner of his mouth, then remarked, "This picture is better-looking than you are! But you've done good work, 'Lije, and now you're getting credit for it. Also, the President of the United States is your patient and your wife has a new fur coat. But, for God's sake, be careful. Don't inflate! Vanity and dexterity never co-habit!"

Then he tossed the photograph upon the desk, put his shapely head, which was graying at the temples, back against the dent molded by the heads of countless patients and blew smoke rings toward the ceiling. They were contented rings and through them he imagined he could glimpse his father's twinkling eyes, see the chiseled curl of the old man's lips and feel him say, "Before there was any proof whatever, *I* knew it, and *you knew* I knew it. You didn't go to pieces then. Why swell up, now? It's too late to be conceited, boy!"

Dr. Howe clapped his hands upon his knees and bowed. He had decided to get out that bottle of old sherry, which, because of Maria's prohibition leanings, was hidden behind his *Archives of Surgery* and drink to his dead father's faith, when there was a sharp knock upon the door leading into that section of the house occupied by his family. The door opened and his wife's little body moved firmly across the sill.

Her pompadour, stub nose and dark eyes were all controlled and yet alertly incensed.

"Doctor Howe"—and her voice was so ominously low that her husband cut his eye hastily toward the *Archives of Surgery* to see if the bottle had jumped from its hiding place—"please step into the front hall with me."

"What's the matter, Maria?" His measuring eyes studied her face.

She pursed her lips and said stonily, "I cannot tell you, Elijah."

Dr. Howe rose immediately, screwed his cigar across to the other corner of his mouth, then remembered that Maria didn't allow smoking, either, in her part of the house; he reluctantly poised the delicious weed on the marble mantel edge and followed his wife.

"I don't see anything," he announced gruffly when they reached the hallway.

She rested her hand upon the umbrella stand and said coldly, "In the vestibule."

Dr. Howe sighed irritably but eased open the front door. As it swung inward, he heard a voice say thickly and huskily, "Heyo!"

"Hello, son," he replied casually and opened the door wide.

"Elijah," his wife said sternly, "he's drunk!"

"You nevva saw a drunk man in yo' protected life. H'd'yo'kno'?" her son announced.

The sarcasm made Dr. Howe's lips twitch, but his voice remained casual and friendly. "Come on in, son."

"Naw." The boy's hat began rolling around upon his head and his collar button popped. "Naw, I guess I—better not. It's her house, Doc!"

"Elijah!" Mrs. Howe's voice was cutting.

The doctor turned his back squarely upon her and said to the boy, "But you are my son."

When his arm was securely around 'Lije's shoulders, Dr. Howe blazed his eyes into those of his wife and ordered, "I'll see you later in the upstairs parlor, Maria."

"This is disgraceful!" she announced.

"Very!" Her husband replied caustically and closed the door.

He waited until she had mounted the stairway, then hung the overcoat and hat of his first-born upon the hatrack and supported the inert figure into his office. After his son was settled in the black leather patient's chair, Dr. Howe walked over to the mantelpiece and picked up the cigar again. Then he loosened 'Lije's clothes and said calmly, "Where did you go?"

"I dunno."

"Why did you go?"

The boy sat up and hiccuped his words.

"Wanna kno'? Well, I tell you—" his voice was conciliatory—"I tell you—" He propped his hands upon his knees and continued, "I'm tired. I'm so-damned tired. Tha's why I went. I wanted to get drunk and forget it—all ——"

One hand swept out to encircle "all," and then two minutes were spent getting it back upon his knee and rebalancing his head. His father leaned against the mantelpiece and watched him with mingled chagrin and amusement.

"All what?" he prompted presently.

"All this grind. Medicine. Dead niggers. Stinking guts. Glass eyes. Jews. Studying six nights a week. Bein' yo' son ——"

His mother now stood in the open door and said breathlessly, "Oh!"

His father turned around and ordered again, "Go back upstairs."

"No!" she defied.

"All right. Then close your mouth and listen. Perhaps"—the word came bitingly—"you'll understand." He turned back to his son and said in the same pleasantly inquiring voice, "Why did you want to forget—bein' my son, 'Lije?"

The boy laughed scornfully, worked his nose around his face, and
the words began to cascade from him.

"Son of a famous man." He spit the phrase. "Think it's any fun
bein' a son-o-famous-man, d'you? It ain't. I c'n tell you it ain't.
Nobody treats you right. Nobody lets you be nat'rul. Jes' cause your
pa is the best eye stitcher in Baltimore, Snell rides the hell outa you
if you can't dissect a brain first go. I ash you—is it right? I ash you?
Is it fair? I ash you, Docta Howe, is it?"

His mother gathered all of the indignation in the room into her
lungs. Her fury left his father limp and amused. Made him calm
enough to sense the high humor of his own situation.

"Go on, son," he said casually.

"It's jes' like livin' unda a shadow day and night. Unda a shad—o—
shad—unda a sha—I ash you, Docta Howe, is is—is it ——"

"What?"

"I dunno. I dun—no!"

'Lije's head fell forward; he crumpled onto the floor. He was
asleep. His father took the fine cigar from his lips, foregoing the
last few puffs, settled it on the edge of the mantel to die; then picked
up his son, placed him upon a couch and said over his shoulder to
his stunned wife, who stood rooted in the doorway, "Get me a
couple more blankets."

After she was gone Dr. Howe went quickly over to his desk, thrust
the A.M.A. photograph of himself into a drawer, took out a sheet of
clean paper and scrawled, "No, it isn't fair—but you are man enough
to take it." Then he leaned over the boy again, ran one button of his
son's vest through the sheet of paper and pulled up the steamer rug
just as his wife entered with the blankets and a hot-water bottle.

After 'Lije's shoes were on the floor beside the couch and the hot-
water bottle at his feet, Dr. Howe said sternly as his wife leaned
over the boy and started to pat him, "Come away from there, Maria!
I want to talk to you."

Then he snapped off the desk light, followed her through the door
into the hall and shut the door behind him. Upstairs in her precise
parlor with its Victorian furnishings and unerring landscapes, he
took from his pocket a second Corona Corona, cut the end and struck
a match.

Mrs. Howe drew in her breath, but she did not protest.

The doctor sat perfectly silent and smoked. His faculties were automatically returning. For the first time in fifteen years he was realizing that if he sat silent long enough, Maria would behave like any other woman.

"Elijah," she said presently, "I'll never be able to express how hurt I am about—about what he's done."

"Why?" The word was grunted out between puffs; the tone in which she had called him Elijah was precisely that she used when referring to him as Doctor Howe, but her husband decided to ignore it.

His "Why?" did not seem concerned enough. Mrs. Howe drew herself up and answered, "I cannot forgive him. I cannot! He knows how *I* detest liquor. And when I think of how *you've* worked to send him to the University, to prepare him for medical school—he—he should be grateful, not—not! I cannot forgive him! Ever!"

"I didn't think you could." Her husband made a flat statement. Then he sighed and muttered, "So, it's up to me to make you."

"I wish you could," she replied. "Tonight makes all of the years of struggle I've had over him seem so wasted!"

Dr. Howe had been fortifying himself with deep puffs. "Now listen, Maria," he said, and held the cigar in his forefinger eyeing it as he spoke. "Sometime—and I guess it might as well be now—you have got to grasp the fact that out of your body there came a man, and as such you cannot expect his reactions to coincide with yours. Now being a man is only part of the trouble. Being a medical student is only part of the trouble. Being the son of a—successful—man is the rest of it. That drunk is the best thing 'Lije ever did for himself. Perhaps it saved him a nervous breakdown. And taught me a lot. 'Bout him and you, too. Taught me how utterly innocent I've let you remain."

"Why, Doctor Howe!"

"No use being modest about it. I'm ashamed of it. Makes me wish I'd gotten drunk every six months myself."

"Now, let me tell you something—" His wife pursed her lips and sat indignantly upon the edge of her chair.

"After while," her husband interrupted. "First I've got to show you some facts. Studying medicine is probably the worst nervous strain you can put any man through. It's like having a wife who is pregnant all the time and never delivered; only when the time for the delivery comes, as in a nightmare, it turns out to be you and not your wife, who has to be delivered. Now you think that over for a while and after you've thought it over—say four days—I'll sit down and give you *two solid hours*, no matter *how* busy I am, in which to 'tell me something.' One more thing: by tomorrow morning you must have entirely erased from your mind and your memory what happened so far as your behavior toward 'Lije is concerned. Thank God the girls were in bed. As a matter of fact, though, it'll take years of careful handling ever to make up to him for what you did. The memory of that and his own chagrin when he wakes up will be punishment enough to last the rest of his life, Maria Howe."

He had risen and was towering over her silent little body.

"I'm glad he got drunk. Damned glad! Shows spirit. The lad's a horrible inferiority complex and I'd been too blind to see it before. Always thought he'd inherited your temper!"

"Elijah Howe!"

"Now, I see it's just your ambition and my sense of humor. Which is worse. A hell of a combination!"

"You may think this is a joke," his wife defied, standing up, "but I——"

Dr. Howe put his second cigar upon the second marble mantelpiece and turned wearily around.

"Maria," he said slowly, "in two weeks you'll be the wife of a much discussed man. Don't be premature, my dear!"

The weary note in his voice touched her heart.

"Instead I'll be proud," she replied graciously as she walked toward him and lifted her lips to his.

At about the same time that Dr. Howe placed the hot-water bottle between 'Lije's feet, Pug Prentiss untied the laces of Clay Abernathy's brogues and said to Silas over his shoulder, "Where did you find him?"

Clay lay upon his own bed in the fourth floor of Miss Susie's house and snored loudly. Silas's even voice weighted down the snores as he answered, "On the corner. Sitting on the curb. Crying."

"Oh, for Gawd's sake!"

Pug slung his head irritably and Silas continued, "No use being profane about it. Nobody saw. I took him around into the alley and brought him up the backstairs. Miss Susie's gone to bed and Hizer's out."

"Who was he with?" Pug asked flatly.

"I dunno, Prentiss. The first I saw of him was on the curb."

"I see. How did you manage to get him in by yourself?"

"It wasn't hard. I'd been for a walk. This city kinda cramps me sometimes. I'd been for a long walk, and I felt fine. So I slung him over my shoulder."

Pug dropped one shoe and swung around.

"Say, Holmes, you mean you carried this ox?"

Silas turned fiery red and apologized, "Why not? He's nothing but a big sack of meal. It was easy."

"You get drunk much, Holmes?"

"No. Why?"

"Don't. If you do that sober, you'd kill somebody drunk!"

Approbation, upon Silas, had precisely the same effect as condemnation. He switched the subject immediately.

"What'll we do with his clothes, Prentiss?"

"Why don't you call me Pug, boy?"

" 'Cause you don't look that way to me. Sometimes I think you're— aw, what'll we do with his clothes?"

"Drop 'em by a dry cleaner's on our way to Otto's. Come on."

"You go, I'll stay."

"Listen, Holmes, that kind of drunk lasts at least twelve hours. The kid's so loaded he couldn't move if he wanted to. Cummon!"

Fifteen minutes later, Ben Mead said to Elbert Riggs, "Slide over, here comes the menagerie."

"Where?" Elbert cut his eyes toward the door.

"The elephant and the chimpanzee, see 'em?"

Silas and Pug reached the bar.

"Where you been?"

"Pall-bearing, Ben."

"Who, Pug?"

"Your interlocutor."

"Abernathy?"

"None other."

"Well, I'll be damned. Where'd he been?"

"Search us. Sandow," he motioned toward Silas, "found him lost on the street and carried him home."

"What are you doing, Holmes, taking Lydia Pinkham 'fore breakfast?" Ben's voice carried admiration and pleasant banter. Silas blushed miserably and Ben continued, "So Clay soaked down his anatomy. Then I lose a bet."

"With whom?"

"With Ashby, Riggs. He said you'd be the first drunk."

"Hunh, he's got his nerve!"

"Way you sneer, sounds like he's got yours."

Elbert squared himself.

"Aw, can it!" Pug ordered with infinite casualness. "What Alex Ashby said was that you were silent enough to like your liquor. That's all. I heard him say it. And he was right. You are."

The restaurant was almost deserted. Only a few men down the bar and the fellows from Miss Susie's were present. They were being tended by an assistant. The arrival of Otto created a commotion and silenced conversation. Otto, resplendent in a cutaway coat, black Stetson hat, pin striped trousers and highly polished black shoes, entered the front door. An air of excitement exuded from him.

"Say," Ben called, "Kaiser come to town, Otto?"

Otto unbuttoned his coat carefully and his gold watch chain festooned his protruding abdomen as he announced, "De Boston Orkestra. Brahms Secund. Sooplime und peautiful!" His right hand took its butterfly sweep. "Dat secund moofment vas grand. Yo' frien' Ashby und Docturr McMillan, dey vas der."

"Who was with Ashby, Otto?"

Otto removed his hat and cocked his head slowly; then massaged his tuft of front hair with gentle precision and replied, "A man I nefer zee pefore." He raised his hand to his own nose by way of explanation and continued, "I gonsider him a Jew—but a Jew mit a fine head!"

"Aaron," Pug confirmed the description.

Otto narrowed his eyes and poked his head forward. "Hiss name?"

"Aaron. Isidore Aaron. He's in our class," Pug replied.

"Aaron. A-aron." Otto's lips formed the word twice. Then he threw back his head and became jovial. "Vhere hafe you peen, poys?"

"Aw, jes' aroun'," Ben Mead responded carelessly.

"Aroundt vhere?"

"Aroun' misery," Ben smiled.

Otto returned the smile and nodded; as he smiled he looked at Silas out of the corner of his eye, then tripped over beside him, scrutinizing every feature. His hand went to his lips and picked off the word, "Holmes! Dat right?"

Silas nodded slowly.

"Pefore," Otto remarked, "I toldt you I—knew. How ish yo' fadder?"

"Dead," Silas said, but his eyes never wavered from Otto's.

The little bartender turned, slipped under the end of the bar, made crooning noises in his throat and reached in the bottom of the cellaret for five hollow-stemmed glasses which he put silently side by side. The bottle whose sparkling contents he poured into them was long and narrow. His concentration was so immense that an interruption, even a movement, would have been an insult.

Gravely in front of each boy he placed a glass. Then lifting his own he said, "To de memory of Si-las Holmes und de future of hiss son: Prosit!"

When the glasses were drained, Prentiss remarked appreciatively, "That's a fine vintage."

Otto gave him a rare and elderly smile; then turning to the others he said, "So you hafe peen studyin'. De relentless tide of learnin' ish closin' in. Yess. Yess, I hafe zeen it pefore—many dimes. I oondershtand. Medicine ish takin' de blace of bier. But peware too mooch medicine! De bes' learnin' ish done py res'ed minds."

Chapter Seven

EASTER AT MISS SUSIE SLAGLE'S

At eleven o'clock on March twenty-third, 1913, Miss Susie Slagle was seated in her pew at Old St. Paul's Church. She wore her black silk, which now was very brown. For the last two months, because he looked thin, she had made Alex Ashby drink milk and cream, and the extra cream bill had consumed her new dress savings. Her black sailor hat was also "last year's," furbished up with a new grosgrain ribbon.

That corsage of violets and sweetheart roses pinned over the mended place just above her high busted corset had become as much a part of the Easter service as the presence of Miss Susie; and its donors were as well known. The same florist prepared it and always enclosed the same card, "With love from your boys."

The flowers obliterated her clothes, matched her face and created unspeakable envy among her contemporaries; they caused as complete a readjustment of her posture as if they were a man's hand against her waist.

She began carefully removing her new white kid gloves. Yesterday, at lunch, Alex had turned the conversation to the corresponding sizes of feet and hands, in anatomy, and she had told her measurements. Last night the gloves had come in a gift package—with no card; they were the nicest she had ever owned, the finest which could be bought and as white as the altar lilies.

The odor of flowers, knowledge of love, and assurance of faith filled her senses as invisibly as the organ music filled the waiting church, when it swung, after the prelude, into the familiar lilting tune of "Welcome Happy Morning, Age to Age Shall Say."

At that same moment across the city, Hizer, with a sweeping gesture, swung inward the front door of Miss Susie's house and said, " 'Mornin', gentmen. Happy Eastas t'you all!"

"How are you, Hizer?" Dean Theodore Wingate asked as he gave

110

Hizer his hat, and he and Dr. Elijah Howe stepped onto the worn carpet in the parlor. Dr. Howe said with his usual gruffness, " 'Do, Hizer."

As he closed the door, Hizer dispensed with his gravity. He turned toward the two prominent men. "Well, suh!" he replied, "it certain'y do give me pride to look at you all! I nevva 'spected whin you was our boys dat you'd be where you is today."

"Nothing to be 'sprised about. Nor proud of, either," Dr. Howe replied. "Top of the ladder is a dangerous place."

The old negro shook his head deprecatingly, "Nuthin' fur you to worry 'bout, Docta 'Lije. You bin at de top long 'nough to be at home dere: an' 'nyhows, afta seein' you go up dat stairway whin you was drunk, I ain't ever bin afraid ob yo' makin' out on high places. No suh! Nevva!"

Dr. Wingate laughed and then became aware of Alex Ashby at the rear door of the parlor. Alex said cordially, "Morning, Dean. Morning, Doctor Howe. Thank you for coming. Won't you sit down, gentlemen?" Then he continued, "Those juleps are ready, Hizer. You'd better get them."

"Who made 'em?" Hizer asked relentlessly, backing hallward.

"Prentiss," Ashby answered.

"Dey'll do!" Hizer said and passed on toward the dining room.

Wingate took the love seat as Dr. Howe eased into one of the morris chairs and said flatly, "Never can tell what's in a man's head. Had no idea you were house champion, Ashby!"

Alex laughed. "Hizer still knows all your originals; I listened one night when everybody else was out!"

"That's fair enough!" Wingate chuckled turning to Howe.

Alex extended a box of Corona cigars and Dr. Howe took one, groaned appreciatively, and then groaned again as Hizer entered with the two thickly frosted juleps. "I told dese boys," Hizer said, "t'give you juleps, even if it t'weren't summertime, 'cause dey's a heavy drink, ez well ez a *slo'* one."

"I'm dry as a chip, Hizer," Dr. Howe answered and took the glass from the tray.

Hizer sputtered, "But you gittin' too old t'drink fas'!"

Ashby remarked, "I'll go and get them started, gentlemen. Hizer knows where the bottle is, but you'd better make him bring it in here where you can keep an eye on both of them."

"Bof ob whut, Mista Alex?" Hizer said reproachfully. Then he brought his cane-bottom chair from the rear hall and placed the contents of his pockets upon the marble-topped table; among the things he put there were the full quart of rye whisky, his old biscuit watch, rabbit foot, and a small tin cup. He brought, also, a bowl of cracked ice.

As Ashby disappeared up the stairway, Doctors Howe and Wingate settled into solid comfort and Howe asked Hizer, "Is that the same cup?"

"Yassuh," Hizer grinned and uncorked the whisky bottle.

"And still straight?" Dean Wingate asked.

"Yassuh. An' still three fingers."

"How can you tell through that tin, you ole black bastard?"

"I can't," Hizer grinned, "I jes' jedges. An' sumtimes I misjedges: but whin I does, nobody dies frum it."

Both doctors smiled; then Wingate remarked, "I remember a pie you 'misjedged' once. Had soap in it 'stead of soda."

"Dat," Hizer responded a trifle reprovingly, "was 'fore Docta 'Lije seen I needed spectickles."

"Where are they?" Howe growled between sips of his julep.

"I got 'em!" Hizer said quickly.

"Ever wear 'em?" Howe asked sarcastically.

"Only whin I'se cookin'," Hizer announced as he poured his three fingers into the cup.

Dr. Howe pretended not to notice his actions, and Dean Wingate watched the two of them with silent amusement. Since Howe first came to Miss Susie's, a pugnacious, belligerent boy, the affection between Hizer and himself had always assumed the outward appearance of repeated insults. As Howe's fame increased the only person whose manner toward him never altered was this old black negro cook, and because it never altered Dr. Howe bore Hizer an attachment which was always affecting to see.

Hizer put the bottle on the table and continued defensively as Howe sank into a hurt silence, "Whin I'se sweepin', or totin' drunk doctas upstairs, or snatchin' de telephone off de hook, I ain't got no

way ob protectin' dem, an' dem glasses is done fur me whut a microscope does fur you, Dean."

Wingate nodded understandingly and Dr. Howe relaxed his silence,
"Wear 'em! You know I'll get you some more if they are broken."

"I got 'em fixed oncest myself," Hizer remarked.

"Where?" the ophthalmologist asked skeptically.

"At a eye-glass man's on Pennsylvania Avvenu."

"You ole fool! How in the hell do you know you got the same
lens?"

Hizer gulped the remainder of his drink and explained, "Oh, no, it
t'weren't patched. He gave me a new one."

"Listen," Dr. Howe said succinctly, "you be in my office tomorrow
morning at nine o'clock and bring your glasses with you."

"Docta 'Lije," Hizer whined, "you kno' tomorrow is Easta Monday
an' I *got* to be on de Avvenu 'longside ob ebery other nigger in
Balt'moor City."

"My office," Howe said relentlessly, as he extended his glass for
replenishment, "at nine."

Hizer eyed the glass and said, "I told you dey was a *slo'* drink!"

"Those boys are too young to fix a julep," Howe answered.

Hizer grinned and took the glass, then continued reverting to the
former topic, " 'Nyhows, even if it weren't Easta Monday, you kno',
Docta 'Lije, ez well ez I does dat Miss Susie don't nevva 'low me
outta de house on Monday. Since you got so highfalutin' is you
furgot how I spends Mondays? Is you?"

Dean Wingate ignored his julep, lit a cigar and enjoyed the interchange.

Dr. Howe repeated, "Monday morning: tomorrow: nine o'clock."

"I ain't cumin'," Hizer announced defiantly and turning his back
upon the renowned ophthalmologist said deferentially to the Dean,
"Is you ready, suh?"

Wingate held his glass aloft, displayed its contents, and shook his
head.

Dr. Howe picked up his cigar, took several puffs and said, "If it
has a thumbnail frost, we'll make it Tuesday, Hizer."

"I ain't cumin' Tuesday, nor Monday, nor no other time. I c'n see," the old man announced stoutly, as though endeavoring to convince himself; or by his own stern defiance to defend himself.

"Then I'll send the police for you: I know what is wrong with your eyes—damn you! And you are not going 'round with those blasted window glasses on while I'm practicing in this town, not if I have to get the sheriff, himself, to haul you in!"

The stream of whisky began to flow fitfully. Hizer's words turned pleading. "Docta 'Lije, you ain't gonna do dat. I ain't nevva had no words wid no sheriff an' I ain't gonna start now."

"He's a patient of mine. Would raise the roof off anything if I told him to."

"An' ez fur de po-leece," Hizer continued, ignoring Howe's statement, "many's de time I'se kept 'em frum shovin' you in de hoosegow whin you was havin' yo' fling in de old days. Dat's howcum my eyes is bad, now—cum t'think 'bout it—dey ain't nevva bin de same since dat time you hauled off an' hit me whin you was ——"

The old negro and the doctor had so long been friends that the current of pain which flowed from Dr. Howe's stocky body at the mention of his pugilistic exploits was so intense that, Hizer, out of mercy, ceased to allude to them. He said gently, holding the glass he had been fixing toward the man he had been heckling, "In yo' old age, you think you c'n handle dat, Docta 'Lije?"

Dr. Howe grinned, but did not speak and Hizer, sensing that he had hurt him deeply, chattered as a mother croons to a child, "Dere was a time—I 'member it jes' ez well—dere was a time whin you'd a laughed me downstairs fur askin' you if you could handle a drink, I don't care whut kind nor how much. Gee, you was a reckless boy! But I ain't ever furgot how good you was, too. You was de fust one whut ever took a notice ob my eyes. You kno' dat? Even whin you was livin' heah you was tryin' to git me to go to de hosbittle an' have 'em x-zamined, an' you nevva gave me no peace, neither, till I wint. An' dat time it wasn't nuthin' wrong wid 'em. Now, howcum you so sho' dat dere is sumthin' wrong wid 'em dis time? Huh?"

As he moved the mint in his strengthened julep, Dr. Howe replied, "I'm not sure, Hizer. But I just like you too much to take a chance. It won't cost you anything, not even if you have to have new glasses. And it won't hurt you. Now, you can tell me when you *can* come?"

Dean Wingate blinked and then riveted his gaze upon his glass as he heard Howe, whose patients frequently waited three weeks or a month for an appointment, ask this ancient negro cook that question.

"I'se off Thursday aftanoon frum two to four, but I got t'pay my *in-surance* an' ——"

"I'll see you at two-thirty, and I won't keep you waiting," Dr. Howe answered.

Hizer slung three fingers more into his tin cup, gulped it and then said, "C'n I see—aftawards? Does you put drops in me?"

"You've been in medicine long enough to know people past forty-five don't need drops, usually," Dr. Howe remarked as he sipped the julep and gave a satisfied moan.

"Howcum you think I'm dat old?" Hizer protested in a high falsetto.

" 'Cause you claimed to be that old when I was a post-graduate student—and that's been twenty-odd years ago. If you aren't pushing seventy, I'm ——"

Hizer gave a wild negroid laugh and then asked, referring to his eyes, "Will dey las' ez long ez I does, Docta 'Lije?"

"Sure!" Howe answered heartily. "If I put the proper glasses on you, they will. And if you've got sense enough to wear 'em after I put 'em on."

Hizer gave a sudden grateful nod and then raising his grizzled head said proudly, "One thing dat ain't goin' t'fail me is my years. I c'n heah jes' ez good now ez I could whin I was a chile. An' de reason fur dat is ——"

Wingate shook his glass and Hizer interrupted himself to replenish it. Dr. Howe prompted, "What's the reason?"

"Ain't none ob our boys," Hizer announced, "ever had to sink to bein' skin doctas, nor year doctas, nor th'oat men, an' so ain't nobody ever meddled wid dem organs in dis heah body, so dey's good ez dey was de day I was bawn."

Dean Wingate patted his foot on the floor and laughed. Then he shook his head with slow amusement and waited.

"Before my generation came along," Howe said, "eye, ear, nose and

throat all went together. Don't see why you trust me, Hizer! I'm
pretty near down to skin!"

"Dey's two things in dis world I ain't nevva goin' to 'low my
years to lissen to: one is to 'nybody lowratin' you, an' de other is to
you lowratin' yo'self!" the old negro said gravely. "I kno's yo' faults,
better'n you do, an' I still has ——"

"Ready?" an excited tenor voice called from the third floor down
to the second.

"Ready!" Alex Ashby's reply sailed upward and he asked, "How
about the men on four?"

A voice from the fourth floor which Hizer recognized as that of
Abernathy yelled, "Give us a chance! Four's full of thilth."

Hizer stepped into the hallway and raising what was a strong and
surprisingly hale voice to be housed in such a frame, called, "De
jedges is lissenin', Mista Alex!"

The fourth floor group were seated in the hallway: Clay Abernathy,
beginning to sweat, tilted his cane-bottom chair precariously to and
fro. Pug, watching, felt that its motion was a pretty good barometer
of the condition of Clay's stomach. Beyond Clay, his flat feet placidly
resting on the railing, his plain face altering under the influence of
liquor as an ordinary building alters with sunset reflections, sat
Silas Holmes in another cane-bottom chair. Nearby Elbert Riggs, his
features more chiseled than ever, began to hum a recognizable tune
as though assuring himself that his reactions were all right; occasionally Riggs would recross his feet and solemnly wiggle his toes
within his shoes as if inquiring if they were not of the same opinion
as himself.

Pug, who never achieved oblivion through liquor but suffered
from increased perception, narrowed his glittering eyes to slits, set
his mouth into a vacant blot and watched. He had seen enough drunk
men to enjoy the deadly seriousness with which these medical students faked an intoxication. His amusement grew as he studied them.
He and Ashby had decided as an experiment to cut the liquor three
ways and serve it with plenty of ginger ale and ice. One factor had
been their determination to have no maudlin drunks at Miss Susie's
Easter dinner; another had been money; still another had been

Prentiss's theory that a man believing himself drunk would react as though he were drunk; and Ashby skepticism.

Of course for the judges and Hizer, they had known that only the best rye whisky would suffice. "They," Ashby had pointed out, "are connoisseurs, particularly Hizer."

But for the fourth floor boys Prentiss had won Ashby's approval of an experiment. Every man before him had thrown three highballs under his belt since Miss Susie departed for church; yet none of those highballs had contained more than a finger of whisky, and all of them together hadn't been even one stiff drink. Prentiss realized that if the singing began and he had the will power to refrain from opening a window, within twenty minutes Abernathy would be hiccuping and within thirty trickling with vulgarities.

Alex, in solitary glory, settled his body in the comfortable chair he had slid from his room into the second floor hallway. He placed his highball on the floor and in response to Hizer's statement about the judges called downward, "Thank you, gentlemen." Then he craned his neck and inquired, "Four, are you ready?"

Minnie Otts and Ben Mead, for whom Pug was also bartender, lolled in their chairs in the third floor hallway and turned appraising, critical ears upward. To Ben, this was one of the pleasantest events of the year; he had been so properly reared by a widowed mother that his capacity for being shocked was not dulled during adolescence and his ability to remember what had shocked him seemed to increase with age.

Minnie Otts enjoyed it as respectably married men do a burlesque show; it was so foreign to his upbringing and native to his inclinations that a pleasant twinge of shame invaded his veins.

"Sure, we're ready!" Pug answered Ashby's question. The men upon four eyed each other, struck up a chorus, sung like a Gregorian chant, which was based on anatomical terms in relation to human passions. They had practiced the passages so that Clay Abernathy's tenor stressed with a tremolo quality different words; and then Pug's bass would pick up those words and put them down so that they rolled into the ears of the men on three, of Ashby on two and reverberated to the judges.

"Good voice," Dean Wingate remarked, and the other judges understood that he was referring to Prentiss.

"Cums outta a good man," Hizer answered and poured himself another three fingers. He sat in his cane-bottom chair and tilted his head in a respectful, "After you, Doctor," attitude.

The Dean, in response to Hizer's pantomime inquiry, slipped his glass forward. Dr. Howe did, also, for it was an unwritten rule of this event that if Hizer began drinking heavily the judges must never refuse dividends and had to consume the liquor quickly. As Hizer replenished their juleps, the chorus completed its final flourish and it became the duty of the men on three to offer their song.

So Minnie Otts and Ben Mead took a final gulp, braced their feet on the banister and began. Ben had a fair tenor and Minnie was blessed with what Ashby had aptly termed an hermaphrodite baritone; they sang, nevertheless, a neat duet about a doctor whose center of gravity was his pubic arch and the troubles resulting therefrom. He closely resembled an instructor encountered by second and fourth year students, and Wingate's eyes began to dance. When the duet concluded, Howe said, "Good description of Appleton."

"Jes' like him," Hizer answered knowingly as they waited for the house champion to sing.

The intense and spreading stillness was broken as Alex Ashby began to sing a lewd and witty song about the proclivity of medical professors when in doubt at clinic and then, later at autopsy, as to the cause of a patient's death, to "say syphilis." Ashby's gift of rhythmic singing, which only men raised in open country and negroes ever attain, made his words roll with perfect diction up and down the stairway. The last verse pointed out that since Ehrlich, in gratitude for a fellowship grant, had sent Rockefeller a thousand doses of "606," many medical men from this vicinity had gone to the Institute. A bellow of laughter arose from the judges!

The excitement brought a sudden gleam to Hizer's eye. Wingate and Howe tossed off their juleps nonchalantly and pushed their glasses forward again. Hizer fixed them; but before measuring the whisky, he put on his windowpane glasses and looked gravely at the bottle.

As Alex finished his final refrain, from the fourth floor there came an unexpected and indecent hiccup. Pug Prentiss stood up, yanked Clay Abernathy into his room and shut the door; then leaned over the banister and slung a half dollar at Ashby's feet.

As Riggs, Holmes and he settled into a circle of unspoken relief, Silas remarked, "Well, one thing's sure: Abernathy won't be house champion."

"It's between Ashby and Pug, anyhow," Riggs replied.

"You're crazy!" Prentiss said. "It's Mead and Ashby."

Hizer stepped into the downstairs hall and announced, "I'se *de*cided we ain't got time fur eberybody to *com*pete 'cause de Dean an' Docta 'Lije is goin' t'sing 'Little Elize' in a duet."

The mingled shouts and Ben Mead's "Hoorah!" made the two startled men in the parlor understand that they'd have to go through with it.

"You ole bastard!" Dr. Howe rumbled. "I've forgotten the words."

Hizer said, in an aside, "Ain't you drunk up all de likker? I'se got to have sum fun, ain't I?"

Then to the students he called, "Choose yo' floor champions an' we'll heah frum dem while de jedges is gittin' dere wind up."

Silas hollered, "Prentiss!"

Minnie Otts called, "Mead!"

And Alex Ashby said, "Ashby: defending Ashby!"

"Go 'head!" Hizer ordered. Silas and Bert Riggs heaved Pug to his feet. So much of Prentiss's life had been spent in utter loneliness, that now, among a group of really jovial men, a spontaneity and a confidence ran through his veins; he sang, in a voice which was ribbed with amusement, a vastly ludicrous song about the indubitable relation between crabs and cancer, oysters and arterio-sclerosis, and terrapin and impotence. For Clay Abernathy, back in the group again, there remained a lifelong aversion to terrapin.

It wasn't that Prentiss's voice was good or that the song was so funny, but the others sensed that at last this man was gay. During their resounding applause, Hizer announced in a tone which brooked no denial, "Dat Prentiss sho' is a caution, but he can't tech Mista Alex. Jes' wait."

"Like the sound of that fellow very much," Howe growled. "Want to meet him."

"Whin de others is finished, you will," Hizer replied, preparing to doctor his three fingers. The observant medical men shoved their glasses swiftly forward and Dr. Howe realized that he was getting pretty loaded. He wondered what he would say to Maria, and if it would be necessary for 'Lije to stand by him!

Suddenly, he was back into the boy he had been when he had lived at Miss Susie's; before he knew how to make a living, or satisfy a wife, or pretend he wasn't frightened when performing a delicate operation. The sight of that crazy Christmas-tree bird teetering on her mantel lattice made him recall precisely how he felt when he came back the night Maria promised to marry him, and sat in this same chair, too ardent and too restless to go to bed, watching that bird flutter in the air.

Dr. Howe was rocked from his reverie by the effort required to complete the unfinished lines in the song which Mead was singing; Ben had concocted a ditty which mentioned the first line of many of the most rancid medical jokes and never completed the sequence. You could have heard a pin drop in that house; every man listened acutely and tried silently to complete the unfinished lines. Ben concluded with a story of a colored woman's malapropisms when she informed the interne that she was "lookin' fur de fraternity clinic."

The audience howled. Hizer shook his head and said, "I kno's 'em all. I ain't missed a one!"

"No man in America been as exposed—except, perhaps, the cook at the Pithotomy Club," Dr. Howe snorted.

"Ssh." Hizer rolled his eyes, ignored the possibility of a rival at that well-known medical club, turned his good ear toward the stairway and remarked to the other two judges, "Mista Alex is got de voice an' de mem'ry, too. Jes' you lissen."

Ashby's eight-line song gave two of his auditors infinite delight as they watched its effect upon a third. His effortless voice rolled through the house to the tune of "Four More Years of Grover." He sang:

> When the Pithotomy cook killed his wife
> The Club decided to save his life
> So they threw their brows in creases
> And went to court and pled paresis!

Oh, Hizer'd better be careful
Hizer'd better be clean
For the Judge has caught on to paresis
And turned just too-damned mean!

The men on all floors yelled; Dean Wingate patted his foot on the
floor and laughed so hard that he choked. Between great, indecent
belly guffaws, Dr. Howe staggered to his feet and pounded Wingate
on the back.

Cloaked in his dignity, Hizer sputtered. "Whut dat boy talkin'
'bout? I ain't got no wife! I ain't *got* no wife."

Nobody paid him the slightest attention. As the students came
downstairs to receive the decision of the judges they sang the last
verse. Wingate, who had gone back to an almost adolescent giggle,
threw in his baritone with Dr. Howe's bass on the final lines. All of
them were now crammed in Miss Susie's parlor and the Christmas-
tree bird swung to and fro in a perfect frenzy.

Hizer sat in his cane-bottom chair and protested. "I ain't got *no*
wife. Me an' Dean Wingate we's bachelors—fur good!"

"Difference 'tween you and the Dean," Dr. Howe said belligerently,
"is *he* knows enough medicine to realize you can have paresis—without a wife, Hizer!"

Everybody roared again. The old negro stood up. "Docta 'Lije," he
said in a high falsetto, "you orta be 'shamed ob yo'self. I 'member whin
you didn't kno' no more medisun thin a June-bug! Dat Pithotomy
Club takes de trashy-ish niggers in town!"

Again the men laughed; and Dean Wingate, who couldn't bear to
see Hizer upset, remarked in his professional tone, "Gentlemen, may
I suggest that we get on with the business in hand."

The boys understood that the guying was over. Wingate continued,
"As Chairman of the Judges, Hizer, will you please take the vote for
house champion?"

With a negro's fine sense of sound, Hizer responded to the deference in Wingate's voice; he drew himself up to a height which vastly
exceeded his physical measurements and announced:

"Dean Wingate, Docta 'Lije an' you gentmens who hopes to enter
de perfession—" To the latter group he applied a summary and critical gaze, then continued gravely, "Ez de onlies' permnent jedge ob

de Easta champion choosin', I is pleased to welcum you heah. Ob all de men, famus an' unfamus, I is de onlies' one whut is always bin present. An' 'fore we choose dis champion, I wants t'say—in all my mem'ry—dere ain't ever bin two men in Americun Medisun who is writ a song to tech de one dese two other jedges is t'sing afta we gits over de annual matter ob pickin' de champion.

"We ain't nevva kno'ed who writ 'Little Elize.' De onlies' thing I c'n say is: dat we started dis boardin' house in '86. De med'cal school didn't open till '93, but in dem years 'tween '87 an' '93 dere was post-graduwait students 'lowed to study path-ology, or look on at de hos-bittle, which opened in '89, an' sum ob dem boarded wid us. Takin' in *all* de med'cal students I'se ever seen, dere ain't nevva bin a group whut could tech dem boys fur low-down thinkin'."

The song which Ashby had sung was forgotten as Hizer warmed to his subject; Wingate blushed and Howe grumbled. Hizer continued, "One ob dem boys had bin to de Univurs'ty ob Virginny Med'cal School—an' dey *are* ruff-minded!"

Wingate shot Howe a side-glance which was not lost on the boys. Hizer said, " 'Nuther was a Yankee frum Harvard an' I put him t'bed drunk 'nough times to kno' dere ain't nuthin' pure 'bout no Puritan."

A laugh, led by Dr. Howe, engulfed the students; Wingate colored and Hizer continued, "An' I still thanks Gawd dat Miss Susie was vistin' in Norfolk dat Easta, 'cause de night 'fore Easta-day, dem two boys wint to Otto's an' de next day, durin' de champion choosin' dey sang a song which I done ast 'em to re-peat dis mornin'. Gentmen, I gives you Docta 'Lije, ob de Univurs'ty, an' de Dean, ob Harvard! Who fust sung 'Little Elize,' Easta, '88. (De champion choosin' c'n wait.)"

The last remark was to the boys; when the clapping subsided, the two embarrassed judges took their places in front of the fireplace, cleared their throats and began that song which is known to all of the men who ever lived at Miss Susie Slagle's.

They were both pretty high; both back, in their mind's eye, to the days which Hizer had been describing. Wingate's baritone led off with a plain statement of fact:

> "Pregnancy is a germ disease.
> Pregnancy is a germ disease."

Howe cocked his head and the imps in Pug's green eyes danced as he heard the deep bass rumble:

> "It's outrageous
> To say it's contagious!"

Wingate began in Hizer's eyes to appear as boyish as he had that Easter of '88. A twisted smile fled from his lips and he responded with polite seriousness:

> "The case of Little Elize,
> PROVES that pregnancy is a germ disease."

Dropping his voice down into his ankles, Dr. Howe inquired:

> "And if you please,
> Who's Little Elize?"

The students rocked with silent mirth, as Dean Wingate's baritone launched into that well-known explanation:

> "Elize is a virgin—young and fair,
> Possessed of the loveliest—golden hair,
> Who boards in a house—run with care,
> And lives in a room on—the backest stair."

Howe listened with growing interest and then asked, skeptically:

> "The backest stair?
> What happens there?"

Wingate ignored the query with precisely the gesture he had used Easter '88, and a throat chuckle from Hizer was his compliment. The Dean went on:

> "Boarding on Elize's floor,
> In a room with a connecting door,
> Is a pregnant dame,
> Who claims a married name."

Howe lifted his eye-brows:

> "A married name?"

Wingate insisted with acid politeness:

> "Mrs. O'Hara, a primipara."

Spontaneous laughter filled the room; after it died down, the Doctor and the Dean threw their arms over each other's shoulders and sang, with infinite relief:

> "Who claims a married name,
> Mrs. O'Hara, a primipara."

The boys snickered: then Dr. Howe stepped away from Dean Wingate and remarked, in his best consultation manner:

> "I'm still leary,
> Prove your theory."

Dean Wingate folded his hands with a sepulchral gesture and continued:

> "Mrs. O'Hara is friendly with Elize,
> Gives her fudge and India teas,
> And talks about her Davy,
> Who's an ensign in the Navy."

Howe snorted, jammed his thumbs into his vest pockets and bellowed:

> "I still hold it's outrageous
> To say that thing's contagious!"

The Dean's face became expressionless and that to Alex Ashby was the funniest part of the whole performance; then, after the proper interval, Wingate gave Howe a withering look, as if to imply that in the light of the foregoing evidence he was a fool, and sang, slowly:

> "Two months later, in despair,
> As she combs her gold-en hair,
> Elize has a siege
> Of mawnin' sickness."

"Mawning sickness?" Howe was shocked.

"Mawning sickness!" Wingate affirmed, heavy with grief. Howe tossed his head and replied caustically:

> "It's true she's been exposed,
> But has that girl no beaux?"

Wingate shook his head, and then Howe began some highly technical and unprintable verses citing recorded cases in medicine and history of famous pregnancies and emphasizing the basic difference of those cases and that of Little Elize.

Wingate and the students listened attentively and the Dean and Hizer were amazed to find that Howe remembered every line, many of which were new to his younger auditors. He concluded with a very scathing verse about Elize's night life.

The Dean folded his hands piously and sang:

> "Elize retires at eight,
> And behaves most sedate.
> She brushes her hair a hundred strokes,
> Then writes a letter to her folks."

Then they extemporized two new verses which neither the students nor Hizer expected.

Howe grumbled slowly:

> "If Elize's case be true,
> Men are forever through!"

Wingate replied:

> "And now it's proven true,
> Men are forever through,
> With shot-gun marriages,
> And baby carriages."

Howe lost his gloom and skepticism instantly. He grinned broadly and then answered:

> "On the evidence presented,
> I certainly have relented,
> And it would be outrageous,
> To say it's *not* contagious!"

Before the students had time to laugh, they threw their arms over each other's shoulders, again, and sang the final two stanzas:

> "That's the case of Little Elize,
> Which PROVES that pregnancy is a germ disease.
> And it would have been the same,
> Regardless of her name.

"Whatever his text book in O—B
Any fair-minded student *must* see
From the history of Little Elize,
That pregnancy is a germ disease."

They brought down the house! The boys hurrahed and Hizer was
so overcome that he replenished the juleps and handed them to the
duet before realizing that by doing so, he had completely emptied
the bottle. After the laughter subsided and the men stood about
chatting, Hizer interrupted, authoritatively, "She's due 'most any
minnit, now. Docta 'Lije, you an' de Dean hurry up wid dem
drinks. Mista Ben, you collec' de glasses off de floors an' take 'em to
de kitchen." He gathered his own valuables from the table as the
other men obeyed. Hizer continued, "She kno's we has a mos' popular
boy. We c'n choose de champion afta she's heah, if we has to, but I
ain't nevva let Miss Susie see no man drinkin' hard likker in dis
house!"

When the doctors' empty glasses had followed the others to the
kitchen, students and judges relaxed and lit the cigars, which Ashby
passed. To these men, none of whom was drunk but all of whom
had had a rattling good time, a good cigar was precisely the proper
touch.

Ashby introduced to Dr. Howe the boys he had not met. To Clay
Abernathy, Howe said, "How is your father? Is he ever coming back
here?"

"I hope so, sir."

"So do I. He's a fine rascal."

To Prentiss he said, "Didn't know you in a previous generation.
Didn't need to."

Pug understood that it was a compliment and grinned; then Hizer
announced:

"De house champion choosin' will pro-ceed if you jedges ain't done
gone an' furgot whut dese boys sung?"

"We haven't forgot, Hizer," Wingate assured him.

Hizer, ignoring that reference, continued, "It ain't necessary fur me
t'tell you whut de house champion does: Docta 'Lije, de Dean an'
Mista Alex kno's frum x-perience, but fur de rest ob you I *re*mark

his rights. He sleeps in de room, on de floor wid Miss Susie's, in de double bed wid de box-spring, whut belonged to her Mamma an' Papa. Ebery mornin' whin I bring Miss Susie her 'fore-breakfas' coffee he gits a cup, too. He has a desk all his own wid a student lamp an' a fly-roun' chair. He c'n use Miss Susie's bathroom—but he still has fust call on de third floor bathroom any hour day or night. Now, jedges, who is he?"

He lowered his kinky head and peered over his glasses at the Dean. Wingate coughed and said gravely, "As I understand, this choice is made upon medical knowledge—not on a broad understanding of human nature, in which case I should be at a loss whether to vote for the future Doctor Mead or the future Doctor Ashby—but it being based as I said, on a knowledge of medical terms, I vote unquestionably for the future Doctor St. George Prentiss!"

"Thank you, Dean. Dem's my sent'ments, too," Hizer said hastily, "So no matter whut Docta 'Lije says he's 'lected!"

"The vote is unanimous," Howe bellowed above the resulting din and the cries of "Speech!" "Speech, Prentiss!"

The men ranged themselves about the room. Hizer took his trappings to the pantry and then rushed up the hall again. But Prentiss was saved, for Hizer hissed, "Ssh! Sit down! She's cumin' up de steps!"

Ashby, who was still official host until his possessions were removed from the champion room, said, "Doctor Howe, will you and the Dean please stand near the door, and the rest of you make room for her in the morris chair."

They moved to their stations and innocence exuded from their countenances as Hizer opened the door, and Miss Susie stepped across her own sill. She smiled instantly, extending her hands toward Howe and Wingate. "My dears, what a lovely surprise! You boys must stay to dinner. Hizer, please put two more places on the table."

The Dean held her small hand in his, and Dr. Howe kissed her upon the cheek. That phrase "you boys," was the best thing they had heard that morning; it made the sensation of youth which they had experienced when singing Little Elize seem an actuality.

"Can't stay. Should have been at church with my wife. Came to keep an eye on the Dean, Miss Susie," Dr. Howe said.

"But you'll stay, my dear," she turned to Wingate. "And you'll sit next to me like you used to."

Wingate tried to protest, tried to be dignified, but his affection for the old lady was so intense that he could not bear to disappoint her.

Hizer said quickly, "I'll set de place fur de Dean right away . . . an' give him his same silver napkin ring."

Then Miss Susie saw the students in the parlor, saw the aisle they had formed to the chair, and heard Alex saying, "Miss Susie, we want you to sit in that chair for a few minutes, please, while we inform you of my successor as the most popular boy. I've been voted out."

"Oh, Alex! You—" Her face clouded then she controlled herself and said, "Certainly, my dears, I'll be delighted to." She walked over and sat down in the morris chair and the students grouped behind her.

The two doctors were shocked to see that with the boys' faces as a background, Miss Susie looked no older than she had in their day. The only difference was that her hair was now distinctly white; but her eyes still shone with innocence, her cheeks were still plump and the ridiculous little nose still perched expectantly between them. Her hour-glass figure was precisely as it had been. She sat upright, without touching the chair back, her eyes gravely upon them, like the eyes of a child. This queer old parlor they wouldn't have seen changed for the world, and Miss Susie, surrounded by her boys, was a memory which afterward they treasured.

Ashby's voice invaded their thoughts. "Miss Susie," he was saying, "as the last duty of a student who has been privileged to sleep in your mother and father's room for a year, and enjoy Hizer's excellent morning coffee, it gives me great pleasure to inform you that the gentleman who has been voted my successor is St. George Prentiss."

"Oh!" she said with surprise and there was pleasure in it, "I'm so very glad!"

Pug bowed his appreciation, and Alex sensing his embarrassment turned to the judges, whom Hizer had rejoined, and suggested, "Doctor Howe, may I offer you an opportunity to speak?"

"I've resigned in favor of the Dean," Howe replied gruffly, and Wingate, in his most dignified tone, began:

"My dear lady, and you gentlemen of medicine, to be invited to return here for a few hours upon Easter morning is an honor which I have always coveted. In fact, I would much rather be chosen to come to Miss Susie's on Easter morning than to be a Hunterian Lecturer!"

"Bravo!" cried the audience. Miss Susie's eyes filled.

Wingate gestured for silence and then continued, "As the unwritten rule has always been that no medical man can ever be so honored more than once in a life time, Doctor Howe and I have decided that we should like to commemorate our honor, by presenting you, Miss Susie, with a small token of our affection."

The murky March atmosphere seemed suddenly dispelled. The sun shone through the old lace curtains and lighted the dim parlor as he took from his inside coat pocket a long slender package and handed it to her.

"My dears, you shouldn't do this! I ——"

"Untie it, Miss Susie. Open it!" the boys behind her chair insisted.

The package had evidently come from Kirk's. Wrapped as a gift, in tissue paper and tied with ribbon, it was the length of two decks of cards. The curious students observed silently as the little old maid's plump fingers unknotted the ribbons, unwrapped the package and came upon the leather jewel case. Every man watched her release the catch and raise the lid.

Lying there, in separate velvet plush grooves, was a set of six silver crochet hooks of varying sizes, each flattened at one end to the dimensions of a dime so that it might carry her initials.

Chapter Eight

FIRST HOSPITAL WORK

That night Ashby came to claim his slippers which he had forgotten when he moved from the champion room, and found Prentiss lying luxuriously spraddled to the four corners of the famous double bed.

"Alex, you are a fool! You knew darn well that after you sang that song the judges had no choice. They couldn't offend Hizer."

"Forget it!" Ashby said, throwing one leg over the footboard. "Not all the boxsprings in Baltimore could have made me refrain from that ditty! Hizer was tickled pink!"

"Well, if it suits you, it suits me," Prentiss replied. "God knows it suits me." Then pulling his body to a sitting posture, he asked solemnly, "How long has this been going on?"

"This—what?"

"This business of her crocheting table mats for every bride and caps for every baby?"

"Since the first one of her boys was decently married and had a legitimate heir, I imagine."

"You haven't seen enough of all kinds of people to realize that there is nothing like it in America!"

"Without seein' 'em, I understand that!" Alex observed. Then he smiled, "But, boy, we did well, you know it? The liquor lasted and the cigars were swell!"

"Say, who chooses the judges?"

"The floor champions and Hizer."

"And the judges pay for that present, don't they?"

"Yeah, Pug, that's part of the rules. They are not on paper—but they are known just the same. Hizer, of course, never contributes, though his judgment is always sought."

"Of course," Prentiss grinned, and then remarked, "It is one of the best things we've got: tradition."

130

"Why?" Alex, who could never resist an argument, seated himself upon the side of the bed pleased to find Pug's reticence gone.

Prentiss continued, "Because it is an Anglo-Saxon's way—when it is good tradition—of acknowledging that he has been praiseworthy in the past. *You* have a tradition of bravery: it is written all over you. You are not afraid of any man alive!"

"Only of women."

"Yeah. I know. Well, this is the first time I've ever run into a group of people who had a tradition of love, of kindness." He checked himself; then inquired, "Do you think she knew we had been drinking, Alex?"

"Don't know, but I suspect that she did. Miss Susie's great virtues are that she never scolds and that she always believes you to be fine. I've never seen a student yet who didn't respond to that creed!"

After he had gone Pug lay thinking about Ashby's statement— which was true. Presently he picked up his *Rabelais* and lost himself. The other volume of his library lay on the mantel; it was *Don Quixote*.

When vacation came the personnel of Miss Susie's disbanded. Alex went back to Texas and spent a month riding the range on a ranch over which, as far as the eye could see, his family owned the land; then he returned to work in the dispensary. Mead went home and fell out of love, fell in love and drank corn likker. Clay Abernathy returned to West Virginia and talked of the famous professor as intimately as he spoke of the students; his father said nothing, but was hurt when he realized that the boy was partly his wife's progeny. Silas, having gotten out of the perineum, determined to go back into it again, alone; he obtained a cadaver for his own private use, worked at the anatomy building and stayed on at Miss Susie's. Elbert Riggs went back to Pennsylvania, made occasional flying visits to Baltimore and ate numerous dinners at Uncle Emil's. Ford's was closed; it was too hot to climb the Monument, so Uncle Emil's became the rendezvous.

Just before the close of school in June, when his itching foot was bothering him again, and he was thinking of going abroad, Pug Prentiss, under Ashby's guidance, spent a Saturday night in the accident room. The experience scotched the trip; it scotched everything but his nightly appearances there, and a fierce pain which his ugly face caused in the hearts of several nurses.

Once, when he discovered that Miss Susie had never been to New York, he renounced the accident room for three days and took her as his guest: a trip which neither of them ever forgot and of which they never told anyone but Hizer.

Miss Susie was afraid it would be talked about, that she had gone unchaperoned, and Pug was not the sort of man to tell any person that he had spent money on his friends. The way he finally persuaded her to go was to dangle in front of her mind's eye the exhibits of handmade lace at the Metropolitan, for since the advent of the various-sized needles Miss Susie had begun to make caps which were gossamer.

Before they left, Silas being away for the week end, Pug offered to give Hizer five dollars provided he "drank it up in twenty-four hours and was sober when Miss Susie returned." Hizer accepted the challenge.

So it came about that in the fall of 1913 when the personnel of Miss Susie's household reconvened and medical school reopened, everybody had had a change which in some way stimulated his ego.

Silas had dissected his cadaver, alone. Prentiss had become such a favorite about the accident room that occasionally in a push, the internes allowed him to assist, a signal honor for a man just entering his second year. But no one ever thought of Prentiss "by years"; he seemed to many of the internes as seasoned as the residents. They saw that to hysterical, terrified people he represented comfort and wisdom; when they walked into the accident room and looked over the men, they invariably made a beeline for the tall, homely fellow with the startlingly beautiful smile.

Ashby and Ben entered their third year and Minnie Otts was gone, having graduated and taken an internship in a hospital in Delaware. Pug, Clay, Silas and Elbert Riggs were still in the grind of the first two years of medicine. "Still in hell and outta the hospital," as Ben put it one night when all of them were draped in their favorite seats in Miss Susie's parlor.

"I call what I'm in fair enough," Elbert remarked practically. "I'm like a bank teller now, who knows why he learned the multiplication tables. What do you say, Ashby?"

Alex stretched his long legs. "Depends on how you look at it."

"Gosh!" Ben said in disgust, "I thought a month in the wide open spaces would have rid you of that rotten word. You scientists are afraid to make a definite statement about anything. What in the hell is the good of you anyhow? Got your eyes glued to microscopes always claiming you are learning everything and know everything, but damned if I ever heard you tell any of it to anybody!"

"Ah, Bennie," Alex replied sadly, "you surgeons all have complexes even when you are students! Even before you know that you don't know! Sadistic tendencies and superiority complexes. Never saw one yet without 'em."

"Bosh!" Ben growled while the others laughed. "That's just the kind of thing I'm talking about. I ask you a simple question and instead of answering it you evade me and harp on my personality!"

"Bennie!" Alex mimicked his own tone; then continued soberly, "As a scientist, perhaps in the abstract sense you are right; but as a diagnostician, in this case, I think I've done brilliantly. You show perfect symptoms."

Silas, on whom these encounters had little effect, boomed, "How long does this pharmacology last?"

"How do you like it?" Ben asked.

"I don't," Silas said and there was such a wealth of despair in the two words that Pug, who concurred with his sentiments, laughed heartily.

"Better learn it, old timer," Ben suggested cheerfully. "Because when your senses fail, you can resort to drugs, when your diagnoses fail, you can resort to drugs, when you ——"

Ashby interrupted caustically, "When you fail, you can resort to drugs!"

Prentiss, seeing the expression on Holmes's plain face, realized that Ashby's words had missed fire. Pug said, "The only thing wrong with that last diagnosis, Alex, is that Holmes won't fail, and I'll take even money on it."

Silas blushed and Ashby cleared his throat and explained, "Don't be so literal, Pug. 'You,' in my vocabulary, performs the same function as 'one' does in yours, or the editorial 'we' does in print."

Ben burst out, "Thanks, Alex. Thought you meant me."

Ashby gave him a scornful look and Silas understood that all this was somehow an apology and changed the subject. "If you've got to learn to give drugs all the time, I think I'll be a pathologist!"

The group howled and Silas looked aghast. When they had quieted down Pug remarked, "You like that, don't you, Si?"

"Well, er, yes, I do," Silas admitted coloring.

"Why?"

Silas's reply was as serious as Alex's sudden question had been, "Because it is the best way I've ever seen for a man to catch up with his own blunders."

Pug whistled slowly and Mead asked, "After you've made 'em what is the sense of knowing 'em?"

"To convince yourself that you've made 'em," Silas responded. Ashby shot him a sudden glance of admiration. Prentiss whistled again.

Ben asked teasingly, "Going to do autopsies on the ones you murder, Si?"

"Probably won't be allowed to if I go back to my father's practice. Country people are against autopsies."

"So are surgeons," Alex inserted. "Don't let Mead's joshing get under your hide, Holmes."

"It won't," Silas answered.

Ben said, "After the heckling I've been subjected to under the renowned Doctor Ashby, I reckon I'll be able to take my lickings over autopsies in the years to come."

"Way you intone that 'In the years to come' you sound as redundant as Boyd, Bennie."

"Who is Boyd?"

"He is the man you'll get in normal physical diagnosis next quarter, Riggs," Ashby answered. "Makes all simple statements with great emphasis and all emphatic statements with haste."

"Men who do that," Pug put in, "usually use the time they are speaking slowly to do their important thinking."

"Gives the classes an impression of vagueness, nevertheless. Makes 'em feel like every time their attention is focused they've been hit on the head with a heavy-ended hammer."

"Speaking of such things," Pug said good-naturedly, "I'd better go hit a few of my brain cells with that excellently obtuse textbook in clinical mike. So long, boys!"

"Things as hard as clinical microscopy have no right to affectionate nicknames," Riggs said.

"Hard enough to learn it—without talkin' about it," Silas agreed.

Ben followed Pug upstairs and Alex decided that with his chief protagonist and his chief antagonist gone, he'd better clear out too, so the session broke up. As a third year man, Alex found he was pretty well swamped with trying to apply all of the knowledge which the first two years of cramming required one to assimilate; the application he found, while vastly more interesting, was not one whit easier than the accumulation had been.

Even the boys in the second year were beginning to catch a glimmer of that sad fact. With the beginning of the second quarter the pharmacology let up and the pathology continued, but was interspersed with normal physical diagnosis, neurological diagnosis, ophthalmology, and psychiatry; the heavy courses in ophthalmology and psychiatry did not come until the third and fourth years, but the introductory courses began in the second quarter of the second year. Neither subject interested any of the boys from Miss Susie's.

The course in normal physical diagnosis under Boyd interested everybody; every student was assigned a classmate who, as Ben Mead put it, "was presumedly normal" and gave him a complete examination. One night as the boys sat jawing in Miss Susie's parlor, Pug drawled, "Before Laennec and Ehrlich I wonder how a second year medical student spent his time!"

"Who were they?" Silas asked. Clay Abernathy wanted to ask but was unwilling to show his ignorance.

"If they weren't surgeons I don't know who they were," Ben stated.

"Laennec developed the stethoscope and opened up the whole region of man's chest to exploration; and Ehrlich invented the treatment for syphilis," Pug explained.

"Well, of course a surgeon wouldn't know about Ehrlich," Ben said airily.

"One of the few things he can't cut out," Alex put in dryly. "Then, too, the treatment is so recent, only invented in 1906, one would hardly expect a surgeon to have heard of it."

"I hope to hell I get a chance to do a prostatectomy on you some day!"

"Thanks, Ben," Alex bowed.

"What is the sense of learning normal physical diagnosis, anyhow?" Bert Riggs asked.

"So you can distinguish it from abnormal, I presume," Clay ventured.

"Doctors shouldn't presume," Alex's voice was cutting. "The only people who can get away with doing that are surgeons."

"Quit riding me, can't you?" Ben said. "Anyhow, I'm thinking of being a neurologist."

"Huh? You?" Alex grinned disparagingly and then he continued to Clay, "Surgeons, you see, are the only people who can cut out their presumptions."

Such conversation always made Abernathy ill at ease and while he smiled knowingly, he also began to sweat profusely.

Silas, who had dropped into a well of silence, practiced his irritating way of turning the conversation back to where it last penetrated his memory and asked, "How can they be certain we are normal?"

"They can't," Alex answered. "But we are the nearest thing to it hereabouts. You certainly don't think they are normal, do you?" The boys understood that he referred to the professors and chuckled. Pug said, "I don't feel complimented by it."

"By what?" Clay queried.

"Being taken for normal: normal people rarely do anything except be normal."

"That in itself is quite an art," Alex suggested.

"I'd rather be less artistic and a little more alive," Pug replied.

Silas began chewing his mental cud on the last remarks. Again Abernathy felt at sea and when Clay felt confused, he always resorted to words.

"Is a normal man 'stable'?"

"I think he belongs in a stable," Ashby answered jokingly. For some reason he could never explain, he found it impossible to treat Abernathy either seriously or gently.

To Prentiss he was neither that effecting nor that amusing; he felt genuinely sorry for Abernathy and now interrupted, "Is any man stable? Isn't that just 'front'?"

Ashby replied, "I've seen one or two with whom it was natural. Jack Cameron hereabout is one."

"You may be right, but he is rich. Happily married. Four beautiful children. Tops in his line. Why shouldn't he be stable?" Pug's voice had a challenge to it.

"Why should he be?" Ashby shot the question.

"Because his conditioning is perfect," Pug retorted instantly.

"Renouncing psychiatric terms and talking in a way that even a plain surgeon can understand," Ben said. "Do you mean, Pug, that a stable person is a person who keeps steady under adverse conditions?"

"Precisely."

"Sir William Osler calls that equanimity, and he rates it as the best quality any medical man can acquire," Alex remarked.

"How do you acquire it?" Clay asked in the same tone in which he might have inquired the price of a fetching tie.

"Dunno," Ashby shrugged his shoulders.

" 'De-pends,' " Ben mimicked and then suggested, "Surgeons have to be exposed to medicine, and from the medicine we are being exposed to now, I'd say it is largely a question of glands. If your glandular balance is good, you are calm. If it's not, you are not."

"Is anybody's?" Silas asked.

"Sure. Occasionally. But you can take it from me, that they're not surgeons, they're not artists, they're not ——"

"Are surgeons artists?" Alex evinced surprise.

"Hey, you two, quit it!" Pug said.

"Anybody going to *answer* my question?" Riggs asked.

"Better repeat it."

"I asked, Pug, why normal physical diagnosis is valuable?"

"It is valuable," Prentiss answered, "because half of the people who come to you aren't physically sick. They come for a physical ailment because they hope to escape through it."

"By the way, Riggs," Ashby intervened. "I heard Boyd ask Doctor

McMillan if he could take you all, your group, into the hospital this quarter."

"You mean to work?" Silas's face lit up.

"I don't know, but I doubt it. Probably just to show you how the routine interlocks, let you get the hang of things and give you a look-see. Mostly, second year men don't go until the latter part of the third quarter, you know."

They all nodded. Alex turned to Prentiss, "Say, Pug, about this escaping-through-ailments business, you sound like you've been shining shoes for psychiatrists. Planning to go into that, are you?"

"Not until I've had a bath," Pug said as he rose and gave Ashby a friendly slap on the shoulder.

"Yeah, you've got to be pure to succeed at it," Ashby replied. And as Prentiss began to mount the stairs, Alex continued in a loud tone, "Definitely anti-social, rooms to himself, bathes to himself, thinks ——"

"Hey, that reminds me!" Ben turned to Abernathy. "Can you think of three good reasons why a woman wears a sweater?"

"To keep warm—" Clay began and Pug, as he rounded the stair landing called, "The other two are obvious."

"Oh!" said Clay. Alex broke into a deep laugh, and then Elbert Riggs asked a question which had long been in his mind.

"Ashby, how much is equanimity tied up with a man's sex life?"

Alex replied soberly, "Less than it is with a woman's, I suppose, but only a surgeon could answer that question."

Riggs turned to Ben, who sputtered and said, "According to the medical men, the psychiatrists over-rate the relationship; and according to the psychiatrists the surgeons ignore it too much or explore it too much; and according to the surgeons, the gynecologists are not disinterested enough to have any perception! If you really want to know, I reckon you'd better ask the pediatricians!"

A few days later, upon a Monday morning, Dr. Boyd took the group over to the hospital to observe the resident staff, third and fourth year men and the consultants caring for their dispensary patients, and to begin to comprehend the relationship between their training in normal physical diagnosis and physical diagnosis.

It was an experience which Ashby warned Prentiss would be different from that of the accident room, and watching the long lines of waiting people Pug understood what Alex meant. Accident decisions were keyed through tension and emergency. Here, under that first impression of people, hundreds of people, people everywhere, lay the vicious circle of permanent poverty and recurrent illness. Black, brown, white and yellow, in every clinic benches deep, people sat waiting, waiting with the relaxed resignation of the poor, waiting with a ray of hope beating through their set faces.

Boyd said, "The things of which a man sees only an occasional case in private practice come here by the tens and twenties, daily. Pregnancies from the first month on, with every type of heart and kidney involvement, and every pelvic complication; tuberculosis in all guises, all stages, all ages; Graves's disease with all its resulting maladies. *Everything* walks into a dispensary."

Pug's thoughts ran past Boyd's words to what Ashby had said about the sensation of a wall of onrushing humanity engulfing the dispensary at nine, taking its divergent courses by ten, being adjusted and handled in those courses by medical men and then receding by noon and rebounding by afternoon.

It was Riggs's practicality which brought Prentiss back into the present. "How, Doctor Boyd, do you keep them straight?"

"Every patient seen has a case history and a physical examination taken," Boyd replied. "That history is on file in the history room and brought up each time the patient is seen. The doctor seeing him studies it before considering his current illness. Dispensary admissions, when they are hospitalized, are generally ward patients and therefore the decisions of the dispensary doctor are rechecked again—internes, assistant residents, residents, and professors, to say nothing of medical students, all study the case. In many cases, if a ward patient dies, and the relatives give permission for an autopsy, one's conclusions are again checked at the autopsy table. A teaching hospital must have more patients than beds, and therefore a free patient, in a teaching hospital, gets quite as good care as a private patient. It is an exacting service, gentlemen!"

"Do the people pay anything?" Riggs asked.

"Fifteen cents each dispensary visit, if they can. And if they can't, nothing. All of the medicine practiced in a dispensary is given. No man working here receives a salary for dispensary cases. All he receives is a chance to learn, and if his work merits it, eventually, staff recognition in the medical school and visiting privileges at the hospital—a chance to bring his own patients to the hospital."

Prentiss began to understand quite clearly where that hope which beat through the fatigue in the countless faces of the dispensary patients came from; and he saw why, as Boyd took them from clinic to clinic, dispensary service is a work which with many men lasts every morning from their second year medicine to their graves.

Boyd joshed an elderly and famous consultant about that, and the man turned on him and said, "There is no such thing as an unselfish act. I come here because I want to come. All kinds, all colors, all ages, all diseases—I don't want to be paid! I want a chance to see." He turned to the group and said gruffly, "My best teachers have been students. Get some white coats on these boys, and bring 'em back, Boyd."

En route to get the white coats they walked again among the waves of people and their reactions were revealing. Pug's profound sympathy gave him an instant and lifelong duty toward them; Elbert Riggs wanted to help them to get well, so that they could help themselves; Silas just stood ready to help them; Clay Abernathy was prepared to help them, condescendingly; they shocked 'Lije Howe and then under his irritation moved him; but they thrilled Isidore Aaron, for he no longer felt sick with agony at his own uselessness.

After Boyd had dealt them a lecture upon the necessity of observation, and the duty of a good doctor never to reveal his true opinions in the presence of the patient, they were issued the white coats. Even to those, their reactions were interesting and dissimilar. Silas accepted his, regretted it had no breast pocket and then accepted the regret and forgot about it and the coat; Riggs resented the fact that they did not fit, and that his sleeves were too short. Prentiss, who had been permitted in the accident room to wear one when he was assisting, slipped into his with sheer joy; to Abernathy it was like a reporter's press card and gave him privileges; to Isidore it was like the armor of the knights of old, to be worn as a sacred trust; to Elijah Howe it didn't mean any more than a pair of pajamas and was a darn sight less comfortable.

But from some patient in that jammed dispensary within an hour of the time they had put on the coats, each of those second year men received his baptism, not in jest, but in earnestness, as a panic-stricken voice referred to him as "Doctor."

No matter how material the student's outlook, there was an emotional thrill that came with the utterance of that word which none of them ever forgot. Pug had heard it before, but he enjoyed and treasured hearing it again. The first time he had heard it was when the negro woman brought the child scalded by boiling starch into the accident room, placed it in his arms and begged, "Tell me, Docta, will de baby live?" The baby had lived. Now, a small boy with a mashed finger walked up to Pug and asked, "Doctor, will you fix me?" Prentiss grinned and the kid grinned back; then Pug took him to Dr. Boyd, and on to the accident room.

To Elbert Riggs the word "Doctor" came from a terrified woman who was trying to find the maternity clinic; to Abernathy it came from a blind person; and to Silas it was first pronounced by a stevedore, a day laborer whose foot had been crushed.

The first person who used it when addressing 'Lije was a bent cotton-headed old negro leaning heavily upon a gnarled stick who asked, "Docta, is you goin' to count fo' me?"

"What do you mean, 'count fo' you'?," 'Lije's belligerence overcame his equanimity.

The negro, no more upset by 'Lije's vehemence than Hizer was by that of his father, explained, "I means count fo' me. Lots ob people is come up heah, an' dey ain't bin seen since. Can't nobody count fo' dem. I ain't goin' to be x-amined if you ain't goin' to count fo' me." He began edging doorward past the crowded benches.

'Lije yanked him back and said, "Sit down. Sure, I'll count for you."

As it developed later, it was wise that he did, for the case proved very interesting. Eventually Boyd, who had taken over in one of the medical examining rooms, got the old fellow onto the examining table, listened to a recital of his symptoms and then allowed the students to check his heart action. He was arthritic, had a bad heart and the usual complications of his age, but there seemed to be no explanation for what the old fellow aptly described as "a stitch in my back."

As the examination progressed he kept his eyes fixed upon young Howe and 'Lije grew profoundly embarrassed. He wished that the old negro were dead; that mesmeristic word "Doctor" had inveigled him into this ridiculous position. When Boyd, the interne and the assembled students had held a grave consultation, even Boyd had to tell the old man that he could find nothing which could have caused the pain.

He looked so pitiful when he begged, "Take one mo' look, Docta. Jes' one mo'," that Boyd relented and scrutinized the man's spine, again.

Isidore Aaron, who was observing, narrowed his eyes, tilted his head further forward, waited until Boyd reassured the old man that there was nothing there, and then asked, "Doctor Boyd, may I—that hair— er—this one." He leaned closer, caught hold of the ends of the hair to which he referred and pulled.

The negro groaned, but before Boyd or the interne could protest or intervene, they and the other students saw, dangling upon that half inch of black thread clenched between Isidore's thumb and forefinger, a slim steel needle.

"Thank you, Docta! You done stopped it!"

Isidore silently passed his findings on to Boyd and while the interne disinfected the wound, and reported it in the case history which he was preparing, the professor and the students looked at the needle. Had they failed to extract it then, all of them knew that it might have taken months of searching, many X-rays, and then have ended in just another unexplained pain.

"Thank you, Aaron," Boyd said calmly. "Very much."

"I'm sorry, sir, that I—" Isidore had meant to apologize for taking the case in his own hands, but even as he spoke he knew that he had been justified and stammered.

"What you did was your duty," Boyd said, "and I appreciate it."

When the elderly patient was off of the table, still unaware that the stitch in his back had actually existed, he remembered his manners and said to 'Lije, "An' I'se much obliged to you, too, suh."

'Lije acknowledged the remark with a gruff, "Welcome," which was such a good imitation of his father's way of saying it that several of the boys snickered; which made him feel still more foolish. He thought that they were grinning at his coming off second-fiddle to Aaron in the estimation of an illiterate patient.

After the old man was gone, Dr. Boyd asked Isidore, "How could you distinguish that hair—er—thread—from the hairs?"

"My eyes are very good, Doctor. I've never needed glasses," Isidore replied. Boyd wore glasses.

The true reason Isidore did not care to acknowledge. He had helped in the tailor shop many summers and knew that hair lies differently from thread.

"Wonder where he got it?" Abernathy asked, trying as usual to insert himself into conversations where he was not concerned.

"His wife had been sewing, I daresay, and perhaps she stuck that needle in the bed," Dr. Boyd replied.

Pug swallowed a smile; he had long since noticed that Boyd regarded all negroes as legitimately married.

Of course, the only person who knew that the first time any patient ever called Isidore "Doctor" was to thank him for his services was Isidore, himself. In a way he could never discuss with any one it was the best thing which had ever happened to him. He wasn't any longer a Jew being polite to Gentiles; he was a doctor being important to people who were worse off than himself and who thanked him for his help. This was the first time he had ever had any faith in what Alex Ashby had said during their first walk when he had prophesied that medicine was a profession where being a Jew was not a disadvantage.

And forever, privately and completely, this experience set him apart from and above the people on lower Broadway. They were all trying to wrest a living from the world: to get the world to help them. Of course he would have to try to wrest a living from it, too, but from now on it was, as Boyd put it, his duty to help the world. In a hidden sense, Isidore had always felt that this was so, but in another sense he had never dared to permit himself to believe that it was. Now, he knew that it was so, and the knowledge gave him an intangible kind of magnanimity and of happiness. Also, a strength: other things beside his own aspirations rested upon his shoulders.

Some things in life can happen only once, and this was such a thing: he had entered the hospital as an active participant in medicine and had acquitted himself with brilliance. He hated Jews who boasted, so all of these emotions were locked within his own breast and stayed locked there throughout the day and until he started down Broadway in the late afternoon.

Then it swept over him with a wave of ironic clarity: it wasn't any knowledge of medicine which had made him acquit himself so well today. It was a knowledge of tailoring! And with that short-sighted-ness which lifelong poverty brings, he couldn't comprehend that at last privation was going to be an advantage to him. He could only know that the things he had always hated had stood him in good stead and, therefore, he hated them more fiercely than ever. His desire to sever his life in the slums from his life in the hospital had not been as successful as he had imagined, and probably it would never be.

When he arrived home he permitted himself an hour with *Religio Medici*, and then went about his studying furiously. The only way to sever his life in the slums and his life at the hospital was to do such brilliant work that he would be given an opening at the hospital and could live there, altogether.

The boys from Miss Susie's sauntered home in high good humor and Pug said to Silas as he offered him a cheroot, "Have one, doctor?"

Supper was good; Miss Susie seemed especially gay, and after she had gone to the Altar Guild meeting, Mead fell to telling Abernathy a couple of jokes he had heard during the day.

No one remembered to tell Ashby when he came in, late from an autopsy, about Isidore's diagnosis, which was regrettable for although it was after ten, Alex would have gone to congratulate him. As it was, by eleven Isidore had completed his studying, the elation had worn off, the despair had worn off and a vacant kind of hopelessness had set in. He sat slumped over his desk, in the dark, so that if his brothers looked through the keyhole they wouldn't know; had he been a man with less emotional control, he would have sobbed.

Chapter Nine

FORSAKING ALL OTHERS

"What's the matter?" Dr. Howe growled. His wife was standing in the doorway which led from his office into the family section of the house. Maria, during office hours, never interrupted except for emergencies and to see her now startled him.

"May I speak to you a minute, Doctor Howe?" she said primly and nodded toward the hall as his office nurse went into the waiting room for the next patient. When they were alone in the hall, Mrs. Howe said, "I need your advice. I'm sorry to bother you, Doctor Howe."

The formality with which she always addressed him when fully clothed never failed to amuse her husband, but he was too intent upon her anxiety to chide her now. She continued, "Bessie McMillan is having a dinner dance tonight and ——"

"Who's she?"

"Doctor McMillan's daughter who is the same age as your eldest daughter. You know perfectly well who she is, Doctor Howe!"

"Even when you are provoked, Maria, you certainly have an inviting mouth," he remarked as he took her chin in his hand and put his lips to hers. She struggled and pretended to push him away.

"Behave yourself. What will the servants think?"

"I don't give a damn what they think," her husband said.

She made a fluttery gesture of disapproval and then went on, "What I want to consult you about is—this: Bessie is having only third and fourth year medical students. 'Lije isn't invited, of course, but Sally is and Sally can't go."

"Why?" the doctor made no endeavor to move across the hall to where his wife had fled; instead he busied himself cutting the cigar which he intended lighting as soon as he had finished with his patients.

Mrs. Howe hesitated and he said, "Hurry up. It's nearly three o'clock."

"She can't go because—I've got her in bed. She isn't very well."

"What's the matter? Why don't you send for a doctor?" His eyes twinkled. She stammered,

"She—she doesn't need a doctor; she—she just isn't well enough to go."

"Got the cramps?"

"Ssh! Don't talk like that, the servants will hear you."

Her husband put the cigar in his vest pocket and shook his head in amusement. "How on earth you ever manage to be such a satisfactory wife in private and such a pious prude in public is a mystery to me!"

"Doctor Howe! Stop teasing me. I need your help!" She moved over beside him, put her arm through his and explained, "It's too late for Bessie to ask anybody else and Sally really can't go. Mrs. Mc-Millan wants Margaretta to come in Sally's place and I said I'd have to have fifteen minutes to think it over and call her back."

"Sure, Gret can go. That fixes it."

"But Margaretta's such a baby. All of the boys are older and she's *so* impressionable. I wonder if it is wise?"

"For heaven's sake, Maria! Gret's eighteen. And not half the baby Sally is. Never was."

"She's terribly young. You don't know how young she is. She's really just a baby."

"She hasn't been a baby since she was eighteen months old and kicked 'Lije in the pants for pulling her curls."

"Really! You do remember the worse things, Doctor Howe."

"No. Just the ones which are medically important, Mrs. Howe!" His wife said nothing and pursed her lips; the way he copied her tone when he said, "Mrs. Howe" irritated her and he knew that it did.

"Trouble with mothers," he patted her hand and said soothingly, "is they never believe their daughters grow up. Gret was born grown. You be a good girl now and telephone Mrs. McMillan that she'll be glad to come. Has she a pretty dress? And a decent evening coat?"

"She can wear Sally's coat."

"No, she can't. Won't allow it. Take her downtown and buy her one of her own."

"But she's not old enough ——"

"And don't come back with any rose-bud, school-age party dress, either," he interrupted. "Get her an evening dress. Maybe that will take your mind off the fact that she's no longer a baby. But if it doesn't—why——"

"Why what?"

"Why, if you are determined to have a baby, you'll just have to *have* a baby, I suppose."

"Doctor Howe, don't you dare to talk to me ——!"

He placed his arm about her. "Ssh! Don't tell the servants, Maria. Not yet!" Then with boyish haste he ran toward his office, opened and shut the door, after himself.

Mrs. Howe sat quickly down upon the hatrack seat and tilted her head in a gesture of commingled satisfaction and reproof. The office door opened slightly. Her husband's head slid 'round it and he muttered, "I wasn't joking about those evening clothes, either!"

The door closed quickly and Mrs. Howe realized that if she didn't humor him about the evening gown and coat he might think that she was trying to keep his favorite daughter in swaddling clothes; at that moment the daughter in question was returning from the Peabody swinging her music roll and bemoaning her fate.

She knew that it would be at least two years before she would be invited to any parties like the one to which Sally was going tonight. If only Mamma would let her go to one Pithotomy dance—with 'Lije, if necessary—but go, just once, and see if she couldn't hook something better than a prep school beau. Sally wouldn't like the same kind of boys she did, they wouldn't get in each other's way. Why in Hades did Mamma say she was too young for anything but school-age dances, where the kids were fifteen to eighteen? Might as well go to dancing class as go to those!

The afternoon was dull and sunless. Margaretta's spirits were in keeping with it as she entered the hall at home and found Mamma sitting on the hatrack seat smiling to herself. Then, within half an hour, as a result of Dr. Howe's threats and Mrs. Howe's impetuosity, the girl had been whisked to O'Neill's and clothed like a fairy princess.

That evening between six and eight, the Howe household seethed with excitement. After office hours Dr. Howe had gone up and given Sally some aspirin, so upon their return Mrs. Howe put Margaretta in her room to rest. 'Lije, home from medical school, suggested through the keyhole, "Better let Mamma put your hair up, baby—so it'll *stay* up!"

When dinner was announced he asked, "Is Sally eating in bed?"

"No, she's asleep. Your father doped her," Mrs. Howe answered.

"What for?"

"So she wouldn't be jealous."

Dr. Howe pretended that he hadn't heard and devoted himself to his dinner.

"Never saw a time yet when Gret couldn't eat. You better send *her* something on a tray, Mamma."

"She's too excited to eat," Mrs. Howe replied.

"Damage her infant digestion," Dr. Howe said sarcastically. "Any rosebuds on that dress?"

"No!"

"What color is it?"

"Wait—and see! She picked it out, herself. The only thing *I* suggested was that the slippers be trimmed to match it. And they took them *right* away and had it done. The clerks were just *as nice* as they could be. All of them came to look at her while the dress was being fitted."

"Nice?" Dr. Howe snorted. "Many an old maid's gone home tonight cherishing that memory."

'Lije winked at his mother. Mrs. Howe rose and said, "I'd better begin to dress her."

When they were alone, Dr. Howe remarked, " 'Lije, Gret's not the only one that's excited; your mother didn't eat a thing."

"You better finish your salad, sir."

"So I had," Dr. Howe replied fingering his fork.

"Want me to take her, Papa?"

"No. I'll do it. Your mother told Mrs. McMillan she was too young to come with an escort, so—I'm going to take her."

'Lije grinned; then they sat silent a few minutes and Dr. Howe suggested, "Come on down and have a cigar, son." 'Lije gulped back his astonishment and when they were down in his father's office, he tried hard to smoke the cigar as though it were a daily habit. Their mutual excitement over a minor crisis concerning a female relative left them too keyed to talk.

Presently, 'Lije interrupted their silent puffing, "Papa, sounds like they are coming!"

Dr. Howe stood up as his wife opened the office door and announced, "Here she is. Look at her!"

The tall, slender young woman was aglow. Her flashing brown eyes and humorous mouth were now balanced and accentuated by the broad sweep of her brow from which the curly brown hair had been brushed and piled on top of her head. It was knotted at precisely the proper angle to offset her upturned nose and well-proportioned jaw. Even the way she held her head and her small ears set to it was so much like the portraits of Dr. Howe's dead mother that his voice was husky when he spoke.

"Come in, Miss Margaretta Howe. My, you are beautiful!"

Her eyes sparkled as she stepped into the room, "Oh, Papa, you like the dress as much as I do!"

"Baby, you're a knock-out," 'Lije shook his head convincingly, and while there was reverence in Dr. Howe's voice, there was pride in 'Lije's. "Stand in front of the fireplace, where we can see you."

Made with a close fitting bodice, the neck of the pink velvet dress was heart-shaped in front, rounded in the back and outlined, as were the arm bands of the pink tulle puff sleeves, in double rows of tiny white seed pearls. The long skirt had flared insets, one of which made a short fishtail train in the rear.

"And look, Papa! Instead of baby-ribbon loops with which ladies lift their trains, mine has seed pearl finger loops. See?"

She put her little finger through one, raised the train, tilted her head and stalked to and fro in front of the fireplace. Dr. Howe grinned like a pleased school boy and 'Lije said, "Gee, baby, you walk in high heels like you're born in 'em!"

"High heels, too?" Dr. Howe's eyes were keen with interest.

Margaretta lifted her skirt and showed for his inspection the toe of a daintily made pink velvet pump with a seed pearl bow.

"Maria, you've got good taste," Dr. Howe said gruffly. "Those bows are lovely. Come on, Gret, let's go."

Mrs. Howe answered, "I've known that I had good taste ever since I married you."

As he came over and kissed her, she knew that he was deeply pleased. He said, "Maria, your taste is mediocre compared with mine!" Then helping Margaretta into the gold-brocaded coat he continued, "Like this, too. See you later, Maria. Take care of her, 'Lije. Come on, Gret!"

"Thank you again, Mamma!" Margaretta breathed.

Mrs. Howe waved the enthusiasm aside and said, "Remember—" and Margaretta interrupted, "Yessum—to give Mrs. McMillan your love."

"No, I'm speaking to your father." Mrs. Howe handed him his hat and suggested, "Remember, Doctor Howe, that you are *not* invited."

"You'll ask me as many questions when I come back as if I had been! I'm not going any further than the front steps."

When the automobile was two blocks from his house, Dr. Howe drew in against the curb and asked, "Anything your mamma did to you that you want to change?"

"Unhuh."

"What is it?"

"She just choked up the front of my dress with tulle, 'cause she said it was too low for a young girl to wear and it looks tacky."

"Only kind that can wear 'em low. Can you see anything without the tulle?"

"Of course not."

"Well, let's fix it. I've got some scissors in my surgical case. Wait a minute."

He pulled the surgical case from the back seat, got the scissors and by the light of a street lamp, to the rhythm of the chugging motor and the orders of his young daughter, he removed the offending tulle. "I'll put your mamma to bed before I come for you, so you can get the dress off 'fore she sees."

"Papa, you are a darling!"

"No, I'm not."

There was hidden pleasure in his stubborn reply. "Everything else suit you?"

"Perfectly, Papa."

"Remember to sew that tulle back in tomorrow."

"I will."

The winter wind whistling through the bare trees and the noise of the motor laid between them for several blocks; when Dr. Howe had turned from Cathedral into Charles Street, Margaretta said, "Papa?"

"Huh?"

"I'm scared to death."

"What of?"

"I don't know how to talk to grown men, Papa."

"Bosh!—darn your mother—you talk to me, don't you? You talk to Doctor McMillan when he comes to dinner, don't you?"

"But it's so easy with you, Papa. All I have to do is—is—just be myself."

"That's all you have to do tonight. Grown men! Fiddlesticks! Those whippersnappers'll be nothing to talk to—after us."

"Well, Mamma says——"

"All your mamma knows is how to get on with me. You've always been friends with Dean Wingate. You get on with him, don't you?"

"Of course. But he's so sweet and timid; I just try to make him feel at ease."

"Gret, all men are timid. The boys there tonight will be wondering just as hard how to get on with you as you are how to get on with them. You already know how to get on with 'em; treat 'em like you do Wingate. He's as sensitive as they come. Think about their side of it: those boys are like convicts on parole in a governor's mansion. Scared you'll go home and tattle to your Pa if they don't dance with you, and he'll flunk 'em. They are in a worse fix than you are."

"Why, Papa, they're crazy!"

The indignation in her voice amused Dr. Howe, but he replied calmly, "Sure. Most medical students are crazy. 'Nother thing you ought to know, though, is that a man hates to be refused anything, even little things, like filling your water glass or dancing with you. If you are going to refuse him, do it politely."

"Yes, sir. And by the way, Papa, now we are by ourselves will you answer another question?"

"If I know the answer. Shoot!"

"If a man wants to—to kiss me before I'm married must I let him?"

Dr. Howe answered calmly as though such questions were put to him daily, "Not unless you want to, Gret—but if you want to, you bet you let him! Kisses are to love like thermometers are to fever; can't tell how badly you've got it without 'em. But don't you go 'round kissing every Tom, Dick and Harry."

"Thank you, Papa. I won't."

They drew up at the McMillans and Dr. Howe said as he looked at the windows on all three floors of the row house, "Lit up like a Christmas tree. Damn, I wish I hadn't said I wouldn't go in. I'll take you to the steps."

"Never mind," Gret opened the door. "I'll be all right."

"Sit still, Gret. Men should always be allowed the illusion of bossing. You better practice up on me."

Margaretta giggled gaily as he came around, helped her from the car and they walked across the sidewalk toward the white stone steps.

At the foot of the steps Dr. Howe said, "By the way, if you want to come home with one of those boys, you do it. Otherwise I'll be here at twelve-thirty. Have a good time, baby!"

He moved back toward the car, as Margaretta put her foot on the steps and the butler opened the door. Half way up, the girl turned and called,

"Wait, Papa!"

"For what?"

"This," she said and ran the few paces which separated them, threw her arms about his neck and kissed him.

He gave a pleased growl, then she skipped up the steps and the butler closed the door behind her.

After leaving her coat with an admiring maid, it was like a vivid dream to Margaretta to walk into the double parlors and be thanked by Bessie for coming. All of the girls were Sally's age, but they weren't a bit snooty and everyone said how beautiful she was. And that was strange, too; strange as wearing these gorgeous clothes, for nobody ever said it except Papa. Suddenly her fears began to recede and she felt glad; glad that the roses were as pink as her dress, glad to hear the fire crackle and watch it reflect the high polish on the mahogany furniture, glad that she was tall enough to look into the eyes of the men over the heads of the other girls.

The butler passed the dry sherry and Gret took a glass and sipped it before she realized that the other girls had taken none. She placed her glass quickly on the mantelpiece and looked shyly at Dr. McMillan who stood beside her. "I didn't mean to be the only one."

"Now that you are," he suggested kindly, "let's finish ours together. Unless you're not accustomed to——"

Gret lifted the glass and smiled. "I'm used to it. But I feel it ought to come from behind the *Archives of Surgery*."

Dr. McMillan laughed so spontaneously that the others began to look at them. He turned his back. "Margaretta," he said, "I want to drink a toast to your happiness: may your father live to see it!"

They touched glasses and when both were empty, the physician remarked, "That behind the *Archives of Surgery* is better sherry, I think."

"Oh, I don't," she said quickly. "And thank you, sir, for—for the toast."

Other guests were arriving; Bessie brought them up to her father, for Mrs. McMillan was too much of an invalid to appear at parties. Margaretta slipped away and went upstairs to speak to her.

Mrs. McMillan was an older edition of her daughter, cornflower beauty which had faded yellow, not white; in the presence of her fragile body one felt uneasy, helpless and too vital. Gret thanked her for suggesting that she take Sally's place. The gentle little lady smiled.

"Confidentially, my dear, I'm glad you are the one who came, because you are exquisite tonight! I shall enjoy remembering how beautiful you look."

"Oh, Mrs. McMillan, I—I ——"

"Come here." She motioned Gret down beside her upon the chaise longue. "When a person has been ill as long as I, all of the senses are more acute. I wouldn't tell the Doctor so, but I always know from the time he mentions a patient's name, if that patient will recover. I don't know how I know, my dear, but I do. I told you the truth about yourself just now because I know that your coming tonight is the beginning of some train of events which will matter to you as long as you live—more than anything else."

"What do you mean?" Margaretta asked the question with the same sort of intensity she used when arguing with her father; the inflection of an equal querying an equal.

Mrs. McMillan's sensitive ear caught it; she replied with similar intensity, "I can't say what I mean. I don't know, Margaretta. But as soon as you find out, I'd like to know, my dear, very much."

"You shall," Gret promised as she leaned forward and kissed the purplish lips in the sallow, peaked face.

Mrs. McMillan's thin hands touched the girl's cheeks. She said, "How vital and vivid you are! Whatever it is, Margaretta, happiness or unhappiness, you'll never be mean about it. Now go find it, my child."

It found her. She had just closed Mrs. McMillan's door and was strutting and swishing in front of the full length gilt framed mirror in the end of the upstairs hall, tilting her head and easing her train, when she found a tall, square-shouldered man with black hair and gray eyes, there in the glass beside her.

She was very close to the mirror, he quite a distance—yet with that strange unity which existed between them from the first, both knew that they would continue their acquaintance mirror-wise.

He said, "Lord, you are beautiful!"

"Do you think so?" Margaretta threw her shoulders back and watched him, those flashing sudden lights in her eyes matching the copper tints of her hair.

"Even a blind man would think so," he said slowly, in a singularly deep voice. "Now that you are in the mirror and will, of course, fade away shortly," he continued with great dignity, ignoring her challenging eyes, "I may tell you all of those things which I would never dare to say in life, mayn't I? Your figure is divine. Your waist tapers perfectly. I like the arch of your brow and your generous mouth.

And the damnably devilish way you toss your head and carry it, as though neither hell nor high water will ever cover your chin.

"Is there *anything* you like about *me*?"

Gret, mesmerized both by his voice and his appearance, answered into the mirror, "You have beautiful hands, but they are masculine, too. I like them. And aristocratic shoulders. I like them. And I'm glad there is more to your chin than to mine and that you are taller than I am, and your hair is black. Thank God, your eyes have those black edgings, too. Close 'em a minute—please——"

The last word came so gently that involuntarily the man obeyed. And he opened his eyes almost immediately to find he was gazing in the mirror at his own image. The radiant girl in the pink velvet dress had vanished.

For a second Alex Ashby wondered if it had happened. He started to go downstairs to find her, then shrugged his shoulders and dismissed it as pure fancy—the sort of experience one has in a mirage on a desert. He moved back into the room where the men had laid their coats, desiring the presence of other people. Only a negro maid was there. He came out again and went by to pay his respects to Mrs. McMillan.

Their greeting was formal, and so was their conversation, and her not being quite alive, although she was alive, fitted into his mood. On the way downstairs he wondered if he were ill and should go home immediately. At the foot of the stairs, Bessie McMillan collared him and apologized for having to put him beside Sally Howe's little sister, because Sally was sick and couldn't come. Then Bessie led him over to be introduced. And Alex saw her, out of the mirror and in the flesh, and had her hand in his.

It was a moment which neither of them ever forgot. Bessie fluttered away unnoticed, as Alex said wonderingly, "So you are real!" Margaretta's cheeks matched her dress, and she refused to look at him. Alex continued, "I meant everything I said in that mirror, Miss Howe."

The doors to the dining room were thrown open and Dr. McMillan, before going up to join his wife, was shepherding his guests in. Alex still stood holding Gret's hand. Once she tried to pull it away and whispered, "It's no fair, doing things you didn't do in the mirror, is it?"

"I intend to hold your hand," he said firmly, "from now to the end of the world unless you let me see whether your eyes have actually got devils in them. Anyhow, I kissed the curls on your neck—in the mirror—so it should be all right for me to hold your hand in real life, I guess."

"If I look up, will you turn it loose?"

"Do you want me to turn it loose? If you answer honestly, I'll do whatever you say."

"No, I don't want you to," she breathed. "So turn it loose."

"All right—for the moment."

They were the last couple into the dining room. Dr. McMillan remarked later to his wife, "Those children are mates: born mates! And it took all of my professional guile to keep the attention of the others focused toward the dining room, while they were discovering each other."

What the food was at that meal, Alex and Margaretta never knew; as soon as they were seated, he reached down and found her hand again. Margaretta struggled a moment or two and then permitted it to lie within his. Then a warmth of such intensity they could hardly eat, began radiating from their fingertips into their entire beings. What other people said, they never knew; they conversed with others, even danced with others between courses, but as soon as they were seated again, Alex's hand found hers and hers rested and throbbed in his.

"May I have this dance, Ladykins?"

"Why do you call me that?"

"Partly because that is what you look like. Like you never had your hair piled on top of your head before. Did you?"

Gret lifted her chin. "Hundreds of times."

"Don't believe it! Nobody could look as charming as you do tonight—hundreds of times."

Alex swung her into his arms and began to dance. She looked up at him and said, "You are wrong! And I'm *not* Ladykins."

"In or out of the mirror, you *are* Ladykins. *My* Ladykins." This time his voice was not jovial, nor teasing, but it enfolded her and his eyes caught hers.

A quick, complete blush suffused her features and she said primly, "I'm Margaretta."

"Margaretta Howe," he replied gravely. "Impulsive, impetuous and the baby of the family."

She threw her head up and Alex said, "You can't tilt that nose any higher, it's foolish to try."

"I shouldn't criticize the defects of a person I scarcely know."

"Oh, Ladykins, how can you say that? Surely you don't believe that exquisite ——"

A little smile began running about the corners of her tightly closed mouth and Alex's voice was almost beyond teasing when he said, "I warn you. I'll kiss you if you swallow that smile. Out of the mirror, I can reach your lips."

"Oh!" Gret was breathless; then she threw her head up and looked him squarely in the eye. "Satisfied with my teeth, too?" she said and gave him her broadest grin.

"You are a she-devil!" Alex muttered.

Margaretta pretended not to hear. "Tell me why you call me Ladykins?"

"You are a beautiful dancer, you know."

"But *why* am I Ladykins?"

"Oh, because when I'm an old man forty—five—you'll have dignity, poise, elegance and perhaps a touch of austerity; all the things I'll want most then. Now, though, you are just—Ladykins."

"Why bother to dance with me, now, when I'm only eighteen, Mister Ashby?"

"Say 'Alexander' and I'll tell you."

"Alexander."

"Because I know so definitely that I'll want you and only you and nobody but you—when I'm forty-five—that I'm getting myself in training, now. Do you object?"

"No—Alexander."

"Who brought you tonight?"

"Papa."

"Well, I'm taking you home."

"Are you? Does Papa know you?"

"Of course he does, and I know 'Lije, too. Ever hear 'em speak of me?"

"Papa never talks about medical students, and 'Lije always talks about himself."

Alex laughed heartily, and Margaretta, slightly ashamed, changed the subject.

"Where do you live?"

"At Miss Susie Slagle's. Do you know her?"

"Of course! She made the cap we all wore when we were baptized, and I think she *is grand*."

"She certainly is."

"And she's the only person Mamma is jealous of. Papa just worships her."

"So do I. And now that Miss Susie has made me acceptable, Ladykins—I'm taking you home."

"Couldn't you ask me—if I'm willing for you to?" she gave him a sudden coy glance.

"No!" Alex said and drew her to him tenderly. They danced in silence for some seconds, then leaning downward so that his words just lay within her small ear, he whispered, "Will you permit Alexander to care about you *before* he's forty-five, Ladykins?"

"Do you really want to?"

"I do."

"Then say it in both ears, so it will meet in my head and I'll know you mean it."

As Alex obeyed, he folded her closely in his arms, they took a deep breath together and spun away into a gliding waltz.

"Did it meet in your head?"

"Yes," she whispered.

"I'm coming to see you, often—whenever you'll let me."

"I'm a freshman at Goucher College all week."

"But there are Saturdays and Sundays."

Sudden lilting laughter filled his ears, and he knew and she knew that he had her permission to come as often as he liked.

The music of the three-piece orchestra swelled toward a finale as Ashby asked quietly, "Happy, Ladykins?"

Margaretta, her face unguarded, innocent and lovely, lifted her eyes toward his shining gray ones and answered, "Entirely, Alexander."

Then with an utterly sweet little gesture, she nestled her head against his chest and Alex led her through a swerving, swinging, satisfying series of circles as the music increased its beat and finally faded away.

Chapter Ten

HERALD ANGELS SING

"And still their heavenly music floats,
O'er all the weary world."

Throughout the hospital, down corridors, into laboratories, penetrating kitchens, filling waiting rooms, suffusing a thousand memories, resting a thousand hearts, the music of the negro choir came. As a consequence, it was as though all things seen had fallen away and all things unseen—those hidden centers of real life—were revealed in every passing face.

Dr. Elijah Howe stepped into a darker corner of the ward corridor and relaxed his world-envied, dexterous fingers against his thighs. The lids descended over his eyes and a deep peace bathed his features as he listened motionlessly, avidly, shamelessly.

In a linen closet nearby, an elderly Supervisor of nurses wept into a bed blanket; cried for "Chris'mus Gif'" upon Thousand Oaks plantation, for the taste of sugar cane, the blue veins of her mother's placid hand, the new red rocking chair and the little girl who sat in it. She wept so silently that the notes of "Climbin' Up de Golden Stair" sifted through the cracked door and into her lonely heart.

Further down the corridor an orderly from Dublin, homesick because it was Christmas Eve, gave his head a startled jerk; then an Irish lake reflected in his eyes and the eagerness of a pilgrim broke through his hard features.

On the floor below a Chinese interne, with a precision denoting immense surprise, ceased to move. His imperturbable eyes grew black with pleasure. His face was still waxen, but spreading into it was a slow realization of beauty. Distant beauty toward which, as soon as he had accustomed himself, he must move. Their talk of their Christmas and then their failure to worship Their Shrine had strained his cloak of politeness, but this exquisite melody floating

160

down the concrete stairway, gold-flecking the last moments of a bitter twilight, was like a forgotten vision from the Great Wall.

In an ascending elevator the old operator, Thomas, tilted his ebony head and nodded his approbation; then his face clouded and he looked with astonishment at his only passenger, Dean Wingate. Had he forgotten his usual Christmas tip? Apparently he had for the Dean's eyes were shut and as the notes reached his ears, a relaxation resembling sleep spread over his fearless features.

Half a block away in the lobby of the Administration Building, beyond the marvelous melody, Ben Mead stood chatting with Prentiss. Pug was watching the last pale daylight touch the fingers of the outstretched hands of that immense marble statue of Christ which stands in the cross-corridors. The inscription upon the base shone clearly in the waning light:

"Come unto me all ye that are weary and heavy laden and I will give you rest."

At the moment, they were alone in the lobby and a hasty flinging of the front door of the hospital, a sense of bustle preceding an entrance made them turn. They saw a buxom, black negress, in a fur coat and her third pregnancy, toiling up the inside steps. Beside her walked the first child, aged about five, clothed in a ragged gingham dress, a sagging sweater and high shoes without laces. She had no hat and her black fingers clutched the hem of her mother's coat. The second child lay contentedly against the woman's breast, indistinguishable in a dirty pink blanket.

The negress gasped with indecision, saw the students and smiled benignly. Ben Mead recognized her, not by sight, but by the three golden upper teeth an instructor had mentioned, inadvertently, when discussing her case history.

"Isn't your name Verbena?" Ben asked.

The negress replied with an almost imperceptible nod.

And suddenly Pug Prentiss understood the psychology of the negro race, for the oldest child saw Jesus and as naturally as we might raise our hand, ran forward and kissed His feet. Then turning to her mother, she demanded, "Whar's Gawd?"

"Ressin Hisself!" the mother's voice carried finality.

With polite obeisance, she continued to Ben Mead, "Docta, I don't 'member you, but 'nyhow c'n you please, suh, tell me whar de choir is?"

"What?"

"De chech choir, whut sings in de hosbittle et Chris'mus. Howcum you kno'ed my name and ain't kno'ed dat? I jined again afta dis baby, Jehu, was bawn. Dey sings in de Woman's Wards. I *kno'* dey sings in de Woman's Wards!"

Her conviction was vocal, but with its reverberation upon her own eardrums decision came, and Gawd's Chillun passed on into the main corridor of the hospital.

"Gee," Ben said a sudden light breaking over his face. "So she's that Verbena, too! Cummon, Pug, you'll want to hear this. And I'll tell you afterward how it began."

Ahead in the twilit corridor, they could see Jehu's mother ambling along. Slightly behind her, flopped the first child. Her little pigtails were electrified with an emotion transcending imagination. Through open doors, past wheel chairs, to and fro, into Thomas's elevator, awed and eager ranged her chinquapin eyes.

Arriving upon the floor from whence the golden voices came, Jehu's mother deposited him in the arms of the first student nurse she passed, and maternity gave 'way to melody. But the face of the first child never altered. She peered expectantly into every bed:

"Gawd was ressin Hisself," and she was looking for Him!

Harmony and the soprano of Jehu's mother swept through that ward of ill negro women as the leader of the choir, an elderly negro —tall, resolute, square-built and regal—admitted the late member with a curt nod. The wonderful cadence of his gigantic bass beat relentlessly on.

Behind him Mary Alice tilted her head in approbation at the arrival of her daughter-in-law, and her worn jacket filled with effortless joy as her contralto burst forth:

> "Sinnahs do y'u luv yo' Jedus,
> Sinnahs do y'u luv yo' Jedus,
> Sinnahs do y'u luv yo' Jedus,
> Soldiahs—of—de—Cross?"

Pug Prentiss standing among the growing crowd opposite the choir recalled a phrase a famous teacher had once told him: "If you doubt the goodness of human nature study it relaxed—if fortune ever allows you the opportunity—in the mass."

Relaxed it stood in the persons of doctors whose names are revered around the world, relaxed it lay in these wilted, wan women, relaxed it sang and through its relentless rhythm spread into this heterogeneous audience a beauty individual, indiscreet, and almost unearthly.

The thirty voices of that negro choir transported the twenty hearts of the desolated patients into Their Father's House in the twinkling of an eye; through spiritual after spiritual, Prentiss caught phrases which left any man trembling—"Dig my grave with a silver spade"— "Lay me down with a golden chain"—"To wake a nation underground"— The spiritual in which that line occurred killed his critical faculty. The leader's bass took up:

> "Y'u heah de trumpet soun'
> To wake a nation unda'groun'
> Lookin' to My Gawd's right han'
> When—de—stars—begin—to—fall."

Then the choir burst into:

> "My Lawd whut a mawnin',
> My Lawd whut a mawnin',
> My Lawd whut a mawnin',
> When—de—stars—begin—to—fall."

Faith! A hope beyond our present, a better future toward which wearily we stagger. To those who dreaded death, to those who saw it day after day, to the patients and the doctors and the nurses now crowding the ward and the corridor, that negro choir revealed:

> "Ezekiel saw de wheel,
> Way up in de middle of de air,
> Ezekiel saw de wheel,
> Up in de middle of de air.
>
> De little wheel moves by faith,
> Way up in de middle of de air,
> De big wheel moves by de grace of Gawd,
> Up in de—middle—of de air."

There was no argument, no dogma, no creed barrier. Race unto race speaketh knowledge. Shelley's moon, the Pleiades, the Wise Men's star, belonged to God and therefore became perfectly touchable to His Chillun. Beyond the declaring heavens the bass led them:

> "Steal away—steal away—
> Steal away to Jedus—
> Steal away—steal away—home,
> I ain't got long t'stay heah—"

Three score years! And frequently before their infirmity, Dr. Howe, the elderly Supervisor and Dr. McMillan who now stood together, had seen hard journeys closed; sometimes in pain, sometimes in fear: but occasionally, as that glorious bass suggested, closed with the same wonder which made the fright of Ezekiel's vision understandable.

> "My Lawd He calls me,
> He calls me by de lightnin'
> De trumpet sounds withina my soul,
> I ain't got long t'stay heah."

And then, as though it had been already given to all of them—that miracle of eternal rest—the choir leader carried his listeners on into heaven. Dr. Howe rumbled deeply, his bass mutterings vying with the Moses-promise in the leader's sonorous cadences.

The pickaninny with the electric pigtails jumped instantly onto a chair and fastened her gaze upon Dr. Howe. Her popping eyes never wavered.

The promised land began to vista out:

> "Y'u got a crown
> I got a crown
> All Gawd's chillun
> Got a crown.
> When I git t'Hebben
> Gonna put on my crown
> An' walk all ovah Gawd's Hebben."

Pug Prentiss hummed his into place; Dean Wingate picked his up with his baritone; Ben Mead and Dr. McMillan adjusted theirs with their tenors and the tremulous soprano of the Supervisor added a sweet note which was smothered by Dr. Howe's "HEBBEN."

Mary Alice reached swiftly forward from her end-row position in the choir and hissed to her grandchild, "Git off'n dat cheer!"

The pickaninny never moved. She never heard her.

As the spiritual ceased, the Supervisor said, "Let's finish with 'Hark the Herald Angels Sing,' please."

Ever since the choir began singing in the hospital at Christmas, Mary Alice had led them in that carol and pride overcame discipline; she forgot her grandchild and enticed them out of heaven into an earthly Christmas Eve.

As the choir and the audience and the patients began that carol, the Chinese interne began to smile. The terrible beauty of the spirituals had relaxed his age-old reserve. Prentiss eased toward an eastern window and his heart lifted with the music as he saw that snowflakes were falling.

Jehu's mother, her voice wild with joy, took up the "God and sinner reconciled" and stroked her fur coat, contentedly.

Dr. Howe's deep bass rumbled on——

The wondering gaze of the pickaninny never shifted from his face. She had found God——

Half an hour later up a Broadway fast whitening with snow, Ben and Pug walked toward Miss Susie's house. Ben said, "They say that the negroes began singing in the hospital at Christmas as the result of an accident."

"How, Ben? What do you mean?"

"Well, a September afternoon some years ago, two negroes working on an ice cream truck—a man about forty-nine and a boy about nineteen—had a fight over a colored girl named Verbena. Yeah, the same one I spoke to. Supposedly, Verbena was the property of the man, but Jehu, the boy, had bought her a pair of red satin slippers. He and the man had what niggers call 'words' and when they stopped at a filling station for gas, the man turned the hose on Jehu, while the proprietor wasn't looking. He was bull-mad, I guess, 'cause then he threw a lighted match on that boy.

"When they brought Jehu into the accident room only his feet, covered with high shoes, and his kinky hair, covered with his cap, were unburned. Over two-thirds of his body area was burned. Some of it third degree, too. Nobody thought he'd live.

"His mother, Mary Alice—that contralto in the choir—reached the hospital almost as soon as the ambulance arrived with Jehu. Niggers, you know, have a funny grapevine. He was so horrible to look at they wouldn't let her see him, and she caused such a furor that they had to put her out. But at the accident room door she turned to the surgical resident and said ominously, 'Ah done ast Docta Jedus t'watch you.'"

Prentiss whistled appreciatively.

Ben continued, "And it was like a curse, somehow. Everybody worked to save Jehu more than if he'd been the President. Cases in which over two-thirds of the body area is burned hardly ever recover; especially if much of it is third degree and his was. Just the same, though, they jammed Jehu full of liquids, and put him in circulating tubs every few hours and——"

"How did they lift him, Ben?"

"By his ruff of hair and by his feet. They were the only unburned parts. The way people worked over him is tradition, almost. He was painted with gentian violet, fed intravenously, put under a light cradle and it was weeks and weeks before anybody thought he had any chance, whatever.

"And when he continued to live in spite of all predictions, the whole hospital grew interested. Everybody became fond of his mother, Mary Alice, too. He was always pretty sick but one day when they thought he was going out they sent for her, and she walked right up to the bed and said to that bandaged little charcoal, 'Baby, Ah gwine bring yuh a stalk ob sugar cane in de mawnin'.'

"They were Louisiana niggers, Pug, and some of her relatives had sent her some sugar cane, but Jehu was running such a temperature that nobody thought he'd live to have the juice from it. Then after she had promised him the sugar cane, Mary Alice rolled her eyes heavenward and said, 'Jedus-Gawd, holt onto him!' and went home.

"Her Rabelaisian body and her reverential mind brought humor, wild, negroid and childlike, into the hard routine and hidden fright of the people watching over Jehu. Her gratitude and faith, I guess, did all of 'em good. Niggers are like that, you know.

"Infection or pneumonia in those cases is what frightens you and either seemed imminent that night. The interne, and the resident, the private nurse, the floor nurse and the Supervisor—that old one who was up at the singing today—practically held an all night reception over him. But the next morning, Mary Alice came trudging in with the sugar cane and in a few days Jehu had some of the juice!

"He had crisis after crisis and his temperature chart looks like a mountain range—all peaks. I'll show you his case history some time; I've just been reading it in connection with a burned case I'm—er, working on, and Dr. McMillan was telling us all of the fine points the other day.

"As the months rolled on and Jehu continued to live, they decided to try skin grafting on him. Lord! He got nursing! People say that the nurses were as fond of him as if he'd been a kitten, and the doctors were as proud of him as if he'd been a bird dog. In a way he was their own special cinder into whom they were blowing life, again.

"And—er, I sound kind of maudlin, I reckon ——"

"If you told this story without emotion I'd never speak to you again. Where does the choir come in? And what happened to Jehu?"

"Mary Alice is responsible for the choir," Ben said. "She began bringing them on Sunday afternoons to sing to Jehu and the other ward patients. Sneaked 'em in one Sunday and after that nobody could do without them. You heard 'em and—*can* they sing!"

"You bet they can! Did Jehu get well?"

"Eventually by pinch grafting and warm salt solution compresses, and a couple of full thickness and a Thiersch graft, Jehu was repaired. They gave him new eyelids and a new nose, among other things."

"What do you mean—a new nose, Ben?"

"Just what I say: a new nose. Loosened some skin from the left shoulder and brought it around to make the nose. Has to stay attached to the shoulder, as well as the face, for two weeks while it granulates. The left shoulder must remain in practically the same position during that time and the dressings must be saturated with absolute regularity. Tricky work—all of it. I guess that nigger is the prettiest piece of plastic surgery alive.

"Seems that he was dismissed on Christmas Eve and ever since, each Christmas Eve, Mary Alice brings her choir to sing in the hospital.

"But upon the Christmas Eve when he was dismissed, Florence Nightingale's descendants and the Sons of Hippocrates saw—actually saw—Jehu walk past the statue of Jesus out of the hospital. Beside him walked Verbena and she wore red satin slippers."

Chapter Eleven

LIFE IS FINE

Alone outside the main entrance of the hospital, a student nurse stood trembling. Her milk-white skin, blue eyes and red-gold hair were invisible in the darkness. Underneath the blue cape, her willowy body turned taut with the weight of the delivery bags drawing at her shoulder muscles. Her nose, which looked brand new, and the mouth to which nothing had happened—yet—lost their frightened air as she tilted her chin and decided, "Shucks! There's no sense being scared! Last thing before going to bed I read over the entire chapter on externe O-B. First ask the patient about her pains. Then clear the room of people; and if you have time, get hot water, prepare the patient, time the pains. Probably I've got the jumps because the cases I saw in the hospital were primiparas or abnormal. Our home deliveries are normal cases!"

Two headlights drew a semi-circle against the hospital fence, and an old Ford roadster rattled up the driveway. A long-legged young man swung out and leaped toward the doorway. The nurse stepped from the shadows.

"Are you——?"

Alex Ashby halted, took off his hat and when his eyes focused he whistled once, long and softly. Then he said, "I am. Come on!"

When she heard his voice, the girl ceased trembling.

"Give me those bags!" he ordered. "Mind climbing over the door? It's got adhesions." And when the car began clanking down the hill he asked, "Know where we're going?"

"Yes, I do. 1035 Dallas Street. Flossie Johnson."

His voice imitated hers, "Multipara. Negress. Been out before?"

"No."

"Afraid?" his word was almost a caress. This time her "No" was firmer. Ashby laughed. "If you continue saying 'yes' with 'no' you'll scare me, too."

Her defiance crumbled. "Oh, please, she might die if you were scared!"

"Gee, little girl, you are frightened! Forget it! I've been out before. Matter of fact, I spent part of last summer in the O-B service. Go off my externe work tomorrow. Just put in some hours studying Flossie's case history. She'll be all right."

The nurse said apologetically, "I've never been out at night when a city's asleep like this. Perhaps that has something to do——"

"Perhaps. Partly my fault, too. I was late. Liddie-P had gone dry and—I—I beg your pardon!"

The girl laughed. "Is that what you call her?"

"So her owner says. I borrowed her. The compound says a baby a bottle and Liddie can deliver one every trip! You didn't get cold waiting, did you?"

"Nnuh. It was fun, sort of. Having the stars to myself——"

"I know! I've felt that way summers riding the range down in Texas."

"Are you from Texas?"

"Yes. Been to Texas?"

"No, but I like horses."

"Then, you'll have to see Texas, Miss—er—er."

"What do you think it should be?"

"Let's make it Princess, because nothing scares princesses! Have you a home, Princess?"

"Not a real one."

"I'm sorry. Haven't you even a parent?"

"A father, but he married again. So I came in training."

"Oh!" Alex's voice carried sympathy.

"Why did you go into medicine, Doctor Texas?"

"No, not doctor—yet. And not Texas. Alexander Ashby, to be exact."

"I'd be exact with anything as beautiful as that name."

"Thank you, little lady!"

"You're welcome. Now, why did you go into medicine?"

"To get a chance to ride around in old Fords with fairy princesses between midnight and dawn."

"Please, Mister Ashby, don't tease me! By the way, that sign says 'Dallas Street'!"

"Dallas Street? How does Dallas Street concern us, Princess?"

"Don't you remember? Dallas Street is the street where Flossie Johnson lives. The street where you and I——"

"Are going to forget to be afraid," Alex said as he swung the car about. "1035, wasn't it?"

"Yes. That's a fine phrase—'forget to be afraid'—I'll remember it all my life."

"Then I won't need a tombstone. Any numbers ahoy, Princess?"

"We just passed 807."

"Should be two blocks further down, then." The Ford rattled sociably along. "Any more numbers, Princess? Probably aren't any more. Do you know what stage she was in?"

"No, I don't. First, I think."

"Then we should have plenty of time, still, with niggers you never can tell. I'll park Liddie here. You knock at the shanties across the street, I'll take those on this side. Quickest way to find her highness." The old Ford wheezed to a halt. The night seemed thick and liquid.

"What shall I do with the bags?"

"You take one, Princess, I'll carry the other. Can't chance having them snitched." Ashby climbed over the door and helped her from the car. "Say, are you trembling again?"

"No."

"All right?"

"Yes, I am." Her voice was very firm.

"I'm glad you are," he replied gravely. "Take the flashlight and don't go into any house without me."

The girl had the sensation of being watched by many unseen eyes as she knocked upon the flimsy white door of a two-story brick squatting. There was no answer. She lifted the heel of her low black oxford and rapped with it. A feeling of eyes above as well as behind came over her. The sliding of a window shutter made her step back and look up. In the distance she heard Ashby's voice. She raised her own.

"Anybody here?"

The shutter closed stealthily. There was muffled whispering. Then it flung back with a bang and a deep female voice, as powerful as the dark, descended.

"Who dat?"

"It's—are you having a baby?"

" 'Deed, Lawd, I ain't. Dat is—not as I kno's—I ain't!"

"I'm the nurse from the hospital," the girl said apologetically. "Does Flossie Johnson——?"

The negro woman leaned forward. "Two houses up dataway. Yassum. Two houses. You want me to go wid you, chile?"

"No. No, thank you. I have the doctor."

To persuade the negro in the designated house to unlock the door, Ashby turned the flashlight upon the uniformed nurse. The colored man saw that they were neither cops nor night-doctors, and while he fumbled with the lock, Alex shined the light toward the girl again and said, "Blue! Gee, Princess, how many years have you had 'em?"

"Nineteen," she laughed softly.

The negro pulled the door inward; the student doctor and the student nurse stepped into the room. A kerosene lamp sputtered on the shelf over the table. The room contained one double bed and two pallets. Upon the pallets were huddled two pickaninnies with staring eyes. Around the bed stood three negro women moaning and praying. Flossie lay in a deathlike relaxation. The student nurse thought, "She's dead!" and then, "Clear the room!" She tried to open her lips, but Ashby's voice filled the pain-laden atmosphere.

"I'm the doctor. You women take those children to your houses and put them to bed, please. And don't come back into this room, unless I send for you."

The negresses began backing respectfully away from the bed. Ashby ignored their retreat, "John, build a fire in the kitchen stove right away. We'll need plenty of hot water."

The negro man's face worked, "I ain't got no wood, Docta. I——"

Ashby moved toward the patient, but his words were directed to the other women. "One of you take the children. One go home and bring enough wood to keep the fire up all the rest of the night. And the other one get all the large-sized kettles in the neighborhood and keep them on the stove, please."

Three obedient, "Yassuhs," and the women and children hustled toward the door. The nurse turned to the negro man, "May I have three chairs, please?"

"I ain't got but one, miss."

"I has two," one of the women said.

"John, go get them," Ashby ordered. "Then build the fire and start heating the water."

"Yassuh, Docta, I is."

After they were gone, in the same authoritative tone Ashby asked, "Flossie, where is your other lamp?"

The patient replied calmly, "Behindst de playa pi-ana. Ovah in dat corna', suh. I keeps hit fur 'casions."

"Well, this is an occasion!"

" 'Deed hit is, Docta!" Flossie grinned; then she realized that she was "actin' " too well. Her great body heaved. "Jedus— Ho, Jedus!"

"Have a pain?" the nurse asked.

The woman wilted into suffering, "Yassum. A big un!"

Ashby held high the freshly lighted lamp, picked up two packing boxes, set them on end beside the bed and put the lamp upon them.

"Flossie, you've had other babies. How you gettin' on?"

"Hit'll be plenty ob time, Docta, fur a bed-bath an' one ob dem akahull rubs, too."

Alex laughed, "Got some alcohol, Miss—er—Nurse?"

Five minutes later, the student nurse's equipment had been laid out upon the chairs according to the order prescribed in the O-B text book. The girl had washed her hands, put on her white gown and was beginning to do the routine preparations upon the patient prior to giving a sponge bath.

"Call me if you need me. I'll be by the kitchen stove," Ashby said.

His executive ability had brought to the nurse a sudden confidence; she no longer felt frightened for the Supervisor and the Assistant Resident to come tomorrow and check their work.

Between pains, the negro woman enjoyed all of the luxuries and inconveniences of modern hospital technique. The girl was too busy to think. Her fine white hands flew with a precision which would have delighted her superiors. She comforted, rubbed, examined, crooned. Everything was going to be all right. Negro women were so appreciative and wise. They knew how to use their pains.

One of the women brought a kettle of hot water and the student nurse prepared to give the patient the sponge bath. As the water cooled in the covered kettle, she checked her equipment and sent the woman for a market basket. While she was gone the girl gave the patient the sponge bath, remade her bed with the tight sheet, the oil cloth, the draw sheet, and placed the thicknesses of old newspapers covered with old muslin. All of this equipment she took from her bags. Next she put upon Flossie's legs a pair of white cotton hospital stockings and upon her body a hospital nightgown. The patient enjoyed every movement of the girl's hands. Every timing of the pains.

Occasionally she moaned, "Oh, Gawd! Do, Jedus!"

The woman returned with the market basket. The student nurse took a pillow from one of the pallets, eyed it gingerly, then covered it with a hospital blanket and put it into the basket. She also took from her bags a hot-water bottle. This she filled and tucked into a fold of the blanket. Then she checked again the doctor's instruments, his gown, his gloves and began to scrub her own hands and prepare to finish cleansing the patient. One of the lamps sputtered and went out. The woman who had brought the basket, and sat unnoticed on one of the now rolled-up pallets, rose and carried it from the room.

With the lessening of the light the cold seemed to gain headway. The girl was not aware that there was now only one lamp and that it was beginning to flicker. She was not aware that she was cold. She was only aware that she was beginning to be frightened. Desperately frightened and that something was about to happen. That she needed——

The patient began to cry softly with animal pain. The girl tried to fill the air with words, "Flossie! Are you all right, Flossie?"

The remaining lamp went out, and in the darkness, the nurse ran toward the kitchen door and screamed, "Alexander Ashby—come quick!"

She had wiped her dripping hands on her white apron, but for the next twenty minutes that was of no consequence for as soon as Ashby saw the situation he ordered, "Go over to my overcoat, get my flashlight and hold it! Hold it steady, Princess. Everything's here, isn't it? Good girl!

"All right, Flossie. All right. The doctor's come. Wait till I wash my hands and get my gloves on, Flossie. Hold that pain—just a minute. Hold it, Flossie."

At three A.M., above the din of Liddie's rattles, Ashby asked, "What was that street sign?"

The nurse did not answer. He glanced toward her and under the glare of a street lamp saw that the tears were falling off her chin and onto the buttons of her cape.

"Princess! Why, Princess!"

His soothing voice brought the sobs.

"That's all right, honey. You just cry!" Alex steered the car into a dark alley and switched off the lights. Then he put his arm around the girl and asked gently, "Were you so very frightened, lady? You never showed it. You were fine straight through! You never allowed that light to waver an inch. You mustn't be frightened. That's life and life is—fine!"

She buried her face in his upper arm and sobbed uncontrollably. Bitter, racking sobs through which the words jumped and stung, "Oh, no, I—I think it's terrible. Life's ugly! I don't see why women ever——"

"Ever what, Princess?"

"Ever have babies and tear and nearly die. I thought she was going to die when— And there wasn't any gas or ether, just nothing we could do. Life's not fine. It's—it's a trap!"

"Lord, you are young," Alex said and laughed suddenly. "Listen, Princess, when you find the person you really love you'll see. Life's fine, then—very fine."

His words stung her pride. She drew primly over into her own corner of the seat.

"I'm sorry I was hysterical."

"Aw, forget it!" Alex answered. He understood that she had cried herself out and talked herself out and that silence was the most acceptable thing he had to offer.

A few minutes later each window of the looming hospital seemed to that student nurse opened and aware of her self-disgust. As the automobile halted in front of the main entrance she said, "You won't tell anybody?"

"Of course not!"

Then, with a bag in each hand, she ran up the steps and shoved in the swinging door. Alex saw that she did not look back.

After he had returned Liddie and was walking toward Miss Susie's he wondered why he was so depressed and had been for days. The nurse's hysterics weren't responsible. Poor kid! Life was tough when you had a preview, and were a woman. He'd been depressed though before she went to pieces. Why? Margaretta sounded all right over the telephone yesterday afternoon; with his father no news was good news, he never wrote except to send remittances. Since the only two people he really cared about were all right, what was it that had him so down? Exams were over and he'd come out fine. Maybe he was catching cold, or just tired. Come to think about it, he'd snatched a quick dinner at Otto's, read Flossie's case history, gone out on her delivery and not been home since breakfast. Now, there would be time for some sleep before breakfast.

The night light burned in Miss Susie's hall. Alex eased open the front door and tiptoed in; then automatically lifted the letter on the hatrack and found it addressed to himself. The handwriting was that of Jim Peters, the foreman on his father's ranch. He had received the quarter remittance from his father three weeks ago, why was Jim writing?

Alex settled in a morris chair in the parlor, turned on a lamp and opened the envelope. The still house, the furniture, even the air, seemed to be waiting for the letter to emerge. A cashier's check fell out, and without looking at it, for Ashby had suddenly become frightened, he stuffed it into his pocket. Then he unfolded the lined sheet of tablet paper and the labored ink words of the letter began to stand out:

Ashby's Ranch, Texas.
February 18th, 1914.

Dear Alex,

I never seen an Ashby yet who couldn't take it straight. Your Father died two weeks ago tonight. He was riding the south fence on Proxy when he keeled over with a heart attack. Him and me went to a doctor in San Anton last month—he's been having 'em since September. Made me swear not to tell you. The doctor said he could last ten years if he took care of himself and rested. Old Alex said he'd rather be dead.

When he keeled over Proxy brought him in and he lived about three hours. Spent most of 'em giving me instructions. Said it was your examination time and made me promise not to tell you for two weeks. In a way it's a good thing for him that he went. The last two years has been pretty bad for ranchers and the King Brothers would have taken him over March 1st, but he wouldn't let anybody tell you last summer how things stood. They'd of paid him a salary to run his own ranch. I'm glad he's gone. Enclosed is a cashier's check for $2000. They was the gold pieces your Mother made him bury. He told me afore he died to dig 'em up and get this check. He figgered it would see you through. If it don't King's paying me enough to let you have $50 a month.

Now listen, Alex, there ain't any use in you coming back to Texas till you're useful. I buried him beside her and got his books and saddle in the bunkhouse, along with her furniture. I'll keep 'em till you want 'em.

Having you left did a lot to make him happy. He was mighty proud of you. The last thing he said was "Tell Alex the Ashbys ain't afraid." God knows he never was.

His friend and yours,
Jim Peters.

The letter slipped to the floor unnoticed, and the old familiar objects —Queen Victoria's picture, Miss Susie's sampler, the Christmas-tree bird—stood by and accepted the knowledge as Ashby said, "My father's dead. Been dead—three weeks!"

At the sound of his own words, his eyes swam with tears and his mind became paragraphed with pictures. He saw his mother the day she had made his father bury that two thousand dollars as penitence money for cutting off his own curls. He was only four then, but he could see right now the way she had stiffened, like a fresh lace curtain, at the sight of his haircut and then, without warning, burst out crying. Two thousand dollars! But that year Old Alex had come back from Kansas City with twenty thousand.

Then the years between the curl-cutting and his first long pants rose in his memory—his first pony—the *Encyclopedia Britannica* for his tenth birthday—the tooled leather saddle from Mexico City. The phrases of his father became honeycombed in the scenes. "Kill that snake, son, don't be afraid. Ashbys ain't afraid— Ride him, Alex, stick on his back!—If you hit that target forty times, I'll give you four dollars— What do you think of those cows? What's your opinion of that pasture?"

Lord, how Old Alex could ride!—"Here come the Ashbys!"— In sight of the ranch porch, they always threw their hats in the air and hallooed those words to his mother.

The way his father insisted on saying "ain't" had been another of his forms of teasing her. Over and over the summer that the three of them went abroad he'd say, "Ain't anything in Europe to touch Texas. Ain't it so, Alex?"

On the way back they had taken him to Sewanee, and his mother talked Europe with her cousins while his father took him to the Vice-Chancellor.

"He's a good judge of cows, and can shoot straight, Bishop, but he don't know much Latin. His name's Alex—as usual."

The following summer, when he was sixteen, on his first vacation from Sewanee, he and his father had stood by—a hundred miles from a doctor—and watched his mother choke to death with diphtheria. That night decided him to be a doctor. He never wanted to be so helpless again.

Now, he could see what his decision must have cost his father. Blood had meant a lot to him. The things he'd said that summer after she was dead and they rode side by side kept ringing in his son's head now— "The most expensive thing a fellow can buy is favors— The way to keep a secret is to swallow it— A man's happiness comes out of his emotions. But when he trades on his emotions for material advancement he wins to lose. Son, don't you ever forget that— You've got blood, Alex, fine blood. Blood tells in cattle and in crises. There's been an Ashby in every war this country ever fought. We Ashbys have seen a lot. We've been poor and lived through it; we've been defeated and risen again. The only thing we don't do is to marry before we can support a wife. The kind of women we love will wait."

Alex's mind shifted to the picture which Jim's letter had evoked. He could see his father riding the south fence, where he knew every hummock, every post, and see his gray-blue eyes narrow, his firm jaw tighten as his eye sliced over the land. Old Alex loved that land— every square mile of it.

Ashby's head dropped into his hands and he stifled a moan. Probably the realization that the King Brothers would own it was what had really killed him. Sometimes a little cash, no matter how you stood on paper, could save things, for a breathing spell. Perhaps if he had used that two thousand dollars— But how like him to stand steady to the promise he had made his wife that it was his son's money! How like him to die alone and give his son a free mind through exams! And how like him to say "ain't"— "Tell Alex the Ashbys ain't afraid."

Alex saw that the letter was wet with his own tears. He picked it up and carefully put it into his pocket. And the memory of the cashier's check cut him back into his present problems. He didn't want to face them in this room. It wasn't decent to let other things come between him and these memories.

He went into the hall again, picked up his hat and overcoat and slipped out of the front door toward Broadway. Before morning he knew that he must make up his mind how to face this. Must he keep it to himself, or let other people know?

He was on the boulevard pathway and walking toward the harbor before things began to clear in his head. Yesterday, he'd thought that his father was alive and well and that he owned two counties in Texas. Tonight he knew that his father was dead and that he owned two thousand dollars. Those were the facts, but what did they mean to his future?

They didn't frighten him. He could meet them provided nobody sympathized with him—or—or pitied him. The one thing to avoid was pity. The last thing in the world he wanted was to cash in on pity. So long as he kept his mouth shut nobody, at Hopkins, would know either that his father was dead or that he was broke. Since his father only wrote at quarter remittances, it would be easy to say that he'd sent the money by the half year, if Miss Susie questioned him. Thank God he'd written every week—and thank God he hadn't told Old Alex about Margaretta. Because now, he'd have seen as clearly as he, himself, saw, that he'd have to give her up.

She was the one person in the world he wanted to tell, and therefore from now on she was the one person he must not permit himself to see. Old Alex was right! A man couldn't trade on his emotions for material advancement, and if Gret knew, she'd try to get her father to use his influence to get him an internship at Hopkins. Any loyal woman would. No! The way to do was to tell nobody. He had been and he could continue to be first in his class. Then using his record, he'd go to New York next summer and try to sign up with the Rockefeller. They didn't take many men until after graduation, but being first at Hopkins ought to have some value. Anyhow syphilis was what he wanted to go on in, he thought, and their work in syphilis was outstanding. If he applied to them first, then the Hopkins staff—McMillan, Wingate and Howe—would recommend him without realizing that he needed the fellowship for pocket money. What he wanted to be certain about was that he got his appointment on merit—not on pity, or on sex-pull. After it was a certainty—along about October, say—it would be all right to go to see Margaretta, and tell her—tell her everything.

Tell her that now he couldn't marry for ten years, probably. Tell her that he never wanted to come back to Hopkins on anybody's pull. But until he could open his mouth entirely on his own merit, he'd better not trust himself, he'd better not see her.

When the dawn came it was gray and weary. It revealed the ugly row houses in frames of gray black light. It took all the leafless trees and smothered their fine limb fibers with fog. Through its long thick waste the heavy streetcars clanged; the hoofs of the milk-wagon horses and the corresponding clink of the bottles were hollow and discordant. They labored along and made a loud noise. The papers the newsboys slung upon the miles of white stone steps were limp when they landed. As the minutes wore on, there was no sensation of lifting, no change in the heavy breath of the fog. It closed, oppressed and widened.

Four times from the foot of Broadway to North Avenue, Alex Ashby walked fighting the same battle over the same ground where many another poor young doctor has trod.

When he returned to Miss Susie's his mind ached, his body ached and his soul ached. For the next ten days he lay ill, ostensibly ill with the "flu."

Chapter Twelve

AND SO IS DEATH

The first Sunday afternoon Ashby was up, he refused all invitations to poker parties and gab-fests and went for a walk. He went alone, purposely, for he wanted to test his strength and also to destroy the note which the student nurse had written him apologizing for her instability. Now that he felt so much older, he was sorry that he had told her that life was fine.

The attack of "flu" which followed his decisions had left him spiritually shaken and bereft. As he walked down Broadway, the ground was still covered with patches of ice and piles of dirty snow filled the flower beds. Although it was early March, the earth was as dreary as his thoughts—melancholy and running into gray and black landscapes. Even the unleafed branches of the tall trees, instead of being etched against the sky were as black as cobwebs against a dirty wallpaper. He wanted to see Margaretta badly; he missed her more as time went on.

Except for an intangible odor of spring which could only be ascertained through his nostrils, his fatigue would have driven him back; but no emotional crisis ever kills one's sense of smell. And young blood and new odors have forever understood each other.

Then, too, in that warm breath of sudden spring there was a faint tinge which reminded him of some flower of the Texas plain; of some blue blossom in that profusion of spring covering which ran for miles and miles in all directions and which from the back of a horse mingled with horizon and vied with the heavens. What was it? Wild bluebells? Texas bluebuttons?

He tilted his hat over his eyes and narrowed them. And unconsciously his body fell into its old jauntiness. The odor seemed to pull his nostrils forward; it became stronger with his steps. But what in the wide world——?

And then he forgot it altogether, for a cardinal lit upon the low branch of a tree just ahead, and Alex Ashby stood in his tracks and drank its color. Pictures, sunsets, cities at night—all forms of color— had for this man a fascination which amounted almost to a sensual sensation. Their gradations and their toning could set his every fiber atingle. This fine vivid painfulness of red was like only one thing in the world, was associated in his mind with only one sight beside that of a cardinal.

What sight?

Ah, he had it! An autopsy. Only in an autopsy did one get such vital beauty. Only in an autopsy. Alex's eyes began to explore his whereabouts and he found that he was within a block of the autopsy room. A sudden desire to go back, drop in and see if anything were going on, overwhelmed him. That cardinal, in this gray landscape, had been like the profound exquisiteness of organs beneath a dead man's skin; and filled his undetermined footsteps with anticipation and with hope.

The sensation of spring propelled his body, but the sight of the cardinal reawakened his mind.

Up a deserted Monument Street, flat with Sunday despair, he hurried. A streetcar with screechy brakes slid down the long incline. Two dilapidated automobiles rattled after it. In the distance a stooped thin man pushed a baby buggy uphill; beside him trudged an undernourished woman with brave shoulders.

Otherwise the street was empty and sad.

At the door of the pathology entrance Alex found Dan, the autopsy room helper, and Dr. Scott, a research pathologist, who also taught in the medical school. They were smoking and gazing vacantly out upon the grimy street.

"Hello, Ashby," Dr. Scott said in his deep quiet voice. "I'm glad to see you again."

"Thank you, sir. Anything going on, sir?"

Scott flicked his cigarette and his steady clear eyes watched the ashes mingle with the concrete of the hall floor. "Yes, Ashby. Something I think you'd like to see."

Dan lit a new cigarette from the butt of his old one and grinned acknowledgment of Alex's greeting as he announced, "I'll get along and get things ready, Doc."

Scott nodded his thanks with a graceful gesture and continued to Alex, "Research worker from Toronto University. Down here doing something special with monkeys over in Anatomy. Contracted some kind of virus. Most peculiar symptoms. Came in with a slight fever, which increased. Later developed appearance of polio—infantile paralysis, you know—but it wasn't. Strange! He requested an autopsy. When the paralysis reached the respiratory organs, it was over."

Ashby took his hands from his pockets and slapped them together. "Too bad, sir!"

"Mmm," Scott replied slowly and lifted his head. "Too bad! Well, let's see what we can find out. Twenty-seven years old."

Then he turned and started down the corridor and Alex walked beside him. They were tall, composed and gentle. They might have been Osler's sons. At the door of the autopsy room, the pathologist said suddenly, "Prentiss told me you were sick, Ashby. I missed you."

"Thank you, sir."

"It wasn't much, was it?" Scott's kind eyes met those of the medical student.

"No—" Alex breathed the word, "it ——"

"Well," Scott interrupted straightening his shoulders and moving through the doorway. "There is always medicine. I found that out some years ago. By the way, you are not afraid of this virus, are you?"

"Afraid, sir?"

"The other students seem to be."

With that single sentence, Scott walked over to the far corner and ran his eye over the contents of the culture table. Alex climbed into the "bleachers." His legs were trembling and he felt almost as though he might faint. But neither his illness nor the memory of its cause occasioned his sensations.

In front of him, down by the autopsy table, Dan was sponging and cleaning the equipment. And watching him, Ashby was suddenly conscious that somehow all of this seemed new and knife-edged; this marble table into which over 4,200 autopsies had ground the contour of a man, these two spigots streaming water over its surface, and Dan whose lip muscles, from years of shifting the position of his cigarette while his contaminated hands were occupied, had as much expression as most men grow in a whole face; they were now scissored against his senses as differently and definitely as Westminster Abbey had been in actuality, as compared with his childhood impression. A haze had gone from them, and an understanding of their relation to each other and to him had superseded it.

Behind him, rising and falling above the splash of the water was the conversation of the waiting men. Carlyle, the resident who was to perform the autopsy, said, "Fine brawl, but my feet have killed me all day. Did two this morning and then this came. Had them in salt water when Dan 'phoned."

"You're growing too old for that sort of thing, Will!" Scott remarked.

"Right now, I believe you," Carlyle replied. Then he said over his shoulder, "Want anything, Dan?"

Dan swung his diminutive body past and shot back, "I'm ready. If you ——"

"Certainly," Carlyle answered and they fell into step. Alex Ashby turned around and watched. Directly behind his "bleacher" were two stretchers. Upon one lay the body of a man about sixty, with dough-like features mushed on; but now, surrounded by the casual spit curls in which his damp forehead had nestled, he looked like a sleeping child. Precisely as he must have at six years of age. Only his large purpling feet confirmed his death.

Carlyle gave him a passing stare. "That's the rheumatic heart, isn't it, Dan? I was too busy with his organs to remember his face."

"Yeap." With that single word Dan threw back the sheet from the other body and said, "Feet, Doctor?"

"Yes," Carlyle replied and stepped toward the foot of the stretcher. Dan took a long knife and cut the gauze waist band, and then unwrapped it from the leg, and cut it again, leaving only the small knot around the penis; then he said, "Ready?"

"Ready," Carlyle replied. Dan shifted his cigarette and raised the body under the armpits as Carlyle took the heels of the feet, whose big toes were tied together with gauze bandage, and lifted. From the stretcher to the scales was a distance of about three feet and Carlyle held the body steady, by the toes, while Dan re-mouthed his cigarette and adjusted the weights.

"What is it?"

"Hundred and fifty-eight," Dan peered over his horn-rimmed glasses.

"Humph," Carlyle said.

"Sturdy," Scott remarked to Andrews, the bacteriologist who wore yellow glasses over thick-lensed glasses and perched both pairs casually upon an intelligent, inquiring, understanding face; a little body which didn't matter much held up his intellect, but a long association with death had permeated it with gentle motions.

"I hope the cultures *show* something," Andrews replied fretfully.

Dan and Dr. Carlyle lifted the carcass of the research worker onto the marble table.

With all his new acuteness, Alex Ashby hunched his elbows against the iron bar of the "bleachers" and watched. The man had been a sprinter. Legs like iron, molded by motion, and his chest and torso belonged to a tennis player, not the rangy, but the stocky type. The wooden pillow threw his head backward and accentuated the firm youngness of his jaw, the shortness of his eyebrows which were so new they still lay calmly against his unwrinkled forehead. The mouth, and eyes of course, were closed, and the ears were stuffed with cotton, but the jet black hair still held its unruly cowlicks, and every muscle of the body, even in relaxation, showed determination.

To confirm his estimate of that, Alex sought sight of the hands. They were small-boned, covered with black hair, and the fingernails were cut square. It was the shape of the wrists which showed that he had been a prober, and the width of the fingers which indexed his relentlessness. So vital had this man been that Alex almost expected him to open his eyes and step back again.

It was Carlyle's voice which shattered the illusion: "Right?"

"Right," Dan responded and the long knife penetrated the drab ivory skin under the right armpit and cut, under the nipples and through the black hairs of the chest a semicircle to the left armpit.

And Alex Ashby leaned forward and forgot to breathe. The inch of fat beneath this man's skin was precisely canary yellow. It was like sunshine on egg yolks, and as Carlyle, with Dan's help, rolled upward the semicircle of skin and exposed the ribs, it formed against the red of the muscle a background of unbelievable beauty. Then the long knife ran down the center of the body, shaving past the navel and laying open, beneath the outer surface of black hairs, the golden inner lining. As Carlyle folded back the flaps, that exquisite mauve beauty of the peritoneum was revealed.

"Want to sear this spleen, Doctor Andrews?" Carlyle asked.

The old bacteriologist answered, "Yes, let's take no chances."

Scott took the searing iron from the gas rack, handed it to Carlyle and then prepared the sterile tube and stepped forward. After the culture was in the tube and the tube in its sterile container, Scott passed it to Andrews who held it prayerfully before his eyes, which by their failing sight, gave his face that same fine power into the distance that a life in the constant sun contracts into a man's features.

Carlyle took his long knife and began cutting the cartilage just an inch inside the ribs and outside the sternum. He cut them down, V-shaped, and lifted the V out. Then he grunted, reached under the ribs and lifted out the lungs.

And that ruby redness, which neither precious stones nor man can ever duplicate, swam before Alex's eyes as he thought,

"Lungs. Life. No larger than a hand apiece. Tuberculosis. Not in these—but in an area, when a man speaks of an area he means a small section of one of those organs, no bigger than eight by four inches. Anywhere in the body, that is the way we die. That is what finally gets us—an inch here—there—a stoppage!"

Carlyle had again called for the searing iron and was applying it to the heart of the research worker. Scott was holding the culture tube and old Andrews, over his shoulder, was begging, "Anything—to—SEE?"

And Alex watching them thought, "It may be death, but his relaxation is so complete and so alert, he almost seems to be helping us—to be watching, himself."

Another man had joined the group, the resident in medicine, under whose desperate care the stranger had died a slight three hours before. He was bothered, baffled, beaten and busy. At his appearance, Dan moved back toward the telephone and began taking his calls. Between calls, Dan's stubbed nose twitched incessantly, lifting his slipping glasses into focus again. In his contaminated hands he held the Sunday paper and continued his perusal of world affairs.

The door into the corridor opened. Alex felt the draft and turned around. The man standing inside the doorway said, "Is he ready?"

Dan looked up from his paper and replied cuttingly, "I *told you* he wouldn't be ready till seven-thirty. No, he *ain't* ready. The King of Italy is dead."

The face of the man, which through a lifelong association with utterly inert and relaxed faces had grown blank itself, fell into an expression of irritation. He scoffed, "That's old stuff! *He's* got to make the seven-forty-five to Toronto."

Dan allowed his glasses to slip so far forward that they pointed his nose before he spoke. Then he looked over them and gasped, "I told you seven-thirty, and I *meant* it."

With that dismissal his attention again centered upon the newspaper, and the vacillating undertaker drooped into the corridor and closed the door.

Carlyle began carefully lifting the small intestine and slicing away the fat, and Alex Ashby became seduced by the beauty again. Became drunk with the majesty of man.

"Dead or alive, we are beautiful," he reflected. "The gorgeousness of color of the liver, those lungs nestling their rich redness against the silver grayness of those intestines and the golden beauty of that fat lying upon the old marble table: colors of the interior of the human body excel all other colors because they have a transparency, an illumination, a glory, almost as if the sun were shining through them. An aliveness of tone, a quickness of texture. Yes, that's it: the quick. The quick!"

Trembling with that realization, Alex turned and heard Scott saying in his fine slow voice, "No, Doctor Andrews, there is nothing visible."

But Alex hardly heard him. For invisible, to him, much was present. Later, a gnarled and weeping lady in Canada might request that indecent display which civilized men called a funeral, but now— for these next two hours his body—and the research worker's organs for as long as science survived—belonged to medicine.

Far from home, among total strangers, with his head thrown back and his shapely legs only untouched, this research worker was receiving a tribute which would last forever. In the gracious towering figure of Scott, in the wrinkled fineness of Andrews, in the harassed resident, and the nimble hands of Carlyle, there was a common knowledge. He belongs to us. He belongs to medicine.

But in his young strong body as it lay with all its inner beauty splashed upon that table and placed in pans, from which later it would be put into formalin and turn gray, there seemed to be a questioning. In the way his hands had fallen and his head rested, as though listening, there whispered no acceptance of their tribute, but rather one continuous sentence, "What is it—what did it?"

And the hunching of Andrews's thin shoulders seemed to reply, "We can't tell—yet."

And the soothing movement of Scott's hands fanned through the air, to his eager questioning, "A good pathologist mustn't try to hurry time. Some cultures grow slowly."

When all of his viscera was panned and awaiting examination, Dan suddenly appeared across his body from Carlyle and began applying sponges to the chest cavities. The well-developed legs became circled in jets of red, and Alex Ashby found himself thinking,

"Twenty-eight years ago, a man turned over in bed. A cold winter night ——"

Dan wrung a sponge clean and washed the face of the research worker as gently as a mother washes a baby; then he and Carlyle lifted the body back onto the stretcher, and Scott said to Andrews, "Spinal punctures and a brain puncture, too, Doctor?"

"Everything," Andrews's voice was definite, as they followed the cadaver into the embalming room.

Alex eased around in the "bleachers" and watched. Carlyle and Dan laid the empty body upon the embalming table, and even then, as though he knew precisely what was coming and wanted to help, the boy quietly flopped his hands against his thighs. Dan took a pair of clippers, as large as ice tongs and began clipping out sections of the spine. His glasses and his cigarette accompanied his motions. And Carlyle lifted a section of the scalp, folded it over the features so that the hair made mustaches against the upper lip, as Dan said, "You wanted a pure culture, didn't you? That's why I didn't insert the paraffin into the face, first."

After the spinal punctures were carefully tubed, Dan sawed out a section of the ribs, extracted bone marrow, and then helped Carlyle saw the skull and extract the fluid from the brain. As they were extracting the throat organs, old Andrews and Scott backed into the autopsy room, and waited.

From where Alex stood he could obtain a full view of the whole proceeding. Now, only the fine shapely legs of the young body remained unmutilated. And Alex saw Andrews's eyes go carefully over them, saw his thin old mouth expand but not smile, and overheard him say to Scott, "I understand he was a fine lad."

Scott nodded slowly and replied, "Promising."

The cultures were finished, but the part of him belonging to medicine floated in all its pristine glory, awaiting exploration, in the pans on the top of the table upon which over 4,200 autopsies had been performed.

Two hours later, Alex Ashby swung up Broadway through the clear, crisp night. The stars had come out and denied the drab day.

He was thinking, "In Canada, tomorrow, they'll cover him with snow. But in medicine, forever, he'll live. Through Andrews, through Scott, through me. Death can be fine, anyhow! Very fine!"

Chapter Thirteen

OUT OF DEATH COMES LIFE

After he had finished his work on the remains of the research worker and the undertaker had removed the body, Dan came out of the embalming room. Doctor Scott was checking his cultures, the others had gone.

"Go on out and get your dinner, Doc. I'll stay around till you get back."

"No thanks, Dan. I want to get these cultures started. It will be four or five hours before I'm ready to eat. You go get yours."

Dan shifted the stub of his cigarette and moved over to the scrub-up basin mumbling, "It ain't human for a man as young as you are to spend his nights with stiffs! I'm telling you, Doctor Scotty, when you have been around 'em as long as I have an unexplained death don't amount to nothing—they happen every day—only there ain't many docs with guts enough to admit it."

Scott said nothing. Dan rinsed his hands, picked up a towel and said, "I'll help you take those pans up to your lab, Doc. Do you mind if I switch the 'phone calls there? My wife's having sauerkraut and potato dumplings tonight and I said I'd get home, if I could."

"Go ahead!" Scott urged. They began stacking the pans on a stretcher. Dan switched the 'phone connection, then remarked confidentially, "I don't know how I'd managed to stay around the dead so long if I hadn't of had some happiness—in life."

"Ever see any doctors who did?" Scott asked.

"A few. If they don't love the women, they love the children."

"How many have you, Dan?"

"Two."

"What are their names?"

They steadied the stretcher toward the elevator and some extraneous, casual conversation intervened before Dan replied. "My kids are named for two—we did," he said settling the pan on Scott's labora-

190

tory shelves. "One is named Henry for a medical student, about the age of that one today—but you are the first person who knows he's named that—why, I mean. It was an early spring day just like this when we did him, and I got to thinking about how his father must of felt 'fore I went home."

"And the other one?" Scott asked in a tone which completely relaxed the embarrassment of other men.

"The other one's a girl. She's named for a head nurse——"

"One you liked, Dan?"

"No. She was a head nurse who had plenty of chances to marry, but didn't." Dan jockeyed the last pan into place. "She died when she was thirty-five of spinal meningitis and when her lovely body was there on the table, and all of the men who had respected her were standing around, one of them asked why she had never married. Dean Wingate, who was watching, answered without looking up, 'Epilepsy in the family.'

"The way he said it—I've known him so long—the way he said it just hit me between the eyes like a sledge hammer. And with a crazy sort of clearness, I felt that she was the woman he loved. He was still a young man then, and it just come over me like lightning what that autopsy was meaning to him. I couldn't get home quick enough that night. So when my little daughter was born, I come to the conclusion that the Dean and that nurse hadn't been wasted exactly, and that her being a girl had a funny kind of meaning—a sign sort of—and so I named her Ethel for that nurse."

"Does Wingate know, Dan?"

"Till you got it out of me, Doctor Scotty, nobody knew how come either of my kids was named. My wife didn't care—she's always teasing me about liking names the way she likes flowers and I just let it go at that."

"But Dean Wingate ought to know," Scott insisted.

"No. It would spoil it if he knew," Dan said decisively. "I couldn't stay around here if anybody told him."

"All right, Dan. It's your secret, I won't give it away."

"I know you won't. I guess that's why I told you. Well—" Dan moved toward the door, "don't work too late, Doc. I've checked the clinics and nobody expects any of 'em to go out tonight, but if one should, you know how to get me—my number's on the wall over the 'phone in the autopsy room.

"Thanks, Dan. If anything turns up, I'll give you a ring."

It was the same old sentence which all pathologists pass between themselves, but the tone in which it was uttered convinced Dan that no matter what turned up, this pathologist had guaranteed him a night off.

As Scott turned back to the cultures he was thinking, "Well, you may have a namesake, Doctor-from-Canada."

Later that same night in the old double mahogany bed which she occupied with her sister Sally, Margaretta lay taut, still and racked with anguish. Beside her, Sally slept peacefully.

Margaretta was wondering what was the matter with her? What had she done to offend Alex Ashby? Was it something she had said? Or something she hadn't said? There wasn't any sense deceiving herself longer. Now that everybody had gone to sleep and the house was dark and private, she could acknowledge to herself that in some way she wasn't sufficiently attractive. Because it was three weeks— three weeks this very Sunday—since Alex had last come to see her. He had come every Sunday night after that McMillan dinner dance and then when he went on night call in externe O-B he'd come on Sunday afternoons and still telephoned twice a week. The last time he had 'phoned, he'd said he'd be off externe O-B the next day and would call her right away—and—and then he'd never come back—he'd never called.

Her heart gave a sickening flop as she wondered if he had ever come to see her? Could it be that he was crazy about Sally and that Sally wasn't crazy about him and that Alex knew it and just couldn't stand coming over any more?

Oh, God! Could that be it?

If it were, then she hadn't failed in just one little way—instead she'd failed in everything and those things he had said when he first called her Ladykins were—were just talk.

Compared with Sally she wasn't any good. The tears welled in her eyes and that dreadful uncertainty about her own personality hounded her mind again. She wasn't as gay as Sally; she just couldn't love people, the world and life the way Sally did. She could love only Alex Ashby with his beautiful, kind eyes and the calm deep way he'd say, "Happy, Ladykins?"

As she remembered that, she recalled, too, how his eyes had widened and included her inside his heart, almost, when he had asked that question. And the way he had looked in the mirror! How right Mrs. McMillan had been! No, it wasn't Sally who had stopped his coming. Thinking it was Sally was just a form of excusing her own inadequacy.

What probably stopped him was that he had been shocked when she let him kiss her that last time. But she was only trying to see if Papa were right about kisses and love—and he was. No, it couldn't be that kiss which had stopped his coming, because afterwards when she felt so weak he had said, "That's love, Sweetheart. It makes women that way," and carried her to the parlor sofa and knelt beside her. The way he looked then, now that she let herself think about it, had taught her something, something true—if Alex Ashby loved any girl, she was the girl.

Lying there in the friendly dark, she whispered over and over to herself the words he had said, as he knelt beside her. "Ladykins, I'll buy you a horse, a high spirited horse, and all of our little boys will have ponies."

Then he'd put his cheek against hers and kept it there for the longest kind of time. Remembering it made you feel like drinking sherry did. Made you hear again how he said, "I love you, Ladykins. I love you." After he said it, the weight of his head against her cheek was the sweetest heaviness on earth; even now thinking about it could put her to sleep sometimes.

When a man loved a girl that way, didn't he want to be with her? Talking about your children was 'most like being married and having them. Didn't he want to see her, too? To—to touch her, just as she wanted to see and touch him?

Didn't he?

Chapter Fourteen

EXPERIENCES OF THE
FREE QUARTER

"What is going on in the witenagemot?" Alex asked, sauntering into Pug Prentiss's room where Ben Mead seemed to be delivering a lecture.

Pug listened from the bed, Silas from a rocking chair, Clay was draped against the mantel and Bert Riggs perched on the corner of Pug's desk.

Ben turned to Ashby and said, "With all of the things you've got to remember professionally, how in the hell you've time to pack your head full of queer words stumps me!"

Alex seated himself on the bed and drawled, "Etymology is to me what kheirergo is to you!"

"And what in the hell is that?" Ben scowled.

"What were you doing when you were supposed to be taking Greek?"

"Never took it. Spill it: what does the word mean?"

Pug grinned, and Bert Riggs who had had a fine apprenticeship in a backwoods Pennsylvania college bit a smile from his lips. Alex cleared his throat and then in the tone in which Dr. Howe made intricate things so clear, he said, "Kheir means hand, ergo means work: in American, surgery, Bennie."

Ben colored and sputtered, "I hope to God I get a chance to ——"

"You've previously performed the prostatectomy on me."

"Alex, that reminds me," Pug said. "What do you think of my taking some urology next quarter?"

"Better make it G-Y-N. Hizer says you are a lady doctor," Ben intervened.

The group laughed. Alex answered, "Leave it alone, Pug. I don't know what you are: but you certainly are not that."

"Which?"

"Certainly not a urologist. Those fellows—gosh, it's the most depressing field next to psychiatry. Do your free quarter in something else. Is that what's got you all wrinkled up?"

"Yeah." Clay inserted himself into the discussion. "Ben was telling us it didn't matter what we took, we'd find it wasn't what we wanted later."

"Ben's right," Alex remarked.

Ben said sarcastically, "If I'm right you must be ill."

Alex ignored the slur and Ben continued defensively, "I wasted the whole quarter taking advanced bacteriology and immunology, and I ask you what in the hell good did it do me? Not a damn bit, I'd of been better off quartering beef in a butcher shop. Nothing to it, so far as I'm concerned. Nothing!"

Alex's eyes began to dance. He lowered his chin and looked up at Ben. "You'd better go to bed. Sounds to me like you've got a bad case of lalorrhea. What do you think, doctor?" He turned to Pug.

" 'Fraid so," Prentiss replied and gave Ben that keen, impersonal look which doctors visit upon patients when wishing to see the actual letters of their diagnosis spread across the victim's chest.

Both of them looked so entirely, but so calmly, worried that the grin fell from Ben's face and he asked, "Hey, what's that?"

Again Riggs bit a smile from his lips. Alex answered slowly, "We may be wrong, Ben. I'd rather wait a few minutes before we tell you."

"Is it contagious?" Clay put in quickly.

"In some cases. Not always," Prentiss replied. Then he and Ashby fixed their gaze upon Ben Mead again.

"For God's sake," Ben said pleadingly. "Tell me."

"Not yet," Alex's voice was judicial and he suggested, "What do you think they ought to do with their free quarter?"

"Whatever they want to," Ben replied sullenly. "Just like I said, though, whatever they do is wrong. A man in the second year medicine hasn't any more idea what he wants to be than a baby in diapers. He's just floundering around and he might just as well flounder one way as another. Look at you, Alex, you spent that whole damn quarter in Department L working in syphilis. Ten to one you'll never research in it, you'll never have it, and you won't know it when you meet it on the street."

"Oh, come, Bennie! You don't tip your hat to a person because he— or she—is syphilitic! Whether I can tell it on the street or not, at least I'll know enough not to marry a girl with knots behind her ears!"

"Is that a sign?" Clay asked in a high-pitched tone.

"Aw, rats!" Ben said. "Forget it. Why, when Alex was taking that course, you know as well as I do, that he'd have done a Wassermann on Miss Susie, even—if he'd dared. And any old surgeon knows that virginity, through the centuries, was so prized because virgins were not diseased."

Those two facts, coming one so closely on the other, left Clay speechless.

"That reminds me!" Pug interrupted, sitting up. "Your diagnosis, Alex, is correct; it's certainly lalorrhea."

"Well, if I've got it, what is it?" Ben asked abruptly.

Alex eased doorward, and when he had one foot safely across the sill he replied, "According to medical dictionaries, Doctor Mead, lalorrhea is an abnormal or excessive flow of words."

He bounded up the stairs as the text book Mead slung after him slid along the hall floor and collided with the banister.

"Hey!" Pug hollered, "that's my clinical mike and it cost ten bucks."

But as Ben had prophesied, what each man took during that quarter turned out in later life to have been a mistake, with the exception of Silas; he had long ago made up his mind to return to his father's old practice and was, therefore, systematically covering every course which would be of value to a general practitioner. He split the quarter between a course in ophthalmology and one in laryngology and otology.

During that second year, under the guidance of Alex Ashby, the group from Miss Susie's made a careful inspection of the Pathological Museum.

The exhibits, housed in the different basement rooms of the building, were all pickled in jars and numbered. Ashby showed how by taking the number one could refer to the corresponding number on the typewritten sheet tacked against the wall and ascertain the diagnosis. In many instances the jars were like earthenware pickle jars and Ashby's long rubber-gloved fingers delved in the formalin, brought up the different organs and he explained their condition.

But in each room the prize exhibits were in sealed glass containers. One such jar contained a pair of Siamese twins, which bore a card, "Gift of McGill University."

"Gee!" Clay said. "Think of having 'em to give away."

"Probably already had an exhibit themselves," Alex said, "and when these were born—and died—they just passed 'em on to Welch. We've got a list down here of what McGill hasn't and wants in the way of exhibits. That was probably Welch's idea, too."

"Sort of like giving wedding presents," Riggs put in.

Pug grinned, "I daresay they are much more valued by the pathologists to whom they're given."

"You bet they are!" Alex remarked and pointed to another prize exhibit. "She is rare." The jar to which he referred was about three feet high, sealed and contained a two-year-old white girl. Her wide, wistful brown eyes and droopy little mouth seemed to Riggs more pathetic than anything he had ever seen. "See, they removed her brain," Alex continued. "Wish we had it! She was probably an imbecile, which explains the strange look in her eyes."

They fell into a hot argument then as to whether the eyes of a dead person could retain any expression. Years after all of them had forgotten the discussion, Riggs always thought of the effects of syphilis as exemplified in the head of that helpless child: the way the flaps of skin dangled inward made all of the malformations in embryos which came afterward seem inconsequential.

Even the stench of the formalin as Alex took organ after organ from the jars and explained them, even the oily, penetrating heaviness of it, seemed less revolting.

After he had referred to the key sheet, at Ashby's request, and was back in the group looking at the mess of what remained of the uterus which Alex held in his hands, Pug asked, "Aren't there any dates, ages, doctors' names, or case histories on these exhibits?"

"No, not one," Alex replied. "This museum is built to show the results of disease from a pathological viewpoint, not the time it takes to accomplish those results."

"They ought to consider the time element, though. Just look at the room across the hall," Ben Mead, who had joined them, put in.

"It certainly counts there, all right," Ashby agreed as he led the way across to the cancer room. Whereas syphilis is something that medical men often joke about, carcinoma is never treated lightly even by students. When Silas, looking at an elongated strip of tissue suspended in alcohol asked, "What's that, Alex?" his voice was low and calm.

Alex answered without reference to the chart, for he was capable of answering most inquiries about the contents of this room that way, "Carcinoma of the breast: it's been stained with Sudan three."

The section was no larger than the coral portion of a broiled chicken lobster and it was that color, precisely: looking at it Alex thought, as he had often thought, "The exhibits in this room are all so beautiful—and so hideous."

Ben said, "If she had gone to a doctor in time ——"

"Do they ever?" Riggs asked.

"One in a hundred," Alex replied. "Women with false modesty seem cursed with it."

Ashby continued with his demonstration and pointed out the ovary four inches long, shell pink, and perforated; the hand five times its natural size, and the other hand covered with a mussy mess and which looked like a cauliflower.

Still the exclamations came in monotones and the only exhibit which caused much comment was the one which bore out better than an hour's lecture could have done, Ben Mead's plea for surgery and cancer. It was a long group of linked tissues, which resembled a chain of brown islands, suspended in alcohol.

"What's that?" Clay asked, the brown cast having disconcerted him after the coral tint of the other exhibits. "What in a body looks like that?"

Alex waited for Ben to tell them. Ben said impressively, "That is what came from—from behind a mole."

The others were relieved to follow Ashby on into what was dubbed as the miscellaneous room and see the section of the lung which was stained with methyl blue and had been congested by pneumonia.

Even the typhoid intestine with the ulcerated places where the infection had gone through to the abdominal cavity didn't seem so bad after that string of brown links from behind the mole.

Next, Alex displayed the heart with coronary thrombosis. "See the hard sticks of tissue?" The boys leaned attentively forward and watched his gloved finger as he pointed. A murmur of assent circulated, and Silas remembered, though he did not mention it, that Ashby had called the disease the doctor's friend when he had said that his father died of it.

Pug suggested, "What do you say we go on to the leprosy room, Alex?" He had given it a private inspection and some of the things had been so disconcerting that he wanted to scrutinize them in the company of other people. Ashby nodded. As they moved forward he remarked, "Difference between the miscellaneous room and the cancer room is that most of the things in here came out of people who were dead."

"And are therefore related to medicine, not surgery," Ben put in as they moved across the hall again and began eyeing the exhibits in the leprosy and T. B. room.

Every man present had had enough training to know that the bacilli of the two were so closely connected that the exhibits should be housed together.

When the room was filled with living men, Pug took a good, long look at the thing which had made him seek company. Alex watching him said, "That Chinaman's head is a beaut! Never seen another one as good in any pathological museum."

The head, housed in a round glass container, was in the center of a shelf of jars about level with their shoulders. The Chinaman's head consisted of one eye, a porous white streak up the center of the nose, and hair above—the rest was gone—eaten away by leprosy.

To ease their tension the boys fell into a discussion of the methods of treatment for leprosy and one of them mentioned the chaulmoogra oil idea developed in the Philippines. The other things in glass—the hand with two fingers and the white globules throughout the tissue; the spongy lungs and the liver with the hard, white specks—passed before their eyes in a semi-daze. They were experiencing the same sensation which had enveloped Pug after he first saw the Chinaman's head.

"What's next?" Clay asked quickly.

"Worm room," Ben answered. "Got a tape worm six feet long, a long worm inside an intestine, round worms, pretty worms, young worms—cummon, I'll show you."

Pug had conquered his abhorrence and turning to Ashby asked, "Is it very contagious?"

Mead and Abernathy had disappeared.

"I don't think so."

The others understood that they were referring to leprosy. Alex continued, "Doctor Heiser insists that if you take the children of lepers away from their parents at birth, they will grow up free from leprosy—in the majority of cases. Therefore you might argue that it certainly is not inherited. One school of thought holds that it is contracted through the mucous membranes, only. And all schools agree that cleanliness is the best preventive."

"How is it tied up with diet?" Riggs asked.

"Nobody is certain—yet. We know a lot more about T. B."

"But that isn't inherited, is it?" Again it was Riggs who asked the question, and only Alex, with his excellent sense of voice placement, realized that the inquiry came too quietly. "I believe that the ages at which one is most likely to contract it are known," he said.

"What are they?" Silas put the question, and Riggs waited for the answer.

Alex replied, "Early childhood. Early manhood. Few people develop it past thirty."

"A hell of a lot of men around here have had it and gone on and had children, too." Ben and Clay had returned and it was Ben who made the statement.

"Who?" Pug asked.

Again Riggs waited for the answer. Ben replied, "McMillan had it; so did Wingate; and Franklin, in orthopedics, was out a couple of years with it, too."

"Franklin hasn't any children and Wingate isn't married." Clay Abernathy felt that he must get himself into the conversation.

Ashby intervened, "Provided the woman didn't have an open case at the time she was pregnant there isn't much danger if the man's case is arrested. If you ask me, a couple of years of T. B. isn't such a disadvantage after all: the people who have it and come out of it know how to keep from wasting themselves."

"What do you say we go over to Otto's and digest these exhibits with a stein of beer?" Pug flashed his awful grin upon them and everybody felt less doomed and a little more normal.

After their beers, Pug pleaded an engagement and went off by himself for a walk. Baltimore, he had found, is a city of many tints. The shaded reds of the bricks, the rich and varied displays in the markets, even the food seen in the baskets of the street vendors and the flowers sold by street curb-flower men added to the great splash of color. Also, because of the frequent hills and low buildings, it is a city where one is forever conscious of the sky. A sunset in Baltimore, he had learned, meant not merely resplendent cloud banks; it meant, too, a many, different-hued series of brick-reflections almost as intricate in their shading as is the Grand Canyon.

Rarely had Pug observed a block in which the houses were a uniform red, for while they are identical in white steps and symmetrically placed openings, they range in tone all the way from a faded vermilion to turkey and maroon. The whole color study is, therefore, a symphony in the gradations of red.

From the Monument to Lexington Street, most of Charles is on a hogback and Pug walked swiftly over there now, not to study the store windows, but to drink in the beauty, east and west, which the sunset afforded. Whereas in the west the sky dominates the sunset, he knew that in the east, from the Charles Street vantage, the buildings dominate it. One looked west to see the pastel, yellow and blue variations, east to see the many-toned reflections in red which these occasioned from the bricks. East one saw the dome of the hospital cut clear against the pink sky and watched the windows fill with fire.

Here and there a lush green tree plumed out among the brick hues, a robin sang his sunset song and Prentiss thought Baltimore a gratifying place to be.

A city where permanency reigns, it has all of the narrowing disadvantages of permanency, yet, also, all of the charms. Pug had come to sense that people who are born and die in the same row house consider that house home, and the residents of the block in which it is located as their neighbors in a way which apartment dwellers never comprehend. Miles on miles, unseen from the street, he knew that back gardens, no wider than a row-house, but nevertheless carefully nurtured, grew behind brick walls. These gardens he had discovered through alley-walks. He was familiar with them at all seasons, now, and knew that the tulips, blooming violets and lilacs would be followed by exquisite roses. In June climbing red ramblers, yellow Paul Nerons and magnificent Radiance roses would line the beds of the pocket-handkerchief lawns; before the roses came, under the shade of an occasional tree, graceful sweet-odored lilies of the valley lifted their delicate bells, while in the German sections carefully tended grape vines prepared new feelers for their small arbors and parsley and mint beds required more water.

In the poorer sections, Pug knew, petunias, zinnias and morning glories would fill the small plots. The wonderful success which even the poorest of the negroes had with raising plants always interested him. Their ferns were as green as those of the undertakers; their geraniums always bloomed. In rusty cans they created beauty and he wondered if the decaying tin might in some manner increase their blossoms. Baltimore poverty, while as acute as that of the tenement cities, he had found more individual. Was it because they endured it with a pocket-handkerchief of earth which, while too small to cultivate for food, still allowed a man a modicum of pride in his land?

As the sunset faded and he walked back toward Miss Susie's, Pug remembered how in summer when he had been irritated by the ostentatious canna lilies which the city inflicted on the flower beds of Broadway, he had always obtained solace by turning into a nearby alley and using his eyes.

Ahead, he saw one of the things he deeply enjoyed watching: a small negro boy perilously perched on a homemade box-bodied wagon. The front and rear wheels of these conveyances rarely matched and on inquiry Pug had learned that months of saving usually preceded their purchase. At the junk yards they were much in demand, because they had to be sturdy enough to stand fast travel and heavy loads; for these apparently carefree cars of luxury, he had seen, were, in reality, the scavenger wagons of grim poverty. In them were hauled the cast-off cratings discarded by piano and furniture stores; in them traveled the fruit too ripe to sell, tomatoes too bruised to peddle; near the markets of a Saturday night at closing time were lined up rows of these wagons, presided over by alert negro boys whose revolving eyes went from stall to stall scrutinizing the possible refuse.

Around Christmas, if the winter were severe and wood scarce, in the alleys off Charles Street, Prentiss had heard a constant cracking of thin boards as the carefully-minded knocked to pieces their finds, and neatly packed them onto their wagons.

This method, he had observed, required time, a helper and a mundane mind, and adventure, that great unknown driving force which took the shiver out of a child's limbs, ceased to exist if the load were carefully packed. For adventure resulted in teetering as many crates as possible on the wagon and then going downhill at breakneck speed without dislodging the load. To do this necessitated from the little boy who was crouched between the mountainous boxes and the wheels, expert handling of the harness cord by which the direction of those front wheels was determined. It also demanded expert braking with the owner's off-wagon foot.

From repeated observation Pug had found that, generally speaking, wagon accidents were infrequent for, as with sail over steam, men driving horses and automobiles in Baltimore permitted the wagon-boys right of way, whenever possible.

The boy on the wagon which he had just passed, had on the topless brim of an old straw hat. Somehow it made Prentiss think of those lackadaisical, sideless, straw-seated streetcars which moved through Baltimore in the summer. As soon as it got hot, he decided, he would ride out on one to an ample, sway-back, green park bench, smoke a pipe and watch the children lick snowballs—that summertime concoction of shaved ice and fruit syrups which cools their tongues and quiets their stomachs.

When he reached Miss Susie's the grim museum had gone from his mind and after supper the conversation centered around medical fraternities and the ones to which they had been bid.

Pug said flatly that he wouldn't enter any and all of the boys knew that Alex had turned down a bid to Pithotomy. When they had questioned him about it, he replied simply, "Miss Susie's house and Hizer's cooking suit me better than anything I ever hope to run across. Now that I've found them, I'm sticking to them!" After Miss Susie had nursed him through his attack of "flu" he was doubly glad that he had decided never to leave her house until he graduated.

Ben Mead was Pithotomy and the other boys in the house, except Silas, went Pithotomy too, but continued to live at Miss Susie's. Silas was bid to a lesser fraternity but did not join, admitting calmly that he "didn't have the money." Elijah Howe also went Pithotomy.

One man who did not have an opportunity to refuse was Isidore Aaron. The next afternoon as he and Ashby were walking home—to Isidore's home where Ashby had been at last extended the supreme compliment of being invited to a meal—Isidore said, "Are you anti-social, Alex?"

"Not consciously. Why?"

"Weren't you invited to join the Pithotomy Club last year and refused?"

"I did."

"And didn't they invite you again this year?"

"They did."

"Why did you refuse? Had I been invited I would have refused, too, but for reasons which could not possibly have influenced you."

"What reasons?"

"Because having a lone Jew about is embarrassing for the Jew when he senses, as he must in time, that conversation is always guarded in his presence."

"Oh, come, you are exaggerating!"

"I think not."

"But they respect you, and admire you. Any club ought to be complimented to have you for a member," Alex replied hotly.

"Respect and admiration, provided they did exist, are rarely the attributes which lead to jovial companionship."

"That is true—they lead to something better, Isidore."

"Perhaps, but it is lonely," the words had a tinge of pathos which made Alex frown. Isidore mistook that frown for criticism and said quickly, "It *was* lonely, I should say, if I am to be accurate. Since I've known you, I'm no longer lonely."

"Why, thanks," Alex said with feeling, and after a short silence he continued, "Lord, Isidore, belonging to the Pithotomy Club would matter no more to me than riding in a Pullman. I had the fare, could afford the seat, and would have obtained it through no merit of my own. In a way you do not comprehend, to be invited to dine at your house tonight is a much greater honor. Because it does not arise out of money, nor social position, but—but out of friendship. Can't you understand the difference?"

Isidore was silent half a block and at last he said, "All I can ever understand about you, Alex, is what I told you the first time we walked down this street together: and that is that you are an aristocrat."

"Nonsense!" Alex said jokingly. "What are the symptoms?"

"Inexplicable. Something which I knew when you spoke to me and which every action of yours since has verified. Something I'd give anything to be and never shall. Whatever comes to you in life, like Osler, you'll always remain yourself. Distinctly yourself—and I——"

Alex stopped short. "If that is the definition of an aristocrat, then of all human beings I have ever known, Isidore, you have the highest qualifications."

Isidore shook his head. "No. In a crisis which offered a choice between my duty to humanity or my own self-preservation, I should, instinctively, act in a manner which would insure my self-preservation. I should be a hysterical, frightened Jew—or worse yet, a beaten, weary Jew: one of those men who are so detached from their essential Judaism that they are vacant."

"I know. A racially unsexed Jew, you mean. I've seen them," Alex said. "But as to yourself in a crisis, you are wrong. Completely wrong!"

Alex was emphatic, but Isidore retorted as though ignoring his intervention, "While men of your stamp, and Osler's, defeated or victorious, would remain essentially the same."

"All you are describing is a man's ability to stand alone and if any person on God's earth learns how to do that, Isidore, isn't it an intellectual Jew?"

Isidore's eyes brightened as he turned toward Ashby and replied, "Next to being an aristocrat *that* is the best trait any man can have. The very best."

"What?"

"Also on that first walk," Isidore said, "we discussed it and you called it genius: that uncanny ability to know and understand, correctly, what one had never experienced. That is why I think you should be a diagnostician. It is a trait too rare to be wasted on pathology."

Alex colored and lit a cigarette. "You're wrong, Isidore, about me —being one. And as for the trait, it shouldn't be trusted by a diagnostician."

"Why not? Osler relies on it, McMillan preaches it—why shouldn't you trust it?"

"Because it is never valuable unless it has some basis in adversity or in poverty," Alex replied earnestly. "That is why I've always tried to tell you that it is of great import in a Jew: in him it had been weighed and repeatedly weighed by both."

"He never stands outside the curse of hysteria," Isidore said sadly. "Every Jew has thousands of relatives; and if he isn't hysterical about himself he is hysterical about his relatives; and if he isn't hysterical about his relatives, he is hysterical about the fate of his race; and if he isn't hysterical about the fate of his race, he is about his own physical condition. The first thing a Jew does as soon as he gets rich is to go to a good doctor to see if there is anything wrong with him, physically."

"That is good sense."

"In his case, Alex, it is a feeling that if things are right with him financially, they cannot possibly be right with him physically. Hysteria. Fear. The inability to accept what men of your background consider their normal right in a fair amount of happiness. If things are right, they are wrong. If they are wrong, they are right. Defeatist complex: the unhappy race."

"What holds for the race, does not hold for the exception, Isidore. And so far as you are concerned I disagree, completely. If you ever have to make a choice between your obligation to medicine or your preservation, you'll decide in favor of medicine before you have time to think it over. I know that, as certainly as I know that if any of us have genius, you have it."

As Alex ceased speaking they had reached lower Broadway and were below the boulevard pathway going toward Aaron's tailor shop. Isidore came to an abrupt halt, fastened his gaze on Ashby and asked, "Alex, do you honestly *believe* that—about—about me?"

"Yes," Alex replied. "I do."

One of Isidore's adolescent brothers, who was standing in the shop doorway on the lookout, screeched, "Issi! Mumma's feexed food lak Passover!"

The doorway became alive with children and Isidore shrugged, changed the subject and remarked, "When one enters there argument ceases and filial acquiescence begins."

There was ironic bitterness in his voice.

"Hello!" Alex said grinning cheerfully at the assembled children. Isidore lined them up in a prim row and introduced them. The girls were nine and seven and named Rebekkah and Esther; the boys, twelve and sixteen, were Abie and Moses. All had liquid brown eyes, all looked alike and all were dressed in their synagogue best. Alex began talking to them in that friendly manner of his which put other people at ease, and he saw Isidore's quick eye run over their attire. "Abie, tie your shoe!" Isidore muttered and Abie's face went beet red, as he leaned swiftly forward and obeyed.

Alex lifted Esther into his arms and she lisped excitedly in his ear, "Zee! Mine reebons ezz blue."

Alex touched her hair ribbon and replied with the serious earnestness which her statement commanded, "It is a beautiful blue, too."

"I lak hit," she said, putting her head on one side.

"Are you the baby?"

"No. De beebe ezz slipping."

Before Alex could decipher what she meant, Rebekkah said to Isidore, "Mumma hesks you go upstairs and vait."

"Take Esther then," said Isidore, and Alex hastily stood the child on the sidewalk. The children were so dressed up that they didn't dare to play or do anything but be extremely uncomfortable and stare at the cause of their discomfort, but as Rebekkah took Esther's hand, the little girl gave Alex a childish and natural smile.

Alex knelt down beside her and said, "You are a nice armful, Esther, and I like you."

Esther smiled again and the other children smiled too. Then

Isidore led the way into the tailor shop and asked Moses, who followed, where his father was.

Moses replied, "I'm keeping shop. He is dressing to meet your friend."

Moses spoke with such extreme assurance that Alex sensed that he was excessively timid and excessively proud of his lack of accent. As Isidore led the way toward the narrow stairway at the rear of the shop, Alex grinned at Moses and said, "Boy, I certainly like that tie! Where did you get it, Moses?"

Moses grinned too and named a cheap haberdashery of which Alex had never heard. As Alex reached the stairway, he heard Moses saying to the children who were crowding the doorway and still staring, "He likes it! He likes it!"

Alex and Isidore went up into that awful parlor which might have been furnished out of a mail order catalogue. Alex looked at the set table and understood completely the supreme effort which this invitation had called for on the part of the Aaron family. He saw Isidore unconsciously scrutinize the table and give an approving nod; Alex realized that he must have issued minute instructions as to its arrangement, previously.

Isidore's father, Abie Aaron, appeared in the doorway. He was dressed in his best and wearing buttoned shoes like those Ashby had seen long ago, under the bed in the bedroom over this same tailor shop.

Behind Abie stood his wife, her dress a mass of quivering bulges. She had been poured into a corset, protruded above and below it and panted constantly. Both of them looked at Isidore with pleading hopeful eyes, as if to say, "Do we suit you?"

Alex jumped up, gave them an inclusive, infectious smile and before Isidore could speak, he was saying, "How do you do, sir? It's nice to see you again!"

Abie could only nod; then Alex had the hard workworn hand of Isidore's mother in his and was saying to her, "So you are Isidore's mother. I *am* so glad to meet you." The words came in his slow Texas drawl and the couple could not comprehend what they were, but their effect was gratifying. A pleased, embarrassed happiness dripped from both Mr. and Mrs. Aaron. Their eyes watched Alex like the eyes of dogs, but Isidore's mother flashed him a smile with teeth which were still strong and even. His father said nothing, and began to throw out a protective covering, emotionally. Abie didn't want to like a man who was not Orthodox and who was not Jewish.

Isidore had slipped from the room and presently Alex found himself seated with Isidore's parents in that terrifying little parlor. The door was filled with children. They stared at him, the parents stared and nobody spoke. Alex began talking.

"Where I come from there are a great many horses. I imagine Texas is something like parts of Russia must be ——"

The children murmured their assent and Alex, watching the faces of the parents, thought that they had not understood his words. Then it dawned upon him what he had done—they had never seen a Russia like that! He used his smile again and said very distinctly, "We think that Isidore is the brightest man in the school. The doctors all like him."

The stolid expression wilted from the faces of both of the parents. They nodded, smiled and the father said, "A greet ducturr, mine Isidore. A greet ducturr."

They were like a prophecy—those words. Like something certain in the future, which one might not live to see. The mother echoed them, "A greet ducturr," but her echo came in gasps and she mopped her face with her handkerchief.

There was a commotion at the door, the children were brushed aside like leaves as the old grandmother, cane in hand, entered on Isidore's arm. She was a hag whose face was so wrinkled that her small beady black eyes were hardly visible between the crevices. She had a gnarled and belligerent quality which made Alex think of her not as old, but as powerful. As he bowed graciously in acknowledgment of the introduction, Alex noticed that the members of the family were all standing, too. Then he remembered that Isidore had once told him that she had lived through four pogroms.

When the grandmother was seated, Isidore gave his mother a quick nod and she labored from the room. Then his father said to the grandmother, "Dey lak Issi. He tolt; dey lak heem!"

The old woman shook her head in a manner which did not denote surprise, but simply the just truth from a just cause. The children in the doorway whispered the knowledge among themselves. They were hissed asunder and Leah, seventeen, and Ruth, eighteen, now appeared and acknowledged shyly Isidore's introductions as they placed steaming dishes upon the table. Their mother followed with another dish. The children sniffed and remarked its contents, as Alex endeavored to carry on a conversation which would interest the grandmother.

Afterward, the memory of that next hour always filled Alex with such pain that it made him weak. When the table had been completely covered with food and the door shut upon all of the children, the grandmother, the parents, Isidore and he seated themselves. And the expression upon Abie's face as for the first time in his life he broke bread where a Gentile was a guest—the stern, past pain look—lingered in Alex's mind for years. That, and the horrible way the grandmother wolfed her food, and Abie kept darting glances at his plate, ordering Isidore to invite him to have more.

In desperation, after all attempts at conversation had failed and Alex saw Isidore, as Isidore had prophesied, growing hysterical over his relatives, Ashby began discussing Moses Maimonides, the great Jewish physician, and his amazing and accurate knowledge. Isidore belittled it. Yet the occasional mention of Maimonides' name and the realization, from Alex's tone that it was a complimentary mention seemed to please and quiet the parents. Though, until the conclusion of the meal, they kept their liquid eyes fixed upon him and watched Alex's every mouthful.

Outside the room the children began to fight. Their clamor awoke the baby and Ashby could hear the whole contingent break into high-pitched, piercing screams. In complete desperation, Alex turned the conversation to folklore and whether it was good manners or not, he decided to cover up the din by singing. Referring to cowboy songs and their origins, he broke into a verse of "I'm a poor lonesome cowboy and I know I've done wrong."

It worked. The hidden pain disappeared from Isidore's lips, the parents and the grandmother smiled their approval, the children ceased to fight and listened.

After the dreadful ordeal was over and he was walking back up

Broadway again, two things stood out in Alex's mind above the pitiful grooming and above the tension.

One was the way the grandmother had never taken her eyes from Isidore; the way she had watched him as though he were a god. The other was the prophetic sound of Abie Aaron's voice when he said, "A greet ducturr."

Chapter Fifteen

A YOUNG MAN'S FANCY

"Hey, Jack!" Ben Mead bellowed leaning over the banisters. "Are you going?"

"You haven't called me that in years," Alex Ashby answered, stretching away from his study table. "Am I going—where?"

Ben, arrayed only in a B.V.D., flung his arms into the air as he replied, "Where? Hells bells, Doctor Ashby! Didn't you know that Pithotomy's having a dance tonight? If you are going you'd better be getting ready, and if you are not, I want to borrow your dress studs."

"I'm not," Alex answered calmly. "You may. Come on down and get 'em."

Ben came, and as all of this was above Miss Susie's "level" he came as he was. One of Mead's most endearing qualities was that he always responded and now that there was a party in the offing he seemed primed to enjoy it.

"Is that what the well-dressed Pithotomy man is wearing this May, Ben?"

"Aw! What's come over you, Alex? Why don't you come on and go?" Ben grinned cheerfully.

Ashby shook his head. "I'm not a member, Ben."

"Well, you're invited. And so is Pug. He's going."

"Got to study," Alex said shortly. "Much obliged."

"Bosh! I'm in your class. That one won't work with me. What is the real reason?" Ben toyed with the studs which Alex had extracted from the bureau drawer.

"Not everybody's bright as you, Bennie. That *is* the reason."

"You are lying through your teeth and I know it. Are you in love?"

"Only man around here who *claims* to have that disease is you," Alex said caustically. "Didn't you come back last summer and tell me

212

you were engaged? What are you doing running around with other women?"

"What do you think she's doing? Sitting down in Greenville knitting comforters for old ladies? American men don't know how to satisfy women. Don't know how to love and can't teach the women ——"

"Whoa, Ben. You are on the verge of lalorrhea! Do you expect me to believe that you can learn to love on a dance floor?"

Ben made a pass at Ashby and then said, "Certainly wouldn't marry a girl I couldn't dance with. Two things have some relationship, and you know it." Then he warmed to his subject and forgot to be terse. "Gosh, Jack, you know what you remind me of? There are some girls who when you kiss them are just as cold as ice, and in relation to normal outlook you are like those girls. Better get hold of yourself!"

Alex slumped back into his chair again and smiled. "Why do you kiss 'em, Bennie?"

" 'Cause I like to kiss 'em. Oh, you mean why do I kiss the cold ones?"

"Yeah."

"I kiss 'em to find out," Ben answered.

"Have you kissed this one you are going to marry?"

"Yeah—and she fainted. I—say, Jack, don't you ever tell anybody that!"

Ben gathered his emotions under cover and fled from the room He did not see the sudden freezing which came into Alex's eyes.

After Silas, Clay and Miss Susie had all tried to persuade Ashby to go, in sheer self-defense he put on his hat and walked up to the Medical Library. A feeling as instinctive as thirst made him thoroughly aware that the last thing he wanted to do was to take a chance on seeing Margaretta. He found Isidore Aaron in the library, hunched under a desk light, catching up on the current periodicals. His eyes brightened at the sight of Ashby and picking up the A.M.A. again, he pointed out several articles. Alex sat down beside him. They read in silence for half an hour and then fell into one of their discussions; the world beyond their lamp arc receded from Alex's mind.

It was Prentiss who created the excuse which protected him from further prying on the part of Miss Susie's household. While the dance goers were being inspected by Miss Susie and Hizer, Pug said, "About Ashby: I heard somebody say that he lost a delivery recently, and perhaps that is why he—he wants to be left alone. Don't mention it to him, please."

That some change had come over him in his quarter in externe O-B when he had the "flu," all of them were aware. Miss Susie said, "Oh! Thank you for telling us, St. George. When—when that first happens to him, it's a difficult thing for a doctor to bear." Then she turned to Ben Mead and changed the subject, "Now, you remember that you are engaged, and *behave yourself!*"

"Haven't kissed a girl since I came back. Got to keep in practice, Miss Susie," Ben said airily, and walked over and kissed her soundly.

"For mercy's sake!" she gasped.

"Thank you, ma'am. There isn't a girl in Baltimore who could touch my lips after that!" Ben grinned.

Hizer shook his head. "You sho' better watch him, Mista Pug. Dat boy's in a risky mood tonight. Sho' is!"

Miss Susie did not hear; she had turned to look again at Pug Prentiss. This was the first party to which anybody had been able to persuade him to, and she was startled to realize how attractive he was in evening clothes. There was a special light in his green eyes and the way he smiled, when he found her looking at him, wasn't the sort of thing which many women could resist.

"Who are you taking, my dear?"

"I'm going stag. Ben and Clay are bringing the Howe girls and Silas, Bert and I are to meet them, there."

"You'd better watch Ben." Miss Susie tossed her head. "And don't you fall in love tonight, Elbert. Those Howe girls are beauties."

Elbert Riggs turned crimson, and Clay Abernathy said boisterously, "Sally asked Ben to bring some fellow for her younger sister. Said her mother was going to let her out of the cradle tonight."

"She's been out before," Miss Susie said primly, and Hizer put in, "Dat younges' one? Huh! I seed her whin I wint to Docta 'Lije 'bout dese spectickles—dat younges' one is plum full ob de devil, jes' like her Pa."

"Why, Hizer, don't you dare to talk about Miss Margaretta that way. She's a perfectly lovely girl."

"Miss Susie, I ain't blind—yit. An' I'se jes' tellin' dese boys dat Docta 'Lije's baby is a high steppin' spiritid lady, an' dey better watch out fur her!"

Though it was one of the most select medical clubs in America, the Pithotomy, like many another thing about Hopkins, was housed in the most mundane of buildings. It occupied a row house on Broadway, in which a narrow stairway rose abruptly in a narrow living room, beyond which was a narrow dining room containing a feature not often found in Baltimore row houses: a side wall full of windows.

The dining room chairs had been shoved back against the wall, the worn leather chairs in the living room had been shoved back, too, and the orchestra was placed just inside the dining room, directly behind the stairway. At the far end of the dining room a round table, covered with a white cloth, held a punch bowl and cups.

The girls laid their wraps in the bedrooms on the second floor, which were neither as comfortable nor as well kept as those at Miss Susie's house. In 1914 an appearance of continuous modesty still radiated from young females and these parties were carefully chaperoned. No girl penetrated above the second floor and no nurse ever attended. To all outward and visible signs the segregation of the sexes was still in full effect about the hospital. The girls at the party were either debutantes or doctors' daughters who were too young to be debutantes, but old enough to be "beaued."

After the cabarets of South America this gathering made Pug Prentiss feel, as he had feared that it might, emotionally old. The giggles of the girls were flat, their chatter high-pitched and tiresome. The punch was just punch. Completely out of place, he stood lolling around and thinking of going home.

Then Ben and Clay came in with the Howe girls and somehow— Pug never could remember much about it afterward—but somehow he held the one called Sally in his arms and they were dancing together, perfectly. Her hand in his felt soft and warm and permanent. Her head lay against his chest as though it belonged there and always had and always would. Within the first ten minutes Pug Prentiss knew that Sally Howe was the girl for whom he had searched and sought.

When the music ceased, people crowded around her and Sally

began introducing them. Prentiss knew most of the men, but none of the girls; in a quiet haze he acknowledged the introductions and allowed himself to be harnessed into dancing with another female.

Ben Mead came and swept the sunshine and the warmth of Sally Howe away. But over the head of the girl in his arms Pug could still watch Sally and enjoy doing so—her ankles and legs suited him; he was pleased that her hips were full, and that her waist wasn't too slim, nor her bust too small. She was so sweet, so warm, her hair so honey-colored and her eyes so blue. The way she looked at Ben when she laughed, made him envious, momentarily, and then happy because she was happy. He didn't care if her nose wasn't like her beautiful sister's, or that she wasn't tall and graceful. All he cared about was that he felt no longer lonely when she was in his arms and that she was warm, gay, cuddly and built for babies.

When the music stopped, somebody came and snitched the raw-boned skeleton he had away, but before he could reach Sally she was surrounded again. Prentiss wanted to shoo the others aside like flies and since that couldn't be, his next desire was to run away and forget her. He started to the third floor for a drink, but as he mounted the stairs and permitted himself one more look, straight across the room her eyes divined what he was about to do and begged for his return.

She smiled, made a place beside herself and called, "Come over here, Mister Prentiss, there's somebody I want you to meet."

It seemed years to Pug until he could beat his way across that room and feel her arm upon his coat sleeve again.

"Oh, I'm sorry. Some other man took the girl away," Sally said.

"Glad he did," Pug flashed his smile upon her. There were no longer imps in his green eyes, they were no longer teasing. Instead they seemed to Sally as clear as the sea and as deep.

She suggested quickly, "Isn't it awfully hot in here?"

Her arm dropped from his coat sleeve. Pug put his fingers beneath her elbow and steered her toward a window seat. As soon as his flesh touched hers, that sensation of peace returned to him.

When they were seated, Sally began questioning him about himself, and Prentiss told things which he didn't even suspect he remembered. Told her how he had loved his mother; how her hair had been just the color of Sally's and she had piled it on her head just in the same way; he even recalled the nursery songs which she had sung to him.

"Oh, I know that one!" Sally said and hummed a few bars, which Prentiss hadn't heard since he was five, of "Lord Lovel Stood by His Castle Gate."

Sally was thinking, "He's sweet! And not a bit ugly—when you've seen his eyes."

And Pug was thinking, "Is there any way in the world I can ever persuade her to marry me?"

As Prentiss sat watching Sally with adoration in his heart and in his eyes, across the room 'Lije Howe said to Miss Joyce Witherspoon of Raleigh, North Carolina, "It's a knack. You have to learn how. Hardest thing I ever did was to persuade Papa to let me drive it."

Joyce raised her light blue eyes to his snapping dark ones as she drawled, " 'Lije, yuh kno' yuh don' mean thet! I bet yuh drive jes'— wonderfully."

She was too plump, too placid and too pretty for Elijah Howe, Junior to permit any of her statements to go unchallenged.

"When you know me better, Joyce," he said seriously. "You'll understand that I mean what I say. Driving from Baltimore to New York, in an automobile, is—er—er—accomplishment."

She gave an admiring gasp and asked, " 'Lije, didn't it jes' wear yuh out?"

The way her words glided into his ego was as swift as the spreading of molasses on marble. 'Lije cleared his throat, "It was pretty tough."

He stuck his chin in his collar, then lifted his head quickly and said, "I'm boring you, Joyce. Suppose we have some punch."

"Oh, goodness, no yuh not! I'd much rather hear yuh talk, 'Lije. Much—" Her eyes again turned helplessly up to his.

"After you have some punch, Joyce, I'll tell you more about the trip. But I want you to have some punch because you look—" Concern was written over his features.

The girl smiled wanly. "Yuh are a docta already, aren't yuh! It's jes' thet I got up so early to catch the train."

At the punch table Ben Mead spied Joyce. He took her in his arms, swung her around, kissed her on both cheeks and asked, "How did you get up here, Sugar?"

She laughed, blushed and then when she saw that Ben's embrace
had made a sensation, she whined, "Ben Mead, yuh jes' stop thet!
These folks don't kno' we're cousins. These Yankees won't kno' what
t'think o' us!"

When the music began again, the boys began to whisk her away
from 'Lije; the medical students realized that the girl was an excellent dancer, as well as Ben Mead's cousin, and she was popular the
rest of the evening.

No man could say that Elijah Howe, Junior, was without the com-
petitive instinct! And there were two things about Joyce that, to use
a slang term current then, "slayed" 'Lije. One was that he could
impress her, the other that she could impress other people. As soon as
it was decent to do so, 'Lije reclaimed Joyce and seating her safely
against the wall continued relating his experiences as that brave and
exciting creature—the chauffeur.

"Why, 'Lije, I don't see how yuh—ever—could come back home.
Really, I don't!"

'Lije just ate it up. He swallowed it hook, line and sinker and
Margaretta watched him succumb to the Lorelei with both pain and
pleasure. Sally hadn't the slightest idea that he had done so. Margaretta was glad that both of them had forgotten to see that their
"little sister" had a good time. In the last few months she was grateful
to 'Lije and Sally for neither of them had mentioned Alex Ashby nor
teased her, since he stopped calling on her. Mamma was the only
person who ever tried to probe her about it and tonight she was sorry
that she hadn't stood Mamma down and stayed at home.

Because this awful pain inside of her was like a sword against her
heart. Hoping against hope, she kept an eagle eye doorward, just
wishing to God that for one single second she could see Alex Ashby
standing there and too proud to ask Ben Mead if he were coming.

As Hizer had prophesied, Margaretta deviled everybody and had a
dozen men dangling from different strings, adroitly managing
never to get them tangled. But her eyes kept returning to that front
door, and each time that it opened, her heart beat so swiftly that she
thought she would faint.

When eleven-thirty came and there wasn't the remotest chance of
Alex's coming, Margaretta persuaded Clay Abernathy to take her

home. She called it a headache, got rid of him at the door and tiptoed up to bed feeling the lump rise in her throat with every step.

Clay went back across town mad with her for "piking" on him, and mad with himself for being unable to kiss her. She had even edged away when he tried to put his arm about her shoulder. His collar was uncomfortable, his clothes didn't fit, he didn't feel at home in them, he didn't feel at home with the people at that party, and he didn't see any sense to going back there, again. Instead, he went to Otto's and got drunk. Otto, who had been out, found Clay so drunk when he returned that he would not send him to Miss Susie's and locked him in the washroom. When Alex and Isidore showed up after their walk, Otto told them, "I vas apout to shutt him der oontil morning. Shtudents like him, I kess nefer vouldt hafe sense."

"You ought to kick him out," Alex said succinctly. Then he went into the telephone booth and called Ben Mead at the club, told him of Clay's whereabouts and said, "Didn't he bring a girl? How about her?"

"Oh," Ben answered, "he brought Gret Howe. She went home hours ago with a headache."

"I see," Alex said shortly. "Then that's all right."

But it wasn't all right; somehow he felt that he had done Margaretta a dirty trick; she should never have been subjected to Clay. When he and Isidore had at last put Clay to bed at Miss Susie's, Alex said, "Mind if I take a turn down Broadway with you again?"

"Never object to that," Isidore answered. Alex walked home with him, then up past the Pithotomy Club again where the lights still burned and the dancing continued. For the last few weeks he had been studying so hard that he had almost forgotten it was spring, but there was a warm breeze through the leaves tonight and one could almost hear the grass grow. The last time he'd walked Broadway after midnight was when he'd received the letter about his father. Then the flower beds were bare, the trees were bleak and there was frozen ground in the center circles. Now the trees were in leaf, the octagonal and diamond-shaped beds were filled with pansies, and in a way they were a fruition for him. He wasn't sorry for the decisions he had made that night. He did not regret a single one of them—except—

except he wished that there was some way to let her know and at the same time be sure that she wouldn't tell Dr. Howe.

Phrases of his own father came back into his mind again—"The most expensive thing a man can buy is favors"—"A man's happiness comes out of his emotions. But when he trades on his emotions, for material advancement, he wins to lose. Son, don't you ever forget that." "A strong man is one who knows where he's weak. After your mother died, many's the night I wanted to cry my eyes out. Darkness is a big help, sometimes. It lets you be yourself."

Alex made the decision which he had been mulling over in his mind and turning west walked swiftly toward Cathedral Street. Within twenty minutes, he was standing across from the Howe residence staring up at the windows and wondering if she were very sick and whether she had gotten home safely.

From an incident Margaretta had once told him, Alex was aware which room the girls occupied, and as he stood in the shadow, he saw the light in their room come up, for a second, and then die down. Gret had climbed out of bed to get a clean handkerchief. The tears had come at last and she wanted, desperately, to complete her cry before Sally and 'Lije came home. After he saw the light, Alex felt easier in his mind and turned east again to Miss Susie's. Afterward he never permitted himself to think of that excursion and he studied with a renewed fierceness. The way his pipe had tasted and the sense of sudden peace after he had seen that light in her room, though, lingered in his memory for months.

And that party lingered in hers as a sort of white hell through which if she could help it, she would not put herself a second time. No matter what Mamma said, she wouldn't do it. A week later Margaretta strained her ankle and was thereby given the chance for which she longed. The chance not to see him, unless he called. He never called. She never thought that he would, but day after day when the telephone rang and it was for her, Margaretta hobbled to it with such a fluttering heart she could hardly make her bound leg move. Always the voice was that of some other student, though, and the way her heart sank before she could continue the conversation didn't get any easier as time went on. It didn't help in the least either, to think that when Pug Prentiss 'phoned Sally, nightly, he was talking from the house in which Alex Ashby lived and that perhaps Alex was listening.

Nothing could have been further from the truth; for if ever there was a man secretive about his emotions, St. George Prentiss was that man. Nightly, before the after-dinner conversation got under way he went out to a nearby drug store for "cheroots."

"You reckon he thinks he's got us buffaloed?" Ben Mead asked one night.

"Might ask him," Ashby suggested.

"I'd rather ask the Dean if he's got any bastards!" Ben made a wry face.

"Well, why don't you?"

Ben grinned and shook his head. "Glad I'm not in the same town with my heart trouble. Gosh! I'd never get through medical school if I thought she was in kissing distance every night and I couldn't kiss her."

"How you going to get through your internship feeling like that?" Silas asked soberly.

"Why bring that up? I got to get appointed before I face that, haven't I?"

"I daresay you've heard, Doctor Mead," Alex said, mimicking Dr. Halsted, "that it is against our rules for internes to be married men."

"I'm not worried about that, Doc: just give me the interneship and I'll teach her to wait!" Ben answered.

Pug reappeared and Ben said, "How about giving me one of those cheroots, Doctor?"

"Glad to," Pug answered and eased himself into a morris chair. Their affection was so intense that they did not guy Prentiss, further. The conversation returned to medical topics.

Clay, whistling, and wearing his best tie and a clean collar, came downstairs.

"Where are you going, sweetheart?" Ben asked.

"To buy some cheroots," Clay answered with a glance at Pug.

"Prentiss has already bought some," said Ashby.

"But not my brand," Clay pushed his pug nose skyward. "See you when I get back from the Altar Guild, boys." Then glibly resuming his whistling, he went down the street toward Broadway.

"Takes his gynecology seriously," Ben said, ignoring Clay's second remark.

"Is she on that service?" Ashby asked, also ignoring it.

"The redhead from Kansas with the pretty stems," Ben explained.

"Anybody see them together they'll both be canned. He ought to know better than to play around with nurses," Ashby made a plain statement.

"What's wrong with nurses?" Ben insisted. "You sound pure as the doctor who was asked by a colleague if he had married a nurse ——"

"What did he say?" Bert Riggs asked.

Ben replied, "He said, 'No. He'd married a lady.' And the colleague, who had married a nurse, answered, 'Well, it's too bad your wife lowered herself so!' "

The boys laughed heartily, and Ben insisted again, "What's wrong with nurses, Alex?"

"Nothing that I know of. But the segregation is a good rule on the whole—no matter how nice the nurses are."

"Why?"

It was Silas who asked the question. Ashby answered, "Because when people's emotions get gummed up in their work, they're not responsible for what they are doing half the time."

Silas replied, "The reason it seems wise to me is because no medical man is in position to marry until about five years after he graduates, is he?"

"And what is he to do with his 'inspirations'—in the meantime?" Ben asked sarcastically.

Alex said, "Osler advises that he 'put his emotions on ice for a few years.' "

Pug rose. "I've got to study, boys. See you later."

After he disappeared up the stairway Silas said calmly, "The reason I defended nurses is that I intend to marry one."

"Have you told her?" Ben inquired.

"No. Not yet."

"Well, tell us then—who is she?"

Alex intervened. "Hey, don't be so rough on him. Good luck to you, Si. And when she says, 'yes,' let us know."

"She won't have an opportunity to do so until I'm established. But the only reason I'm telling you—now—is that all of them are not redheaded—by a long shot."

"Gosh, I know that!" Ben said.

"So do I!" Riggs remarked.

At midnight when Clay returned, he found Holmes sitting in the parlor.

"Pretty late for you to be up, isn't it, Si?"

Holmes disregarded the chatty note and putting his big hands on his knees looked straight at the other student and said, "I waited up until you came home, Abernathy, because I want to warn you. If you ever make fun of the things Miss Susie respects, again, while I'm in this house, I'll beat you to a pulp."

"Oh, for mercy's sake, Si," Clay's voice was full of false gaiety, but his face drained of color. "I was just joking! Want to *know* where I've been?"

Silas rose, moved toward the stairway and Clay retreated to the vicinity of the front door. At the foot of the stairs Silas turned, "I don't give a damn where you've been, Abernathy. Good night."

Clay silently watched his broad back as he mounted the stairs and decided that it might be a good idea to walk around the block before going to bed.

He felt as if an ox had breathed upon him.

Chapter Sixteen

THOSE HIDDEN CENTERS
OF REAL LIFE

'Lije, feeling almost upon the verge of nausea, threw back the bedcovers and stood up. As his bare toes sank into the deep carpet, his eyes became adjusted to the darkness. Then, through some instinctive knowledge, now that he was erect, he knew that the feeling of nausea was not physical and possibly not nausea; it was like nausea is physically but it wasn't happening to his stomach; he dared go no further in self-examination.

A faint glow from the street light filtered into the room as he made his way to the single open window and lit a protective cigarette. It must be after eleven-thirty because there was no light in old Mr. Simmon's library across the street and he never went to bed before then. Also, the night had turned silent as it does after one, when patiently finishing its course and waiting to spread into dawn. Below was the selfsame Cathedral Street and across the identical row houses at which he had peered ever since he was able to peer. But somehow tonight they were animate. Instead of looking at the fronts and thinking "pasteboard," 'Lije's mind went skipping on into the living rooms, bedrooms and pantries.

Except for hall nightlights, all of the houses were in total darkness and against the thick, dampish mist they appeared to be breathing deeply in unison. Their individual discords were obliterated in the settling quiet.

Elijah lit a fresh cigarette, threw his stub into the street, watched it hit, skid and roll into the gutter. Then he placed his hands under his jaws, rested his elbows against the sill and tried to rationalize.

But it was no use; there was something as heavy, fecund and damp in this half-mist as there is in the atmosphere of a greenhouse. A quality more disquieting than moonlight: like sitting beside a devastating woman after a tennis match, when she has ceased to perspire and begun to glow; a deepish feeling full of tingles and desire.

She was like tonight—not piercing as moonlight is—but moist and alive. Few men can walk in moonlight indefinitely, but many men are imaginatively pleased by mist, and something sensed but never grasped. Or—now that he had acknowledged that much he ought to really think it out—could that thing about her which now he adored be as mist, an inbetween something, not night, not day? Did he want it so fiercely because he had never seen it before in anybody else—or because inside it suited him completely? She really wasn't terribly pretty, nor too well built: lots of the girls he had known all his life were better looking and richer; but if just once he could have Joyce and get to that quality, would he ever be unhappy again?

That awful penetrating desire was what made him feel like nausea; precisely the same kind of thing, only emotionally, which that patient had tried to explain in the maternity clinic when her child quickened. That was it, all right! Might as well face it: he, Elijah Howe, the unattainable, was woozy with love.

Well, what could you do about it, anyhow? Tell Papa? Tell Mamma? Tell her? Tell her! Gosh! He took his cigarette from his lips and whistled with the same sort of alarm with which one recalls a truant dog, as though hoping, thereby, to recapture his emotions and exert his common sense. Why, all together he had only seen her six times! What sort of an ass would she take him for, if he told her, and what could he tell her?

With a gesture of despair he replaced the cigarette and smoked furiously. His mind, or whatever you called it when it got involved like this, still informed him that he had two years more in medical school before he could secure an interneship. Then with Papa behind him, he ought to get something, easily; but even if he did, after he interned there'd be a residency and then a grind before he'd be in a position to tell her.

"Aw hell!" he said despondently and slung the other cigarette toward its mate in the gutter. It fell wide of the mark and all of him that was not his mind continued to inform him that if he had any sense whatever he'd chuck his mind and swoop down on her in the dead of night.

The young man shook his head as though besieged by gnats, then eased it between his hands and groaned; and the hard old street, caressed and calmed by night, breathed up a sympathy which comforted Elijah. It was as if the old paving stones said, "People lived here before these present people. I've seen so much in my time, just tell me. Other people have told me. Even if there is nothing I can do, I can understand."

Young Howe lifted his head with determination. The street was right. If he couldn't tell her, he wouldn't tell anybody. Mamma would try to talk him out of it, Papa would say he wasn't old enough to know what he was talking about; the girls would giggle. And if he told Joyce, she might be so surprised and frightened she wouldn't see him again. Because if he did tell her, he couldn't just say, "I love you," he'd have to say it all: about wanting her—really.

His body applauded his emotions, the old street seemed to rise and turn, and the black softness changed to pink-gray. Then the tiny fronds of green leaves on the corner trees were shocked by a sudden breeze and abandoned themselves into trembling gaiety. But as the cornice of the house intervened between them and the east which was fast suffusing with light, 'Lije did not actually behold, but only sensed their transformation. And in a sweet agony of pain he stumbled to his bed and buried his miserableness in the familiar pillow. The groans changed to sobs, but there were no tears.

After Maria was asleep with her finger safely locked in his palm, Dr. Howe lay thinking——

When the children were young, after a day harassed by tragic patients, he had gone to their nursery and received from them the strength, the power, the touch-spring of energy with which to go on. 'Lije in the small bed; Sally's curly head beyond; and in the crib, Margaretta—*he* had made them, *he* had decided to place them within Maria's body, steadied her through their growth, held her hand while they were delivered and calmed her nerves through their infancies.

They were his. All of them. Back in that old nursery with the silhouettes of playing children tacked upon the walls and the live children which he had created relaxed upon the beds, a sense of power, infinite and invincible, always flowed through his limbs and into his brain. They were his. This house was his. All of the food they had ever eaten, he had supplied.

Out of that feeling of competency against the vicissitudes of childhood, his mind swung back into this present complex world of his established reputation and their real problems. Was a father able to influence his children only so long as his influence was of no real value? When they frequented that nursery these children of his flesh didn't need him, actually, in the slightest. Had he died then, someone would have seen them through their childhood. And whether it had been happy or unhappy, they'd soon have forgotten.

But these present painful years when 'Lije was so unsure of himself and of medicine and probably of sex, why was a father so isolated? Was it his own fault? Why couldn't he manage to throw off their hideous reserve, now, with the audacious ease with which he used to throw off the burdens of his day when reading the *Just So Stories* to the boy after supper? Wasn't this part of life as natural as that?

These intense pains of first love—male and female—lasted as long as life, often; too many patients had described them to him long years afterward, for him to doubt that. And now when his own offspring were facing real, personal tragedy why was he so incompetent? Did fathers always seem so infinitely helpless when their children suffered? So bitterly unnecessary?

Of course it was true, in the ultimate sense, that a man must do his suffering alone; perhaps that was what made him so thoroughly impatient with and baffled by this suffering of his children. When a patient suffered from a purely physical cause, it was usually possible to relieve the suffering, or—at least, to lower it and estimate the extent of its duration. But, when the emotions first came into conflict with the desires, could any outside person teach a human being how to regulate them?

Was it really true that the only way we ever learn is through pain?

In Gret, for instance, there was a kind of iron which made her capable of infinite suffering, infinite feeling, infinite joy, yet, also, capable of standing whichever came her way with steadiness. To be so strong a woman was almost as much of a disadvantage as being a hunchback; it frightened off all lesser men. But it also gave immense courage to every person with whom she ever came in contact. Was it just his imagination or was it being tested too early? Should he do as Maria pestered him to and talk to Alex Ashby? Or should he talk to Gret? Or should he follow his own inclination and leave it strictly alone? So long as the boy stayed in Baltimore there was always a chance that they could patch it up for themselves. Probably it was too bad that he hadn't listened to Maria and kept Gret home from the McMillans. What in the thunder could have happened to them, anyhow? Dr. McMillan said they fell in love at first sight; Maria said they were in love; and they certainly had looked that way to him. McMillan's advice was to leave it alone for six months, and to make Margaretta go out as much as they could. And Maria wanted to take her back to Maine for the summer, which probably would be a good thing. At least she wouldn't jump out of her chair every time the telephone rang and perhaps she'd get some flesh on her bones. But there wasn't any use believing in that guff Maria slung about the child forgetting Ashby. Unfortunately Gret wasn't the forgetting kind. He knew that, and that was why he was so concerned about her. Her intensity came straight from himself, though; if anybody was to blame for this suffering he was.

Sally, now, was incapable of such pain. Sally's great attractiveness was her femininity; it arose primarily out of her sex, her obvious fitness for maternity. Ruffles; babies; the instinct to protect her was the first emotion which arose in any man—and he was glad that it had arisen so plainly in Pug Prentiss. There couldn't be two finer sons-in-law than those boys. And with Prentiss, at least, the attraction seemed lasting. That was one of the baffling points about Alex Ashby's behavior—the attraction had certainly looked lasting there— and no matter what Maria said to the contrary he still believed that it was.

But, however one argued the individual case, certain generalities held for them all: from these first encounters one often got one's libido either warped or straight for life—and the later happiness was born out of the confidence or the lack of it, established then. The only real living we ever do is in our emotions and probably this was the most important time emotionally that most people ever had to face. And was there anything a father could do to assist a child in such a facing? Should the girls go out more? Should 'Lije have more allowance? Was there any way to pry him loose from that North Carolina young woman without damaging him permanently?

Dr. Howe eased his head sidewise upon the pillow and watched Maria sleep; now that his hand was securely locked about her finger, she slept with the confidence, abandon and security that the girls and 'Lije had exhibited when they were little. How gigantically complicated a process life was! He and Maria through a completely right relationship had begun these children whose frightening futures were filling his fancies now; in a sense, things in life being "right" created in the end almost as infinite a variety of problems as things being wrong!

A little silent chuckle filled his throat and with it came an intense desire to smoke, which he curbed on account of Maria. The fumes would awaken her, and at the moment he preferred morose solitude to marital conversation; yet since his sense of humor had asserted itself, a sense of hope had entered his outlook. He remembered that he had often thought when he was frightened about a patient, "A great many people have passed through this sort of crisis before—and survived."

Being in a philosophical mood he continued thinking, "Those who survived, maimed, often accomplished fine work. Happiness isn't always necessary to the display of a man's best talents. Some—flower under adversity."

Yet, he had never been able to convince himself that the flowering would not have been more complete under the influence of happiness. For when he tried to imagine how hideous a thing his own life would have been without the eternal comfort of Maria, the ever-present feeling of her hand upon his shoulder, a fear of great depth rose within him, and he realized a cowardice which in broad daylight when meeting and comforting countless people he never allowed himself to acknowledge.

The fear of death: not for himself, with the children provided for and Maria secure; not for his patients when they were weary of life and defeated; but the blank, starved pain which would be his if Maria died.

In that deep silence during which 'Lije had stumbled to his bed yearning, his father, too, lay utterly defenseless against his emotions, knowing, as he had so often known, that a man who is emotionally happy with a woman is the most fortunate and the most unfortunate of all creatures, for the possible death of that woman holds for him a darkness opaque and endless.

Maria stirred in her sleep and cuddled closer to him. Nestling his lips against hers, he awoke her. When she was asleep again, he recalled that Balzac had said somewhere that a husband should be the last to go to sleep at night and the first to awake in the morning; and bathed in an utter contentment he lay watching the dawn suffuse the world.

A sudden breeze caused the tiny fronds of green leaves upon the corner trees, visible through their open window, to abandon themselves into a trembling gaiety. And a phrase for which he had hunted and never found words grew clear and fell into sequence in his mind. It was: a man who sleeps with a woman he loves is as a tree with roots.

Margaretta rose from the breakfast table and said calmly, too calmly her father thought, "Mamma, will you excuse me?"

"But, baby, you haven't eaten your cereal!"

"Mamma, I'm *not* a baby. And I got permission at college to switch a class and play piano duets before my lesson this morning. *Please,* I've got to go."

"But child, you haven't eaten a thing. Three weeks from now, when we get to Maine, I hope your appetite will have improved!"

Dr. Howe saw Margaretta stiffen suddenly at the word Maine and he said quickly, "Think you've still got enough strength to kiss me good-bye, Gret?"

There was no irritation in his voice and no vehemence in hers as she replied, "I'll never be too weak for that." She walked around the table, kissed him on the lips and tossing her head backward fled from the room.

The sun still shone, the day was still bright, but Dr. Howe felt as though an early morning breeze had died down. He continued his breakfast in silence and wondered if that bracing of her head had been to avoid tears.

Margaretta ran upstairs, put on her big straw hat, picked up her music roll and then slipped down the back stairway, for she was afraid that they would call her into the dining room again and that she'd break down.

Sneaking out through the back garden she resorted to alley walking; there were nobody but niggers and dogs in alleys. There wasn't any danger of seeing the people she knew in them, and if she walked through them to a section of the city where she knew no one—one of those little parks in West Baltimore—then she could sit down and stand it alone.

And until she found some place to sit down she mustn't think. It wouldn't do to think. It had been cowardly to run away, but if she had sat at that breakfast table another minute, after Mamma said they were going to Maine in three weeks, she'd have burst out crying and then all of them would have known.

As it was, nobody really knew; you could stand terrible pain when nobody knew. You could stand years and years like this by yourself, if you had to, but you wouldn't be able to stand even one day of it if Mamma and 'Lije and Sally and Papa knew. They just thought Alex Ashby was another beau; they'd forgotten him by now.

But what was the matter with her? Why couldn't she forget him? Why couldn't she be glad to go to Maine? It used to be fun in Maine —sailing and meeting people. How did she know so surely that it wouldn't be fun any more? It wouldn't be. Never again would it be fun anywhere out of the same town with Alex. If—if he wanted to 'phone her she wanted to be where he could reach her. But if he didn't want to call her, then why couldn't she stop wanting him to want to? Where was her pride? Why couldn't she stop loving him? What was wrong with her?

It was damp in the alley and puddles lay in the uneven sections, but in her misery Gret did not notice them. Too weak to walk further, she leaned against a garage door and decided to close her eyes in an endeavor to cut out the pain which was as clear as the sunshine; perhaps if she shut her eyes, it wouldn't seem so terrible. Sunshine and pain didn't go together, but darkness and pain did; when she hurt this way at night, she could get up in the morning

and go on all right but, until right now, it had never been awful like
this in the daytime.

Maybe if she shut her eyes——

She shut them. Her unlined firm hands tightened around the music
roll; her slender body pulled away from the garage door; she stood
erect and closed her eyes, quickly.

Fortunately, the alley remained deserted of human beings; then
a robin sang in some back-garden tree and without warning Alex
Ashby's face, his fine gray eyes and a warmth, the warmth he had
and nobody else ever had, bore down through the darkness toward
her as his deep voice said, "I love you, Ladykins."

Instantly, Margaretta opened her eyes and shook her head violently
to keep from fainting; the music roll slipped from her fingers, and
landed against a garbage can.

The robin began again. The girl, her eyes wide and defiantly open,
searched the trees for him and murmured: "I won't suffer. I
just won't!"

But inside she knew that when she went to dances, she would
still be lost; no matter how many men danced with her, and asked
her for dates and took her places, there wasn't a single one of them
who had that warmth which Alex Ashby had. No other man could
sit in a room with her, so there wasn't any air left over, so that everything was alive and breathing.

Oh, God, couldn't you ever stop loving? Couldn't you?

Well, even if you couldn't, there was some comfort in music. She
leaned down, picked up the music roll, brushed her big hat backward
upon her head and walked gracefully out of the alley, the same way
that she had come. It would be no use to go to a park and fight it
out. Fighting it out couldn't cut it out.

In the warm May air, the front doors of the negro shanties stood
ajar, and somewhere nearby, a voice began to sing, "To dem dat
hath, it shall be given," and then a defiant sort of refrain followed,
" 'Nything dey want."

The part of Margaretta Howe which was akin to her father
brought something rather close to a smile to her lips and she thought
it was true—that phrase. Sally had Pug Prentiss, so at every opportunity he was given to her. Mamma had Papa, so they were always

invited places together. But she didn't have Alex—now. For some reason she couldn't understand he wasn't hers. So nobody would ever help to give him to her.

But how did them that hath get their start?

What was it in Mamma that Papa wanted, which Alex, after he kissed her, didn't want in her?

Why, when people were happy together, did everybody always help them to be more happy—and when people were like she was and needing help they never got it?

Instead they got piano duets. Mozart and Haydn.

And even in their music, there were parts which seemed to moan and cry, "Ladykins, Ladykins, Ladykins."

Chapter Seventeen

FENCING WITH DEATH

As Alex strolled up Broadway he found that he was restless and decided to take a walk; go all the way up to North Avenue, then take a turn through Clifton Park and come back to Otto's for a glass of beer before going to bed.

Several blocks above the hospital he ran into Prentiss.

"Been looking for you, Alex. Where are you headed?"

"To take a walk. Come along. Where're you going?"

"To the accident room and then to Otto's for some Bock beer. Come along with me."

"Sure," Ashby swung around.

"Where have you been?"

"Talking with Isidore. What's stirring at home?"

"Ben still has lalorrhea; Clay has the jumps; Hizer's got the toothache, and Riggs and Holmes aren't home. Everything is fine!"

"Sounds like it! What are you planning to do this summer, Pug?"

"Stay here," Prentiss said instantly. "And you?"

"Thinking of doing the same thing, if I can get a chance to work in one of the clinics."

"Not going to Texas?"

"Not if I can get a chance in one of the clinics."

"Which one?"

"Department L, I think. Depends: either that or medicine."

"Think you'll go on in syphilis, Alex?"

"Probably. What do you want to do?"

"I don't know either. That's why I'm sticking around this summer: trying to decide."

Ten minutes later they entered the accident room, but things were in a lull. Alex began contemplating a foaming stein of Bock beer—that heavy, rich, black fluid which is obtainable only during the spring months. Also, he was anticipating a conversation with Otto.

He had just opened his lips to suggest leaving when the door of the accident room opened and two firemen bore in a stretcher from a municipal ambulance. On it, covered with the gray-black blankets of the city, lay a mature and robust negro woman. She was groaning and praying, simultaneously.

The nurse directed the firemen to roll the negress into the adjacent examination room and with a nod Prentiss suggested to Ashby that they follow.

"From the way those blankets lay, she's pregnant."

"I'm not too certain, Pug. Did you notice the size of her arms? That may be only fat."

They found the obstetrical interne leaning over her. He had ascertained her name. "What seems to be the matter, Pearl?"

As she described a pain in the stomach which had started two hours before, the interne took her pulse, the nurse took her temperature.

Alex murmured to Pug, "As you know, when they complain of a pain in the stomach it's usually salpingitis—inflammation of a fallopian tube, caused generally by gonorrhea. Very frequent among negroes."

The interne had found that Pearl's blood pressure was 100 over 60, her temperature a hundred point two, and that the pain localized in the region of the left fallopian tube; also, she might be one month pregnant. She had previously had a midline incision for a Caesarean delivery.

Pug and Alex assisted where necessary. Pug was surprised at the large hips and the midline scar. Alex explained, "Contracted pelves are common among negroes: result of rickets. One reason why this school is so famous for manipulating a delivery through a contracted pelvis—had more experience with it than almost any group of men in the country."

At the interne's direction, they had placed a chair under the foot of the bed which was not the self-winding type, and Pearl's feet were now higher than her head. The interne went to telephone for the assistant resident. He came to confirm the examination and then the doctors went to consult with the resident over the 'phone. Alex, standing near the head of the bed calming Pearl, taking her pulse, said hastily, "Pug, get him!"

Prentiss understood that he meant the interne and did so.

"Her pulse is gone," Alex reported. As the three men watched, the patient's feet turned yellow-gray, gray and were turning white-gray. The woman had lapsed into coma. "She's in shock," the interne said to the nurse. "Get some morphia quickly."

He applied his stethoscope and heard the heart beat faintly. They stood helplessly about the bed. Was she dying? There was nothing more to do except to operate.

The resident arrived and the assistant resident reported, "Ectopic pregnancy, I think, but no vaginal blood, no subnormal temperature."

Pug stood watching intently as the resident examined the patient. Alex relinquished his position to the interne and thought, "That's pregnancy in the fallopian tube which has ruptured. She's bleeding to death internally—if the diagnosis is correct."

Within seconds, Pearl had her injection of morphia.

The resident confirmed his belief that the diagnosis was correct. The assistant resident continued watching Pearl and the interne kept feeling for the pulse in her temple, on the side of her nose and then listening with his stethoscope over her heart. Turning to the students he said, "She's in shock, all right. Here! Feel her skin."

They did so and it was cold, clammy, and still gray-white. The doctors put more blankets over her. The interne found a faint pulse in the temple which the resident checked, and then he went into the accident room and made the telephone call which decided Pug Prentiss's fate.

"Give me the G-Y-N operating room, please," he said. "G-Y-N operating room? Doctor Allison speaking. I'm going in on a midline exploratory. Probably in twenty minutes, please."

Returning to the men standing about Pearl, he began dividing up the work. To the assistant resident he said, "Will you check her heart and lungs and watch her." To the interne, "Take her blood and get her typed for transfusion." Turning to Ashby he ordered, "You do the hemoglobin. I want to determine the extent of hemorrhage." To himself he muttered, "I'd better glance over her case history. It's just come up." Then recognizing Pug as a medical student and assuming that he was of an advanced year, the resident said, "There is a brother outside. Take his blood for matching, will you? And ask the nurse to get the policeman on the beat to call all available relatives and friends. She will need two or three transfusions and as many matchings as we can get."

Nobody remarked that Prentiss was second year; Pug's acute observation had taught him that he must get two samples from the donors; one for matching, the other for Wassermann. The Wassermann test, he knew, would take several hours to determine and be useful for determining later transfusions, the typing would take about ten minutes; in the present emergency Wassermanns must go by the board, temporarily. For the next two hours what Pearl needed was blood, from a husband, a brother or a sister, regardless.

It was the first time in his entire life that Prentiss had been an active participant in a scientific battle against death. Pug called the negro man into the accident room, cleansed his arm and took the samples with a fine professional assurance. Then he took them to the interne to be sent to the laboratory.

The nurse from G-Y-N arrived and prepared the patient; removed clothes, put a hospital nightgown and flannel leggings on the woman; then, with the help of the doctors, the orderly placed the patient on the stretcher and Pearl was rolled up the corridor en route to the operating room. The assistant resident reported that the heart action was no worse.

After they had finished their portion of the work-up and were in the G-Y-N dressing room putting on their gowns, caps and masks, Alex said to Pug, "The reason they didn't give her any glucose when she was in shock was because if she is bleeding to death, increasing the liquids in the body would only increase the pressure."

They went on into the operating room and sat behind the glass screen in the observation "bleachers," gazing down at the nurses checking their equipment, fixing the basins of bichloride of mercury solution, awaiting the doctors and the anesthetized patient. Ben Mead arrived apparently from nowhere and eased in beside Alex and Pug. Ashby brought him up to date on the case and concluded, "I think he's right to go in. Another sinking spell and she'd be out."

Ben said gutturally behind his mask, "I think he is, too. By the way, I heard the lab said that her brother's blood matched."

"That's good. She's going to need it," Alex answered.

The doctors came from the scrub-up room into the operating room. Their shirt sleeves were rolled above their elbows and their scrubbed arms, hands and faces glistened. The scrubbed-up nurse handed them their caps and held their gowns. While they adjusted their masks, she began sorting the packages of sterile gloves. The men put their hands in the bichloride basins, dried them on the sterile towels which the nurse provided. Each doctor opened the powder envelope in his sterile glove package, flicked his hands with the powder and slipped his fingers into the gloves. Then, with his gloved hands in a sterile towel, each man stood by waiting.

The patient was rolled in, draped and put in the Trendelenburg position, with her head lower than her feet; and although her head was toward the students, her position incidentally allowed them a perfect view of the operation.

Somewhere in the distance Pug heard a clock striking midnight and realized that within forty minutes of the time that she had entered the hospital, Pearl was on the operating table. Some of the younger men standing about her body were on the verge of changing their minds about her diagnosis. The gray-white had disappeared from her skin. Had they been gotten out of bed on a fluke? Was she really bleeding, internally?

The interne swabbed the pulsating abdomen with iodine, which blended into the color of Pearl's flesh so that its only evidence was a puddle in the navel. Gowned and gloved, the resident and the assistant resident looked over their masks at his work. Above the operating table the huge circular light blazed. Within its radius the tables of instruments, all freshly laid out since the resident's 'phone call, were presided over by efficient, experienced operating room nurses, who were also gowned and gloved and masked. The interne finished and re-draped the patient so that only the former midline was visible.

Then he stepped back. The resident took his position beside the patient, the assistant resident stood across, ready to assist, and the nurse rolled the instrument table into place at Pearl's feet.

The resident picked up his scalpel and Alex whispered to Pug,

"He'll probably excise that old midline." Then the scalpel penetrated, made an opening upon only one side of the scar and Alex murmured, "He's afraid of wasting time. He's going to get in and get out. And she is something to get into! Look at that fat!"

It was white and extended a full three inches before he reached the abdominal muscles and the assistant resident began applying an occasional hemostat clamp which the instrument nurse handed to him.

The room cleared with the sudden stillness. The assistant resident said, "Clamp. Clamp. Another clamp, please."

At the resident's direction another interne started giving Pearl an intravenous injection of 5 per cent glucose solution. He failed to find the vein first go and had to cut down on it. He found it, and then the fluid flowed from the elevated glucose bottle into the copper-colored arm.

A waiting spread into the stillness of the men about the table. A sudden change of tempo through which Pug Prentiss realized that the resident was now down to the peritoneum. He wondered could they see the blood in the abdominal cavity through the peritoneum? Was Pearl bleeding internally, or—? The students leaned forward. The operating team leaned forward.

Then experienced fingers laid the scalpel-blade upon the tough yellow-white surface of the peritoneum. Lifting a small portion of the peritoneum with an instrument, the surgeon began the incision. Instantly, his glove, his scalpel, the clamps, the fat, and the draping sheet were covered with blood.

A murmur of approbation went up from the men assisting and Alex said to Pug, "It's that, all right! She was—*bleeding to death*—inside."

"Sponge. 'Nuther sponge! Sponge! Still another sponge!"

The voice of the resident made the hands of his assistant fly with a gorgeous precision, made the hands of the scrubbed-up nurse weave to and fro.

The sponges weren't fast enough. The surgeon laid his scalpel aside and began digging out the blood clots with his gloved fingers. They lay like rubies on the draping sheet—several slid onto the floor.

"Don't throw that blood on the floor! It's valuable," he said, and his assistant and the nurses jumped for sterile containers in which to catch it. "Filter it with gauze and then pour it into the glucose bottle," he ordered.

As a nurse did so, the men across the operating table continued applying and removing the sponges.

"Good diagnosis!" the assistant resident said admiringly.

"Hope I can get at it," the resident answered.

The students leaned forward and waited. The clots were out, the resident's fingers packed aside, using large gauzes which had been soaked and wrung from warm saline solution, the large intestine. Ashby said to Pug, "He's looking for the uterus. He's found it. See! And that's the tube. He's *got* it!"

The surgeon's swift fingers worked like lightning, churning with knowledge. He raised the fallopian tube, which should be no larger in diameter than a lead pencil, and was in this case swollen ten times its diameter, with a small hole in it from which the blood was dripping. He applied two Kelly clamps between the tube and the uterus and two more between the mass and the pelvic wall. Then, using a fresh scalpel he excised the tube and the ovary, lifted them with the attached clamps out of the body and slung them onto a white-covered stand nearby.

"No time to save the ovary, and that's what gonorrhea will do to your tubes!" remarked Ben Mead, who had watched the operation wordlessly.

As the suturing began the resident said, "Can't think about suspending that uterus. Patient would die. Got to get out as fast as possible. She's lost too much blood to tamper with her."

The three students watched the three men suture, unclamp, suture, unclamp, suture their way out of a human body and into an operating room again.

Twenty-five minutes from the time they had made the incision, they tied the last suture.

Ben Mead hunched forward, watching every movement of a wrist, every knotting of a suture, utterly absorbed in the sight before him. Pug Prentiss hunched forward, too, but he was absorbed in a very different vision.

Against the opposite wall, beyond the arc of the operating table light, he could almost see the men stand out—the men on whose shoulders these surgeons before him had stood—Lister, Crawford Long, Sir David Brewster, Ephraim McDowell, Howard Kelly and 'Buck' Edwards. And he felt drawn to them with a kinship which was deeper than words; he felt that as libraries bear testimony to brilliant minds, *he* wanted before *he* died to leave some testimony either in technique or in instruments which would be valuable upon a gynecological operating table. He wanted to be a rung in the ladder of female surgery.

As the resident tied the last stitch, he ordered, "Prepare to transfuse from her brother as soon as we get her off the table."

Ben Mead looked up and said, as though he had been reading Prentiss's thoughts, "Those abdominal clamps were called after Kelly—our Doctor Kelly—because he uses them in his operating room, and in G-Y-N surgery they are used more than any other clamp."

Pug nodded silently. He was thinking that within three hours from the time Pearl had first been stricken with pain modern surgery had saved her life, and he had found a branch of medicine in which he no longer felt an onlooker, but a participant.

There was a dawn quality in the night as the three students strolled back toward Miss Susie's. Otto's was closed. Bock beer had been forgotten.

Chapter Eighteen

THE SUMMER OF 1914

After dinner one night toward the end of May, Dr. Howe called 'Lije into his office and said, "Sit down, son." 'Lije obeyed.

His father took several puffs on his cigar and asked, "Got any idea what you want to do this summer?"

'Lije cleared his throat. "I'd like to go up to Maine with Mamma and the girls for a month, sir. Then, if you could get me a position in a New York hospital, I'd like to—er look around up there for a while."

"What's the matter with getting yourself a position and looking around here?"

"Nothing, except—er."

"Er—what?"

"Er—I'd just like to be on my own, for a little while, sir."

"You only 'sir' me when you are trying to get something out of me. Stop it! And another thing: if I get you a job you certainly won't be on your own. You'll still be under my shadow." Dr. Howe leaned forward and his eyes twinkled. "You know you are dead right when you think it is a disadvantage to be the son of a man who is already established in medicine."

"I wish you'd forget that, sir—I ——"

"Forget it! Hell, it is the wisest thing you ever said."

Few people had ever accused 'Lije of wisdom, and as he began to expand his father noted the change. Dr. Howe continued, "I want you to get away from us, son, for the summer. Is your girl going to be in Maine? That why you want to go there?"

"No, sir."

"Then, don't go. If a man stays too much around the women he is kin to, they cramp him. I want you to go where you'll meet people you never saw before and may never see again. I want you to go to London."

"To London, sir?"

"That's what I said."

The expression on the boy's face was one of such infinite surprise that his father found it comic, but Dr. Howe refrained from laughing and continued, "I'll give you money to pay your passage both ways. And money to live off of for one month. Now, there are four months vacation, so you can take your choice of what you'll do. I'll also give you letters to my friends in the profession which will get you a job at some hospital. And I'll get the Dean to give you a letter which simply says that you are a medical student and hasn't a single damned word about your being my son in it. After your money is gone, you can use either of the letters you please. The only stipulation I make is that you don't come home until the last boat before medical school opens in the fall. What do you think of it?"

"I—" the boy stammered. Then suddenly standing up he grasped his father's hand and grinned, "I think it's fine, sir! Just fine!"

Dr. Howe patted 'Lije's hand with satisfaction. "It'll do you good, son. I'll be glad to see you go."

"I wish you were going too, sir."

The doctor answered gruffly, "After you start practicing, son, you can't get away. Be lucky if I have ten days with your mother in Maine."

"May I tell 'em I'm going?" 'Lije asked, easing doorward.

"Certainly, but don't tell 'em *why* I want you to go."

After he was alone Dr. Howe lit a fresh cigar and sat for a long time trying not to be disappointed. He had hoped against hope that the boy would say he'd prefer to stay home and they'd keep bachelor hall together. But that was foolish sentimentality! What boy wouldn't hop at a chance to spend the summer visiting the clinics in London? Still—Hopkins clinics were as good as any in the civilized world. But being young and inexperienced 'Lije couldn't understand how he missed Maria during the summers; how he yearned for his children; how secretly he had thought that when the boy grew up they would be together.

With the closing of medical school and the coming of summer, there was little difference in the personnel of Miss Susie's house. Prentiss stayed on, went to work as a voluntary assistant in the G-Y-N dispensary and wrote weekly letters to Maine. Ben Mead stayed on and took time out from operations only for sleeping and eating; otherwise any time any two or three gathered together to cut upon the human body, Ben was among them. Clay went home, then decided that a small town wasn't of any interest as compared with a city, even an old moth-eaten city like Baltimore, and returned to spend the summer sticking around the hospital. His father was relieved when he did so, for Clay, one of the first of that type who believe that only specialists can save human life, corrected Dr. Abernathy upon every turn and left the honest, hard-working country doctor with the seeds of a fierce inferiority complex.

Silas Holmes quietly returned to North Carolina and humbly apprenticed himself to a country doctor for the summer. Bert Riggs returned to Pennsylvania for six weeks and then to his own amazement found that the farm didn't satisfy him, even when it was making money. He came back to join the students observing at the hospital, and thereby get a daily look at Nan Rogers.

Alex Ashby, at McMillan's invitation, spent the summer substituting for internes who were on vacation—an honor of signal importance and one which was rarely extended to a man who had just concluded his third year. Before reporting, Alex took two days off and went to New York to apply at the Rockefeller. At his suggestion they promised not to investigate him at Hopkins until August, so that his interne work might count in their final decision. Of its outcome, he felt reasonably sure, but until he actually had the appointment, he was still unwilling to see Margaretta. Anyhow from the increase in Prentiss's leisure, he learned that Mrs. Howe and the girls were away.

Against furious protests from his family, Isidore Aaron spent the summer dissecting brains. He seemed obsessed with their functions and their malformations—with correlating man's past knowledge upon the influence of different parts of the brain upon different functions of the body. From early morning until way past midnight, Alex could find him in the small laboratory which Snell had assigned to him, or in the Pathological Museum.

Once when Ashby questioned him, Isidore justified himself replying, "Insanity is either to be controlled through endocrinology or purely through the psychic approach."

"And you think?"

"I do not permit myself to think—yet. The whole field is too uncharted for any man to make an authoritative statement about it."

"Even for a man like Cushing?"

"Because Halsted's radical operation for carcinoma of the breast works doesn't mean, in the slightest, that Halsted knows the cause of carcinoma."

Before the summer was over Rigman, whose work in brain surgery was renowned, became so accustomed to finding Aaron in the "bleachers" when he operated that he questioned Snell about him.

Snell said, "He may be unwilling to take an appointment upon your service when he graduates. Anyhow, the boy has two more years of medical school before he will be in a position to begin an interneship."

"What do you mean, may not want to be on my service?" Rigman, a blond giant of a man, roared.

Snell, who had been an instructor years before when Rigman was a student, had a pretty accurate knowledge of Rigman's personality. Snell answered calmly, "Some men know what they wish to do even when they are young. Aaron is such a man. Now, what he is doing—alone—is deciding whether he thinks your field is interesting enough for him to enter."

"Just like all Jews! Conceited and——"

"—unless I'm very much mistaken he is not at all certain—yet—whether he prefers to work with you or with Cushing." Snell, who was genuinely fond of Isidore, completed the sentence for the surgeon and thereby cinched Aaron a job upon the brain team after graduation.

The menus at Miss Susie's altered during the summer. Instead of stewed fruit there were sliced bananas and cream for breakfast, or Eastern Shore cantaloupes and peaches when they came in season. The house altered, too; the rugs were removed from the floors and the dark-blue window shades replaced the straw-colored ones, as they did almost by sacred right at the windows of all of the identical row houses in Baltimore. The parlor furniture was swathed in "dust covers"—homemade, heavy muslin things which were always wrinkling, always having to be removed and washed. During their reign, Hizer stoutly refused to make hot bread and the boys "had to do on baker's bread."

Whatever the season, though, the courtesy remained and no man living on the fourth floor would have acknowledged to Miss Susie that it was any hotter up there than in the parlor. As she never penetrated above the second floor, the way the men from there on up stood the blistering, stifling, humid hell, was to bow the outside window shutters so that no one could see in from across the street, and go about strip, stark naked. This completely modest old maid, serenely unaware, lived on in a house all of whose occupants, except Prentiss, who still had the room near hers, and Hizer, who had a cool lean-to behind the kitchen, pursued their education completely nude.

The tub in the bathroom adorned with the phosphorus ceiling lady spent the summer filled with cold water. Each man when he got home hopped into it, smoked a couple of cigarettes, re-filled it with fresh water and left it for the next comer.

The Baltimore summer wore on, and the city lay smothered in layers of a heat which sunset did not alleviate. By some quirk of mass insanity these houses, so constructed that they should never have been permitted in a climate where the temperature rose above eighty degrees, stretch for miles in a city where it often soars above a hundred. And miles on square miles, the bricks hold that heat for weeks at a time.

Pug Prentiss did not mind the heat. The only thing which he did regret was that he was contented in a way which must, in the nature of things, soon cease. Ashby's absence at the hospital this summer accentuated his sense of impending loss. In the bathroom with the ceiling lady, he would lie in the tub smoking and trying to hold on to the sensation of contentment. Every man in this house he liked, in some way, and the one he liked best would be gone from it in another nine months. When Pug tried to look ahead to what the place would be like without Alex's teasing, his singing, his brilliance and his kindness, a black despair would enter his mind and perch there—like Poe's raven. The knowledge that Sally Howe would be home in the fall was the only thing which could decrease his sadness.

It wasn't that he didn't want Ashby to move forward in the profession, but simply that for the first time in his entire life he was a member of a group who suited his every imagined desire. He didn't want it nor the outlook it occasioned in him to alter. Kipling knew the feeling—the lama had referred to it when addressing Kim as "the red mist of affection."

Everywhere Alex invited Pug to go he went feeling as if it were the last time they should ever be together. When Alex and Isidore took an afternoon off and went to the Army Medical Museum in Washington, Prentiss accompanied them. For all three, it was a day hung outside of time in congeniality. The only person who understood Pug's depression was Aaron. When Alex had gone to the washroom on the train, Isidore turned to Pug and said, "The ancients spoke of it, too. That despair when friends must separate. No man knows how I shall miss him."

"Perhaps he'll stay on at the hospital. I think McMillan wants him to," Pug answered colorlessly.

Isidore shook his head. "I believe he'll go away. There is something in Baltimore which we don't know that he wants to leave—for a time."

"What makes you say that?"

"Because— I don't know, Prentiss."

"Got any idea what it is?"

"The only way anybody would ever find that out would be to do an autopsy," Isidore remarked wryly.

To still another person the fact that Alex Ashby would soon graduate was a constant pain, but she had been through similar pains before though none of similar depth, and learned to accept them silently. One night after she was in bed, though, she broke down and presently there was added another line to Miss Susie's prayers which remained part of her nightly petitions to the end of her life. It was, "God, whatever Alex Ashby wants, please, allow him to have."

During that summer still another person was feeling, as he had sensed that he might, that when young life becomes adult life, the life which has nurtured it becomes lonely. And in a way that men do not understand until their offspring become fledglings, but women know early through the pangs of childbirth, there grew locked in Dr. Howe's chest a steady agony. The only thing which made it at all endurable was that he still had Maria. After this part of life was over and the children had obtained their own footings, he and Maria would still have each other. But there wasn't much assurance in that comfort, for it caused him to desire her with a fierceness which gave him restless nights and made him curse the distance between Maine and Baltimore.

Late in July Miss Susie chanced to hear Ben Mead say one night at supper that 'Lije Howe was a lucky devil to be doing the clinics in London.

"London? Why, Ben, I didn't know a thing about it. Are Doctor and Mrs. Howe in London, too? When did they sail?"

"Mrs. Howe and the girls are in Maine," Pug drawled.

"That's what I thought," Miss Susie said and then insisted, "Is Doctor Howe in London?"

"No'm. He hasn't gone anywhere," Ben replied. "I saw him at the hospital today."

Miss Susie sputtered, "You boys should have told me long ago. Since Alex moved to the hospital I don't know anything! I thought Doctor Howe was in Maine, too. You know very well that I'd have made him come to dinner every Sunday. He must be frightfully lonely. Excuse me, please." Placing her napkin primly on the table, she went immediately to the telephone.

So it happened that upon the first Sunday in August, 1914, Dr. Elijah Howe, as well as the regular boys, was seated at Miss Susie's dinner table. Miss Susie finished saying grace, and the men had just removed their napkins from their rings, when Alex Ashby rushed in.

"I'm sorry I'm late, Miss Susie. I could only get away for an hour. I—*they've done it!*" Alex stood by his chair without remembering to sit down.

"Done what, dear?" Miss Susie asked.

"The English and French," Alex answered slowly, "have ordered twenty-four-hour mobilization. The Germans are invading Belgium. It means—*war!*"

Hizer put down the dish of fried chicken, and said before any other man could open his lips, "I'se goin'!"

Miss Susie retorted, "You are not! I'm the only living person who knows exactly how old you are and I'll tell if necessary. You are not going! Pass that chicken, please, before it gets cold."

"Yassum," Hizer replied meekly.

Dr. Howe put down his knife and fork and asked with studied calmness, "Are they taking Americans, Ashby?"

"I don't know, sir, but I believe from the way the extras read that anybody can enlist. Here's the extra, sir."

Dr. Howe brushed the paper aside with a bluff, "Thank you." Then he rose and asked Miss Susie if he might use her 'phone, and went into the hall. As he called the editor of *The Sun*, Hizer held the chicken platter and waited; the boys laid aside their knives and forks; everybody listened intently.

Turning back into the dining room, Dr. Howe said, "Anybody can enlist. May I send a cable over your 'phone, Miss Susie?"

"Certainly, my dear."

Then Miss Susie put her chin in the air and ordered, "Hizer, please close the door."

Dr. Howe leaned back into the dining room and announced, "Please, leave it open. This concerns them, too."

The cable was addressed to his son in care of the hospital in London where, with the Dean's letter, 'Lije had obtained a chance to observe. It said:

The first two years of medicine do not prepare a man to do anything useful in a war. Come home and finish your training. It will last a long time. Please cable your mother immediately.

Dr. Howe re-entered the dining room and before seating himself he said to the students, "You are far enough along in medicine—all of you—to know that emotional instability and hysteria cannot be tolerated in a doctor. A lot of people who are misfits will escape to this war within a month. But remember this—all of you: *you might live through it.* Any man who lives through a war and has to live in the world which continues afterward, whether he be defeated or victorious, needs every ounce of preparation he can get to exist. You've had enough education, you know enough history to be aware that the world which follows wars is always tough.

"Whoever wins, there will be maimed, crippled, insane, weary people to care for. From the moment when the first patient refers to you as 'Doctor' to the day you die, you will find that you can rarely do what you want to do.

"But whether you do what you want to do, or what you don't want to do, a medical man has to *know* what he is doing, and you don't *know*—yet."

"But if one were driving an ambulance and giving first aid—?" Ashby pleaded, still clinging to the back of his chair.

Dr. Howe turned on him and answered, "Because you didn't have the guts to stick to your training, I'd call that being a coward."

It was the first time any human being had ever used that word in Miss Susie's presence. The man who did so did not apologize, and from the tilt of Miss Susie's head as she listened to it, the students knew that no apology was necessary. Guts was the proper word.

"You are right, sir," Alex said and dropped into his chair. "But I make no promises—after next June."

A little half moan escaped Miss Susie and Dr. Howe cut her a look as if to say, "If you show any emotion we are lost." She stiffened immediately and remarked, "Alex, after you are prepared, the decision, of course, rests entirely with you. None of us would want you to go against your conscience—then."

It was such a brave speech that it entirely took the wind from the students' sails. Pug Prentiss began to cut his chicken to hide his emotion. Ben said to Clay, "Please pass the bread." Bert Riggs, who was seated beside Dr. Howe asked, "Would you like some gravy, sir?"

With a very gruff "Much obliged," Dr. Howe took the gravy boat and saturated everything upon his plate before he knew what he was doing.

No student at the table missed the action. Alex quickly turned the conversation to the reversal of seasons in South America. Pug picked up his lead and gave an amusing description of August being rainy and one of the coldest months there. Then he spoke of coffee plantations and eventually they drifted into a discussion of the effect of high altitude on persons with thyroid disorders.

After the dessert was finished Miss Susie asked, "My dears, will you please do me a favor?"

Dr. Howe laid down the cigar which she had given him permission to light. Miss Susie blushed as their eyes turned toward her. Taking a quick breath she continued, "There is one person who must be horribly upset by this—and needs to know his friends. Instead of sitting here and talking, would you mind going—going to Otto's?"

By three o'clock on the afternoon of August second, 1914, Otto's restaurant was jammed with men; many had come from a restless desire to be in the company of other people during an exciting epoch: a mass urge toward mass hysteria. Whatever brought them, though, each man shook Otto's hand and had a pleasant, friendly word for the little bartender.

McMillan sat at the table which he always occupied and Dr. Howe sat beside him. McMillan said, "This must stop! Otto will have a heart attack."

Howe growled, "Best thing that could possibly happen to him would be to die right now. Men can't remain neutral long when their ancestry is involved. Predominating influence in this medical school is English. Know of any other one in the country where the four principal personages all had English, Irish, or Welsh names?"

"No," McMillan answered vacantly, his eyes upon Otto.

"Take your eyes off him, Mac! You had a reception once when you were honored by the A.M.A. I came to it. This is Otto's party. Let him have it."

"But he hasn't the physique to stand it."

"Physique? Aw, hell! Ever know a doctor who did have the physique to stand anything?"

"You have."

"Well, the point is I haven't stood much, nor done as much as the ones without physique. Look at yourself."

McMillan changed the subject. "I was in New York yesterday and went over to the Rockefeller. Simon asked me about Ashby. He's applied there for next year. Impressed Simon very much. Said Ashby was the first fellow in years who said 'why' instead of 'yes sir.'"

"What the devil! Didn't you offer him a job?" Dr. Howe frowned and forgot his whereabouts.

"Not in so many words—until this morning." Dr. McMillan replied. "It never occurred to me that he'd want to leave Hopkins."

"Does he?" Dr. Howe said stonily.

"Says he does. Talk to him yourself if you want to."

"What are his reasons?"

"Doesn't give any. He's very reticent. Something's happened. I don't know what, but he seemed so eager for the job I'll see he gets it. Simon wants him. Very much."

"Don't like his running away."

"I'm not sure he's running away, 'Lije."

"Did he mention Gret?"

"No. He wouldn't to me, of course."

"Did you mention her?"

"Thought it best not to. How is she?"

"Maria says she's no better. Wants you to order her appendix out in hopes of bringing 'em together. Female foolishness. Gret would die, first."

Dr. McMillan was silent a minute, then suggested, "Now that the boy has brought his problem to a solution, why don't you talk to him?"

"Whole thing's my fault," Dr. Howe said hopelessly.

"Oh, I wouldn't say that. I hate to see him go as much as you do. I'm devoted to that lad."

"It is a crazy way to be, but so am I."

Dr. McMillan did not answer. He was already on his feet and the men, who had sensed his presence, parted and made a path for him. Within a few seconds of the time Otto keeled over, the famous internist was kneeling beside him. And a hush which seemed louder than noise hung over the entire assemblage. Men did not replace their beer steins, they held them in mid-air and waited.

Mead and Prentiss, who had been standing near the door, returned from the hospital with a stretcher. Still nobody spoke. McMillan completed his examination and said, "Good! Get him onto it, please."

The boys obeyed and after the stretcher was en route to the hospital again, the physician turned to the men packing Otto's restaurant. "No matter how long this lasts," he ordered, "nobody must ever discuss it with him. He can live for years—without excitement." Then, he turned and followed the stretcher.

The men in the restaurant drank a round of beer to Otto's health. As the assistant bartender filled the steins, the person who helped circulate them was Dr. Howe. His "Sit-down-boys" lowered them about the tables, but even his brisk good humor couldn't efface the loss. Within half an hour the restaurant was deserted and, for the next six weeks the men who drank their beer there drank it out of duty, not out of joy.

To those who had spent their youth visiting the German clinics—men like McMillan and Howe—what happened at Otto's on that fateful second of August was in a symbolic sense an unavoidable and sad severing of all that was pleasantest out of their youthful memories. This war would not only do things to people physically, it was going to destroy many of the things which they treasured emotionally.

Chapter Nineteen

LOVED I NOT HONOR MORE

For the next ten days Dr. Howe was pulling diplomatic wires to get 'Lije passage on an early boat, steadying his wife over the long distance telephone, attending to his patients. Underneath these duties, though, he felt a growing determination to talk to Ashby. The first time he met Alex alone in the corridor, Dr. Howe wheeled around.

"Can you come into my office five minutes? I want to talk to you."

Alex understood that he meant the hospital office. "Be glad to, sir," he said and fell into step beside the ophthalmologist.

When they were seated in the office with the door closed, Howe said bluntly, "Isn't Hopkins good enough for you?"

"Of course it is, Doctor Howe."

"Well, then, what's all this talk about you going to the Rockefeller?" Howe clamped his cigar in the corner of his mouth and blazed his eyes into Ashby.

Alex stood his ground. "I applied for a fellowship there to do some work in syphilis, sir. I had a letter last week accepting me."

Howe snorted, "You leave the hospital with the largest free negro work in the country to get a chance to research in syphilis! Don't hold water! What's the real reason?"

Alex answered slowly, "I need the money, sir."

Howe snorted again, "It's true Hopkins don't pay anything and Rockefeller does. But men like you don't want money. Anyhow, hasn't your father a big cattle ranch?"

His direct question wrung the truth from Alex. "My father died last February, Doctor Howe."

"Aw, I'm sorry! I hadn't heard, Ashby." His belligerence had vanished, his voice was sympathetic.

"Thank you, sir. You—you're the first person in Baltimore I've told."

"I appreciate that, son," Dr. Howe answered. Then a kindly silence emanated from him and presently Alex said, "He had a heart condition, but made 'em keep it from me. And it must have been mighty lonely there on the ranch, by himself. Also, things hadn't been going well in the last few years, but I didn't know it. King Brothers took over the ranch in March. I'm glad he didn't live to see another man own his land."

Dr. Howe nodded, then jerked his head upward and asked, "Need some money to finish your education? Be glad to lend it to you."

"No, sir. Thank you very much. He left me two thousand dollars. And—and a lot of other things which are worth more than money." Alex's voice was husky; he concentrated his attention upon the design of the rug on the office floor.

"You bet they are!" Dr. Howe said stoutly. They were silent again and finally he took the cigar from his lips.

"Alex, do you love my daughter?"

Ashby's eyes met those of the older man as he replied, "I certainly do, sir."

The silence settled again, but now it was relieved and peaceful. Suddenly Dr. Howe cleared his throat, reached out and put his hand on Ashby's knee and said, "Alex, I'm as proud of you as your father would be. I understand now why you've left her alone. Not many medical students, shocked into reality, would refuse to cash in on their emotions."

Ashby's eyes brightened, he gave a slow smile and replied, "I—I was afraid, sir, you'd say I was a fool."

"You are: a quixotic fool. But damn it, I'm *glad* you are! And I'll tell you something which no other human being knows—Margaretta's my favorite. Women ought to marry men of their own weight, or better, mentally, spiritually, and sexually. She's lost ten pounds. Her mother's trying to get McMillan to have her appendix out."

"Does she need it out, sir?"

Dr. Howe grinned at the alarm in Alex's voice. "Nope. Mrs. Howe's idea of the way to bring you together. I refused. Gret's proud. She'd die ——"

"Of course she would, she's a thoroughbred."

"Much obliged. Thought maybe you considered her beautiful," her father remarked dryly.

"There is *nothing* ugly about a thoroughbred."

Dr. Howe's eyes twinkled. "Thank you, son. But they are devilish."

"Down in Texas, we used to think that was only another way of saying they're brave. A spirited horse, when he's bored, is hell on wheels, but when things are too tight for the man who owns him—he—he can always count on the horse's help."

Dr. Howe gave a pleased growl. "Now that I *can't* help you, professionally, when you coming to see her?"

Alex's brow clouded, "It'll be ten years, now, before I'll be in a position to marry her, Dr. Howe, because I *won't* marry her until I can stand up to it, financially."

"Are you the only living Ashby?"

"Yes, sir. By the way, sir, there is no tuberculosis, cancer or epilepsy in the Ashbys."

Dr. Howe nodded the information into his mind and asked, "Any chance of your coming back to Hopkins, later?"

"Not unless I come on my record."

The older man drummed his fingers on his desk, "Hog-tying me for life, are you?"

"On that score, yes, sir."

Dr. Howe chuckled. "Alex, there are some people you can't give anything to—and they are the ones you always want to help. But I wouldn't take anything on earth for the way you've thumbed your nose at me. The money side of life can alter, but for people like you and Gret the emotional side doesn't change. She'll be better off engaged to you—and waiting—than married to any other man alive."

"God knows I've missed her!" Alex muttered and dropped his head in his hands.

Dr. Howe remarked, "One thing about this Rockefeller job—it'll keep you out of the war."

Alex threw his chin up, "There's been an Ashby in every war this country ever fought, sir. If we go in— That's another reason I wondered if I had a right to see Margaretta."

Dr. Howe replied decisively, "Bosh! Any woman is better off with a dead fiancé than with a damaged ego. You come on over to supper tonight. My wife and Sally are stopping off in New York to meet 'Lije, but Gret will be down on the four o'clock train. She and I'll be glad to see you. 'Bout seven. I better warn you, though. When you've done a thing a woman ought to be proud of, she's likely to be furious."

From four-thirty Margaretta roamed from one empty room to another. Now that there were so many places where she could be by herself, she didn't want to stay in any of them. Last spring she could close the way she felt about Alex Ashby up in certain rooms, but now—it was just everywhere. The pictures, and books and chairs, seemed to remember as well as she did, how terribly she missed him.

In desperation she slipped down to her father's office. The secretary was gone for the day, and as the girl sat in the patients' old leather chair, the misery and self-pity receded from her mind. She flung her leg across the chair arm and decided that when Papa came she'd be gay, so gay that he wouldn't have the courage to question her. As a preparation she began humming and singing snatches from "The Mikado":

"And that singular anomaly, the lady novelist—
I don't think she'd be missed—I'm sure she'd not be missed!
He's got her on the list—he's got her on the list,
And I don't think she'll be missed—I'm sure she'll not be missed."

The witty song raised her spirits; she was planning to go upstairs and change from her navy blue georgette to a flowery chiffon which would knock Papa's eye out, when the telephone rang.

Gret ceased singing and answered it.

Dr. Howe said, "Baby, did you get in all right? That's good. I won't be home for dinner. Going to Doctor McMillan's and then on to a consultation. Sorry."

He hung up immediately. Margaretta slowly replaced the receiver, relief flattening her mind. Then she began to wonder why he sounded so happy. Was it because Mamma was coming home? He'd looked preoccupied at the station and now he sounded carefree as a bird.

She began to hum again, *I don't think she'd be missed— That singular anomaly . . ."*

The door bell rang, and Margaretta went listlessly into the hall to answer it, almost certain that it would be a telegram from Mamma announcing the landing of her precious son.

When the door was open, she swung on to the knob for support and gasped, "Oh!"

"Oh, yourself!" Alex said. "May I come in?"

An intuitive lightning flashed through her mind, "He's the same— he still loves me," but she said coldly, "Why yes. Of course, come in."

As he closed the door, Alex could see that confusion lay under her acid politeness. "Your father thought it would be a good idea if I came to dinner," he drawled. "Has he come in, yet?"

"No. He just telephoned. He won't be home." The words were prim.

Alex picked up his hat from the rack, "Then perhaps, I've mistaken the night. I'm sorry."

"Don't go!" For an instant honest entreaty broke through her politeness.

Alex's gray eyes danced as he asked, "You mean, *you* want me to stay?"

"Well," Margaretta threw her chin up in the air, "it's a long way over to Miss Susie's. There's nobody here but me— I—I guess there'll be enough for both of us."

Alex disregarded the irony in her casual little speech and silently laid his hat down again. His silence bothered Margaretta, and she asked quickly, "Would you mind sitting in Papa's office while I go and change my dress? If I'd known anybody was coming——"

Alex caught her by the arm, "Stay like you are. Please!"

"Why?"

" 'Cause I don't want you out of my sight, Gret. Not even for five minutes."

His fingers tightened about her arm; she pulled away and led him toward Dr. Howe's office as she replied, "It's taken you a mighty long time to realize that."

Alex decided to try silence—the kind of silence he used to use when sitting on a corral fence and watching a horse he'd had trouble with frisk about him.

They were dueling and both of them knew it. Margaretta sat in the patients' chair and Alex took a straight-backed one.

"How are things at the hospital?"

"Busy. How were they in Maine?"

"Cold. And tiresome."

Still the flatness held, and the silence began spreading between them. The air became loaded with their mutual stubbornness. Alex loved the way the curls at the nape of her neck laid sassily against the round white collar, and Margaretta loved the sound of his voice, the warmth he brought into the room, so many things that she was dizzy tabulating them. Their silences seemed to meet and the impact made the corners of Gret's mouth twitch. Alex kept his eyes gravely upon his cheroot.

He continued smoking.

The minutes continued passing.

The tension continued rising.

Margaretta went quickly and pushed upward the window which the secretary had carefully lowered before leaving. Alex stayed in his chair and said reprovingly, "I would have done that for you."

"I'm getting pretty well used to doing things for myself, now."

Alex did not reply; she continued looking out of the window. They were testing each other's mental weight. The fatigue was frightening. Her back was still toward him and she had the advantage. It was a fight, a real fight. They were both so tired they could hardly keep from screaming and they were both enjoying every second of the conflict. Here was the thing for which she had looked all of her life! A man who could stand up against her and match her mood for mood! With him she had been the underdog. Now she was going to make him crawl if she could, and she hoped from the bottom of her inexperienced young heart that she couldn't.

Alex knew all of this perfectly. To him her back spoke quite as plainly as her words might have done. He took a deep breath, changed to the comfortable chair, then enjoyed studying her slim ankles and remained perfectly still.

Gret gave an unexpected giggle and Alex said instantly, "What are you laughing about?"

She turned abruptly, her face perfectly blank, her words too slow. "I'm not laughing, Doctor."

His eyes measured her calmly and she pretended not to notice the measurement. Then his voice bridged the distance between them, "You are too thin, Ladykins. Drink a glass of milk with your meals, won't you?"

She switched closer and replied, "And I'm older and more decayed than I was when you last saw me. You'd better mention that too, Doctor."

Her waspishness made Ashby angry. He flung his cheroot into the empty fireplace, caught her by the shoulders and when his eyes had captured hers, said, "I had my reasons for not coming to see you. I thought that they were good reasons—but whether they were good or bad, I've never stopped loving you for one single moment. And if you don't believe me—in words, then perhaps you'll believe me—this way." His arms slipped to her waist, his lips covered hers as the belligerence and then the pain flew from her mind and heart, and that old sweet inactivity of love spread through them again.

By the time the kiss was completed he laid her upon the sofa and eased his cheek against hers. As he knelt beside her, there came upon them an utter, unspeakable contentment. An undeniable fusion which took from him all of the harassment and agony of the past months and from her all of the fear and uncertainty—melted them away like sand in a swift river and in their stead permitted a peace past all understanding.

Little by little Alex told her of his father's death, of his father's phrases and the Rockefeller job. Told her the things which he had felt and remembered, and little by little the lonely, hidden ache for other Ashbys went out of his heart, and a joy too deep for probing began to grow in hers.

Chapter Twenty

NOT FOR A YEAR AT LEAST

On the hospital internes and residents regarding the war, the older men employed a restraint similar to that which Howe had exercised on the medical students; but they were also reminded that they had contracted themselves for one year and had no right to break their word.

During those six weeks Otto spent as a private patient, he received so many gifts of fruit, candy and books, all from men with Anglo-Saxon names, that McMillan remarked, "If you don't get out of this hospital, Otto, all of the doctors' children in Baltimore will be without any Christmas!"

Finally, McMillan was persuaded to permit him to go back to his restaurant and "take his chances," and the war was six weeks old before the bartender saw a newspaper. From then until the Armistice, though, the order which McMillan had issued was rigorously obeyed by every man who ever drank a glass of beer at Otto's.

Those first six weeks passed for the boys at Miss Susie's in almost as much of a haze as they did for Otto. Alex and Ben were entering their fourth year coming directly under the tutelage of McMillan and swamped in the sea of internal medicine. Everybody was studying medicine. The medical quarter came first in the third year, too, and while Alex and Ben were in direct contact with the patients, the third year students were in direct contact with the textbooks. Symptoms took the place of guns in their minds, and only a short period after dinner could be devoted to fighting the war. Anyhow, as McMillan aptly phrased it, "The war will cease, sometime, but the sick are always with us."

The straw-colored shades had replaced the blue ones at Miss Susie's windows, the rugs were put down again, and the last remaining rose on the parlor carpet began to have its petals walked away. Symptoms were sprinkled like sugar about the breakfast table.

"Do you have a headache with smallpox, Alex?" Clay asked frowning.

"Depends—" Ashby began.

"If you do, you don't notice it," Ben remarked.

"Osler's *Principles of Medicine*, pages fifty-six through sixty-two," Pug put in.

"Do you have smallpox with a headache, Clay?" Alex asked teasingly, then finished, "Well, then I'd say you don't have a headache with smallpox!"

"Doctor Higgenbottom says a headache is like a temperature—the sign of something else, and usually something arising from a stomach upset," Silas said.

"If you want to learn some medicine without reading it in a book, Clay, just ask Silas," Alex suggested. "He learned more in the three months he spent with that country practitioner last summer than the rest of us will assimilate in ten years."

Silas blushed. Clay asked, "What sort of lab did he have, Si?"

"Didn't have one."

"Who did his lab work, then?"

"I rigged up a few things."

"Could you persuade him to use them?"

"Only occasionally."

"How in the devil can you claim that a man like that knows medicine?" Clay scoffed.

Alex turned to Silas. "See him pull any patients through tricky illnesses?"

"Seven."

"Could we have pulled them through with equipment?"

"I think so."

"Think so!" Clay bellowed.

Alex ignored him. "How do you account for his ability to do it without equipment, Holmes?"

"He knows the patient's background," Silas replied. "He uses his eyes and he's had a long experience getting along without aid. He has gotten so he doesn't need it, I reckon."

"Well, what did you see him do that was so remarkable?" Clay demanded.

"Manipulate twins through a contracted pelvis. Save a pneumonia with a rheumatic heart. Set a broken hip so that the old lady could walk again."

Clay did not pursue the matter further, but Alex said. "How do you account for his success in those cases, Si?"

Silas answered calmly, "He didn't have to get 'em out of the hospital in three weeks. All of those things require time and patience, and remember this: because a man has practiced in the country ever since he got out of medical school don't mean that he hasn't learned anything."

Nevertheless, the boys entering the medical quarter found that the first way in which they became an integral part of the hospital was in doing the routine laboratory work upon the ward patients—a procedure which Dr. Osler had instituted years before. Men in the third year medical quarter spent most of their time observing at Hopkins and the city hospitals while men in the fourth year, from the time a patient came into the dispensary, worked with the interne handling the case—a method which as the years passed proved its value as a teaching adjunct.

Once when Isidore and Alex were discussing why this medical school, in a few years, had progressed so far ahead of older institutions, Isidore said, "I think it is because every man who has graduated from it, and remains attached to the hospital in any capacity, is teaching somebody. This keeps every person from the most insignificant interne to men like McMillan and Howe on his toes all of the time. Makes him learn that part of his duty is to impart knowledge—and a man must possess knowledge to impart it."

Later, when Alex broached the system of interlocking instruction at Miss Susie's, Ben Mead remarked, "Yeah, it's like a railroad. If you derail an engine everybody knows about it—every damn fellow from the divisional superintendent to the man who shovels coal. And if a patient 'goes out' through your stupidity, eventually everybody—from McMillan, if you're interning in medicine, to Dan, in the autopsy room—knows you've killed somebody. Damn it to hell, it's awful—and it's grand!"

"What's the batting average? How many mistakes can a man make?" Silas asked. "What happens to him if he does make 'em?"

"Nothing happens. There is no punishment—and that's the worst kind of punishment. The only thing that happens is that he just doesn't advance. His appointment is unlikely to be renewed at the end of the year, or he just *stays put*."

"Bosh, Ben! Men advance through politics in medicine as well as anywhere else," Clay Abernathy said.

"Oh, sure, to a point," Ben conceded. "But a politician is only up against the public. A professor is up against medical students, and the public is a damned sight more lenient than medical students!"

"But medical students are always changing; it's how a man stands with his own contemporaries which cinches his job, I believe." Clay pronounced the last two words as though he had considered the matter carefully.

"They get him the opportunity," Ben replied. "But it is the students who give him his rep. That rep doesn't change and from class to class it is passed on. When you came here—remember all the stuff we told you about the faculty?"

"Sort of. But you didn't tell me *how* they had gotten their positions."

"Well, how had they, Clay?"

"Dean Wingate was a nephew of one of the Board of Trustees. The man is dead now, but he wasn't when Wingate was made dean. Old Snell is a cousin of Mrs. McMillan; McMillan was Osler's pet; Boyd got in through that Princeton clique. If you ask me, it's politics, all politics."

"Say, you ought not to be studying medicine," Ben howled. "You ought to be running a social register. You've got a memory for family relationships like a society reporter."

"Laugh all you please," Clay said shortly. "It's the truth. Isn't it, Ashby?"

"Depends on how you look at it," Alex answered. "That they are related is true. But that doesn't mean that they're not good at their jobs. What Ben is saying is that if a man isn't good at his job, due to his student rep, when a full professorship falls vacant elsewhere he won't get it. Professors in medical schools are chosen for their ability to teach, and if students dislike them they are not considered good teachers. Marry my sister and I'll make you a full professor?

Bah! Won't work—unless you have enough ability to get by with the students. Of course there are exceptions."

Silas, to whom politics in medicine was as uninteresting as paper curlers in a patient's hair, had risen and gone upstairs to study. Miss Susie was at an Altar Guild meeting; Hizer was out paying his insurance and Bert Riggs had disappeared directly after dinner announcing that he was going to take a bath.

Pug, to whom learning always came easily and conversation was an endless delight, had delayed studying and was enjoying the argument. He drawled, "Iniquity in high places is one of the proofs that the places are high, I think."

Then Silas's voice came down the stairway and put a stop to the discussion. "Ashby," he said. "Will you come up here a minute, please?" It was the first request that Silas had ever made of any of them. Alex jumped to his feet and asked, bounding up the stairway, "Yeah. What's up?"

It was early November and Hizer had just started the furnace. Above the creak of the radiators, Silas's words echoed through the house and dropped with deadly terror into the ears of every student who heard them. He replied, "Bert has had a hemorrhage."

For a second nobody said anything. Clay's loose-lipped mouth lay open as if he were trying to absorb the knowledge through that aperture; Pug put his upper teeth inside of his lower ones and sat staring at the single rose left upon the carpet; Ben Mead said, "Good God!" and jumped to his feet.

He entered the room which Riggs and Silas occupied almost as soon as Ashby entered it. The same study table at which Doctor Howe and Dean Wingate—in their day—had sat poring over Osler's *Principles of Medicine* was splattered with blood and the old carved initials were outlined in it.

The medical student lay sprawled on the floor. His own copy of Osler's *Principles of Medicine* had been pushed under his head—and it and his shirt front were also covered with blood.

"He's unconscious," Silas said, kneeling beside him. "Can we move him, Alex?"

"Only to the bed. Then we must telephone for McMillan."

"I'll do that," Ben suggested stoutly, and leaped down the stairway again. To the boys in the parlor he said, "Clay, get all of the rags you can find and a dishpan from the kitchen. Fill it with hot water and soap and go on up." To Prentiss he remarked, "Newspapers ought to help, too."

Pug rose silently, went into the back hall for a bundle and mounted the front stairway as Clay went up the back one. In the hallway below, he could hear Ben talking with the Professor of Medicine.

As they reached the third floor hallway, Clay said to Prentiss, "You never can tell from the way people look, can you? He certainly looked healthy." Pug did not reply. As they entered Riggs's room only Abernathy had the indiscretion to continue talking; the others sensed that he was covering his fright with words and permitted him to chatter on until he finished cleaning the floor. Then Ashby said, "Mind going to the drug store and getting some ammonia, Clay?" There was plenty of ammonia in the bathroom, but Alex felt that if he had to put up with Abernathy's insane chatter he'd go mad.

Clay put down the rags and said cheerfully, "Sure!" Prentiss picked them up and continued cleansing the table. When it could be removed without danger of spotting the halls, Pug wrapped the drenched copy of the *Principles of Medicine* in newspaper and started with the things toward the cellar.

Now that Abernathy was gone the students worked silently; Alex sat beside the unconscious boy, holding his pulse; he and Silas had washed and eased him into the clean bed and pajamas. Silas went for a hot-water bottle. Prentiss, meeting Mead on the stairs, asked, "After you tell Ashby what McMillan said, please wrap his clothes in newspaper and bring them on down to the furnace, too?"

"Sure, I will," Ben replied and went on up toward the room where Elbert Riggs lay.

When Clay returned, Prentiss met him at the front door and put him to work in the cellar burning the table and textbooks. Ben brought down the clothes bundle and then went to wait in the hall-way, beside the front door. Pug took the ammonia on upstairs.

Silas and Alex still sat by the bed and watched the features of the boy who lay in a coma. Against the white pillow, even with his face so chalk white, the twenty-four-year-old student, now that his calm features did not show his intense shyness, looked strikingly handsome. All of them had grown to like his reticence, had become particularly fond of his silent consideration of others; now they understood, at last, from what that reticence arose. Alex said, as they watched his peaceful, almost gentle expression, "I think he'd been expecting it for a long time. Remember that day at the Pathological Museum how he questioned me?"

"Very well—now," Prentiss answered.

"You burned the things, didn't you?"

"Yes, Alex. There wasn't anything else to do. He won't be needing a *Principles of Medicine* for some time, will he?"

"Not for a year, at least." It was Silas who answered that question.

Then the doorbell rang and the student upon the bed opened his eyes and closed them, wearily. Silas looked at Ashby. Alex rose and tiptoed downstairs to join the gray-haired professor and Ben Mead. After they had reported minutely the events of the last hour, Mc-Millan mounted the stairs and Ben and Alex followed.

Clay Abernathy was still in the cellar: it took the *Principles of Medicine* a long time to burn, even when placed on a bed of red-hot coals.

The room which Dr. McMillan entered bore no evidence of the hemorrhage; the student lying upon the bed was spotless.

Pug and Silas rose to leave, but McMillan said, "Stay, boys. If Riggs doesn't object?"

He turned to the young man who lay watching him as if he were the only hope in a desolate world. As the first thing McMillan said was put in the form of a trivial question, Elbert began to feel better instantly. His grim lips parted and from their expression, the students knew that he did not object. And they also knew that Dr. McMillan had eased him past the first point of danger in his disease—a point on which McMillan never ceased to caution them—the danger of shame.

The internist took the chair which Silas had vacated, took Elbert's hand in his, found his pulse and said chattily, "Did you stage this just to give Ashby and Mead an opportunity to show me how much they've learned?" Everybody grinned. McMillan chuckled, "They seem to have learned a lot! You did well, boys."

To the patient, turning suddenly serious, he said, "Ever have one of these before, son?"

"No, sir." The words came faintly.

"Wonder if your family history is as bad as mine. I know of three beside myself. And you?"

"My father and one aunt."

"His sister?"

The student nodded. McMillan caught the quick fatigue in Riggs's eyes and said, "I want to listen to your chest a minute. We'll talk, later." He adjusted his stethoscope and made a thorough and careful examination. The other students stood silently by. Realizing that the boy's fists were tightly clenched beneath the covers, McMillan remarked as he laid the stethoscope aside, "The first rule in dealing with an intelligent tubercular, Riggs, is to tell him the truth. Like some types of heart ailments, it is one of those things in which the patient's recovery is due largely to the care he takes of himself. And beyond that, doctors shouldn't lie to doctors, no matter what the trouble. About your case: I can make no accurate diagnosis until that lesion quiets down. The only way it can be made to quiet down is for you to remain in this bed and to remain absolutely quiet. After it has quieted down, we'll take all of the X-rays necessary, hold as many consultations as you like, and tell you exactly what is ahead of you: precisely what you have to face. Until then you have got to content yourself with forgetting about everything except rest."

Then observing the bed in which Silas slept, McMillan continued, "You must be alone, too. There must be no distractions. And—you can't study."

The lips of the boy in the bed drew to a tight line. McMillan said to the others, as Silas began moving his books from the room, "Help him, please." They understood that they were dismissed and closed the door behind them.

After he was alone with Riggs, the physician drew his chair nearer to the bed and said, "The chance to grow up doesn't come to most men until around middle age. Then they fail to get their full professorships, or have an unexplained problem child, or their wives die—but if they live through those defeats they've got a victory, and nothing in God's world can ever frighten them, again.

"Most people go through life frightened of their own shadows, frightened of what people will think of them, frightened of their own short-comings—for three years of medical school you've been frightened of this. Well, it has come. I know how you feel, boy; it came to me at just the same time—in just the same way. And through it I found all of the happiness I've ever had. I met my wife, because her brother had the bed next to mine, and we had to wait until our love was full grown and I was well again.

"I learned not to waste myself and I got over being afraid. If you can stand these ten days alone, you'll pull through: and whether I can get to see you often or not, I'll be thinking about you. Good night, son. Good night."

During those ten days life around Miss Susie's continued as normally as possible under the circumstances. Silas moved down to room with Prentiss, and Dr. McMillan left rigid instructions about the boiling of dishes and the wearing of masks in the handling of a case of open tuberculosis. Miss Susie carried out the instructions to the letter as far as other people were concerned, but stoutly refused to obey, herself, declaring that she was too old to catch anything.

The memory of the pleasant suppers which he had eaten at Uncle Emil's, the many times he had met Nan up in the Monument, the first time he had kissed her, the day she had promised to marry him when he was established, the sound of her voice that Christmas Eve when she had said, "I hate tuberculosis," hummed through Elbert's head and haunted him as he lay in the darkened room.

Now, of course, she couldn't risk coming to see him. If they knew at the hospital that she had been engaged to a medical student, they might refuse to let her graduate in the spring. Anyhow, Dr. McMillan had said he must have no excitement, no visitors.

Aware that he needed companionship, hour after hour Miss Susie sat near the bed in the dim room, crocheting.

"Don't you need some light?" Riggs whispered once.

"Lor', child, I've been doing these things so long, I could do them blindfolded. Of course I don't need any light. But you mustn't talk. If you talk I'll have to leave and I don't mind acknowledging to you, Elbert, that I'm enjoying having somebody in the house during the day. I've been lonelier than I suspected, my dear."

"You certainly keep me from being lonely," he said simply and turned over and went back to sleep.

Later, McMillan protested the companionship, but Miss Susie tossed her head and defied him. "When a man is sick, a dog in the room helps. I'm performing that function for this child. I won't get out!"

"Well, one thing which you must promise me is not to feed him every hour. No matter what you think he'd like, Miss Susie, his stomach has to have some rest, too."

"All right. Lay down a diet and I'll follow it minutely. But that boy has never had anything but old maid aunts. His parents are dead. Until—until you decide what to do with him, I'm going to see to it that he's not lonely."

So for the first ten days of his illness, Bert Riggs was privileged as few men had ever been and he derived from Miss Susie's silent presence a comfort and a strength not unlike that unspoken camaraderie which develops between chess players.

He also derived something else which helped him in the long months which followed: the sense of a woman's touch, not offered in passion, but in gentle kindliness. Miss Susie resolutely refused to allow Ashby and Prentiss to bathe him before they went to medical school. When the question had been broached, she turned it down with the same vehemence with which she had vetoed the trained nurse idea. "He's going to sleep until he wakes up and then Hizer and I'll do it," she said.

And they did. Each morning Hizer brought the basins of warm water, and Miss Susie washed Elbert's face as lovingly as if he had been a baby. He protested at first and tried to wash himself, but she put a quick stop to that. "I know Doctor McMillan said that the way to make that lesion heal was to lie still, and my dear, you are going to do it! Turn your head so that I can finish your left ear."

While she went down to see that his breakfast tray was attractive and dainty, Hizer finished the boy's toilette and got him into clean pajamas, remade the bed and prepared the room for the day. Then Miss Susie returned, gave him the final instructions about the tray and picked up her crocheting again. As she was too polite to enter the boys' bathroom, even in their absence, Miss Susie remained completely ignorant of the artistic adornments and of that famous ceiling.

Early in the second week, Elbert turned to her and asked, "What does Doctor McMillan tell you—when he's out of this room?"

"I never give him a chance to tell me anything, dear. We've been in medicine long enough—all of us—to know that talking doesn't help. And all doctors hate to be hounded about the condition of their patients. Also," she gave Elbert a confidential glance, her voice lowered to a whisper, "I learned long ago that the way to get information out of men was not to ask them for it."

The boy smiled wanly, and took her hand in his. "Miss Susie, you're—you're grand!"

"No, you are," the old lady said solemnly. Then, returning to their previous conversation she continued, "And I got the information out of him that way, last night. He thinks that there isn't any reason why, with the proper care, you can't be as fit as he is—in time."

The last two words had tears in them. She pulled her hand away, gave him a sudden pat and ordered, "Now turn over and go to sleep. I've almost dropped a stitch!"

In the darkened room it was impossible to see what she was crocheting; Elbert presumed that it was just another set of table mats. But the other students had noticed that she was using her largest silver hook and working in very soft, very fine, brightly colored wools.

It was Alex who finally teased her into admitting what she was making. All of the boys, except Elbert, were seated around the dinner-table as he said, "Your cap on a medical baby's head, Miss Susie, is about as important as the Cross on his forehead at baptism. These boys—since you gave up making table mats and caps—are beginning to feel hurt. Don't you expect us to ever have any children?"

"Oh, Alex—you! How can you say that? Of course I hope all of you have—sons."

"Well, why don't you encourage us by making caps, then?"

"Because—I——"

"What are you working on, Miss Susie? We're curious."

She blushed and then stammered, "I—I'm making an afghan for

him to use at Saranac. It's *cold* up there and he'll need something
like that."

When the lesion healed and Dr. McMillan sent Elbert Riggs up
to Trudeau, instead of a *Principles of Medicine* he carried a many
colored patch-squared afghan into every stitch of which had gone
an old lady's hope. A month later, Dr. McMillan sent the boy his
own copy of the *Principles of Medicine*.

Also, among Elbert's cherished possessions were three colored postal
cards which Nan Rogers had sent him soon after he arrived in
Saranac. On the card-back of the Washington Monument she had
written, "One is for love"; on that of Ford's Theatre, "One is for
memory," and upon that of the Johns Hopkins Hospital, "One is
for courage."

Nobody at Miss Susie's ever mentioned the pity of it, the blight of
a young man cut down. So early in medicine do even young men
learn to laugh to keep from crying that the casual sentimentality
which laymen exude in the face of trouble is erased from their characters, and in its stead there grows a repressed and silent understanding of the real pity of it, which takes the form of outward gaiety.

Within forty-eight hours of the time Elbert Riggs had been moved
from the house everybody, except Miss Susie who still maintained
that she was too old to catch anything, underwent a thorough
"check-up"—tuberculin tests, X-rays, and complete chest examinations which in all cases proved negative.

The only person who came out of the ordeal in difficulty was
Hizer. Ashby kept insisting that his diagnosis wasn't complete and
that it would probably take a month to decide, but they feared it
would certainly be, like that of the Pithotomy cook, a clear case of
paresis.

"You is de lieinges' boy to be an honest man I ever did see!"
Hizer replied nonchalantly. "Ain't nuthin' de matter wid me, 'cept
I'se tired ob med'cal students, an' dere everlastin' sass!"

"Well, there's not but seven more months of me," Alex said
solemnly and prepared to leave the kitchen.

The old negro dropped into a chair and eased his head into his
hands, "An' don't I kno' it. Dat's whut's grievin' me so!"

"Thought you just said you wanted to get rid of me?" Alex grinned.

"Git outta dis kitchen, an' git out quick!" Hizer shook his head vehemently. "You devil me till I ain't got good sense."

"That's paresis, not deviling," Alex replied, disappearing up the stairway toward the pantry. Then his voice echoed through the house as he began one of the hymns—a concession to Miss Susie's presence —on which he and Hizer enjoyed harmonizing, "Rock—of Ages ——"

From the kitchen came the response, "Cleft—fur me." Alex returned and was sitting on the pantry stairway before he took up the "Let me hide myself—in Thee." As Hizer joined in, he lifted from the cupboard a plate of ginger cookies and set them beside the big man from Texas.

Little by little, references to Bert Riggs dropped from the conversation. Without consulting the others, though, Silas and Pug entered into a pact whereby Silas wrote to him on Mondays and Pug on Thursdays, then each read the other's letter in order not to chronicle the same events.

Chapter Twenty-one

THEY'VE POSTED THE LIST

Early in the second quarter, thoughts of interneships were reflected in the conversation at Miss Susie's and "What are you thinking of trying for?" became a standard phrase. The only two toward whom it could be directed were Mead and Ashby. Alex's appointment at the Rockefeller became common knowledge and Ben announced that he was trying for an interneship in general surgery.

"If you fail to get that, what will you do, Ben?" Clay asked one night as the group sat chatting in the parlor.

"Nothing else I want to do, so I'm not going to fail!" Ben replied.

"Well, if you don't get it at Hopkins, are you going to apply elsewhere?" Clay persisted, blinking his light blue eyes.

"I've already applied to Montreal General, and Massachusetts General and Hopkins. But it's Hopkins I want, and it's Hopkins I'm going to get!"

"What's the matter with the others?" Clay scowled as he began cutting the nails of his pudgy fingers with his pen knife.

"Nothing, but they're not Hopkins," Ben answered.

Then they fell to discussing what made Hopkins Hopkins and Prentiss said, "I think it's being poor. Having splintered floors and no money to build stylish new buildings or put in new-fangled gadgets—and, also—that constant check of every man's work which is maintained regardless of the financial status of the patient. Take the accident room, for example: you get precisely the same attention there if you pay nothing as you do if you pay a full fee."

"How is it at Presbyterian and Montreal General?" Clay inquired, coolly putting away his knife and reaching for his pocket comb.

"I dunno," Pug answered. "But I do know lots of hospitals where the standard of work isn't maintained for the sheer pleasure of being able to sleep with yourself afterward."

"Bosh! What are you talking about?" Clay shrugged.

Pug leaned forward earnestly. "Just this: every man has to sleep with himself every night until he dies. And a hospital which demands that he never do shoddy work and considers the patient before probing the pocketbook has the kind of tradition which makes a doctor conscience-free—even when he fails to save the patient. Know of any other hospital in the world to which negroes come willingly? Do you?"

"I know of plenty to which they won't go under any conditions, dead or alive," Ben remarked.

"That proves it!" Pug growled. "They come to Hopkins. You can say what you please against that old bachelor, Johns Hopkins, and I've heard plenty said, but he did more to lay the ghost of race hatred in this country than any other man who ever lived."

"Because he left the money?"

"No, Ben," Prentiss said with conviction. "Because he stipulated that the hospital was to care for the indigent sick-poor of Baltimore and didn't say a damn word about their having to be white! Mark my words, it's the only hospital in the country which negroes are not afraid of: and the reason they are not afraid of it is that, from the first, it provided a place for them. And you Southerners know there isn't another hospital in the South which did, and few which do, maintain negro wards staffed by precisely the same men who treat the white patients.

"The best thing in Southern aristocracy was that you had to live up to your niggers—that you couldn't let your niggers down. They are the severest critics and the keenest judges of human nature you'll ever run across. Any medical man who has gained the respect of his negro patients is all right! And Hopkins men have had to behave so that they gained it. It is the negroes who have helped to make Hopkins as much as the great men. There've always been plenty of negroes to get sick, occupy ward beds, and be worked upon. There are more patients than beds and always have been, and over a fourth of them are black—and always will be."

It was the longest speech which any of them had ever heard Prentiss make, and it impressed his listeners profoundly. Mead said,

"You are right, Pug. But the way you talk sounds like there has never been a white patient in Hopkins."

Prentiss answered, "I was trying to explain *why* white patients from all over the globe come to a bowl and pitcher room at Hopkins. It's the men who make a hospital, not the gadgets, and that's the reason I'd rather be an interne at Hopkins than anywhere else in the world."

"And I'm going to stay here if I have to tear the roof off the place!" Ben remarked, rising and turning toward the stairway.

"If the niggers have anything to do with it, you'll get a residency!" Alex laughed as Ben went upstairs to study.

Silas questioned, "When are the appointments out?"

"Three weeks from Tuesday," Ben called as he disappeared around the landing.

With the courtesy of future victims, the boys refrained from mentioning the subject again. Pug's dissertation had chastened Abernathy and revealed to Alex his own unconscious regret that he was to leave the Hopkins. As for Silas, he accepted it, digested it and then grew dumbly proud of it, but in Ben's mind it lay knife-edged and increased his tension. For him, somehow, those three weeks passed.

Upon that fateful Tuesday night, Miss Susie and the other members of her household were already at dinner when Ben burst into the dining room, waltzed around the table, kissed Miss Susie and announced, "I've got it! They've posted the list—I've got it!"

"Ben! I'm so glad," she smiled, laughing and crying. The boys rose from their seats and began to cheer.

Hizer appeared in the pantry door and asked, "Whut's de matter? Whut's de matter?" Ben grabbed him and started dancing a jig before Hizer could protest. Then the old man understood and sang, "Hooray! Hooray!"

When the excitement had died down, Hizer said, "You kno' whut done it? I done it! I wint up to de hosbittle an' I jes' says to de Dean, 'Dean, I c'n't let Mista Alex an' Mista Ben bof go 'way. You reckon you could git Docta Halsted to make a place fur Mista Ben?' An' he says, 'I'll do de best I c'n, Hizer.' If it tweren't fur me, you wouldn't had nuthin'!"

"I'm much obliged, Hizer," Ben answered gravely. The old negro, seeing that the boy was too happy to get a rise out of him, changed his tactics and edged forward. "I better git de hot meat pie. You sho' look hungry." Alex persuaded Ben into his chair, then before they could force the food down him, he told them about it.

"Boy, oh, boy! They didn't post 'em until half an hour ago. And we kept on hanging around and smoking and practically every man in the class was there except Alex. You never saw such an awful excitement and such an awful trying to behave like there wasn't any. Two or three times I thought I'd just die standing there!"

Even Miss Susie did not try to make him eat, for she had been through this experience with so many medical students—and through the reverse of this experience, their failure to get the interneships which they coveted—that she reveled in Ben's elation almost as much as he did.

Ben reached for his water glass and drew a long breath. Clay said, "Well, go on! What happened?"

"Along about five-thirty," Ben gulped, "some guy said they weren't going to post 'em on the hospital bulletin board this year, but on the medical school board. We all trouped over there and kept peering at the medical school board and watching everybody who came in the door. Well, it got toward dark and nobody but secretaries were coming through and then two or three niggers came trying to sell dogs. Everybody was so keyed up we couldn't even give 'em straight directions as to how to get to the anat. building."

As the anatomy building was within a stone's throw of where the crowd had been standing, the boys at the table laughed. Hizer, who had deserted the pantry for the event, laughed until Prentiss warned him, "You are going to lose your glasses, if you don't watch out."

"Put 'em in your pocket," Miss Susie ordered.

"Yassum," Hizer obeyed; then asked, "Thin whut happened, Mista Ben?"

Clay, Silas and Prentiss sat with their elbows on the table and their eyes fastened on Ben Mead. Alex Ashby and Miss Susie watched with sympathy, remembering the bashful person Ben had been the first year he was in medical school. Both of them beamed on him.

Ben continued, "And then guess *who* did come up those steps? The Dean, himself. He said, 'What's going on here?' We told him, and he cleared his throat and said, 'It was posted five minutes ago on the main bulletin board of the hospital, boys.' Whew! I wish you could of seen us scatter! That door was like a subway at rush hour. We were down those steps, across the street, into the accident room door, and in front of that board in no time!"

He ceased speaking a minute, his audience waited. Then he continued, "For a minute I couldn't get close enough to see the list, everybody was crowding around so, and then dropping away like they had been hit with a sledge hammer and walking off down the corridor without a word.

"Boy, it was awful! And I couldn't get up the courage to—to have it happen to me, so I just stood there with my knees knocking together like sixty and my throat dry as dust. And then Jake Gaines turned away from the board, let out a whoop, slapped me on the back and said, 'You got it, Ben, and I got it. Hooray!'

"He's such an awful joker I still didn't believe it, but I knew I'd have to learn sometime, so when the boys who didn't get 'em made room, I edged up to the board and there it was—yes, sir— heading the list: 'Benjamin Wilson Mead, Surgery.'

"Whew!"

They fell to questioning him about the appointments and disappointments, and here and there Alex would murmur, "That's hard luck," or "Perhaps Massachusetts General will come through," or "He may get in at Bellevue, they don't appoint until next month." At last Miss Susie interrupted and gave Ben a kindly but severe order to eat his supper and hush.

Clay Abernathy had already checked over in his mind the appointees Ben had mentioned. Clay said, "Two of those in medicine are kin to men on the staff, one in orthopedics, one in psychiatry; and three in pediatrics are sons of Hopkins men and two in O-B have brothers at the Rockefeller."

"Well, one thing you can always say about Doctor Benjamin Mead," Ben remarked, "is that he was without political influence, and was appointed due to——"

"Personal influence: dat's me!" Hizer put in arriving with a plate of hot biscuits.

Later, they all went to Otto's and washed down Ben's future with beer, in company with the other men who had received interneships. Afterward Prentiss said to Alex, when Ashby stopped in his room for a few minutes, "I'd never taken in before, how awful it is."

"What?"

Pug stretched himself out on the bed and motioned Alex to a chair as he continued, "Having your whole future set, and being unable to do anything about it. Fellows who aren't in your class and invited to do special work and who can't make Hopkins, or one of the other better type hospitals, where are they going?"

"The ones who don't make Montreal General," Alex answered, "go to Montreal Jerkwater or Jackson Municipal, or get in at some other city hospital."

"And then they are doomed: as doomed as though they had committed a major crime, aren't they?"

"Not always. Depends on the fellow," Ashby drawled. "If he's got it in him to keep up with the literature and do his research independently, he can do it as well in the sticks as in the centers."

"Yeah, if he has those rare abilities. But he wasn't the man of whom I was thinking. I was thinking of the fellow who is going on in general practice and is forever branded as second-rate."

"No man is branded as second-rate unless he brands himself as such."

"You are wrong," Pug said hotly. "When it comes time to consider men for positions, the first sorting is a paper one: a matter of written records. The man with the best record gets the chance to be interviewed for the job."

"Hadn't thought of it in that light. Guess you are right, at that. Interneships are a bottleneck for any students, and right now they are especially a bottleneck for students with German names."

"Yeah," Pug nodded.

"Isidore believes that they're always a bottleneck for students with Jewish names," Alex continued.

"I doubt that: if his record is good enough to justify his acceptance."

Before Ashby could reply, the doorbell rang violently. Alex said, "Oh, God, Bert's gone!" and bounded down the stairway. Riggs had had a relapse; and although McMillan had not been in the least discouraged by it, the students had steeled themselves for the worst. As Alex opened the door, the telegraph boy extended toward him the fateful envelope and asked, "Does a Mister Benjamin Mead live here?"

"Sure does," Alex grinned.

"It's paid," the boy said. Ashby took the envelope and reached in his pocket, and the telegraph boy held the half dollar up to the light unbelievingly while Alex closed the door.

As he passed Pug's door, Ashby explained, "Probably from his relatives congratulating him." Then he tiptoed on upstairs, cracked the door of Ben's room and found Mead seated at his study table.

"Hey, Bennie. May I come in?"

"Sure, I'm writing to my girl. Wanted to tell her."

"Thought maybe you were boning up to pass your examinations so you could accept that interneship," Alex teased as he handed Ben the telegram. "It looks like your mother's proud of you!"

"No, it's not that. 'Cause I forgot to telegraph her. Sit down." Unable to forego that excitement which telegrams create, Ashby dropped into a chair and waited as Ben tore the flap and read the message. By the sudden stony lines which streaked Ben's cheeks Alex knew that it was bad news.

"Want to talk about it, Ben, or want me to go?" Alex asked and started to rise.

Ben nodded him back to the chair and said, "Nothing to it. Just that she married another man this afternoon. Fellow down home who's got a good job in the bank. Eloped." Ben slumped over his table, his head pillowed in his hands. The telegram covered the letter which he had been writing.

For half an hour they remained silent. And Alex's eyes kept coming back to the picture of the pretty girl upon the mantelpiece. She wasn't beautiful. She was just pretty, awfully pretty, and tonight she was lying in the arms of another man and becoming his wife, while Ben, just a few hours ago, had seemed to have everything and now——

Ben raised his head and Ashby saw the tears on his face. "A man can't have everything, Bennie. And you've still got medicine." It was in substance what the pathologist Scott had said to Ashby; but perhaps old comforts, well tried and adequate, as much as anything can be adequate in such situations, are treasured and handed generation by generation from man to man.

Ben stood away from the table, bit his lips to a line and answered, "I've got to get out of here."

"Well, let's do it quietly," Alex suggested, opening the door, leading the way down the stairs and on up Biddle Street toward Broadway. When dawn came they drifted into a ham and eggs joint out in Towson and ate a breakfast which almost cleaned out the proprietor's larder.

"Shall we take a streetcar or feel like walking back?" Alex asked.

"Let's walk," Ben grinned. "I don't want to get out of touch with my feet, too. Internes have to walk—if they can't do anything else!"

From the time they left Miss Susie's until they entered the restaurant ten miles away, neither of them had spoken.

Chapter Twenty-two

CONSIDERATION OF
SPECIALTIES

Christmas had passed without making much of an impression at Miss Susie's. Alex and Pug had dinner with the Howes, but nobody went home for it. Nobody had time to go home. As Ben Mead put it, "Third year students take more subjects than they ever do again—obstetrics, gynecology, medicine, psychiatry, neurology, therapeutics, pediatrics, hygiene, laryngology, and ophthalmology! They attend more lectures, know more medicine, go to more clinics, and are smarter, wiser and busier than they ever are again. They just haven't got time for Christmas!"

"And fourth year students do what?" Pug grinned.

"Aw, they do physicals and lab work on the ward patients and come to see them twice a day, and then write and write and write on their case histories, till you have to get railroad spikes instead of nails to hold the damn things up. But nobody ever reads what they write, and they can't give orders or prescribe any medicines or *do* anything but talk and write."

"You ought to know, Bennie," Alex said as he picked up his New York *Times*, to which he had subscribed ever since the war began, and went upstairs to study. His interests in medicine and Margaretta were as intense as ever, but he kept up with the war with a daily and growing concern.

Miss Susie's was soberer in many ways, and the Sunday morning singing wasn't so lively as it had been. Miss Susie and Hizer had experienced the change for so many years with so many students that it did not trouble them much. After the second year, medical students had a way of buckling down to hard work, growing abnormally grave and then alternating the gravity with abnormal gaiety.

The only thing which alarmed either of them was Alex's unspoken and continued absorption in the war. Finally one day when she was in the kitchen making the Sunday chocolate cake, Hizer remarked, "Jes' like Mista Bert is got T.B. in his blood, Mista Alex is got fightin', an' if dis heah war goes on too long, ain't nuthin' goin' to hold him."

"Please, Hizer, don't talk to me about it. I just can't bear to think of Alex Ashby going."

"Shucks! Miss Susie," Hizer said comfortingly. "Ain't Mista Alex done gived his word to dem Rockerfellas to do dat researchin'? Ain't he in love wid Docta 'Lije's baby, Miss Ma'gretta? If 'nything c'n hold him, she c'n. He ain't goin'. Dat is, he ain't goin' if it don't keep goin' too long."

Miss Susie nodded and continued beating the cake. Hizer shook his head. "Ain't nuthin' like it to tear yo' heart to pieces—dis keepin' a med'cal boardin' house. Take Mista Alex—eberywhere he wint away frum dey miss him! An' de bes' men marry de wrong wimmen, or dey git sick, or dey don't git dere jobs, or dey go to war an' git——"

"Hand me those cake pans, and don't talk while I'm busy! Hurry up!"

"Yassum." There was a note of pleading and of reprimand in her voice. Hizer obeyed immediately and when the yellow layers of dough were smoothed into the pans he eased them into the oven. Miss Susie fled the kitchen without a word. It was the first time she had ever ordered Hizer to perform any duty other than politely, and the old negro was filled with such remorse that he sat by the stove and watched the cakes constantly.

Alex and Ben that year finished their required medicine, finished their required surgery; in the last two quarters both of which were "free," Alex took more medicine, and Ben took more surgery. Pug, Silas and Clay continued wallowing in the third year and knowing more than they would ever know again.

Alex's determination to advance only on his record had crystallized his ability to work. Ben's disappointment in love had made him determined not to take 'em seriously until he could support 'em permanently and intensified his interest in surgery. Silas's private settling of his love life and his decision not to let it bother him until he was through his training had made Osler's precept of "putting your emotions on ice" function for his advantage.

Pug Prentiss worked over his books with a serene, clear-headedness;

the loneliness which had always hounded him had been so dreadful, that now that it was over he was quite content to wait for love until he could afford marriage. Professionally he had found a subject in which he was no longer an outsider: gynecology, and personally he had found a woman with whom he was no longer afraid to be natural: Sally Howe.

But the turmoil in Clay Abernathy's breast as a result of his flirtation with the redhead from Kansas kept him teetering between elation and despair. His work continued to hold up, but his disposition suffered and his drunks became increasingly frequent. One night after they had heaved him into bed Silas asked Ashby, "Why doesn't his work go blah?"

"Because," Alex answered, "he's a G. U. artist. That's the reason he's drunk tonight, if my guess is right—he's about to ditch the redhead. Saw him in the hospital corridor yesterday talking to Bessie McMillan."

"That's too bad. Her father's a fine man. She ought to be a nice girl."

"She is, Si."

"I can't see how being a G. U. artist explains why Clay's work holds up."

Alex grinned. "In a way it does, Si. Goes with the outlook, just as being a bibliophile goes with internal medicine. You never heard of an internist failing because he was interested in literature, did you?"

Pug Prentiss, lolling in the tub enjoying the ceiling lady but within earshot of the conversation, called, "If he's telling you that internists know everything, don't believe him, Si. But whatever he's telling you, come on in here and finish it!"

They came and Alex explained, "I was saying that internists *know* that they don't know everything, and so they haven't the knack of taking things lightly."

Pug remarked, "I don't know much about internists; the more I see of G-Y-N and O-B the more I like 'em. At least in O-B you've got something for your trouble when you're through: there's a kind of satisfaction to pulling out a baby and its actually being a baby, which few other things can equal—for me."

"Hizer said long ago that you are a lady doctor!" remarked Ben, who had joined the group.

"Yeah, I believe he's right," Pug grinned.

"Apropos of what you were talking about," Ben continued, "I once heard 'Buck' Edwards say that the difference between surgery and medicine and observation and obstetrics is that the obstetrician and the gynecological surgeon don't have a chance to say 'I don't know.'"

Alex pretended that he hadn't heard, and Silas and Pug allowed them the reverence due men of greater knowledge and waited. Ben said, "More than a little truth in what 'Buck' says, too. No wonder medicine is related to witchcraft through the centuries."

"Surgery doesn't come of such a good family itself," Alex retorted.

"Don't claim to," Ben shot back. "Everybody knows that barbers' poles get that red and white 'cause barbers used to be surgeons."

"Bennie, I hadn't any idea you were so smart."

Silas and Pug began to enjoy the interchange. Ben blushed, then answered, "Got to hand it to you all, though, Alex. When you don't know you aren't ashamed to say that you don't. I've heard McMillan say it at least fifty times."

"Thanks."

"Why aren't you ashamed?"

"Because medicine is an art, I suppose. It never pretends to be a science: only uses the sciences to reach its conclusions."

"Exact methods of obtaining indefinite conclusions," Ben scoffed.

"That isn't true," Alex argued. "The conclusions are only indefinite until they are tried. If one method of treatment succeeds and the patient recovers, then no matter how much the conclusions were based on intuition and observation they're no longer inexact."

"Say, I'd never thought of it that way!"

"And if the patient doesn't get well," Alex continued, "the autopsy table is much more damning for us than for you. That was one reason why Osler preached an early familiarity with it, as among the best safeguards against a faulty diagnosis."

"Go on," Ben said.

Alex was glad to see him responding, instead of just keeping up from sheer grit, and continued, "So much of medicine is knowing what you don't know that you know. I mean what you see you must know, but you can't always know what you see."

"Start over: either you are mixed up or I am," Ben said. Silas and Pug waited.

Alex explained, "McMillan said once, 'Remember the first case of every disease you ever see and *know*—if you can. Then put that memory back in your head and hang on to it. After a while you'll understand why; years later, another case without any of the symptoms may come along and you'll get a hunch that it's the same thing and eventually the symptoms may develop and it will be the same thing.' How did you know? Because people with certain diseases have eyelids which droop! The first case you ever saw had them! Does that make it clear?"

"No. Go on."

"Well, put it another way. You *see*: and you don't know. And you *know*: and you don't see. Now in the case of the patient who didn't have the symptoms, you *knew*; but you *didn't see*. It was that back-sense of *past-seeing* which saved your diagnosis."

"Gosh, Alex, are you telling me that people who look certain ways have certain diseases?"

"Of course: within limits; you already know that, Ben."

"Oh, I'm not referring to the protruding eyes in thyroid cases, or the gall-bladder type, or the pointed noses and chins with T.B. I'm asking you if you believe people whose hands are shaped certain ways, whose eyes are set in their heads certain ways, who handle themselves certain ways, may have certain diseases?"

"Ask me that forty years from now and I'll be able to answer you. But without experience, I should say——"

"Not that it depends—" Ben snorted.

"Oh, no! I should say that a good general practitioner in the backwoods had grown the ability to sort out all of those types which the medical texts, as yet, haven't learned to tabulate, and that he quietly reaches his diagnoses by remembering those types."

Ben looked at Alex and said, "Say, I'm sure going to miss you. Like hell!"

"Thanks, Bennie, it's mutual."

"Why don't you stay around here and go on working under Mc-Millan?" Pug asked.

"You ought to," Ben remarked. "He'd make you an assistant resident without troubling with an interneship."

"Don't kid yourself," Alex drawled.

"Well, you're just wasting your time, if you ask me. You're coming back to Hopkins in internal medicine after while, aren't you?"

"Dunno, Bennie. Perhaps."

"Pug," Silas asked, "in your opinion which of all of us will get furtherest?"

"Professionally or financially?"

"Both ways."

"Alex will professionally. Clay will financially."

"Why?" Ben intervened.

"Alex's got the goods and Clay's a sex politician. Men who are steady within themselves don't need to make constant conquests. Clay'll go through life selling out to his vanity. His women patients will be as thick as flies."

"Maybe, because we're both surgeons," Ben said defensively, "I understand Clay better than you do. I think you're too hard on him. He's loud because he's embarrassed. Underneath, I guess we're pups of the same litter."

"The hell you are!" Alex put in. "Different as daylight and dark. Clay's a cat-man. You're a collie!"

Silas nodded his agreement. Pug said, "Lord, that's apt!"

Ben blushed.

Afterward, Isidore could never attribute any logical reason to why he had quickened his pace the day he saw the girl pushing the book cart down the main corridor. Perhaps it was his intense interest in all forms of research, but that warm spring afternoon something made him ask, as he came abreast of her, "Tell me, please, what types of books do patients read?"

The slight young woman braced her hands against the handle bar as a mother pulls backward on a baby carriage, and deftly propelled the cart, out of the traffic, over against the wall. Then she looked shyly at Isidore and said, "Will you please repeat that?"

Around them surged the life of that great corridor—famous medical men, pickaninnies, plutocrats, internes, shy student nurses, mangled day laborers—bravery, skill, self-pity, despair, humor, misery and fame—but for once Isidore was oblivious to its pageantry.

Later, he could never recall the shape of her chin, nor of her nose. In his memory it was her eyes which dominated her face: blue and clean and calm. As he looked down at her he cleared his throat, to hide his pleasure, and answered, "I asked you, Miss—er——?"

"Timberlake. Ellen Timberlake," she supplied gently. The words sounded like the tinkle of Chinese bells.

The man bowed, "I'm Isidore Aaron."

"Yes, I know," and again her words came softly and made Isidore momentarily silent. The girl thought she had offended him. She knew so little of Jews. She explained, "The reason I asked you what you said was I wondered if I had heard correctly."

"What did you hear?"

"You asked me what books the patients read, didn't you?"

"I did," Isidore responded. She gave him a startled glance. "Why be so disconcerted by such a simple question, Miss Timberlake?"

The rhythm of her breathing changed completely. She murmured, "Please let's roll the cart into a waiting room. I think I'm going to faint."

"No, you're not," Isidore answered firmly. They were within a few steps of a side door. He jockeyed the cart closer to the wall, took her arm and led her out to a bench in the back garden. The soft murmur of the spring breeze as it rippled the Virginia creeper on the buildings replaced the roar of the teeming corridor in their ears; except for the scrutiny of people too far away to hear, they were alone in the garden.

"Feel better?"

"Yes," she said, as they seated themselves.

Isidore wondered if she were a psychiatric patient—they often rolled the book carts. Or why else had his simple question affected her so deeply? Then she told him.

"I'm—I'm sorry I was a bother. But—but you see I've looked for you so long."

Isidore held his face a mask; he decided regretfully that the psychiatric diagnosis was correct. "Have you?"

At the casual quality of those two words, the girl blushed. "You are mistaken," she said. "I'm not one of those. What I meant—" she leaned toward him and a vivid lifelike quality suffused her face with beauty. "This is what I meant, and perhaps I ought to be in an asylum, because it is odd. My father died last year. He was a bank president and—he killed himself. I was a freshman at Vassar, and when I came home I got a job in the patients' library here at the hospital. And while I was so unsteady, I formed a tremendous friendship with—with someone I've never seen. Perhaps you won't understand it at all. Perhaps, if there were the money I should be put in an asylum, but——"

"Was it with a person you were related to?"

"No. He was gone before I was any age."

"Gone?"

"Yes. To be Regis Professor of Medicine at Oxford."

At those words, Isidore's whole manner changed; his eyes brightened, then caught and rested on hers. He replied, "He's my friend, too. Tell me about it."

She trembled and leaned forward eagerly. Her eyes matched her blue linen dress. "Of course, he's your friend, too. I knew it and that's why I almost fainted. You see, when I was so ashamed and frightened—every day when I'd roll the book cart past his portrait we'd talk—silently, I mean, in my mind. He'd always ask me about the patients and what they read. And when I told him that two boys with tuberculosis on a medical ward wanted a dictionary and I'd promised to buy them one at the ten cent store, Sir William Osler rebuked me. He said, 'If I were there I'd get them an Oxford dictionary. A long illness can be a great opportunity to obtain an education: it must take the place of college with them—those years in bed.'"

Ellen hesitated and Isidore, whose eyes had never released hers, asked, "And?"

"I—I gave them mine."

"But, you shouldn't! No person should ever give away his dictionary!"

"Oh, you're wrong—when it's like that! Besides, there's a good one in the library. After that I began to read him, and ——"

"I know. The books he guides one to."

"Yes. He was such a comfort to me! Every day he'd ask, 'What do the patients read?' And I'd report; then he began asking, 'Have you found him?' And until right now, I've never been able to say anything but 'No.'"

"Found ——?"

"Yes: his spiritual grandson. The *doctor* who would *want* to know what the patients read."

Isidore rose and turned his back. His eyes were filled with tears. The girl, with a fine courtesy, continued evenly, "I couldn't tell you how many times I've seen a group of internes coming down the corridor when I was pushing the cart and thought, 'One of them will stop. Somewhere in this hospital there is a man who feels as he does.'"

Isidore swung around, found her eyes again and without moving nearer, asked, "Do you like Chaucer?"

"Oh, yes. Especially the 'Wife of Bath's' Prologue. That phrase 'myn owene maister dere'—delicacy and strength and ——"

"Spenser?"

"Very much. And I like the music of the Bible, and ——"

He sat down beside her. His conflicts, racial, medical and mental had vanished. For the first time in his entire life, Isidore Aaron felt happy. Almost simultaneously, he was frightened, and standing abruptly erect he said, "I must see a great deal of you. How do you feel about Jews?"

"I don't know. I've never ——"

"Known one? Or been allowed to associate with one?" The words were bitter and sudden.

Ellen Timberlake stood up too; she answered calmly, "Been privileged to know one—before."

To the distant watching patients, in wheel chairs on the sun decks, they appeared to be having a casual conversation. Isidore carried out that impression, for he made no effort to touch her. Instead, covering her eyes with his he quoted, without preliminaries:

"But since ye deignd so goodly to relent
To me your thrall, in whom is little worth;
That little, that I am, shall all be spent
In setting your immortall prayses forth."

Later that afternoon, he walked with measured, slow steps down Broadway. He wanted to sing, he wanted to skip, but his hatred of hysteria among Jews was so violent, that years before, he had clapped upon himself an iron composure. Now, in the presence of intense pleasure, it functioned by decreasing his speed to a snail's pace. There began coursing through his mind all of the things which they must do together, all of the places which they must see. They would have to go to Washington to the Corcoran, to the Library of Congress—she'd like pictures and before they went to the Corcoran, they could begin with those in the Walters' Gallery, here in Baltimore. And the wealth of English literature which lay before them. For so long he had searched for some person to like Shelley, enjoy Keats, relish Shakespeare, and love Osler as he did. But in a way which he couldn't discuss with another man—not even with Ashby. Perhaps she was interested in the history of medicine, too, and would like to see the books he owned.

Then, for the first time, it flashed over him what such a friendship would mean to his family. They would not permit her to cross their doorstep—and she would consider them—how? So rarely did a Gentile ever understand that a Jew had a racial pride which outstripped anything which any Gentile ever harbored. Only people like Ashby—only students steeped in tradition—comprehended the basis of that pride. The others——?

With the same intensity with which a man in an accident wards off sudden death, Isidore mentally turned his back upon the racial difference. He again considered the exquisite mental and emotional—he was certain that it was there—contact which existed between them. The thought was like a warm fire on a winter evening.

Until midnight he spun through the work which ordinarily seemed burdensome. Instead of responding to that fierce Jewish energy, that refusal to admit fatigue, his studies of their own accord were simple things to master; animate and co-ordinated. There were no obstacles to surmount; in the place of harassment, there had come harmony.

Wearing a new gray suit and a pair of winged-tipped brogues which he considered most becoming, Clay Abernathy stood in Miss Susie's parlor admiring himself in the mantel mirror. He was waiting for two blasts from Bessie McMillan's automobile horn which would announce that she had come to pick him up and go to the country supper which her class at the Peabody was giving.

The other boys, having been loudly told that he had an engagement, were unwilling to act as audience and had scattered. Holmes had gone for a walk, Prentiss was taking a bath, Mead and Ashby were at an autopsy.

Hizer was down in the kitchen washing his dishes while Miss Susie, unknown to anybody, was in the pantry stemming the strawberries which she intended preserving in the morning.

The telephone rang and Clay, thinking that it might be Bessie, jumped into the hall and bellowed to the house in general, "I'll answer it!"

He did so. "Yes," he said. "No. He's taking a bath. I'll tell him. Good-bye."

As he said good-bye, he heard two short blasts from an automobile horn. Before he had time to communicate with any of the other occupants, they were repeated. Clay ran to the hatrack, picked up his cap, bounded down the front steps and jumped in beside Bessie.

In the morning, at breakfast, Pug Prentiss was late. When he came, Miss Susie noticed that he hardly touched his stewed apricots, even refused his customary portion of scrambled eggs.

"Aren't you feeling well, St. George?"

Pug looked up and said absently, "All right, thank you, Miss Susie." He applied himself to silence, again. The other boys continued chatting, Pug grew paler, quieter. During a lapse in the conversation he laid down his knife and fork and asked, "Clay, did you take an O-B call over Miss Susie's 'phone for me last night, about seven?"

For an instant Abernathy's face was as blank as a goat's. Then he grinned and said blandly, "Certainly I took it. Didn't Hizer tell you?"

"Tell him whut?" Hizer asked as he entered from the pantry holding a cup of steaming coffee.

"What I came in here and told you to tell him: that the hospital wanted him to report, immediately. Told you just before that lady er— came by for me. Don't you remember?"

"You didn't cum in heah an' tell me nuthin'!" Hizer said defensively. "I wasn't in heah to be told nuthin'. I was down in de kitchen washin' my dishes, like I orta ob bin."

"I said at the hospital that I didn't receive the call," Pug stated slowly. "They believed me. If they hadn't, I'd have been—kicked out. When you are on O-B, *no* excuse is valid. From now on, when I'm wanted on the 'phone please ——"

"In all de years I bin in dis house, I ain't nevva failed in my med'cal duty 'bout telephone calls. Not once!"

Hizer looked straight at Abernathy and Clay said succinctly, "Until last night."

"You—you—" the coffee cup which Hizer held crashed on the floor, the polite mask drained from his features and an ugly, steady belligerence suffused them.

The students were too stunned to rise. Miss Susie's face blanched. She said instantly, with sweet and gentle calm and an underlying note of authority, "Hizer, my coffee is too hot to drink. May I have some more cream, please?"

"Bring it right away, will you, Hizer? I need some, too," Ashby's words were deferential and pleading.

Without further comment Hizer turned toward the pantry.

Prentiss and Miss Susie began conversing loudly with the persons near them. With great gusto, Abernathy entered into the conversation.

After the boys had gone to school, Miss Susie went into the pantry where Hizer stood jamming napkin rings into the drawer, muttering to himself.

"Hizer," she said ignoring his fury, "when I was in here about seven last night stemming those strawberries and you were down washing your dishes, I noticed that we hadn't put clean paper on these shelves last week. Will you please put some on as soon as you get a chance?"

The old servant's face lit up.

"Yassum. I'll do it right away."

Miss Susie began examining the cruets and Hizer, fingering his rabbit foot, remarked, "He ain't like his Pa, Miss Susie."

"No. Not very much. From now on, you and I will have to take all 'phone calls ourselves."

"Yassum, Miss Susie," Hizer replied solemnly as she pushed the swinging door and went back into the dining room, again.

With a negro's fine sense of subtlety Hizer understood that the incident was closed. When he went to crumb the table and Miss Susie gave him directions about the sugar proportions for the preserves, he behaved as if the Clay Abernathy scene had never occurred. From that day, though, Miss Susie and he treated young Abernathy with unfailing politeness and watched him with unrelenting surveillance.

The nearest any of the boys ever came to referring to the incident was when Silas went down into the kitchen and said to Hizer, "This— er—this was given to me by a patient, a man whose word I value, last summer while I was working down in North Carolina. I've already got a fine one which belonged to my father, and I wonder if you'd like to have this one?"

He opened his hand and held out a six-bladed pocket knife. Hizer's old eyes blinked.

"Yassuh!" he grinned. At supper Silas found his napkin in a silver ring.

As the spring wore on, Alex began to grieve in the privacy of his own heart that he was clearing out of Baltimore, but not even to Margaretta would he have acknowledged how he felt. When the tiny leaves began to turn that delirious new green on all the trees from North Avenue to the foot of Broadway, Alex realized that he loved this old red-brick city with a depth he had not fathomed. The pansies in the round, octagonal and diamond-shaped beds on Broadway had colored so many of his crises, and the way the sun pinked the bricks of the hospital in the late afternoon brought peace into his soul. He loved the old forsythia bushes which made a riot of bright yellow outside the Marburg Building, he was especially fond of the single

Japanese honeysuckle bush in the back garden behind the Nurses' Home. And he treasured his friends, the children who from Biddle Street to the foot of Broadway he knew by name, regardless of their color.

He found himself loving so many things which he hadn't sensed that he was aware of. Loving that walk down Monument Street of a Saturday night when he was going to see Gret. Then all of the negro barber shops were full and the fuzzy black wool dotted the bare floors. He liked to stop and watch the intent demeanor of the clients and the barbers—almost as though barbers were as necessary to their race as the men at the hospital were to all races. Alex found himself walking a block out of his way, to listen to the whistle of the roaster on a peanut cart, to see the housewives going to Belair Market, to look at the cheap toy stores on Gay Street and see the children pressing their noses flat against the windows. He liked to pass that intersection where there stood the statue to Wells and McComas, who had been killed at the Battle of North Point when less than twenty years old. He savored the realization that such a statue stood at the intersection of two streets whose names were Gay and Monument.

In the daytime when he walked along this route everything had a different aspect; but lately, there seemed to be a special note to the cry of the children as they played in the late afternoons, a special significance to the clang of the streetcar bells, almost an especial understanding between this neighborhood and his own soul.

In the afternoon, if there were time, he'd go on to Belair Market, watch the people and study the shades of purple eggplants, red tomatoes, Maryland strawberries and green asparagus. Occasionally, he'd allow himself a rare treat and turning south at Monument and Gay walk back up McElderry Street. There, on the sidewalk, chalked hop-scotch games were marked off; and there seemed a chalkier white to the steps of the poverty-stricken, two-story homes of the negroes. Radiating from all who lived on McElderry Street was a deeper poverty, which manifested itself in ragged clothes and broken windows—but radiating, also, was a deeper living, which somehow Alex liked in a way he could not express but only sensed and silently knew.

It came, of course, from the fact that at the end of this poverty, white steps, low houses and street-living, towering over the marble games and negro children playing with broken dolls—yet remaining not incongruous with such a foreground—stands the Johns Hopkins Hospital.

Rising on the hilltop, serene, dignified, beneficent, calm, and majestic, too, is that old Administration Building with a weather vane which is known 'round the civilized world, and from under whose dome have gone men who make medical history wherever medical history is made.

To a modern architect that brick pile may be a monstrosity, but the place where a man attains his stature has for him a special beauty which the dome of the Johns Hopkins Hospital certainly had for Alex Ashby. And in a way which only men trained in the great teaching hospitals, whose youth is burned out of them ministering to the indigent sick-poor comprehend, there was a thrill which lay outside the power of words and extended from Alex's toes to the crown of his head every time he approached the hospital through the slums. That terrible, intense, fatiguing training had ground into his soul the knowledge that a hospital ought to be approached through the slums, that Hopkins is Hopkins because it cares for a crowded, weary world.

Lately, Alex found that when he came up McElderry Street and saw the white uniform of a nurse flit against the green grass, and the figures of people coming and going through the main entrance, his emotion became more personal. And he thought of all of the great men who had lived in the upper floors of that building and of what had become of them. Of Osler, and that early staff he gathered around him. Of Halsted, who had proposed to his wife in that very building. Of the tradition of it all, and of his own good fortune in being so close in point of generation to those who had created that tradition, that he still felt a vital, living warmth from it. There came a silent understanding that the statue of Jesus was dear to him; not from a religious angle, but from an emotional one. It made the grilling years of work in the free wards a little more valuable, somehow; it made the negroes feel that the hospital was really Their Father's House; it was grotesque, perhaps even hideous, but any man who spends his medical career seeing it daily, grows in time proud that negroes are willing to come to the hospital and expect and get the kind of treatment He promised them.

Alex's thoughts were occupied with the color and the tremendous vitality of the locale and instead of walking through the iron gates and going on up, he turned south and began drinking in the neighborhood between the hospital and lower Broadway. Mundane and quite middle class respectable it looked and the Church Home lent it a certain dignity which did not permit its disintegration until one got below the parkway and came near the water front.

There the street widened; the drug stores had long hourglass-shaped containers of colored liquids in the windows; the clothing stores displayed practically their entire stocks; the people on the sidewalks were no longer predominantly negro, but Polish and Jewish; the men were seamen occasionally. The wideness of the street and of the sidewalk and the many-sided occupations of the people: the seamen, the streetwalkers, the children and the street where a train, instead of a streetcar, crossed Broadway, all made Alex carefree and made him think of Texas. The broadness and flatness and freeness of it all. Of course the boats at the foot of Broadway did not fit in with that impression, but he rarely went where he could see them, for if he came abreast of Aaron's shop, he was invariably stopped and stayed so long that he'd have to hurry home.

Now, he did not permit himself to go that far, but turned east and walked through that spotlessly clean Polish and German neighborhood which surrounds Patterson Park; there the windows, and white stone steps and the faces of the people all looked as if they were scrubbed daily. Signs of spring were in evidence, but it was a middle-class, smug atmosphere with none of the abandon of the negroes, and none of the teeming life of lower Broadway. Alex found it depressing.

Turning about, he approached the hospital from the rear and amused himself picking out the cupola silhouetted against the changing foregrounds—against the terrifically oppressive middle-class neighborhood surrounding Patterson Park—against the two-story, two-window and fiercely clean neighborhood which was Monument Street out beyond the hospital. None of these vistas was satisfactory, so he turned west and approached it from the North Avenue end of Broadway. From that direction, the smaller cupolas were also visible and the whole presented in the soft light of a late spring afternoon, just preceding sunset, a mosquelike appearance: it had that serenity and that aliveness which only a mosque is capable of combining.

En route, the neighborhood was again middle class and respectable. The little girls wore clean socks and the jumping ropes were new with bright red handles. About six blocks from the hospital, he began to run into change, and although the appearance of respectability remained, the houses were poorly painted and the children shabbily dressed.

Alex headed west again and decided to treat himself to another turn down Monument, and then up Gay until he came to Biddle and on home to Miss Susie's. For color, for amusement, for human interest, and for creating in him that intangible feeling of the hospital as a necessity, nothing could touch that region west which lies between Broadway and Asquith Streets, and is a foreground for the Hopkins group.

While Alex was taking his farewell walks during those last few months of medical school, Ben Mead was beginning to suffer from a kind of fright which manifested itself in all of his actions. He didn't eat, he couldn't sleep, and now and then he would say, "If I pass my examinations."

Prentiss said to Ashby one Sunday night as they were coming home from the Howes', "I'm worried about Ben. What are we going to do with him?"

"You mean his fear that he'll fail?"

"Yes. It will make him fail, if we don't counteract it."

"Why don't you talk to the psychiatrists about it?" Alex asked sarcastically.

"It's Ben's problem, and anyhow I wouldn't let anybody know how shaky he is, Alex. It comes, of course, from his girl throwing him over."

"How?" Ashby asked. He had learned to rely upon Prentiss's judgments and grown interested in them.

"Because," Pug answered, "after he got the interneship, for a few hours he—had everything. And then when she jilted him, he lost. What I mean is, if she had jilted him two months after he got the interneship it wouldn't have had the same effect, but the two things coming together convinced Ben that he can never have *all* he wants, again."

"Can anybody?"

"Of course not. But lots of people get over half of what they want by believing that they can have all."

"Interesting psychology, Pug."

"It's one of the reasons we are in medicine."

"What do you mean?"

"If we don't get what we want personally, Alex, there's something beyond our own disappointments we're still interested in. God! If anything were to happen to Sally I think it would kill me—but I know also, that it wouldn't. I'd still be a doctor. Ben's like that. He's still a doctor, but doctors get so used to having to do without what they want, that when they come near to getting it, if they've had a previous disappointment, they are cowardly."

"So you think Ben is suffering from cowardice?"

"I know it. But what I *want* to know is how are we going to talk him out of it without hurting his feelings and yet make him able to pass his exams and get the interneship?"

"Stumps me! Have you any ideas, Pug?"

"Yes. I think you ought to put it up to Miss Susie and do what she says. Surely, she's known some other fellow in Ben's condition."

When they reached home, they found that Miss Susie had already attended to Ben, whose increasing nervousness, and inability to study or to eat she knew, from experience, would be followed by a drunk. When Silas had gone up to his books and Clay had gone out to see Bessie, Miss Susie found Ben pacing the parlor floor. She said, "Sit down, my dear, I want to know what is wrong?"

"Nothing."

But she seated herself and he slid into a chair and dropped his head into his cupped hands. Miss Susie said gently, "You know, Ben, there is a lot which you don't count on which will help you with your exams."

"What?" He raised his head and looked at her. Miss Susie smiled.

"None of my boys has ever failed. You aren't going to fail, either."

"What makes you think that, Miss Susie?"

"Because, I'm sure of it. The thing to do is not to try to study any more. You've spent four years studying just as steadily as you could. You've worked hard, my dear, and you know a great deal of which you are not aware. Just let your knowledge settle itself. Stop stirring it up and mixing it up. Just let it settle itself. Come here, Ben, I want you to promise me something, please?"

He came over, sat on the floor like a little boy and put his head in her lap. Miss Susie's voice had that persuasive gentleness one uses with a child, as she smoothed the cowlick in the top of his sandy hair. "I want you to promise me that you'll go upstairs, dear, and go to bed right away. Hizer is fixing you a hot milk punch, and he'll bring it up in a few minutes. After you drink it, please go straight to sleep and let what you know settle itself. If you do that, you won't fail—and I couldn't stand to have you fail, Ben."

In July, Ben Mead entered the hospital as an interne in surgery. He had been seventh in the class of which Alex Ashby was first.

Chapter Twenty-three

THE LAST YEAR

During July, Mrs. Howe and the girls went to Maine, Alex Ashby began his work at the Rockefeller and 'Lije went down to Raleigh for a further onslaught upon the vanity of Miss Joyce Witherspoon. The day after 'Lije left, Prentiss met Dr. Howe in the corridor and asked if he might come to see him some evening. The doctor answered, "Friday night: eight o'clock."

So upon a hot July evening Pug found him seated in his office smoking a cigar and looking lonely. Dr. Howe said, "Come in. Sit down. Glad to see you, boy."

"Thank you, sir."

"Had any word from Ashby, yet?"

"Letter yesterday, sir. Says he likes it."

"Ought to. Most of 'em are Hopkins men."

Pug lowered himself into the old black leather chair which patients used. The doctor offered him a cigar. He accepted and occupied himself cutting it while trying to get up his courage.

"Light?"

"Thank you, sir," Pug said again, and then resumed his silence. He began to sweat profusely beneath his Palm Beach suit.

Dr. Howe eyed him, cut a smile from his lips and asked, "How is your work? Find it interesting?" Pug had gone back to the G-Y-N dispensary again.

"Yes, sir. Very."

"That's fine," the doctor remarked and rising, walked to the wide window, pushed it higher and while his back was to the student said, "So far as I'm concerned the answer is yes. What does she have to say about it?"

He turned. Prentiss's face had taken on its strange beauty and his eyes were deep green when he answered, "I haven't asked her yet, sir. I wanted to find out how you stood first."

"Great God! What *have* you been doing when you came over here every Saturday night for the last year and a half?" The doctor's voice was gruff, amused and inquiring.

"Looking at her," Pug answered calmly.

Dr. Howe sensed the deep passion which underlay those three words, and seating himself at his desk he remarked, "She's worth looking at, isn't she? Looks very much like her mother did."

They sat a few minutes smoking in contented silence; then the doctor inquired suddenly, "Why haven't you asked her?"

Prentiss turned and faced the man squarely. "Crazy reasons, but you'd understand it. Until I found her, I was a congenital spectator, all I wanted was a ringside seat on life. Just a chance to watch and to see."

"Disappointed in love previously, or what?"

"Being raised an orphan with an income—loneliness, I suppose. No, sir, I've never—never really loved any woman this way before."

It wasn't the speech of a man who was endeavoring to call himself pure and Doctor Howe respected Pug for it, but was too wise to say so. Pug continued, "A congenital spectator is afraid, you see, that he'll never get what he wants. My early wants were all stifled, so that when I found Sally I was afraid—I've been afraid for months that she'd just melt away while I was looking at her. That it was all a dream. Well, before they went to Maine I—I kissed her one night, sir, and it isn't a dream."

"She loves you." Her father made the statement simply, as though he had been aware of it for a long time.

Pug continued, "But—but I—well, you see, sir, I've got another year of medicine, an interneship, and I hope a residency, before we can get married. Is it fair to tie her up emotionally with a man who can't possibly begin to live with her for four or five years? Is it, Doctor Howe?"

Howe laid his cigar aside. "Prentiss, medicine isn't fair to any man who is in love, because it *has* to come first. But if he can stand the gaff and the woman really loves him, then the waiting is an advantage in the end. It's worth going through, provided the man and the woman really love each other. You do. Sally is twenty-two now; that will make it possible when she is twenty-six. And with your income you can afford to have a baby right away. You ought to get that first pregnancy over before she is much past twenty-five."

"That's what I'd figured, sir."

"Then, tell her. And you may have to tell her over and over before she'll believe it, because no woman ever believes a man has self-control when he's in love and Sally has figured that you don't love her."

"Don't love her!" Pug laid the words down like weights.

The doctor grinned, "The last thing she did before she went to Maine was to cry in my arms for two hours about it."

"The night before she left, sir?" Pug asked pertinently.

"No. *Two* nights before. How many times have you written to her since the night before she left?"

"Once."

The older man flung his hands in the air. Prentiss explained, "I—I didn't feel that I could involve her further until I had talked with you, sir."

"Well, now that you've talked with me, you'd better take a couple of days off from that damn dispensary and talk to *her*. I wish to God I could go with you. In the meantime, I'll write her mother. She's been in a fret over you two."

He had risen and was pacing the room. Pug rose, too, and asked, "Will she be opposed——"

"Openly, yes. Inwardly, no. Maria has sense, but she doesn't like to show it. Hot in here! Suppose we go get a glass of beer, son?"

Never before had a man called Pug "Son." To hide his feelings Prentiss said quickly, "I was just going to invite you to go to Otto's with me."

Before they left the house, Dr. Howe put his hand on Prentiss's shoulder and remarked confidentially, "A man feels worried about what's going to happen to his daughters. There's so little he can do about it but just sit and hope that they'll take up with the right men."

"Thank you, sir. Thank you for being her father."

"Don't teach her too much, son. Four years is a long time to wait," Dr. Howe said laconically as they went out and got into his car.

By the time medical school reconvened, Pug Prentiss and Sally Howe were definitely engaged, although Mrs. Howe insisted that nobody must be told for at least two years. Dr. Howe kept silent and

wondered at the occasional obtuseness of smart women, for the change
in Prentiss was so obvious that all of the professors had noted, and com-
mented upon it.

Prentiss no longer observed life; he lived it. The hesitancy with
which he had made decisions in relation to his work had vanished.
McMillan said to Dr. Howe one day, "What did Prentiss do last summer, do you know? The fellow is so changed."

"Worked in the G-Y-N dispensary."

"Anything happen there to alter his outlook?"

"Not that I know of," Howe replied.

"How is my godchild, Margaretta?"

"Blooming, Mac. Positively blooming. How's your daughter?"

McMillan frowned. "Of late, she's interested in a boy I don't care
for, although I certainly liked his father."

"Who's that?"

"Clayton Abernathy's son."

"What do you think is wrong with him, Mac?"

McMillan hesitated a minute and then answered, "Medicine, like
everything else, has its deadbeats and politicians. The profession is not
immune from skunks."

"Not even at Hopkins?" Howe asked sepulchrally.

"Not even in heaven!"

"Well, the two are synonymous in your mind, aren't they?"

Dr. McMillan's eyes twinkled as he replied, "I wouldn't quite say
that, 'Lije. But even if I could, I certainly wouldn't expect a man
from the University of Virginia to agree with me."

"All right, that's a bull's-eye. I admit it. What you going to do
about young Abernathy, Mac?"

McMillan answered slowly, "Not oppose him—openly. But you are
lucky, 'Lije. I congratulate you."

"I won't be, though, if this war lasts. The Ashbys were mated to
war before they were to women. Alex will go, and so will 'Lije; so
will Sally's fiancé."

"Who is Sally's fiancé?"

"Say, Mac, I shouldn't have told. Maria swore me to secrecy. She's
engaged to Prentiss. But don't tell anybody."

"I won't," McMillan said. "Only keep your eyes open for his twin."

But although Dr. McMillan promised to keep the secret and did so, the grapevine telegraph is a puerile, feeble form of communication as compared with the hospital variety. Before many months, it had been whispered in linen closets, murmured over the bodies of dead patients and penetrated to the ears of the faculty via their mates or their sweethearts that Dr. Howe's oldest daughter was engaged to St. George Prentiss.

Nobody ever asked Pug about it; the inmates of Miss Susie's house refrained from doing so, because even the most callous people sensed that if it were not true, they would cause him infinite pain by forcing his denial. And nobody ever asked Dr. Howe because nobody ever dared. But upon Elijah and his mother the curiosity of Baltimore fell with full force and their standard replies became, "You better ask Mamma," and "She is entirely too young to think of it."

As a result Dr. Howe, when about the hospital, assiduously avoided Pug and in the courses Prentiss had under him he treated the student to an added dose of rudeness and hard work. The bond which they had established during the summer remained unbroken. Pug stood up under the grilling like a man. For him, now that life, emotionally, was right, really right, life in all other channels had become amazingly simple to cope with. Each night after he heard Sally's voice over the 'phone, he could go about his studying with a type of concentration which made even the stiff medical courses of the fourth year come easily.

By the fall of 1915, the war talk around the hospital and medical school had increased so much that Miss Susie's household found their missing of Alex Ashby a natural sort of pain. So many people were missing; not dead, but gone. Little by little, the ranks of Canadians doing graduate work had diminished and the German exchange professors and lecturers came no more.

The edict about Otto was strictly followed and his place, after decisive battles, was always filled as though the slaughter across the world demanded an added measure of friendship at home.

The older men still held the younger ones sternly to their contracted word. They spread broadcast the message that Osler had advised to take no man who had not completed his training. They lectured constantly on the folly of men with special knowledge enlisting as common soldiers where their value was slight in comparison with their abilities.

At Miss Susie's, attention was diverted from the war and from Prentiss's engagement by the return of Elbert Riggs from Saranac. His case had been arrested, and Doctor McMillan, after a careful consultation, had decided that it was safe for him to re-enter the medical school and complete his course. To the astonishment of his classmates, he entered the fourth year with them. Elbert had spent the year in bed studying under the tutelage of Doctor Trudeau; McMillan had kept him posted upon his courses.

When Nan Rogers graduated, she had gone immediately out to China to nurse at Peking Union, for after Elbert Riggs learned enough about tuberculosis to realize that it might flare up, even when arrested, he determined never to marry. He also determined that Nan must have a chance away from Baltimore and wrote to his uncle, Doctor Himmis.

Nurses thought she was very lucky to be chosen for China duty immediately after graduation. Nobody at Hopkins, except the Superintendent of Nurses, knew that the man who had asked for her was the uncle of the student who lay in a bed at Saranac.

Occasionally now, Elbert would look across the city at the Washington Monument, but he never dared to waste the necessary energy to walk through Lexington Market or climb to Ford's peanut gallery. Relentlessly he cut his mind from those memories, turned more and more toward the hospital and thought daily of the phrase, "One is for courage."

Pug gave up the house champion room and went back to live on the third floor. Bert Riggs had the double bed in which Miss Susie's Mamma and Papa had slept. He lived on a strict schedule, rested when he came in from school, went up after dinner and rested again, then did his studying and was in bed by ten. He had learned not to waste himself; he had grown up.

Clay Abernathy was finding the fourth year courses stiffer than he had anticipated and Bessie McMillan pretty occupying too. With Ben gone and nobody on whom to test his smutty jokes, Clay spent as much time as he could away from home, courting Bessie. By Christmas he hoped they would be engaged—secretly, at least.

The weight of medicine which had been accumulating upon Silas's shoulders grew a little more arduous and his fund of small talk which had never amounted to more than ten words, now dropped to mere salutations.

Now and then after dinner when the new boys looked especially forlorn, Pug flopped into one of the morris chairs in the parlor and told a few jokes, but even they had none of the old raciness. As a consequence the four new boys who came to live at Miss Susie Slagle's in the fall of 1915 decided among themselves that either things had changed since their fathers' day, or that their fathers were disgustingly senile!

Only once did the house take on its old joviality and that was when Ben, off from the hospital for a few hours, came in for supper. He came unexpectedly, gave Miss Susie a sound kiss and said, seating himself at the table, "Hizer, got anything good to eat? The food at the hospital is so bad my red blood count is below normal. Say, it's fine to be home again!"

"Thank you, my dear," Miss Susie smiled.

Hizer said, "Seems like I kno'ed you was cumin'. I done made sum ladyfingers an' got a great big dish ob charlotte."

"Bring 'em in!" Ben ordered.

Hizer grinned and Miss Susie said, "Not until you eat your roast beef. If your blood's thin, you've got to have some iron. The very idea of letting that happen to you."

"Aw, the hospital is just talking poor and getting us ready to go to war."

"Ben, don't say that, dear. Please don't!"

"All right, Miss Susie. It's all they talk about up there, and I forgot. Excuse me."

"Busy much?" Pug put in.

"I'll say!" Ben said. "Haven't been getting more than four hours' sleep a night for three weeks. Everything's emerging: appendix—er everything." The last word was in deference to Miss Susie's presence, and Clay snickered.

Hizer brought in a heaping plate for Ben.

"Have you heard lately from Alex, Ben?" Miss Susie asked.

"Not a word. Have you, Pug?"

"Not in three weeks," Prentiss answered. "He was fine then, but I think he'd rather be back."

Miss Susie nodded and said nothing.

"Day 'fore yestiddy, he was jes' fine," Hizer said.

"How do you know?" Miss Susie asked frowning.

Hizer replied, "Docta 'Lije's cook pays her *in*-surance same day I does. An' she takes in dem lettas he writes Miss Ma'gretta on Mondays an' Thursdays."

"Whew!" Ben whistled. "What do you know 'bout me, Hizer?"

"Nuthin' dat I could tell in de dinin' room," Hizer retorted and noting the displeased expression on Miss Susie's face disappeared into the pantry.

Ben devoted himself to his food and the four new boys remained politely silent and watched him eat. Although it was November and cool, following the custom of Hopkins' men in that special corner of the world which borders upon Broadway, Ben had come on up in his hospital clothes and thrown an overcoat over the white suit. Hizer and Miss Susie knew that he'd done it to show off: the new boys didn't know why he had done it, but they were profoundly impressed, nevertheless. He'd been through the four years of agony on which they were embarking and was still alive and able to joke about it. In a minor sense, Ben's presence had upon them the same effect that the pictures of the graduating classes had occasioned in the breast of Clay Abernathy years before.

"Ben," Miss Susie said, motioning. "There you are! Dean Wingate brought it to me yesterday." She pointed to the most recent addition to her gallery of medical men: the class of 1915. In the front row still sat the famous older men and Howe, Wingate, Edwards and Mc-Millan—and behind them were grouped the young men among whom were Ben Mead and Alex Ashby.

"Gosh!" Ben said gazing at the picture. "I never thought I'd get there. Never! Miss Susie, do you remember when you made me 'settle my knowledge'?"

She gave her little chuckle and before either of them could explain, the telephone rang. Hizer answered, came back and announced in his best official manner, "De hosbittle is callin' fur Docta Mead."

"Must be true! I reckon that *is* me in that picture." Ben said as he rose. "Will you excuse me, please, Miss Susie?"

"Of course, dear."

Doctor Benjamin Wilson Mead's shoulders squared under his white starched coat as he strode into the hall to meet the demands of the hospital. Prentiss wanted to say, "I'm so glad it happened!" but didn't dare; and Bert Riggs wondered if he had ever been ill, or Ben had ever been the irresponsible cut-up they used to know two years ago. The conversation died out, everybody waited, and Hizer, who had a complete sense of form on important occasions, closed the door carefully.

Within a few minutes Mead opened it again, came back to the silent table, took his seat and Clay said, "Well, who was it?"

"Only a nurse."

"Is that so——?"

"Wanting to be certain that she had not miscalculated the dosage on a patient's chart."

Of all things which could have happened to arouse in the onlookers a sense of the definite difference between Doctor Benjamin Wilson Mead and themselves, that was perhaps the most dramatic. They could attend operations, go to clinics, have opinions on the conditions and the diagnoses of patients, but only a graduate M.D. could give "orders" for prescriptions.

"If it rings again, I'se gonna say you ain't heah," Hizer said. "You gotta eat yo' ladyfingers an' charlotte 'fore you go back to dat hosbittle. Hurry up wid dat roas' beef, Mista Ben."

Doctor Mead replied, in a very professional tone, "What do you mean talking to a man of my importance like that, Hizer?"

Miss Susie smiled. Hizer answered, "Yo' im-portance is so recent I ain't sho' you got it, yit."

The boys laughed. Miss Susie said, "Hizer, bring some hot biscuits, please." Hizer retired to the pantry.

"Ben, did you hear about Rigman and the nurse?" Pug asked.

"No. What?"

The first year students sat forward and waited. Rigman, the brain surgeon, was only a name to them, but he was a name about whom the least fragment of information was worth gleaning. Pug continued,

"He was operating on a patient the other day, before a full gallery, too, and said to a nurse who was assisting, 'Resist me! Resist me!' He wanted her to steady the patient's head, you see, but she answered quietly, 'Doctor, I can't,' and everybody doubled up."

The boys howled and Miss Susie said daintily, "I think that was dreadful!"

"Well, this really was pretty bad," Ben put in. "McMillan, so an interne on his service says, was examining a negro man the other morning over at Bay View, and had a bunch of students standing around—third year fellows. Finally he said to the patient, 'Haven't I seen you somewhere before? Ever been sick at Hopkins?' The negro replied, 'Naw suh.' Doctor McMillan kept on looking at him and then asked, 'What do you do? I'm *certain* I've seen you somewhere before.' And the negro replied, 'I'se doorman at de Gaiety, suh.'"

The boys rocked with laughter. "Ben!" Miss Susie said reprovingly. "You shouldn't tell that—and especially on a nice man like Doctor McMillan."

"How does a nice lady like you know what the Gaiety is, Miss Susie?" Ben asked teasingly. The men at the table continued to laugh. The Gaiety was a strip-act theater for men only.

"Ben," she blushed. "I—I know a great many things which I didn't —didn't——"

"That's all right, Miss Susie," Ben began defending her against his own banter. "You can't take care of medical students for years and years and not know lots of things, can you?"

Prentiss intervened, "Dean Wingate says, 'It takes twenty-five years, thirty thousand dollars and an awful lot of profanity to make a doctor.' How about it, Doctor Mead?"

Ben drew his face to a long mask and replied sadly, "I'm only an interne, how should I know?" The laugh which went around the table was jovial and made it entirely possible for all of them to forgive Ben for strutting, previously. Hizer came in with the dessert. Before they began to eat it, Ben looked around the room at all of the pictures and said, "I'd say at Hopkins it also took Miss Susie Slagle to make a doctor!"

The fine, clear, crisp weather which frequently in Baltimore lasts into December remained that year. It made the news of attacks and counterattacks across the world, in which occasionally one would learn that a McGill man who had previously been at Hopkins, was killed or wounded, seem grotesque and still untrue. When life was so entirely good for him, personally, Pug Prentiss, in spite of his experience as a traveler, found it hard to believe that in Paris, Berlin and London, people had grown grim and desperate.

The same old routine of life continued at Miss Susie's as it had year in and year out; again, only the first year boys went home at Christmas and again the question of interneships arose in the second quarter.

"What are you trying for, Clay?" Silas asked one night after dinner as they sat in the parlor.

"Oh, I dunno. One in medicine first and then one in O-B as second choice. What are you asking for?"

"Anything but psychiatry. Whatever I can get," Silas answered. "But I hope to get pediatrics."

"Rather have that than nose and throat," Clay said airily.

"Didn't know you were interested in medicine, Clay?" Bert said.

"Of course I am," Clay answered hotly. "A doctor's got to know medicine, if he don't know anything else."

"It isn't so much what you'd rather have, is it, in interneships, as what you can get?" Bert remarked.

"What are you trying to get then?" Clay sneered.

Bert did not reply for a second. Then he said, "Doctor McMillan wants me to interne out in Colorado; I've applied to a chest hospital in Denver."

"Oh, I see." Clay's voice was casual.

Prentiss remarked, "We'll miss you, Bert. That is, we'll miss you if we have a chance to."

Bert nodded his gratitude. "What do you want, Pug?"

"G-Y-N at Hopkins."

"And if you can't get it?"

"Then G-Y-N at Montreal General, or Presbyterian, or Jefferson in Philadelphia. I've applied to all of them."

"Would you stay at Hopkins on any other service?"

"No," Pug said. "I wouldn't, Bert. It's the thing I'm interested in and the thing in which I'm going to get a good foundation even if I have to leave Baltimore to do it."

Again, Miss Susie's boys were not among the disappointed, though Clay got the O-B instead of the medicine. But Pug received his interneship in G-Y-N and Silas his in pediatrics. Ben came whooping in one day to announce that he had been made a third assistant resident for the ensuing year.

By the time the third quarter was over, the examination hysteria manifested itself again—but attention wavered from that, for here and there, American hospitals began sending over volunteer units for short terms of service with the Allied Armies. Such a unit went from Harvard and the University of Pennsylvania sent a group; men from all over the country began slipping out of life and were next heard from in the Royal Flying Corps or the Lafayette Esquadrille. At Hopkins, though, the edict about finishing one's training remained in force, and unless one had roots in Canada or in Germany, one was supposed to stick to one's job.

Elijah Howe continued his interest in Joyce Witherspoon, and it became increasingly evident to him that when this medicine business was over, he'd wake up some morning and find himself in France. The Southern tradition of gallant men which Joyce upheld started its insidious work. His father had a hard time persuading him to take an interneship in surgery.

One afternoon, during Easter week, when he was returning from medical school, Silas saw a sight which in these four years in Baltimore he had grown to anticipate.

Halfway up the block a wiry-haired small boy of about ten came out on his white stone steps, looked up and down the street, which was devoid of children, and then devoted his attention to the object which he held in his right hand.

This was a fresh, uncooked, and its owner hoped, strongly shelled egg. Having reassured himself of its merits, the boy lifted his voice and called with a challenging, wailing emphasis on the final word, "Who . . . o pick! who . . . o pick! who . . . o gotta—negg!"

Immediately, farther up the same side of the block a brown-haired, thumpish-looking lad of similar age appeared on *his* white stone steps and replied, with scornful intonation, "Yo—he—oo—EGG!"

Then the young antagonists descended to the sidewalk, covered their eggs with their cupped right hands so that only the butt between the curved thumb and curved forefinger was visible, and with immense concentration approached to joust.

No words passed.

By unwritten Baltimore custom the challenger had first rap. As with all sport between gentlemen, it was presumed that the weapon at hand was not loaded. In other meetings, where the boys were strangers, Silas had seen them examine each other's eggs. A blown egg, filled with plaster of Paris, was always barred, and always suspected among strangers.

These boys he was watching now dispensed with testing.

The challenger took his rap.

The dark-haired boy inspected his egg and grinned.

Then he inspected the challenger's egg and grinned again.

Then he adjusted his own egg in his clenched palm, the wiry-haired boy adjusted his, and the boy he had stirred took his rap.

Their absorption was intense. They failed to notice Silas who stood beside them. The challenger inspected his egg.

It was cracked!

By the laws of this Baltimore custom it therefore became the property of the thumpish boy who promptly took it home and sold it to the family for half the grocery rate.

In the meantime the boy he had defeated went to the store, and with the aid of his mother's housekeeping money, obtained a new and he hoped, thickly shelled weapon.

"Who . . . o pick!" he called again as he ran up the block. Another champion egg-picker responded, they closed ranks to battle, while Silas reluctantly went home to supper.

The last quarter Bert spent catching up on the medicine which he had missed the year before; Clay spent it taking the required work in psychiatry which he had shunned all four years, and Silas decided to devote it to rounding out his course in pediatrics.

May came again and one afternoon as Pug and Isidore strolled down Broadway, Isidore remarked, "Alex's year with the Rockefeller will be up in a few months. I wonder if he'll go then?"

" 'Fraid so. He wrote me that a new Harvard unit is sailing in the summer. Cushing may go with it."

"Cushing!" Isidore almost whispered the word. "How I wish he'd take me!"

"Why don't you write Ashby about it?"

"No. I don't know enough to be of any aid to a man like Cushing—yet. Besides, you know I've accepted an interneship in brain surgery under Rigman."

"Yeah, I'm glad you have; also, I'm glad that you'll be here."

"Thank you, Prentiss. When does Ashby sail? Has the Harvard group accepted him?"

"It's my impression that nothing is to be settled until late June," Pug answered. "But we'll know all of the details soon. Miss Susie said at dinner last night that she'd just had a letter from Alex saying he'd be down for graduation—our graduation. Has five days off."

"Man, I'll be glad to see him!" Isidore said.

"You are not the only one," Pug replied.

But after they had parted a sudden fear rose in Isidore's mind. Was he afraid that Ashby would be killed? Or had he already had the fear before he knew that Ashby was going? It hounded him all afternoon and later when he tried to study. About ten, he slipped out and went for a walk. Suddenly he knew that it was a sensation which, subconsciously, had grown upon him ever since he found Ellen Timberlake. It increased with his happiness, and when his spirits soared, it seemed ever to exert a downward counterbalance. Tonight it was culminating into something which, within minutes, he would be able to locate in his mind and examine.

Emotionally he steeled himself to do so, knowing the while that when he had analyzed the subconscious thought which was now shifting into conscious thought, the result would be pain and the discovery of the trouble would have no effect upon eradicating it. He recalled the radiance of Lin's skin; the gentle, temporary way her eyelashes seemed to touch her cheeks—then suddenly the subconscious thought became conscious and he knew:

The fright arose because of his happiness. He had found the girl he loved, he had won an interneship at Hopkins—he was too happy for a Jew. Their history was not happiness, but strife. When one had achieved contentment, instead of doing as he now did and regarding it as his permanent right, he must teach himself to know it as a transitory blessing.

Suddenly the man sat down on a park bench, and held his head hopelessly in his hands.

Chapter Twenty-four

THE LITTLE ELIZE BED

As the train moved across the Jersey flats, Alex closed *Alice in Wonderland* and slipped the copy into his pocket. The last time he'd gone to Baltimore was in December and then he'd been upon a night train. Now, it was the first day of June, the first morning of summer. His eye ran out to meet the landscape. Little by little the bands of oppression loosened in his brain and instead of thinking clearly in grooved lines, his mind widened to include everything which his eye beheld. Flat land, emerald marsh grass, the potter's field, the sulphur stains from the industrial plants, Elizabeth, Trenton; slowly the train slid into Philadelphia and the sense of mental compression returned. Then the cars rolled onward again. Chester flew by and the run beside the Delaware River attracted his interest. Huge ocean-going steamers edged along and Alex moved over to a seat on the river side. When he saw that several of the steamers were camouflaged, the war came up in his thoughts again.

He decided not to mention his desire to join the Harvard Unit, not even to Dr. Howe, for the first two days of his vacation. For those two days, at least, there'd be nothing to worry about. He'd go to the places he had missed, see the people he loved, be merry, feel carefree. Also, he wouldn't say that the Rockefeller wanted him to continue with them, because his friends would use that as an argument against his joining Harvard's Unit.

As the train drew out of Wilmington, Alex's heart quickened its beat—just a little more than two hours now and he'd be in Baltimore. Gret would meet him at the station and then later he'd have supper at Miss Susie's.

Beyond Wilmington his last vestige of metropolitan strain relaxed as Alex saw plowed fields, green trees, and busy brooks. Picture after picture rose and vanished—a small boy in overalls with an adoring nondescript dog trotting behind; a family wash of bright colors flap-

316

ping against a blue sky; a team of white horses pulling a plow through red earth; the Tom Sawyer island in the Susquehanna River; Havre de Grace and Aberdeen whisked by; two young fishermen with cane poles and a carefully carried can of worms trudged toward the bobbing boats in the Bush River.

A joy like no earthly music began to fill Ashby's heart. It was good to be alive and going back—back to Gret and back to Hopkins, if only for a few days. He'd missed 'em! Lord, how he'd missed 'em.

After the train crossed the Bush River a delirious kind of excitement quickened his breathing. His mind began to race and he thought, "In a few minutes, I'll see it. It will be here, and I'll see it again."

The rows of brick houses with white stone steps stuck themselves into the landscape, the trees disappeared. Concrete streets, bricks, flat roofs: Baltimore! Eagerly Alex looked at them, waited. Then the train rounded a curve and beyond the dancing heat waves of flat roofs, steady and serene, the cupola of the Johns Hopkins Hospital came into his view again. Ashby greeted it with a boyish grin and the old words he had said over and over to himself in the last year surged through his head, "No place on earth is like it." The engine crossed the Broadway trestle and the familiar flower beds, the lush green of the trees melted into his eyes. Then the train dived into the tunnel, from which it would emerge at the station, and phrases dashed through Alex's mind. "I've seen Hopkins! I've seen Broadway and—soon shall my eyes behold thee, Ladykins—soon shall my eyes behold thee!"

After supper, as the boys were filing from the dining room, Miss Susie whispered, "Alex, if you have a minute, will you come to my room, please?"

"Of course, Miss Susie," he replied, as though visits to her room were daily occurrences. But a fear which was gigantic gripped his throat and the muscles under his knees twitched so that he could hardly stand. In all of the years he had known Miss Susie Slagle or known of her, no student had ever crossed the threshold of her bedroom.

Miss Susie continued, "Come up the back stairs, dear. I don't want to cause any excitement. In fifteen minutes."

Then she turned and fled behind the laughing merry men; afterwards Ashby used to get comfort out of the memory of her erect back and proud head outlined against their shoulders. Later, when he knocked on her door, Miss Susie called, "Come in, Alex." That frightened him, too, because he had expected her to open the door, herself. When he was in the room, before he had a chance to see many of the furnishings, he realized that Miss Susie was sitting up in bed.

She wore her nightgown, high-necked with a frill, as he had known it would be, and a pale pink wrapper sprigged with deep pink rosebuds. Her hair was still in a psyche knot on top of her head. Before he could control himself enough to speak, she took the situation in hand and said, "Alex, please lock the door. Then come stand at the foot of the bed where I can look at you."

The grave, kindly man did as she requested, and again before he could question her, she continued, "Don't speak, my dear. Please don't speak! The sound of your voice—right now—would be more than I could bear, and I must tell you this before I lose my courage."

Ashby obeyed. His gray eyes took on their black flecks and steadied her. For a moment he feared that she might cry; such an unexpected change which he took for fear, and then for a refusal to submit to fear, flickered over her features.

She said almost defiantly, "Alex, I want you to examine me. My left——"

Her voice ceased; but still Ashby's eyes held hers. His lips waited for the word, as though they were about to offer it in spite of his will. Presently her lips answered the hidden word on his.

She said, "Breast. My left breast, Alex."

"All right, Miss Susie," he answered lightly, as though she had requested that he examine her toe nail. When she heard his words, Miss Susie swayed back against the pillows and closed her eyes; his voice was like sunshine after pneumonia. Alex Ashby was a gentleman, the son and the grandson of gentlemen, and it was all right for him to see her. It was all right. Everything would be all right, now.

Ashby, watching her face in the mirror as he cleansed his hands at her washstand, remarked calmly, "There is something fine, and solid, and beautiful too, about this old mid-Victorian furniture. You know, Miss Susie, I like to come back from New York to you. This house to me is like the Ten Commandments were to Moses."

The fear and stress drained from her features, a sudden smile lit upon them. She gave her dear, completely happy chuckle and said, "Alex! Oh, Alex!"

As he moved toward the bed, Ashby added, "And you'd never know it, Miss Susie, but sometimes—often—you've been as important to me as *God* was to Moses!"

"Alex, you mustn't say things like that. I've never been important to anybody!"

Before he made any motion to examine her, Ashby sat upon the side of the bed, took her firm small hand in his and went on gently, "I think if I were a woman, I should like to know that at some time my bosom had comforted some man. Miss Susie, when I was so sick that time, it wasn't the flu."

"I knew, dear."

"What did you know?" There was surprise in his question.

"I knew that somehow you'd been wounded emotionally, Alex. Dreadfully wounded. And needed——"

"Just what I got!" Ashby's voice rang the words like a bell. "Succor, peace. You thought I was in delirium then, but I'll remember until I die how you cradled my head against you."

Miss Susie pulled erect, threw her head backward and answered, "That illness of yours was a great satisfaction to me, dear. I—almost felt as though I had a son—of my own. That's why I—I picked you, Alex. That, and because I trust your judgment." Before he could reply she continued, "Now: let's—let's know."

While he was making his examination Ashby asked the usual questions and when he said, "How long has it hurt?" Miss Susie replied, "Since I was housecleaning last fall and fell against the newel post on the landing, it's hurt off and on. But—but that has only been there about two months."

Ashby did not inquire as to what she meant by "that." He kept his face blank, his emotions dead, and verified with his brain the findings of his fingers.

Miss Susie was the one who did the talking. She continued briskly
—so briskly that Alex wished she'd cry instead—"Don't deny it's there
to save my feelings, dear. Don't. I *know* it's there. But—but before
you take me to a surgeon I wanted to be sure that some other person
was sure that it was there, too."

Ashby closed her gown, buttoned it, removed one of the pillows,
and eased her down upon the remaining one.

"Miss Susie, I'm going to do a very unethical thing, and I hope
you won't mind."

"What—what, dear?"

He leaned forward and kissed her upon the lips with reverence
and with love. Then he stood so straightly that Miss Susie read in
his posture, if not in his eyes, his belief. "I couldn't lie to you about
anything," he began.

She nodded, "That is why I chose you."

"You are correct, Miss Susie. There is a mass, and from now on,
since you have chosen me, you automatically become my patient and
are under my care. The worst part of this has been fear: your terror.
You must remember that that is past—over. We can remove the lump,
tell you what it is, tell you what to expect. From now on all of the
worry is mine. Remember that, will you?"

He gave her that smile which no women could resist and which the
women he loved adored. Moving toward the door he said, "I want to
speak to Prentiss. I'll be back in a second."

During the few minutes she lay there alone, Miss Susie discovered
that the things which Alex had said were true. The fear was gone.
Whatever the lump was, he would take care of her. And even if they
removed it, once her breast had comforted a man. A gentleman. The
pink challis wrapper rose and fell with an emotion complex and
courageous.

Outside at the bend of the stairs, Alex Ashby was saying to Pug
Prentiss, "Invite all the boarders to go to Otto's. Tell Otto. Tell him to
get them tight and keep them there until midnight. Tell him, please,
not to tell anybody. Then slip out yourself and 'phone Doctor Howe,
Dean Wingate and Doctor McMillan. Bring back a sleeping potion
which will hold until we get her to the hospital. I know it isn't usual,
but I think McMillan will authorize it, if you tell him that I want

her to be asleep when she is examined. If his diagnosis coincides with mine we'll take her to the hospital and do it tonight. We'll want Halsted. Please ask Doctor Howe or Dean Wingate to get him."

"You are sure it's wise to rush it, Alex?"

"Yeah. She's past crying already. She shan't have to wait like a pig for slaughter."

When Alex returned Miss Susie was still beyond fear and at home in happiness. Ashby had seen that look upon the faces of so many patients who were about to die that it jarred him too much for speech. He sat down upon the side of the bed, took her hand in his again. Presently he remarked, looking out of the window at the sunset, "This is the best time of day to me. When it is neither dark nor light."

"I love it," she replied clearly. "Summer twilight."

"Do you mind a pipe, Miss Susie?"

"Oh, no! It's one of the pleasantest things about boys: smoke. Old maids' houses smell so dead. But where there's smoke——"

"There's usually fire."

"No," Miss Susie said, breathlessly, "Men, minds: medicine."

Ashby sat silent; she continued, "Another reason I like this time of day is that it is so alive. The voices of the little children and the little birds mingle almost hysterically, in an effort to stem off the tide of approaching night, don't you think?"

"I think, Miss Susie, you are a poet!"

She gave her sudden chuckle. Then it froze upon her face and she begged, "Alex, what are you going to do?"

"I'm going to sit by you and enjoy every minute of it until Prentiss comes back and brings something to put you to sleep. Then Prentiss is going to sit by you and see whether or not you snore, while I'm gone to see some of the older men."

"Who?"

"The best in the world."

"Halsted?" she whispered the word.

"Do you think he's so good?" Ashby asked in the tone which medical students use when berating a superior. Miss Susie chuckled again, and then before she could continue questioning him, Ashby said, "You don't know it, but there has been a bet about your snoring for years and years. Doctors all over the world have money on it. We never knew before how to settle it. What Prentiss says will break or make many a man."

"Oh, my dear, don't be so utterly foolish!"

"I've always contended it was medically impossible; that no human could breathe and snore through that adorable nose at the same time."

"Alex!" The chuckle changed to a hearty laugh. There was a knock at the door. Ashby opened it and found Hizer looking as usual, completely as usual, holding the old silver tray upon which were three wine glasses and a decanter of sherry. Alex was too startled to speak.

Hizer explained defensively, "Mista Pug is cumin' up de stairs now. He *said* fur me to bring it."

"Come in, Hizer," Miss Susie suggested, hearing his voice.

Hizer did so and continued, "Mista Pug happened—jes' happened to meet Otto, an' Otto wint down in his 'specialist cellar an' sent Miss Susie de oldes' dry sherry in de world!"

"Oh, heavens!" Miss Susie gasped.

"They declare the glory of her for whom the finest bottle of sherry in the United States has just been opened!" Prentiss responded, standing in the doorway. In an aside to Hizer he said, "Where is your tin cup? I can't find it."

Aloud to everybody Hizer answered, "It's in my lef' rear pocket. You don't think I'd 'low you doctas to drink Miss Susie's health widouten me, do you?"

"Hizer!" Miss Susie's voice was touched and gay.

Prentiss edged toward Ashby and gave him the sleeping potion. "Miss Susie," he said as Alex began to fill the glasses, "you and Doctor Halsted, and Doctor Kelly, and Doctor Welch and Doctor Osler and Otto—you *are* the Hopkins Hospital. And when I told Otto you were sick he told me that for six months when he had that stomach trouble years ago—for six straight months—you sent him wine jelly every single day."

"Tut, tut! As a matter of fact, that's how Hizer turned to drink."

"Off wine jelly, Miss Susie?" Hizer was respectful, but deprecating, nevertheless.

"Don't be a fool! You know very well what I'm talking about!"

She sat up in bed, her authoritative self again, politely but firmly blessing out her own nigger. And her own nigger, grizzled and gray and frightened, stood there and allowed her wrath to fall upon him with sheer joy.

To the boys—men, but boys to her—she explained, "Every time he went, Otto would give him something to drink. Something more than beer, too. For a while, around here, the cooking wasn't fit for anybody to eat, and if Otto hadn't gotten well, why——"

Ashby handed her her glass, gave Prentiss his, filled Hizer's cup, lifted his own glass, and as Prentiss had brought the wine, nodded toward him for a toast. The toast which Prentiss gave was, "To the lady we love. God keep her."

Before she drank, Miss Susie darted Alex a glance as though to say, "We didn't misjudge him, did we?"

When the glasses were empty Hizer, with a negro's fine sense of situation, took charge. "Miss Susie, would you min' if Mista Alex an' me raised a little harmony? Ain't none ob de boys now, c'n harmonize like Mista Alex. I sho' is missed him."

"Do. Please do!"

Prentiss took her empty glass, eased her back among the pillows and Hizer began, "Rock—ob Ages——"

Ashby's magnificent voice took up the "Cleft—for me, Let me hide —myself—in Thee."

In the twilight they all turned vague and featureless to Miss Susie; only Alex's voice steadied, relaxed and guided her out of trouble into sleep.

When he was certain that she was asleep, her gnarled old negro servant who had been left to keep watch, knelt silently beside her bed.

Prentiss and Ashby had tiptoed down to wait for the older men. They found them already arrived. Upon the white stone steps of Miss Susie Slagle's boarding house, three of the greatest men in American medicine sat waiting until she should be asleep, before confirming Ashby's diagnosis.

When they reached her bedroom Hizer was gone. But, later that night as Alex and Pug bore the stretcher toward the waiting ambulance, Prentiss, with that intense observation which accompanies crises, saw that the knob of the newel post on the stairway was gone. It had been sawed off flat with the banister.

After the operation was over, Dr. Howe said to Pug Prentiss, "Come on home to breakfast, son."

Prentiss's eyes changed color. Sally's father, he realized, had stood in that operating room and read his mind; had understood how dreadfully the sight of Miss Susie's mutilation made him yearn to sit in a room with Sally, look at her, and convince himself that she——

As they moved down the corridor Dr. Howe said slowly, "That's one thing our women—haven't got. Thank God!"

Pug remembered his promise and drew back. "The boys at the house, Doctor Howe, and Hizer. I told Ashby I'd tell them."

The elder man answered gruffly. "Already taken care of. Dean Wingate wanted to do it. On his way there now. Come on. I want you to see an old case history I've got in my files. You can look it over while I shave. Probably, the family won't be up yet."

Prentiss went on out and crawled into the automobile beside him. He said nothing, but it flashed through his mind that he was and always would be eternally grateful to that man in B. A. who had ordered him into medicine. Whatever success or failure he attained, would be accomplished among his own kind!

They rode in silence for several blocks; the city lay bathed in that calm which comes before a day actually begins or after it ends; old brick buildings, like the build-up in a symphony, were turning from light pink to rose, to red. Pug thought, "It's not too big: this town. It doesn't smother me."

Again, as though reading his mind, Dr. Howe said, "You know, I love these white stone steps—every mile of 'em!"

"I'm beginning to feel the same way," Prentiss replied.

Dr. Howe changed the subject. "She has even chances, I believe. But not much more. There's always an awful shock to the patient after Halsted's radical. Sense of loss, and with Miss Susie's heart——"

"Don't underestimate her will, sir."

"Well," Dr. Howe remarked as he parked the car at his own curb-stone, "it should take a week either way, I think—unless she decides to die, for when a patient does that, all of our skill is useless. You go on into my office and sit down!"

Prentiss did so, hoping against hope that he had not misread Dr. Howe's intentions. He had not. Within five minutes the door into the family section of the house opened; only a crack at first, and fearing that he had not heard that, Pug kept his eyes upon the medical journal he was reading. The door definitely closed.

Sally's voice said, "Oh, darling, what's the matter?"

The medical journal slipped to the floor as St. George Prentiss stood up, extended his arms and begged, "Sally, come here!" His green eyes were like the sea, his features calmed by a surprising beauty.

A thoroughly feminine reaction entered the girl; she tossed her long yellow plaits, leaned against the mantelpiece, and said petulantly, "Good Heavens, Pug, I thought you must be on the verge of dying, the way Papa tiptoed into our room and told me you needed me immediately!"

She pulled her blue silk kimono tightly about her in a gesture of irritation, which permitted Prentiss's eye to actually confirm what Dr. Howe had understood he needed.

"Oh, Sally. My lovely Sally!" He came across the room, lifted her into his arms and walked about whispering happy inarticulate phrases onto her lips, against her hair.

"Oh, Pug, please, I—" Her whimper was not one of pain; when it reached Prentiss's ears, the effect was instantaneous. The force went out of his grasp and a gentleness which was more forceful than force asserted itself, as he eased down into Dr. Howe's old black leather chair and still holding her, said, "Your father is right. I did need you, beloved!"

"But—but what? Why?"

St. George, beyond words, resorted to masculinity. He placed his lips commandingly against hers and kissed past the girl, which previously he had not dared to do, until he found the woman.

Curiosity fell away from Sally's mind, and for a period which was outside of time Pug Prentiss felt the rise and fall of her breasts against his chest. All of him which was a man desired to strip her; and all of him which her father had trusted refused. But the part which was a man and the part which was a gentleman agreed about one thing:

both of them held within his arms what, for him, would forever be emotional security. He must wait years before he could have her, but now and forever he knew that Sally Howe was his mate.

And the Sally which opened her eyes and looked honestly and adoringly at him, knew it too. Prentiss buried his head in her bosom and said, "You are like sunshine. You are like wine. You're so clean."

Her breathing grew swifter, much swifter. He lifted his head and remarked sternly, "If you don't go get dressed, you'll be late for breakfast and what will your proper Mamma say?"

He held her away from himself, looked at her as a child looks at a beloved doll, and asked, "Aren't you afraid of your proper Mamma, Sweetheart?"

Sally's dimples deepened. She whispered, "Papa is probably doing the same thing to her, darling!"

Then she slipped to the floor, put her lips to his, and the woman he had created kissed him honestly and completely. It left both the gentleman and the man too bewildered to protest, as she fled. The door closed after her and Prentiss understood that forever, he had emotional peace: a woman with whom he was not ashamed to reveal all of the hidden hopes, disappointments and joys too deep for words. She was his to have and to hold for life. All of her. God, how grand!

Waiting for Miss Susie to come out of the anesthetic, Alex Ashby sat in a nearby alcove and thought again of his single question to Dr. Halsted and of Halsted's answer. After the surgeon had finished and while the patient was being removed, Alex, without intention, found himself asking, "Is it inherited?"

Those eyes which were like knives—completely keen—cut into him as Halsted replied wearily, "Nobody knows—for a certainty—yet."

They had, by some twist of fate, been out of ear-shot of the other men. Halsted had continued with his furiously clipped sentences, "Family case histories are dreadfully convincing. Instead of trying to grow carcinoma, I sometimes wonder why no fool has ever thought of approaching it from the negative members of cancer families. Why do some people of the same environment, same heredity, have it and others do not? Why?"

The last question was asked directly and with some sense of interest in Alex's reaction. Ashby shook his head hopelessly, "I don't know, sir."

An intangible irritation, yet energy too, vibrated into the surgeon. His cutting words matched his eyes as he said, "Then why don't you try to find out, Ashby?"

As the descendant of men who had accomplished the impossible, it came naturally to Alex to square his shoulders and answer, "I will, sir."

Halsted remembered him, knew his name, had chosen him! Marked him for a special job. And after he had marked him, he had shyly put his hand on Alex's shoulder and said, "I hope I live to hear you tell me, boy—the answer."

"So do I, sir."

Now as he sat in the alcove, Alex seemed to see things clearly, at last. There was a specific for syphilis; the great work of this generation, now, was cancer. He must ask the Rockefeller to let him switch, or else— His mind reeled with the gigantic possibilities of Halsted's suggestion: the way to fight cancer was not through eradication but through immunity. Through understanding why some were spared and whether with that understanding, the others could be immunized, too.

It would be sort of a liaison work between the healthy and the stricken—but could the healthy be persuaded to submit themselves to such investigation? Easily; the hysteria about cancer was so intense that any person out of a cancer family would do *anything* to avoid the malady.

However, a man who allied himself with such research must accept without reservation the inheritance theory. But didn't a man who allied himself with proving or disproving any theory in research ally himself with one school of thought, and suffer for it, too? Hadn't Pasteur done precisely that in relation to rabies? Hadn't everybody who had ever made any progress in the profession been subjected to criticism? A man like Halsted, when he suggested such research, was aware, utterly aware of such things.

As a matter of fact, to be chosen for this job by a man who once committed himself to a nervous hospital and cured himself of a drug habit, formed in the perfection of local anesthesia, was an honor! When such a person felt one capable of performing any kind of work, he knew what he was about. It might take until he, Alex Ashby, died; it probably would. But at last, through the loss of Miss Susie Slagle's breast, he had been assigned his life work.

The nurse beckoned to him. He rose and went up the corridor toward the door of Miss Susie's room.

Late that night when Miss Susie was conscious enough to ask a question, she inquired of the man who was leaning over her, "What did you do?"

"Operated on you," Dr. Halsted evaded; and Alex Ashby, standing just behind him, said, "I promised we'd tell her the truth, sir."

Halsted bent forward and announced gently, "We removed it, Miss Susie: the lump and the breast."

The hand which rose feebly in an effort to feel, Alex reached out and caught in his strong ones. A faint smile flickered past her lips. Miss Susie looked at Halsted and whispered, "Thank you, Doctor. So much."

Halsted turned away and she lapsed into unconsciousness again. Alex, watching, knew that the will to live had deserted that gallant lady.

Half an hour later when Ashby came out of her room, he found Dr. McMillan waiting.

"Let's sit down, Alex," he said and led the way toward the waiting room. "I want to talk to you."

Alex took a chair and Dr. McMillan said, without preliminaries, "The Carnegie Foundation is going to allow us two full-time men to research at Hopkins in cancer. Doctor Halsted and I are to choose the men. We both want you to be one of them. Will you?"

Ashby controlled himself and replied calmly, "Thank you, sir. Very much. But may I ask a few questions before I answer?"

"Certainly."

"Who recommended me, sir?"

Dr. McMillan gave a wry smile. "You recommended yourself, Alex. You recommended yourself to Doctor Halsted last night. He came to me today and asked if I would approve you. You have an inquiring mind and you are steady. I'd have made you the offer long ago if I'd thought you'd accept it—from me. Halsted knows that you love Miss Susie like a mother, yet last night that didn't keep you from detaching your mind from your emotions sufficiently to ask him a scientific question. You impressed him deeply. Will you come?"

Alex blushed, then squared his shoulders and answered, "Doctor McMillan, there is *nothing* on earth I'd rather do. But—but there has been an Ashby in every war this country ever fought, and——"

"The day we enter, Alex, Doctor Halsted and I will release you for the duration of the war."

"Then I accept, sir—with—with the profoundest pleasure," Alex said huskily.

McMillan grasped his hand and remarked, "I've missed you, Ashby. But the war I'm enlisting you for will last longer than this European one. Sometimes, I greatly fear that I'll be dead before—it's over."

Later that night, after Alex had telephoned the wonderful news to Gret, from Otto's, he returned to the hospital again. Coming toward him down the main corridor he saw a man whose step was brisk, whose manner free, and not until they were almost abreast did he recognize Isidore Aaron.

"Lord, you've changed, boy! You own the world now," Alex drawled.

Isidore smiled and shook Ashby's hand firmly. "My feet are on solid ground. Rigman's taken me on."

"You wrote me. That's grand, Isidore! But it's only the beginning."

Isidore stammered. "You—you look rather well, yourself."

"I ought to. But don't tell anybody; it's a secret, yet. But I'm to be a Carnegie fellow in C-A at Hopkins, beginning in July."

Isidore's eyes filled with tears. He shook his head slowly. "Now, I know I'm *entirely* too happy for a Jew!" Alex knew him too well to laugh.

Isidore controlled himself and asked, "How is Miss Susie?"

"Too early to tell. But, I'm afraid——"

That question, all week, was being constantly answered. As her boys, of all ages, met in the corridors of the hospital they nodded, and then without inquiry passed the phrases, "She's holding her own," "As well as can be expected."

On the third day in the afternoon the "holding her own" had altered to "no change," and on the morning of the fourth day it had become "a matter of hours."

Later that same afternoon, with a suppressed excitement as great as that which followed Paul Revere, man told man, "She's rallied, and wants to see us. All of us. Right away."

From pediatrics, from obstetrics, from ophthalmology, from gynecology, from medicine, from pathology, from surgery—as though drawn by magnets—the men Miss Susie Slagle had nurtured said either to their superiors, or to their subordinates, "Carry on without me for a half hour. Miss Susie's rallied."

Within twenty minutes of the time that Dr. Halsted had said it couldn't change matters if they came, Miss Susie's room was packed with doctors of all ages: students, internes, residents, associate professors, full professors. To Ben Mead it was precisely as if the pictures in the dining room at her boarding house had come to life; and, in their metamorphosis assumed a grave gaiety which was better than joviality.

One by one she greeted them by name; they joked among themselves, quietly, and watched her face with knowledge and with despair.

The rare change which illness brings to some people, it had brought to her. She had gone back to looking eighteen, and her skin had that pearly petal-like quality which all of them had grown to dread. There is an intense life which occasionally precedes death, a sort of inner illumination, and Miss Susie Slagle had it.

"My dears," she smiled, when all of them were packed into the small room. "I sent for you on purpose"—her breath was short—"Alex, please put another pillow behind my head." Ashby looked toward Halsted who stood near the door, and Halsted nodded. When the pillow was in place and before she could resume her speech, there was a knock upon the door. The man nearest opened it, and Hizer entered; he held in his hand a little white napkin square which evidently covered a delicacy.

"Well, I do kno'," he said, "it's jes' like bein' home again."

Miss Susie asked, "How are you, Hizer? And what have you there?"

The old negro moved down the alleyway the doctors had made and said confidentially, "Jes' a little wine jelly, Miss Susie. Taste it!"

He flipped the napkin aside. There was an imperceptible stir among the men, several of whom looked toward Halsted, questioningly. Halsted smiled. Let her have her way. What difference could it make, now? Hizer lifted the spoon, and Miss Susie sampled the jelly.

"Delicious. That's not cooking sherry!"

"No'm. 'Course it ain't. It's de rest ob yo' bottle."

"You didn't drink it, Hizer?"

" 'Fore Gawd, Miss Susie, I'se tellin' de truth!"

The story of Otto's sherry had gone around the hospital and the reactions of Hizer in the presence of liquor were so universally known that the eyes of men who valued control above all virtues, misted.

"Thank you. I'll eat it—later," Miss Susie said with a slight gasp. "May Hizer ask the nurse for some water?"

They understood, then, that she wanted to be alone with them for a few minutes, and Dr. Halsted, who felt that he, too, should leave her with her boys, took Hizer into the hallway.

Then Miss Susie gave them a completely radiant smile and her words were so very clear that they rang into their ears. She said:

"My dears, before I go, I want to thank you for having never disappointed me and for having—loved me. There are two things I want done, please. Sell the house and pension Hizer—St. George, I'd like you to do that. Then—if there is anything over, take it, endow a bed, call it the Little Elize Bed and use it for that."

A stir of blank amazement, of stark incredulity circled them as she took one last breath, which their sensitive ears understood. They smothered the incredulity to be remembered, later, and listened. The doctor nearest the door opened it and beckoned to Dr. Halsted and Hizer.

As they entered, Miss Susie said:

"It's the *passionate* people who make the world progress. Use your brains, my dears, but never stop thinking with your hearts."

The words lingered in the air long after Alex Ashby had caught her head and eased it upon the pillows; while doing so he had closed the eyes, and those doctors whom she had known since adolescence almost, stood silently studying her face.

To no man present was it the face of a corpse: as her character had represented a fineness rarely met in life, so her features became etched with a beauty transcending death.

None of them had ever imagined that she knew of the bawdy song 'Little Elize,' which each of them had rendered at her house some Easter. They had all thought of her as their precious set of virtues which could walk and talk and breathe. Only a few, as the years wore on, had understood what tremendous wisdom underlay that innocent exterior.

Presently, a resident said to an interne, "We'd better be getting back, I suppose."

Before any of them moved, an older man asked, "How did she ever know so much?"

Hizer answered, "She learned it outta all ob you!"

Augusta Tucker was born to be both a storyteller, with the gift of imagining people, and a reporter, talented at factual observation. She is descended from five generations of clergymen, all of whom were writers. Along the way (born in Louisiana, growing up in Mobile, living in New York City, Annapolis, and Baltimore), applying "the seat of the dress to the seat of the chair," she taught herself to write and developed the sensitivity of a healer, alert to other people's illnesses, not just her own.

The writing of Miss Susie Slagle's *took six and a half years of former-patient's patience, but its account of student life at a boardinghouse hard by Johns Hopkins School of Medicine, anno 1912, at once became* the standard portrayal of old-time medical student existence. First published in 1939, Miss Susie Slagle's *was many weeks on national best-seller lists.*

In a later novel, The Man Miss Susie Loved, *Augusta Tucker told about the boardinghouse keeper's origins; she added a contemporary, nonfiction picture of daily life at her favorite hospital in* It Happened at Hopkins. *Sturdily a writer still, she has been working on* Grandsons and Granddaughters, *a third volume in the Miss Susie series. But it is the present book about bygone would-be M.D.'s, their worries and relaxations, that foreign publishers translated, that Hollywood and television glorified, that is deemed a basic book across Maryland and many a medical mile beyond.*